I0678372

THE DREAM LAND

THE DREAM LAND

Dreams of Future's Past

BOOK II OF THE DREAM LAND TRILOGY

Stephen Swartz

TANGENTIAL BOOKS
In Association with

MYRDDIN PUBLISHING GROUP
UNITED STATES · UNITED KINGDOM · AUSTRALIA

Copyright © 2013 Stephen Swartz

All rights reserved. Except as permitted under the U.S. Copyright Act of 1976, no part of this publication may be reproduced, distributed or transmitted in any form or by any means, or stored in a database or retrieval system without the prior written permission of the author or publisher.

This is a work of fiction. Names, characters, places and incidents are products of the author's imagination or are used fictitiously and are not to be construed as real. Any resemblance to actual events, locations, organizations, or persons, living or deceased, is entirely coincidental.

ISBN-13 : 978-1-939296-26-9

ISBN-10 : 1939296269

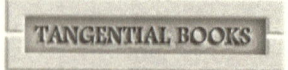

In Association with

www.myrddinpublishing.com

Cover by Marta Swartz

The adventure of the hero is
the adventure of being alive.

Joseph Campbell

THE DREAM LAND

Dreams of Future's Past

Stephen Swartz

PART ONE

Quisque suos patimar manes.

We make our destinies by our choice of gods.

Virgil, *The Aeneid*

Chapter 1

Self-Contained Mutation

Tuesday afternoon. I'm just beginning to see. Now
I'm on my way.

—The Moody Blues, "Forever Afternoon (Tuesday?)"

The yellow sun was beginning to warm the room, the misty,
frayed globe high enough that he knew dawn was coming to an
end. The blue sun was still below the horizon.

Outside the wide, curved window he could observe the
relentless progress of the heavens from dawn until dusk. With
several panels open, he could hear and smell the sea: the rich,
rhythmic riffling of waves against the rocky beach far below, the
odor of sea life washed up and dying. He used to loathe the sea,
fearing its endless depths, an image of sinking into the void
always driving him back. However, he feared the sea no longer.
He still would not swim in it, nor would he easily board a small
watercraft to cross the great ocean, but he knew there was more
to an ocean than endless depths and a dark void. He had crossed
the void of the universe several times, he mused as he stretched
in his lounging chair, the Naugahyde crinkling with each shift of
his body, and what was an ocean of water to that?

He pushed himself reluctantly away from his writing table,

yawning, ready to call another night done. Setting down his pen, he fixed his gaze upon the morning light shimmering across the olive-drab waters below his cliffside perch. He spied a ship approaching. The sight of such a vessel did not immediately alarm him, though no one was expected, much less desired, and he could not speculate who might want to visit his hermit isle. He had time to become excited later, of course. The vessel was yet an hour from shore, he estimated.

The bare crags rising up over his tiny island blocked the suns for a while each morning and he realized the beginning of a day was a precious time, one not to be disturbed by contact with mere mortals—though he had long ago given up the idea that he was special or superior to others. It was really only a matter of perspective. His friends had always reminded him of his mortality, but he had left them behind, his head still spinning from the wars, pounding with the constant shifting of cosmic tangents. Sometimes his head felt as though gravity was pulling him in opposite directions. Safe on his private island of self-exile, he did not care for anyone, but he knew that were he to rejoin society, there would be rules to follow, etiquette to exhibit. He would have to give in and smile occasionally, say something nice, be polite, and sooner or later probably have to give a damn.

He rested in his chair, watching the vessel slide across the now emerald sea, content with what he had written during the night, as he wrote every night. The long, silent hours always melted into a single heartbeat in the cool darkness and he could work without fatigue.

The ship had the markings of an official boat, something sent by a government on diplomatic missions. The powder-blue stripes along its burnished hull, crimson and canary-yellow striped flag flying from its masthead suggested a ship from Sekuate, though one flying the flag of their protectorate, the Kingdom of Aivana. Smoke billowed from the stacks in three shades of gray as the vessel slowed, drifting to shore. He watched a helmsman throw a rope over the post at the end of the short pier, others making ready a ramp to place over the railing. Ambassadors in their finest garb stood patiently on the foredeck.

Rubbing his eyes, he decided he would go ahead and meet whoever had taken the trouble to come out and see him. He had time; the winding trail up the cliffside would take the visitors at least two *peth*—about 40 minutes in Earthspeak. He left his writing table and dressed in clothing suitable for public display: time to get out of the ragged nightshirt he lived in. He often felt it was a useless gesture since he was, as he wished he could forget, a retired king, the *Mexas* of Aivana.

They hailed him, breathlessly, when finally they stood atop the cliff, forming a tight semi-circle on the porch. He waved them inside. They bowed low while his back was turned. When he faced them, their long, waxed, pointed beards touched the hardwood floor.

"Get up, already," he grumbled.

Behind the three ambassadors several porters carried various sizes of treasure boxes—the standard ritual for buying their way into an audience with nobility.

"Just stack it in the corner over there, boys."

Yes, anyone making the journey to his desolate isle must have a serious problem. They must think he was the only one who could possibly provide a remedy. Therefore, any visitor who reached his isle had to be on an important mission. And knowing from their ship's design, their costumes and manner that they were sent from Aivana, he was ready to be pressed into service once more—but he listened to their solemn beatitudes nevertheless. If he waved them off, they would be offended. So he just smiled, politely.

"The Queen requests, from far-away Aivana, that we humbly transport thee to Her Highness, with great payment in advance for your audience," the first official, wearing the stiff ruffled collar of a chamberlain, spoke in the stilted, formal Ghoupallêan speech that was required. "Her Highness begs thee to keep this treasure in exchange for thy brief attention today, if Your Majesty so wishes, and no heavy heart shall be felt against thee among any court member if thou refuse us. However, we do humbly beg thee"—and he dropped to his knee—"in the name of our beloved Queen Tammy Sue Aronstein to indulge the court with a brief audience wherein Her Highness shall invite Your Majesty upon a splendid adventure which shall further

13

illuminate Your Majesty's fame and compel the world to sing further praises of thee."

"Why doesn't she send the *request* with you?" he asked, then decided the chamberlain did not know the answer. He turned from his guests, muttering, "Wonder what she wants this time...." and "That's why I left in the first place...."

He paced the spacious room reserved for meeting guests, separated by seven locked doors from his private chambers, wishing he still retained the dozen or so servants that he'd sent away in anger a year before. He felt awkward. Someone should get these tired guests a cup of coffee, he thought. He shuffled around the kitchen, looking for cups, and his guests were embarrassed that the ex-king was going to serve them. Two of their assistants were nudged forward to help him. He waved them off.

Seeing the steam rise from the boiling water, he imagined the desperate, frosty breaths of his men, his cavalry regiment, lost in the winter of 1533. 'The days when I was a fool,' he always called it. He had survived the Great Northern Campaign across the nation of Tebbicousimankalê, fighting both Tebbi regulars and the Zetin mercenaries on their disastrous retreat over the vast subcontinent. He hated it—and wished he were there again. Then, with his unexpected return from the wars as the top story of the singing *arilor* in the desert land, he had been appointed *Mexas*—King of Aivana, a kingdom whose reigning matron, Tammy Sue, was one of a rare class of residents: an Earthling. Indeed, she was one of the co-workers he had reluctantly brought to this world. He called his new world the Dream Land, for he had once seen it in a dream, though in its cruelty and beauty it now seemed to him more real than his planet of origin. The natives called the planet Ghoupallesz.

He noticed the officials staring, not understanding what this crazy ex-king was rambling on about in his foreign tongue, and only then did he realize that he had been mumbling again.

"I was the *Mexas*," he spoke hesitantly but firmly in their language, "but I grew tired of being a king. The years sitting in judgment of others, choosing the direction of their lives, satisfying all of their grievances, promoting their virtues, celebrating minor efforts and punishing transgressions—it all bored me." He switched to English: "I mean, gimme a break! I've only been here four years. Haven't finished my book—or fixed the back porch, you know. It's a little wobbly. Watch your step. It's a long drop."

He halted his ranting, glared at the head official.

"Will you return with us, Your Majesty?" asked the tall man carrying a peaked cap of bright green plumage which he had removed upon entering the house.

"She's in trouble again, isn't she?"

"Your Majesty, we cannot say which matter causes Her Highness distress. All shall be explained to Your Majesty when we return to Aivana. Her Highness begs us to return thee, the great warrior Set-d'Elous, to her court. Wilt thou consent to return with us?"

He grinned.

"Well, now that you've called me by my real name," he said, then laughed as he recognized the line from an old spaghetti Western, "instead of all that 'your majesty' crap-ola...."

He thought for a moment, wondering when he would be able to return to his writing and finish his extensive tome on the history of Ghoupallesz, now in its seventh volume. He was rewriting history, telling it the way he thought it should be. If anyone insisted on objectivity, he would challenge them to live through it, as he had. Perhaps someday, he pondered, he could re-*right* history. If he did not keep daring the gods to trick him once more. It almost proved fatal the last time.

"Yes, I'll go, dammit!" And he went for his bag, fuming in the language his visitors could not comprehend. "If not me, then who? Who could do it? Who *would* do it? I know she'll want me to go back there. Who would *want* to return there? To that grimy, unjust world? To that land of vanity and insanity, that dimension of decay and whirlpool of—"

He spun around to face them with English spittle on his lips and his K-Mart duffel bag in his hand, clothing falling out where the seams were torn.

"I'm ready."

✳ ✳ ✳

The hand was warm, the voice cool, and he thought he must be home at last. But he could not move. He was locked inside his body, imprisoned in a brain that was mush.

"Mister Talbot? Can you hear me?"

His orbs unsheathed at the sound, but he did not see in the first few moments, not until he allowed the visual input to be analyzed. His rounded antennae recognized the aural experience and proceeded to analyze it, soon accepting what was an interrogative vocalization from the lifeform perched beside him.

"Do you know where you are?"

He regarded the being, noticing the elongated cranial growth falling onto the forearm mountings so limply, of a dark color he could not identify. He could not see any auditory receptors, assumed they must be hidden beneath the...*hair*. That's what it was called! And from the vast storehouse of acquired experience he held within his cranial organ, he identified the coloration of the being's face with the traditional markings of the female gender: pale blue smudges over the eyes, red highlighting the borders of the vocal orifice.

"Do you know how you came here?" the being spoke—and it *was* speaking; he could see the oral apparatus moving, forming sounds. It was correct behavior to perform the same act, his database information revealed.

"Doyouknowme?" was what he could produce.

"Yes," the being uttered.

He was pleased, but the sensations of pleasure confused his brain, sending a bolt of messages down his body, into his sexual organs.

"You must be feeling better," *she* said—he knew that in his social group the females were called 'she' and that he was 'he.'

"Whoamhe?" he allowed his oral apparatus—his 'mouth,' he knew suddenly—to speak, then fell silent.

"You mean, who am I?" she said. "I guess we've never been formally introduced, even though I've been checking on you every day now for...let's see, well, we'll get into all that, hmm, later."

16

His brain scrambled to analyze the new data.

"Now, do you know where you are?" she repeated.

He recognized it as her greeting pattern.

"Doyouknowwhereyouare?" he responded in kind.

"No, do...you...know...where...you...are?"

He stopped, dumped the data he was still processing and focused all his energy on the fragrance his nose detected: spicy and sweet, rich yet delicate, upon her hair.

"Are you okay? You seem confused."

He shifted his eyes back to hers; they were a shade of green. As he held his gaze, her eyes became wider. He adjusted his eyes to the mammalian growths almost visible through the upper opening of her—what was the thing called?—her blue, her bloom, her blow—*blouse*. That's it!

She noticed his change of venue and sat back in her, on her, it was some kind of, piece of fur, fern, furniture, it's a, something—

"Chair!" he exploded, droplets of oral fluid spraying.

The musical pattern again. "Yes, that's right. I'm sitting on a chair. And you are on a bed. Do you know *where* this bed is?"

He ran through the index of responses, categorizing and selecting, sampling and discarding, finally chose: "Here...?"

"Very good. Where is here? Do you know?"

He stared at her for a long time—one second, two, three, maybe a minute.

"Who...are...you?" he spoke.

The woman smiled.

"I'm Toni Franck. You can call me Toni. I'm your doctor. Psychiatrist, actually. I'll be looking after you until you're back on your feet again. We'll be spending more time together in the days to come."

He analyzed her phonemes and intonation.

"Are you...American?" he asked, seeing surprise register on her face.

"Yes, I am. I was born in France, however, near Lyon, but I've lived in the U.S. since I was a child. Twenty years now. I'm surprised I have any accent. I read in your file that you speak five languages. They'll probably come back to you eventually. Then we can speak *en français*."

"Who?"

"Who...?"

He commanded his right arm to move and, to his chagrin, it did, flopping heavily with a thump onto his chest.

"Me."

"You don't know who you are?" she asked—the doctor asked.

"No."

"Your name is Sebastian Talbot," she said, holding up her clipboard and pointing to the letters on the label at the top, "Like it says right here, on your file. See? They spelled your name right, didn't they?"

"No."

"They didn't?"

"Not 'no'—no!"

"No what?" the psychiatrist asked, squinting her eyes.

"Not my name."

"Sebastian Talbot isn't your name?" She spun her head around at the door, returned to him. "This is the right room. You had me worried for a moment, Mister Talbot. We'll be getting everything straightened out in the next few days. I know you'll be anxious to get back on your feet again, but—" she checked her watch, "I'm sorry, it's long over your time now. I'm glad I stayed long enough to see you awaken. It's a good beginning."

"When—?"

"It's Tuesday," the doctor replied. "Tuesday afternoon. Ten past two, in fact."

She stood. Her navy blue skirt clung to her moist thighs.

"See you tomorrow."

She turned to go, stepping lightly toward the door, her white coat hung up on the squashed fabric of her skirt, rolled up against the curvature of her, what was it called, the rear part, the back end, her buzzer, butler, butter, button, *butt*. That's it!

"Bye, now," she said.

"*Au revoir*," he whispered, then rolled his head away and saw the single golden sun outside his window, deciding he would change it if he could.

Chapter 2

Strangers in Paradise

"*Sa'yo Na'a*," the old king whispered to his lovely companion of sixteen years. It meant "I'm dying" in the language of the Rouê people of Aivana. He was not on his death bed, yet he had only a year or so remaining as his illness weakened and tormented him. He swore to his queen that he would not leave her without power—her and the child she had brought into the world a couple years earlier, and the other child born after marrying him.

It was an historic law for the desert people, an ancient race of nomads. Written by the king into the religious texts, it declared that she, his bride and queen, was his sole heir, and that she may appoint to the task of governance any person she deemed wise enough to rule the land. His intention was that she would choose someone from his staff, a Rouê who would know how best to govern the state. However, she had instead appointed to the position of *U'le*, supreme sovereign, the one man she believed was the wisest person on two worlds.

This was the man who had first brought her to this new, vibrant world where her once dull and destitute life had suddenly become a delightful paradise. Sure, they had once been co-workers, tax examiners on the night shift at the IRS service center, back on Earth. They were brought together quite randomly through the misadventures of their mutual acquaintance and co-worker, Michael Fenning. Neither the old king nor his staff, nor his people, knew that the strangers now running the country were once an absent-minded accountant, a lazy mechanic, and an unwed mother living paycheck to paycheck. No, on this world, they came not as employees but as gods, albeit inexperienced ones. Yet Tammy Sue Tucker, whose Ghoupalle rendering had been *Tami'su'o*, wore her official Rouê name with confidence, and welcomed the people's praise whenever they shouted *"Alebafe"*—meaning 'goddess from an island.'

She smiled, thinking back to Agani Isle. While taking her maternity leave there, safe from the gossipy women of the IRS service center, the old king's ship had docked for repairs and he found her, charmed her into returning with him. There she would sit beside him in public, and lie beside him in private. The king had no misgivings about the bloated woman whose unborn child was not his; the youth and beauty she held still provoked his desire, indeed pinned his heart to hers and impassioned his loins. Her blonde hair might have also helped swing the deal. Her child became a regent of the court. Then they made their own child, who became a full-fledged princess.

Then he found he was dying, and spoke his words: *"Sa'yo Na'a, O'helabe Alebafe'o ha'el welamo'o"*—which meant 'My heart is growing cold, dear Alebafe'—and set about building her a new palace.

Now in the tall, gray monstrosity that dominated the whole city, she passed her days beside her new husband, Jason Aronstein, the friend of her benefactor: the man she had chosen as the kingdom's sovereign, the *U'le*, the *Mexas*, called Set-d'Elous in Ghoupallêan, or, as he often was called back in the IRS service center, Sebastian Talbot.

And so it came to pass that three ordinary people from a planet called Earth became the rulers, for better or worse, of the desert kingdom of Aivana, a political unit carved out of the Zissekap territory following annexation by the Sekuatean Empire and subsequent liberation after a hundred years of war. None of them spoke fluent Rouê, though Queen Tammy was, with years of practice, the best. She could even turn an impressive phrase when called upon to speak to her subjects.

Through their comfortable lives—and through Tammy's often tedious days sitting in patient judgment in place of the absent *Mexas*, Set-d'Elous, and especially in the quiet hours of the night after the *arilor*'s last call—she would curl deep within herself and retrieve the lukewarm memories of the child she had left with her mother in that white ranch house with the red trim on that dead end street in the suburbs near the interstate, up the street from the shopping center, the house with the gravel driveway left unpaved when her father died in a drunken frenzy in the family automobile. That was such a distant life, she felt, weeping. She wondered then, in the same pair of breaths, if it was truly her memory rather than some strange obsessive illusion. Or had she always been on this world and only dreamed of a place called Earth? She worried about the thoughts her family must have had when she disappeared, with no word, no call, no warning that she might never come back. Set-d'Elous had told her how he was arrested upon his return, charged with her murder. That gave her family some explanation, even though he managed to escape.

The suns set slowly on the last day of Batou in the subtropical autumn: the larger golden one in the southwest and the small, blue sun in the north, their crisscrossing light giving an emerald hue to the sky. Watching the horizon from the highest tower, she waited long past dusk, composing her request in her head— until her husband, Jason, found her and comforted her, assuring her that Set-d'Elous would come.

Jason, the prince-consort, had once been the builder of high-performance dragsters and the winner of countless street races on Earth. He had briefly been a self-made mercenary in the northern wastes of Tebbicousimankalê while searching for a wayward Set-d'Elous who was himself caught up in the war there. After the war, Jason had served the king of Tebbicousimankalê and was amply rewarded for his creation of the 'electric personal vehicle' and the 'audio spinning-disk sound machine'—enough so, it seemed, that the government looked favorably on the dispensation of Aivana. Visiting the desert kingdom on a trade mission, Jason met the widowed Queen Tammy and, after comparing notes of lives left behind on Earth, they had fallen in love.

21

He rubbed the queen's shoulders, staring at the green sunset, telling his wife of Set's willingness to do her bidding. She refused to rest easily.

There was no one else.

She worshipped Sebastian Talbot/Set-d'Elous, not as a god the way the people of Aivana did, but as the man who had saved her, literally saved her from her loathsome and dreary existence, from the intense pursuit of Michael Fenning, from the depressing life she had, the downward spiral into despair. He set her free, and for that she would be eternally grateful. And eternity on Ghoupallesz was almost possible, it seemed. So she had appointed him King of Aivana. And considering his power and influence across the planet of Ghoupallesz, she knew there was no one else she could rely on to return to Earth and bring back the child of her naïve youth.

"*Sa'yo Na'a o'ha* Set-d'Elous *a'he*," she said with a sigh. She laid her head against the stone rampart. She could not see the caravan snaking its way toward the city with Set-d'Elous as their cargo. "I'll die soon, Set-d'Elous, if you don't come," she repeated in the unused, strange-sounding English, feeling the weight of her longing, hearing the cry of the *arilor* echoing her thoughts.

"He'll be here," whispered Jason, holding her in his arms.

"He's up. Woke up yesterday, around two."

"Can he talk?"

"His shrink was there."

"Can he answer questions?"

"He wasn't very coherent, they said. At least he's awake."

"When can we question him?"

"Said we'd hafta talk to his shrink, the one sent over from Sibley."

"She said we have to wait?"

"We didn't talk to her. We could go on over, strike up a conversation, see if the bastard tells us how he killed'em."

"We can't do that, and you know it."

The detective, his gym muscles stretching his crisp white

shirt taut, slammed his fist on the table, causing the tall stack of papers there to shift dangerously close to the edge. He tossed his sportcoat over the back of a chair and the silver badge clipped to the lapel fell off and clinked on the floor. His colleagues glared at him. He picked up the badge.

"How much more do you need to hear?" he bellowed.

"Calm down, McElroy—and sit down," said Detective Wilson, leaning against the wall next to the window, a Styrofoam cup of lukewarm coffee in his hand.

Chuck McElroy's face was still red as he began pacing.

"You weren't even here when it began," the third man, Detective Henderson spoke, then threw a glance to Wilson.

"If he's come out of the coma," Wilson continued, straightening up and coming over to push the papers away from the edge of the desk, "that isn't any of our concern. He's already in an institute. That's as good as behind bars as far as I'm concerned."

"All murderers need to be followed," McElroy argued with his deep voice and his animated gesturing. "They need to be pursued and never given a second to catch their breath. This one, he's only spared the chair by a cockeyed lawyer and a bullshit shrink. He's living it up over there in that ins*teetoot*."

"Hospital for the criminally insane is what it is," said Henderson. "Besides, he's been in a coma for six months."

"Should've been killed in that hail of bullets," McElroy said. "Never shoulda been any trial, and certainly no—well, you know what I mean, that goddamn disappearing act of his." He paused, rubbing his chin. "Drummond was killed there, in that ambush. He was your partner, wasn't he? Come on, you can't tell me you're willing to sit there and let him go free? How can you live with that? The guy dropped your buddy like a bag of potatoes. You had him surrounded with, what was it, fifty officers? And he gets seven or eight of 'em before he's knocked down. And he's got a nice bed and clean sheets up at Sunnydale Hospital for the criminally lucky!"

"He *didn't* have any gun," Henderson added, "no weapon of any sort—so how could he have shot the men?"

Wilson downed his coffee and tossed the cup in the wastebasket, swept the papers across the table with his arms, and shoved McElroy back against the door—all in the same motion.

"Yes, he was my partner! And I was there, too. It was our case, our serial killer, our guy. And it was my bullet that nailed him. Standing in the center of the quarry, right in the middle, stone walls on three sides of him, holding a piece of wire like he was picking a lock, and grinning as wide as the Missouri River. He said 'goodbye' and stepped back. Someone opened fire and he fell. He got up and others shot. He stepped back, our men went forward and were laid down flat by something or someone firing on them—from *behind* Talbot, in the woods maybe. Nobody was ever found. He was charged with those seven murders—before the incident at the quarry."

Wilson glanced around at the others.

"He was already acting strange. You read the transcripts of his confession. He never said he killed them but he never gave any reasonable explanation of what did happen. Only that talk about being from another planet, and how *they* were there on that world, alive and well. And you saw the photos of the last victim—Davenport, Kenneth J.—his stomach open like he was attacked by one of them goddamn monsters from that *Alien* movie. The burn marks around the opening clearly showed he was hit by something fiery, like...I dunno, a freakin' laser beam."

He stopped to take a breath.

"Yes, I thought of that. I thought of *all* that and I put my own bullet into him. He went down six times, got up six times, and still lived long enough for the medics to get to him. He survived, but in a coma. But he's got *nothing* on the outside—even if he did escape. Talbot is criminally insane. That's done. He'll spend the rest of his life there. That's the court's verdict. I'm satisfied with that. It's finished."

McElroy grinned and Wilson was further unnerved.

"You like my little tantrum, Chuck?"

"No, sir, but I thought you might've saved your breath if you'd just read the report from that jerk, Barkley, down at the Bureau."

"I did read it."

"And you're not at all curious?"

"Curious? About what?"

"The bodies. You want to close the case, right?"

"It is closed."

"But you never found the bodies—except Davenport. No bodies, no crime. Isn't that the way it goes?"

"So Sebastian Talbot is a clever fellow."

"He's lying."

"So what? Guys in comas always lie."

"He's awake now. We've got just as much right to continue questioning him as if he never went into the coma. The bastard can't hide out in a coma. We got to keep up the questioning."

Wilson turned to Henderson, neatly stacking the papers in their file folders. "What about you?"

"I've got no desire to open old graves," Henderson remarked, not looking up.

"Anyway, we've got one of them *carte blanches* there, if we want it."

"What do you mean?" Wilson asked McElroy.

"His shrink. Bitch by the name of Franck."

"And she'll question him for us?" Wilson asked. "You must be out of your freakin' mind. No psychiatrist would pass info to us. Not even on a case like this."

"She's his *shrink*. She's *supposed* to ask him questions. We need to hear the answers. Sooner or later he's gonna talk about the crime. He'll tell her where the bodies are—or how he got rid of them, if that's what he did. I don't believe any of that shit about slipping through some invisible doorway to another world."

"You know we can't do that."

"She'll talk to us—or me, at least. She's a shrink who talks. You heard about her previous job, lasted one month?"

"No, what happened?" asked Wilson.

"Right outta shrink school, gets on over at Sibley, the work farm outside of Saint Charles, ya know. Not criminally insane but crazy enough. You know no broad's got any business being in a joint like that—the worst scum, hardest of the hard criminals, shit of the state. Anyway, first week she's falling in love with her patient, whatever the hell they call'em. Second week, she's helping to get him released from the place. No go. Third week, she's helping him to break out of there. Fourth week, she's fired—but wins a sex harassment case, so her record's cleared. The loony-tune is still in there. Hey, don't worry, she'll talk to us."

Henderson frowned. "Well, I can't allow it."

"Listen, we all know what this guy Talbot's about. He's dangerous, he's crazy. That's the worst combination. Sooner or later he's gonna be let out or he's gonna break out. Before then, we need to get tabs on him, get our questions answered. Remember: this guy overpowered five guards in the truck taking him to Sunnydale, remember? One guy still walks with a limp, another hasn't regained the use of his left arm. You want a guy like that out and about in our city?"

"All right, talk to her," Wilson sighed, nodding his head. "But be discreet."

"Him?" Henderson spoke up. "As discreet as napalm."

It was a great cathedral, a monument to opulence, a vast palace set in *gealan* gemstones and surrounded by the white Ghoupallean gold bled from the Zissekap Mountains. And in the great hall of the great castle sat a pair of great chairs, one his and one hers. He recognized the cushion, having ripped it once before with his sword when he had sat there, overseeing the jurisdiction of the land. He had ordered it be repaired rather than replaced. It was empty now, filled only with the thin memories he projected upon it, and by the warm sunlight screened by the stained-glass windows high on the vaulted walls. There were six years of memories and a dozen lifetimes drifting through the cool, stagnant air of the great hall, like the dust particles he could see in the slanting beams of light.

"You came," Tammy spoke. He was hesitant to face her, but at last he did.

"How could I resist?"

She went to him, kissed his cheeks, held his hand, and laid her head against his shoulder. Her husband entered the room, calling for her to return to where they were needed. She took their guest with her and he found that the family was posing for a portrait. He paused to admire the artist's work over her shoulder: the classic pose of the happy royal family faking grins of compromise and rosy cheeks full of hope and promise. The paints were *daxajo*-based and added a ghostly quality which correctly mocked their superficial satisfaction.

"Are you sure a family portrait is appropriate?"

"Of course it is," replied Tammy.

"You're forgetting, dude, we're no longer just Tammy Tucker and Jason Aronstein of Kansas City, Missouri, America, Earth," her husband spoke. "Now we're something special. We deserve a portrait. What the wife wants, the wife gets."

"Is that why I'm here?"

The royal couple laughed. Their guest settled back, still behind the artist, chuckling.

"Let's not forget our past, Jason."

"The past doesn't exist for us, for you and me, and Tammy. And the future is ours to make as we wish."

"Just don't tell the locals."

"He leaves all of that to me, anyway," said Tammy. "He still hasn't mastered Rouê, so I must do all the talking."

Sebastian, or Set-d'Elous as he was called there, was still the king, the *Mexas*, after all, yet he never felt comfortable with the rituals and trappings of power. He put up with it as he awaited the arrival of Gina Parton, his co-conspirator in tangent-tearing and eternal soul-mate. Her return to Aivana was recorded in historical texts. The date was four years off: the month of Batou, the twenty-first day, in the year 1574 in the Ghoupalle calendar. However, bored with his daily life at court, he had left all the decisions to the Queen and her husband, and left the desert kingdom, sailing north along the coast. He had spent a year at his favorite city, Selauê, the university town, also headquarters of the Second *Coræsz* of the Sekuatean army—his former employer a century before. Then he made his way to the island of Little Biznuik.

It was an island of mystery and myth, a forbidden place. Formed by the volcano which dominated the seascape, its high caldera could hold the city of Selauê and all of its one million inhabitants. Inside that caldera, he searched for the magical doorway through which the race of Ghoupalle people was said to have arrived. He had come to Ghoupallesz through such a doorway—had moved back and forth through several interdimensional doorways, in fact, until his main portal was sealed by explosives he had ordered when the policemen from Earth had chased him through it.

He also spent his nights writing the history of the planet, as he understood it by living it. Twelve lives in different time periods—each the result of slightly different entry points among the doorways of Earth. He and Gina called them tangents, the single point where two worlds meet, the single point where the fabric of space could be pried apart like a curtain being torn, and a dexterous person could carefully step through the tear. Tearing the curtain had been their hobby, and their obsession, until Gina chose to remain on the world they found. That was now hundreds of years in the past, maybe fifteen years of Earth time, and forever in his twisted mind.

"You're right about our portrait," Queen Tammy spoke, diverting him from his brooding. "It won't be complete, not without my son, Chucker, not without my child. Don't you remember him?"

"I remember. But you chose to stay here."

"I know. How could I leave all of this? I never intended to give up him. You said time runs differently between here and Earth. I've made a great life here, and I want my son to join me now."

"It has worked out well for you, but do you really want your son—your Earth-born child—to grow up here, to live *here*? Just imagine what a childhood on this world might lead your son to become. Is that what you want for him? Isn't he better off on his native world, even though it's a simple life, even though he is separated from you?"

Jason waved his hand and the artist cursed.

"You're not listening to her," he started. "She wants her son to be here, and if that's what she wants, then that's what I want. You have to understand how it feels to be without your son."

The *Mexas* frowned, muttered something in Ghoupallêan which to them was unintelligible.

"What did you say?" his friend asked.

"How dare you!"

"I'm not taunting you. So you saved Gina from the Zetin castle and you had a child together, then one morning she and the child were gone. It's not the same."

"That's why I'm here in this time zone, waiting for Gina. I'm waiting for her to return. To Aivana. She'll be here in a few years."

"Think about it: it's a different time zone than the one you two were living up in Kipzon. That girl you had then is now a grandmother, maybe passed on now. And Gina? She won't remember that. She's not looking for you."

"All right. But I still can't go back to Earth, not now. And there are two reasons. I was escaping from the police when I left last time. If I return, they'll arrest me again. And because I was escaping from Earth, I fixed the tangent so that no one could follow me."

The great hall fell silent but for the brush strokes on the canvas.

"You 'fixed' the tangent?" Jason finally asked, eyebrows raised. "How the hell can you *fix* a tangent?"

Set-d'Elous, struck a regal pose, felt silly, and slumped. A smirk developed on his face but he thought it inappropriate and tried to hide it.

"I blew it up."

"You what?" Jason cried out.

"The soldiers you sent to meet me? Well, I had them place explosives at the point where the six policemen came through, and we detonated it."

Jason gasped. "You're kidding!"

"Whatever cosmic door was there, it's destroyed now."

"You fool!"

In big sweeping gestures, Set continued: "I closed the door behind me so no one else would fall through it, accidently or purposefully, and find themselves lost in this place. Also, so none of us could go back there and spread our alien diseases, or our particular proclivities and vices. The 'twain shall never again meet."

Jason broke the pose, stepped forward. "There must be other tangents you can use—like you said before."

"Well, yes...." Set thought a moment. "But they're not so convenient. What I mean is I don't want to end up in the central chamber of the Great Pyramid of Giza!"

The Queen clapped her hands, anxiously. "You could still return to Earth if you had to, right?" She stared desperately at him. "Couldn't you?"

The queen stepped off the dais, wiping a tear away from her cheek. She went over to him, bowing to the floor and taking his hand in hers upon rising.

"Whatever you think of me doesn't matter," she said to him, raising her tear-streaked cheeks. The artist, seeing the ruined cosmetics running down her face shook his head in exasperation. "I beg you to do this for me, for us—Jason and me. It will help ease the pain you hold inside yourself, too. You like helping people. It gives you a reason to go on."

He took hold of her shoulders, regarding her eye to eye.

"Since you asked so nicely...."

"I can see what you hold inside, I always have," she told him. "That's why I welcomed your flight away to that island to be a hermit king. You helped me before when I was at my lowest. I can never repay that. I tried to make you my king yet you reject responsibility. You keep helping people but you.... I'm asking for only one more favor, please. Bring my son to me, so he can join my family here and be a part of my life once more. I know we can't change the past; I want to make the past go away. If I could, I would change a lot of things."

"So would I, but we can't." He gazed at her a moment. "I don't know if I liked you better before or after whatever it is that made you change. Being here on Ghoupallesz, it agrees with you."

"Will you do it?" Jason asked, posed again on the dais. "She's been driving me crazy for six months—six *Ghoupalle* months."

The queen rushed back, gave her husband a playful slap to his arm.

"I have not, goshdarnit!"

The *Mexas* laughed. "That's the Tammy I remember."

Chapter 3

Sexual Poetry

Dr. Toni Franck paused in her note-taking and regarded her patient, knowing that she could make a fortune if she ever published his story.

"What was this new landscape like?"

He let out a long sigh, recharging his mind with the foul air of the machine in the window, considered taking a peek out at the world. He was amused by the way life outside the windows seemed like some kind of television show, the way people came and went, birds flew, dogs shat, the sun shone, the wind waved the trees. They should call it "Saturday in the Park," he thought.

"There's already a song by that name, isn't there?" Toni responded and he realized he had spoken.

He was embarrassed. He could not remember the song.

"Don't worry," she told him, "it's a normal condition when a person has been in a coma. These memories may come back to you in time, the more experiences you have."

"Then shouldn't I get out and start experiencing things, instead of lying on a couch every afternoon? I could revisit places in my past, listen to songs. Then these memories would come back to me."

"Actually, Mister Talbot, they could be new impressions in your mind and not a true recall of memories. I know it's difficult for you, but that's why I'm here to help. Now, let's continue

31

where we left off, shall we?"

"Where's that? I was in the park on a Saturday, or else somewhere in a song—your choice."

"You were going to describe the scene you saw after all of the sparkling lights subsided. You said you entered a new world...?"

"Right."

"Go on, please."

"Well, it's hard to describe. Kind of a ghostly world. Very gray, somber, bland, some kind of limbo. That's how it felt. At first we thought it was a desert, but we weren't sitting on any sand, more like chips of soap. But we walked and walked and came to another landscape—"

"What were your first thoughts when you opened your eyes there?"

"I didn't think anything. Being trained in physics, I thought I was prepared for anything. It wasn't really weird, not like a science-fiction movie, but it was otherworldly."

"And what was your first thought? Were you thinking you had succeeded in your experiment, or were you afraid of something there? Were you excited, worried, disappointed, happy? What?"

"I can't remember now," and he shifted carefully on the couch, found a comfortable position. "I do remember Gina's words. When she was standing in front of it—the lights, I mean—and she pressed her hand into the opening there. She slid her hand forward until it was lost to my sight. She couldn't see it either. That was when I became worried."

"And what did she say?"

"'It's like sex,' she said, 'like the rush of the climax but it doesn't end.' That's what she said. She stood there half-way in the energy field. She slid her hand into it. She said she felt more relaxed but her senses were heightened. Then she said she was being called, something pulling her, so I hurried after her. As she stepped through, a loud roaring sound, like a freight train or a tornado, then nothing. Nothing, because we were on the other side then—and the curtain had closed behind us."

She wrote on her notepad for a moment.

"Some people might conclude, Mister Talbot, that it was most likely a hallucination induced by drugs. Do you see how it might seem that way to some people?"

"Of course." He grinned. "But I'm not telling you this as my attorney, not even as my doctor, but as another human being. I don't care if you believe it. You only have to write that I believe it. It doesn't have to be real. Isn't that how it works in a place like this?"

She chuckled, then stood up from her chair.

"It's interesting to note the relationship between your story and sexual references. This is perfectly normal, and it shows progress. So...."

Usually she kept out of his eyesight, aware of the effect her appearance had on her male patients. He wiggled his toes, at the far end of the couch and wanted to bend his head to see her but the angle was too strained.

"All right, Mister Talbot," she spoke after a minute—he heard papers shuffle and a drawer open and close, "I'd like you to have this, and use it when you feel the need."

She stood over him, gazing down. He noticed his arm was against her calf, and he could touch her if he wished. In her hand, he saw, was a magazine featuring a buxom blond on the cover. He took it from her when she motioned, and set it on his chest. His eyes followed her as she returned to the chair, short skirt riding up on the back of her thighs, hosiery moist in the red circles where her legs had pressed against the upholstery.

The magazine was for men, he saw, flipping through it.

"What do you want me to do with this?"

"Use it," she answered in a smooth alto which had as much emotion as a sheet of glass, "whenever you need to."

"I don't understand. Am I supposed to read it?"

"If you want to." She smiled meekly. "Actually, it's part of your treatment. It's also an experiment of my own design. I can't tell you anymore without affecting the results. But as a scientist yourself, I'm sure you can understand the need not to contaminate an experiment by too much explanation. So, I'll just say to you: 'Use this magazine whenever you need to.'"

He sat up on the couch, found his butt numb as he set his feet on the floor.

"So I'm supposed to go back to my room and contemplate the meaning of whatever the hell you said, and the meaning of 'use' in the context of this girlie magazine?"

"Correct." She turned to her desk.

He watched the navy blue skirt stretch tightly across her rear, knowing he was not a lecherous person in normal life.

"I'll see you again on Thursday. I have an appointment across town tomorrow, so we'll have to pick up your story the next day. Is that all right with you?"

"Sure, whatever you say. You're the doc."

❊ ❊ ❊

The air was musty, like an attic or a closed-off basement, yet this was the top of the hill. Breezes should refresh it. Perhaps it was the breeze itself which held the strange scents of antiquity. It was home, he realized. In the heavier gravity and the caustic atmosphere, he struggled to get his directions from the stony ramparts of the quarry.

Then he put on his clothes.

In the circle of the abandoned quarry all of the limestone blocks remained in place, as they had been one afternoon before when he had stood among them. There, in the noose of law enforcement, he had faced his accusers. He had not killed anyone, though he knew there was no way to prove his innocence. He had placed his fingers on the thickening air behind his hip and felt it give way. He had known it was his doorway to freedom, and as he had pried it apart in full view of the police officers assembled, their guns pointed at him. There was no alternative, he knew, so when the tear in the invisible curtain was large enough, he stepped swiftly through it. They saw him disappear, one leg, one arm, his torso, then his other leg, his head, his other arm—gone.

The police had followed him, pursued him through the closing aperture, and found him standing with a line of soldiers on the other side.

After his men had fired on the blue-uniformed intruders to chase them back, he ordered an explosive detonated at the crux of the tangent. He hoped to seal it so no one could follow him. At that moment, he also accepted that he would stay forever on his adopted world and never return to...

"Earth," he whispered like a long-forgotten secret.

He had trekked back to the location of the torn tangent in the rough Aivana countryside at Tammy's request and found the jagged opening waving solicitously before him, like the wayward flaps of a giant tent. He could see clearly the Earth side ahead of him before he stepped through—then he simply walked through the opening, without any difficulty, without any mental strain or necessary focus or tactile sensitivity. It was open to everyone now, and that disturbed him as much as returning to his world of origin.

"Instead of sealing the doorway, I've blown it wide open!" he gasped.

He stood once again in the same spot, with the same backdrop, the same rocks, the same stars—everything as it was the night he was killed.

Of course, he hadn't actually been killed—a pinch or two of his arm proved it. He presumed the police reports stated as much, however. After all, how could they ever accept that their fugitive had escaped? And escaped through a doorway to another dimension? Hiding out on another planet? There were police who had followed him—and then returned confused, insane. Some of them might still be undergoing psychiatric treatment. What could the official report possibly say about his escape?

He looked quite different now, anyway, due to ascetic living on his island. Who would recognize this gaunt figure now if he were to walk into the police station and greet them?

Down through the forest he went, along the gravel road overgrown with weeds, to the road which cut through the corn and soybean fields. No automobiles went by as he made his way along the crumbly shoulder, heading toward the lights glowing over the next hill. If time had been kind to him, the convenience store would still be there and he could fix his date at the newspaper stand. He might even grab a Baby Ruth.

There would be no Jason to call from the pay phone at the store this time. There might not be any store. He came prepared, carrying a purse from Tammy filled with almost two hundred dollars in cash and coins. He had added an old paycheck inadvertently taken to the next dimension and probably now voided. It was a start, and all that he would get. He recalled the first time he had passed through the curtain and returned dressed in clothing the storekeeper thought was for Halloween. Not this time. He was wearing blue jeans and a Chiefs jersey lent by Jason.

Inside the 7-Eleven, the newspaper blinded him with its dark ink. From the day he had escaped from his police captors up to this evening when he returned, more than three years had passed. It was in the autumn of 1986 when he fled through the tangent. Now it was 1990. Taking a big breath, he looked again: Thursday, March 29. He bought his candy bar, counting in his head.

He checked the phone book at the pay phone outside, found the page of the Tucker residence by Tammy's mother's name and tore it out. He continued walking, now along a broken sidewalk. No new housing had sprouted past the store, but land had been cleared of forest and the pasture plowed for suburban exploitation. Somebody was planning something. He checked into the Greencrest Motel three miles farther on Highway 40, and took a long, hot shower.

The next morning he walked up Noland Road to the bank which once was his. That night back in 1986 when he had returned to his life on Earth after rescuing Gina from the Zetin ambassador's castle, he had gone straight to his job at the IRS service center where, during his midnight lunch break, he was arrested and charged with the murders of his IRS colleagues— completely false accusations, he repeated to himself. He'd had no chance to grab his bank book. And after the interrogation, all of his belongings were surely boxed up and carted away, his apartment rented out to another denizen of the mundane.

Holding the cash machine card he'd saved in his wallet for several years of his Ghoupalle life, he wondered if it would work. He'd had few chances to use the device before he had to flee. He pushed it slowly into the slot. It hummed to life, digital letters directing him to punch in his secret code on the keypad. It was truly secret, even to him. It was something to do with Gina...or maybe Zaura, his Ghoupalle wife. A birthday, a date of death, marriage, anniversary? He had not changed it since he had first opened the account as a place to keep his converted fortune. In good years he would dig for the precious *gealan* stones in the Aivana desert, sell them for gold in Selauê, carry the gold back to Earth and exchange it for cash, then put the cash in high-yielding certificates of deposit, or a few conservatively managed mutual funds.

First, he needed to remember his code. He thought of five combinations of numbers, then felt a surge of energy run through him. The number was in his fingertips: the date he first met Zaura-Matousz, his apartment neighbor in the city of Lyas, in Sekuate-sotos. The screen lit up with a smiley-faced automated teller. His money was still there, and his balance had grown. So he withdrew the maximum daily amount: three hundred dollars. The remaining tens of thousands would have to wait another day.

His MasterCard was still good, having left it with a zero balance, and he was glad that the Avis at the mall took it and gave him a Ford Taurus, gassed and ready to roll. He drove out of the lot, new city map in hand.

His old apartment complex had been repainted—was brown, now beige—and there was a car parked in his old space. He ran a hand through his long brown hair, now tied back in a short ponytail, and spied himself in the car mirror—the ex-hippie look was working well—and decided he wouldn't be recognized.

As expected, there were no bloodstains on the walkway before his former address, nor had it been painted over. After all, the detectives had informed him that the body of his co-worker, the guy everyone called Fat Ken, was found outside his apartment, gut blown open. The name on the mailbox was different, but for his amusement, he rang the doorbell and a woman who looked slightly older than him answered. He asked if it was the Talbot residence, looking for Sebastian, and was told he was crazy—a verdict he had heard several times before. He excused himself, laughing, and returned to his car.

The next stop was the working class neighborhood next to the oil refineries up north in Sugar Creek, along the Missouri River, where Tammy's family used to live and possibly still did.

❋ ❋ ❋

The grin said everything, but Detective Sergeant Charles McElroy spoke anyway: "That is one crazy lady."

"That hooker in D cell?" Henderson asked.

"I'm talking about the one, the only, Doctor Antoinette Franck."

"Who's that?"

"Some woman he's been seeing lately," Detective Wilson explained, turning around from his desk. "Got wrapped up with her following the Talbot case."

"Wrapped up is right, boys. Tight, too." McElroy grinned.

"Oh, her. So what happened? Get laid?" asked Henderson.

"Better than that."

"What's better than that?" someone from the back of the room called.

"I got a lead on the case."

Sighs spilled out all around the room.

"Mister Dedication here, folks," Henderson laughed, returning to his paperwork.

"Getting laid will come later," McElroy assured them. "I feel it building already. But the case is now. She's starting to open up and tell me things. Of course, she don't know I'm on the case, but—"

"Are you outta your mind?" Wilson exploded.

"She's gonna fry you if she finds out!" Henderson shook his head, then glanced around at the faces that had looked up from their own desks.

Wilson motioned for them to lower their voices.

Henderson glared at McElroy.

"Or the department will when they find out."

"You can't go along keeping it a secret," Wilson added, then continued. "And you sure can't keep playing the good cop with her. It's against the law to pump her for info on her patient— even if he is the worst serial killer this town has ever known."

"Would it make a difference if I told her I was on the case?" McElroy replied. "She knows I'm a cop already."

"Probably wouldn't," Henderson mused. "If she's talking to

you now, she's already shown her poor taste. Go ahead, keep it up and see what happens."

"Keeping it up is the easy part. We'll find out about poor taste later, much later."

"What an asshole!" Henderson snorted.

Wilson gestured for them to lower their voices again.

"What did she tell you about Talbot?"

"He's telling her his dreams. Standard psycho procedure, you know. But they match—or she says they match—exactly the events leading up to the murders."

"Nothing new there. That's why he was put in an institute."

"The bastard was walking and talking in his dream world. Something like: 'Oh, there's a tree that's pulling a gun on me, blam-blam, dead; don't mess with me tree-dude.' The world of reality was swirling 'round his psycho head but he saw only what he wanted to see. Thought he was in some enemy fortress and had to rescue some broad from the dungeon. Killed the lord of the castle and escaped on a hang glider, if you can believe that. What he didn't see was that these alien beings were really his co-workers out on a joyride. Blam-blam! Reality is what he should pay for, not some fantasy not-guilty song he's singing up at Sunnydale."

"Calm down, McElroy."

He stuffed his fists angrily in his worn trouser pockets, his habit whenever he found himself shaking them too wildly in the air as he ranted.

"I'll calm down when that bastard is executed good and proper. The hell with crazy-ass defenses and country club institutes. He murdered six people in cold blood claiming he was in another dimension—"

"Why are you taking it so personally, Sergeant?" Wilson quizzed him. "I was at the quarry when Drummond was killed. You don't see me all twisted up in it?"

"Well, that's it. Maybe you should be."

"It's just a case. It's over. We move on. I'm deep into three more cases now."

"Life goes on, ya know," added Henderson. "Like the song. What was it? The Beatles?"

McElroy slapped the desk. "For me, there will always be only one case." His voice was hushed, breathy like a phone sex girl. "That Tammy Tucker who was one of the victims...?"

"Yes? What about her?"

He dropped his head against his chest.

"The mother of my kid."

Chapter 4

Scars Real and Fantastic

The boy acted like a real race car driver, sitting in the seat at the machine, spinning the steering wheel as he followed the video racecourse, dodging video race cars, sliding through pixelated oil slicks. He wore blue jeans and rock concert T-shirt, perhaps fifteen or sixteen, hair slicked back on one side, his right sleeve rolled up over a pack of cigarettes, but his feet held the latest high-top fashion. This had to be the boy he followed to the mall early on a weekday morning with school in session.

"You're Chuck Tucker?" he asked the boy, coming up from behind. The boy did not divert his attention from his task: to win the race. The man repeated his inquiry.

"Who wants to know?" the boy muttered, steering his car through a hairpin turn.

"I do."

"Yeah, and who're you?"

He stayed behind the boy, watching the race over his shoulder. "You might say I'm a friend."

"Yeah?"

He glanced around the arcade: only a few boys of Chuck's age. It was too early for the high school crowd. "Is today a holiday?"

"What do ya mean?"

"Shouldn't you be in school? I couldn't help but notice that it's a weekday."

"I'm taking the day off. So, like, who're you, my truant officer? Forget it. It's okay, I come here all the time. Ask the dude over at the counter there."

"I followed you here from your house." He expected a response, maybe an angry retort, but the boy continued his game, adding a few swear words at the challenging points along the race course. "I'd like to talk with you, Chuck, about something important. You got time?"

"Loads of time."

"It's about your mother."

"My mother?" That made him lose his concentration and his race car spun off the track and hit the wall, accompanied by electronic screaming from the machine. He cursed at the game, then pulled his damaged car back onto the track.

"Do you remember her?"

He shook his head, either as an indication he was not interested in the subject, or he was all too familiar with the conversation to come.

"She died when I was younger," he replied, steering through a hairpin turn with an oil slick and cursing another car suddenly entering the screen. "Don't remember nothing about her now."

"Well, I knew your mother."

"You and a bunch of other dudes. I know you guys. And I ain't interested in what you got to say."

"We worked together—at the IRS service center."

"So what's so important you followed me here?"

He glanced around once more, saw the attendant at the counter watching.

"Is he bothering you, Chuck?" the attendant called.

"Naw, we're just rapping," he replied, keeping his eyes on the screen and his hands gripping the steering wheel, video cars spinning out of control, squealing through their words.

"What do you know about your mother?"

"She was a bitch—I guess. Shit, I dunno. I seen pictures of her, so I know what she looked like. Can't figure why so many dudes wanted to be with her. Guess I ain't never gonna understand."

"Do you know where she is?"

The boy stopped suddenly and the splintering noise of his video car crashing against the railing erupted from the machine.

"Yeah, I know, man. You looking for her? Well, she's dead. Dead and buried."

"What happened?"

"She was killed when I was, like, eight. Some freaked-out maniac did it. She doesn't even have a grave for us to go to. Not enough of her left, they said. That psycho killed a bunch of people at the IRS, too—and trashed all of the bodies."

"Trashed?"

"Yeah, like, buried them or something. I dunno."

"Do you believe that?"

"At first, I thought she just ran away with some new dude and left me with Grandma. She did that a lot when I was a kid. Taking off with some dude—boyfriend, whatever. When I was old enough, Grandma told me what happened. Showed me the newspaper clippings. I read all about it."

"And how did you feel?"

"What're you, the police? Why're you spying on me? Following me around? Pervert."

"Because I have news for you: she's not dead. She's alive and well. In fact, she wants you to join her in her new home."

"Gimme a break, man! I heard all about you old guys. You tell all kinds of lies. I know what you're thinking."

"No, Chuck. I'm serious about your mother. She wants you to join her, and live with her where she's living now."

The boy got up, climbed out of the game seat, scanned the row of pinball machines.

"My dad don't want me. So it's just me and Grandma. We still got all of Mom's shit in the house, but I ain't allowed to get into any of it. Hah! Got my own key to the lock, anyhow."

The kid selected a game and pushed a token into the slot and waited for balls to come into the tray. The stranger stood beside the next pinball machine, dug into his pocket and produced a couple of quarters. He pushed them through the slot and his pinball game came to life.

"Wouldn't you like to be with your mother again?"

"What for? She wasn't too worried about me before. Where is she, anyway? You said she's not dead. She living with her latest boyfriend?"

"She's not dead, but she has remarried. She's a good mother

and her family is in good financial shape. If that matters to you. They're rich. Aren't you curious? How long has it been?"

"The last I remember she was taking us to Grandma's house for the weekend cuz she was going out with this dude named Michael. She was, like, all about Michael. I was six, I think—but I remember that Michael dude: tall, yellow hair, dressed up like a clown, always patting me on the head, like I was a puppy. I thought he was my dad for a while. I hated that. I hated her, too. Shit, I guess I still do. She probably ran away with the dude— whether or not she got killed after that. I don't care no more, man."

He slammed the heel of his hand against the pinball game, a violent strike not to knock an errant ball back into play but out of frustration with the stranger's questioning.

"Man, why don't ya leave me alone!"

And he stalked off to a baseball game across the room.

"Wait, Chuck."

"Wait, nothing! I'm through, man. Leave me alone."

The man pulled out his wallet, retrieved a ten dollar bill.

"I wonder how much this is worth these days," he said to himself before turning to the boy. "Are you hungry? I'm hungry. Why don't we go over to the food plaza and I'll buy you something, all right? Hamburgers sound good? And I'll tell you more about your mother. How's that sound? Some food, in a public place, no strings attached."

He stood back, let the video pitcher throw a strike straight down the plate. The crackling voice of the umpire told him he was out, the third one. He slapped the side of the game and the manager shouted at him to take it easy.

"You can buy me a burger if you want," said the kid, "but I ain't listening to any more of that 'she's *aliiiiive*' crap."

They sat down in the booth at Big Al's, ordered double cheeseburgers and fries, chocolate milkshakes and onion rings. The boy smothered his fries in ketchup. The man drew on his milkshake as though it was fine wine.

"Ah, the joy of a chocolate milkshake...."

"You like this stuff, huh? I thought grown-ups think it's junk food."

"It *is* junk food, but if I don't eat some of it once in a while I

44

can't appreciate the healthy food."

Chuck laughed.

"What do they call you in school? Is it Chuck or Charlie?"

"Chucker is what they *call* me—but I hate that name. Mom was crazy naming me that. Chuck R. Tucker. The 'R' stands for René. Sissy name, ain't it? That was *her* dad's name. Her name was Tucker, and after she got married it was McElroy. Then she changed it back to Tucker. My dad's name is Chuck. That's what Grandma said. So everybody calls me Chucker Tucker—ya know, like Chuck *R.* Tucker?"

"She's not like that now."

"Like what? A bitch? A slut? An airhead?"

"No, she's really quite different."

"You said she's alive, so of course she's different now."

The man set down his milkshake, relaxing in the booth.

"Let me tell you about her, Chuck. Maybe you'll see that I'm serious."

"Whatever," the boy grumbled, amused.

"I met your mother at the IRS Service Center, but I never knew her very well until that guy, Michael Fenning, became interested in her. I never knew what kind of life she had. Then, one night, for some reason the two of them broke into my apartment. Really. They thought I was keeping drugs there. I wasn't, but when I returned I found them going at it, you know, aaa, making love. Your mother became pregnant from that."

"And that's me?"

"No, it's your sister. The sister you haven't met."

"Jesus H. Christ! That's what Grandma says. You mean I got a sister?"

"Yes." He thought he noticed a positive reaction from the boy. "Your mother was afraid of what her co-workers would say—very gossipy bunch of women—so she thought about having an abortion and Michael offered to pay for it. But she didn't really want to do it, so Tammy, your mother—she decided to have the baby, but go away and have it some place where no one would know her or know about it, not even your grandmother."

"That's why she left? Just like that? She dropped me off at Grandma's and just left like that? Not even a suitcase? She left everything behind, man."

"She never planned to stay away so long."

"Then why'd she go away at all? Grandma never said anything about her having any baby."

"Your grandmother didn't know. No one knew."

"Then why was she killed? Or, why was she in the newspaper for being killed? I mean, was she killed or not? Why'd they say shit like that? What's going on?"

The boy dropped his cheeseburger and turned away.

"It was all a mistake, an accident." He watched for a shrugged shoulder, got it. "But it shouldn't matter to you or anyone now. She's fine, very much alive and doing very well. She was never in any danger. Now she's asked me to find you and persuade you to come see her. At least see her, talk with her. After that, it's up to you if you want to stay with her. That's all she asks."

"So you're, like, some kind of dude who finds missing people?"

"Not really." He laughed. "I'm only doing this for Tammy. She asked me to find you. She really wants you to be a part of her family—"

"Why'd she ask you?"

"Because I'm the only one she could ask. I know my way around here. I'm the only one who knows where she is. I'm the only one who can take you to her."

"And where's that?"

"It's far away, a long distance. I won't lie to you. In fact, it's in another country. We can leave today, if you wish. We can leave right now, and everything is paid for. And if you don't want to stay, you're free to come back here to your grandmother and continue as though we never talked."

"Is that Michael dude there?"

"Well, no. Not right there. Not with Tammy. But he went there along with your mother, but then he left and...well, he went his own way, got into trouble. We don't know where he is now. You don't have to worry about Michael."

"Then who'd she marry?"

"That is a long story, too. It would be better for Tammy to explain all that to you. I can tell you, though, that her husband is a friend of mine, a good guy, someone who—well, he loves racing cars, like you. We grew up together. We're kind of like cousins."

"And he wants *me*? Another dumb kid hanging around the house? I don't wanna be just another step-kid."

"You won't be. But you can decide for yourself."

"What the hell...."

"Fine. I'll tell your grandmother where you are after we get there."

"What, are you kidnapping me?"

"No, but we must hurry if we're going to catch our flight. There is only a limited window of opportunity. Like catching the wind in our sails, like catching the right wave on our surfboard, like—"

"I get it, already. So let's get outta here."

✳ ✽ ✳

The afternoon sun breached the office window, blooming exactly where the psychiatrist's face frowned.

"Even an intelligent man such as yourself should be able to see the parallels between your dreams and your fantasy world," said Dr. Franck. "You're a college graduate, and you continue to let your dream state rule your life. These are the observations I've made in these past six months."

"Yes, I know a person could see it that way," the patient responded calmly, compelled to lie still on the couch. "That's why it's so difficult to get anyone to believe me. I mean, if it's so easy for everyone to believe the Apollo missions really went to the moon instead of a movie set, then why is it so difficult to believe me?"

Toni cut in: "The times at work where you slipped out of reality, they were only moments of frustration. You were in another time and place, not sitting at that desk examining tax returns on the night shift. It's very clear."

"Clear as mud to some."

"The incident you described with Gina. It fits perfectly with what you told me about that week at the IRS Service Center. How all of those people were harassing you. It's quite understandable—though not excusable, of course. The fact that you were imagining you were sneaking into a fortified castle to rescue your girlfriend, Gina—who, in fact, you haven't seen for several years—is a classic mind-composed adventure. You got her out. You were wounded fighting. You wrestled with the captain of the guards. You met the lord of the castle, who bowed to you, thinking you were a mythic god. The mercenaries who fought with you, the forces conjured up as your retinue. It's clear what your true feelings are. You are a man of principle who wants to do right. You want to kill dragons and rescue damsels. There are lots of people in this world like you. You described flying from the top of the tower in a hang glider, the exhilarating sensation of soaring like an angel. This is the moment you ascend to heaven, the sacrificial hero, the hero who has given all he has to give and is welcomed into Valhalla."

"I like that part."

"Of course. It's a wonderful scene. Sometimes when I get frustrated, I wish I could fly away. It's a common dream."

"I told you the lord of the castle stabbed me when we fought in the corridor. It was a triangular blade—the style of the Zetin weaponry."

"I'm not going to argue with you, Sebastian. However, I would like you to write another couple of pages on your feelings about my observations."

"I nearly died there, bleeding to death trying to escape!"

Dr. Franck stood and retrieved three sheets of notebook paper from the desk and took them to her patient on the couch.

He bolted up suddenly. "This is my scar!"

The papers fell to the floor. The narrow heel of her shoe seemed to crumple into the carpet and she struggled to maintain her balance.

"Please pull up your pants, Sebastian."

"Do you see it? This triangular scar here? It came within a centimeter of my aorta."

She could not help but look.

"All this talk of yours about wanting to go back, back and change the present by, by changing the past." Her voice was wavering. "It's a dream we all have. That doesn't make a person crazy. It actually makes a person normal."

"If I'm normal, why aren't you looking at my scar?"

She turned her head away. "Mister Talbot, please."

"You don't have to say please, Miss Franck."

"Your pants, please."

"You can't have them. I need them."

"Pull them up, I mean."

He continued, pointing at the jagged line in the fleshy cleft of his hip.

"This scar is from when that Zetin warlord, UT'R-BKANN, thrust his dagger into me the night I saved Gina from his castle. It's the only mark I have from that so-called *other* place. The only time I was careless. The only time I truly faced death and was able to laugh at it. You should have heard me. You know, sometimes the gods play handball with human heads. That's what Gina used to say. That's why we suffer all the trials of our miserable lives. Batted around like a rubber ball. It all depends on whether you're being served or being volleyed. I've been played more than a few times. But I've also refused to be served. I've been lucky in that, *Mademoiselle* Franck. But I have never called myself a god, not even on Earth."

He stopped, noticing the dark glow in her eyes, suddenly sinister, like the eyes of a devil, he imagined—but she told him not to use his imagination so much. Certainly not because things were turning to shit. That was a cop out, she said. Some people hit the walls, others hit themselves. Those who hit other people have to be restrained. That's the rule. Otherwise, everyone is black and blue.

He lowered his hand and felt her sigh blow across his face, standing as close as she was. Her fingers were on his hip, lightly, as though checking the reality of his flesh. One fingertip was pressed against his scar, his mark of humility. When he regarded her, or tried to, her curly black hair was against his stubbly beard, her cheek brushing his chest. And the warmth of her shoulders seemed to melt a sanctuary out of his marble arms, creating a place where she could hide from the world. He couldn't sense her thoughts the way his Ghoupalle wife, Zaura, had been able to with her *senzenaxii* powers. It didn't matter, he decided, taking her delicate face in his right hand and bending her head upward. He felt her hand between his thighs as he moved his lips into the hot cushion of her mouth, where nothing much mattered anymore.

* ✳ *

"That was so *cool*, man!" exclaimed the kid.

With a quick glance back to the wide, wavering opening which sat like a museum painting suspended in the hazy autumn sky, he slung his pack onto his back and started off over the dunes.

"You thought that was cool?" said the man. "You ain't seen nothing yet."

They walked across the gray surface, a vast desert of ash churned from what was once an inland sea. The boy was awed by all he surveyed, accepting it. That pleased the man, knowing that the boy's mother would be happy.

After the first day, the boy became tired and complained about everything. They came to the cache the man had built to keep the things he would need whenever he returned to the world of Ghoupallesz, and disgorged its contents. They changed into the clothes stored there, though the boy did not approve of the alien fashion: the knee-high yellow stockings and blue shorts covered by the reddish triangular tunic fringed with white *papek* tassels.

"I know it looks ridiculous," the man explained, "but Levi's don't cut it here."

"This is for weirdoes," the boy cried.

"It's the fashion. I picked it up just before I came to get you. It's up to date for boys your age. Nobody will laugh at you, I promise. They might even envy you."

"Why can't I wear something like you got on?"

The man looked over his uniform, the khaki and crimson of the Sekuatean military.

"Because you're not old enough for an army uniform, and anyone who saw you might think to arrest you as some impostor."

When he wandered away from the cache, the boy did not see the depression in the sandy soil. His cries for help echoed across the plain and the man rushed to the *tairrag* trap. The meter-long sand lizard was about to take a sample of the boy's leg, caught as he was in the sticky-sloped slime hole. A blast from the AT gun severed the lizard at the neck. With the charred flesh still smoking, he pulled the boy out of the trap and warned him not to wander off again.

"I was just gonna take a piss," said the boy.

Then he wanted to try the pulse-beam rifle himself but the man would not let him.

"What is that, some kind of phaser?"

The man replied that it was not, adding that there was a significant difference between the world of Ghoupallesz and the adventures of the *Star Trek* crew: "On this world, everything is real—except us."

They walked on, and on the third day arrived at the first city. Taking the KOHAX from there—a kind of bus/train vehicle which traveled on tracks between cities and over pavement within the built-up areas—they came to the city of Aivana in less than 100 *peth*, a *peth* equaling about twenty minutes.

The boy was excited, seeing the spires of the tall building in the center of the city, the royal palace. The man was glad too, knowing his mission was about to end.

Chapter 5

Never Neverland

The silvery stone tiles cooled the great hall, and shadows spread out from the deep corners. Their footsteps echoed, magnified in volume, seemed to shake the floor. The boy's eyes were everywhere: the vaulted ceiling and the stained glass windows, the walls covered with tapestries portraying the history of Aivana, the huge thrones sitting upon the dais at the far end of the great hall. He did not know what to think and was searching for clues. Nothing the man had told him on their journey had prepared him for the reality he now faced.

In a distant wall, two magnificent doors creaked open and two guards stepped into the hall, pulling the doors closed. They bowed to the visitors, standing beside the doors.

A woman appeared. She wore a flowing lime-green robe trimmed in gold. Her blonde hair was curly, hanging around her face like a ring of petals around the pistil. In her clasped hands she held the scepter of her office, above its jewel was her smile. Her walk was confident but hesitant, and she seemed as much afraid of her guest as the boy was of her. Her head dipped in acknowledgment when she drew near enough for their eyes to meet.

He heard the kid gasp when she stepped into the light, the multicolored beams of sunlight filtered through the windows streaming down upon her regal robes.

"This is my mom?" he muttered to his escort.

"Yes, she is."

"But...she looks like...my big sister."

"That's because the aging process is slower for us here. She looks the same as when we first came here—except she's put on a few pounds."

"You mean I'll always be fourteen here?"

"Oh, you'll grow up. You just won't grow old."

"So, like, I'm never gonna be sixteen and get my driver's license?"

"You can drive any time you want to here. There are no requirements for licenses. Besides, the cars here are rather primitive. They don't go too fast. You can get a waiver from your mother. She's the queen, after all."

"She doesn't look like my mother."

"But she is your mother. Now go up and greet her."

"I—I can't. What should I say?"

"Tell her how you've missed her."

"But I haven't. I mean, she was gone so I got used to it."

"Then just say that. Make a good start of this. It doesn't matter what you say, as long as you say something to her."

"She does kinda look like some pictures I saw of her back home. Grandma never liked me looking at 'em, thought I'd get too freaked out."

"She's the same person, except now she's a queen."

"How the hell that happen?"

"It's a long story, longer than the one I told you coming here. Now go on and greet her. And call her *Hama*—that's Ghoupallêan for 'Mom.' That'll bring tears to her eyes."

He started forward, paused and looked back at the man who had not long ago discovered him in the arcade.

"Go on, Chucker."

"Don't call me that."

The man gestured again. "She's waiting."

❋ ❋ ❋

Toni remained on the sofa, calmly sipping her espresso and

reflecting on the play downtown she and Chuck McElroy had attended all evening. She had not wanted to invite him into her condo but she thought it was the polite thing to do.

"Put that down," she told him, as she had in the theater when he examined a purse left on the seat next to them.

"How could you let him get to you that way?" McElroy grunted through his clenched teeth, struggling to restrain his rage. Standing beside the cluttered desk, he had grabbed a report.

"It's our patient-doctor privilege," Toni repeated without fear. "He tells me lots of things, but that doesn't mean I believe everything. I write them down, analyze, try to determine the direction of his treatment. Like any doctor does for a patient."

"But this bastard murdered six people!"

"There are worse murderers in history."

"Not in this town. He's evil, pure evil. That's why he's so cool and collected. He's tricking you into believing he's sane, so you'll sign his release papers. Then he's back on the street looking for victims."

"You're totally wrong there, Chuck."

"The hell I am!"

"First, I'm not the one who signs his release, or anyone's papers. Second, it's not up to me alone to decide if he's sane. And third, you silly, silly man, he's a lot more compassionate than some of the cops I've seen. He's an intelligent man, and he speaks intelligently about this mess—all about it—like a rational human being. He rarely shows anger or paranoia at what's been done to him."

"Done to him? He's duped you already!"

"He has not—I mean I'm beginning to believe that—that he's not the murderer."

"Are you crazy?" He raised the report, cranking his arm into a tightly coiled catapult.

Toni finally jumped up from the sofa, seeing the extent of McElroy's anger, vowing never again to date a police officer.

"Listen, Chuck. I'm not any kind of judge or jury, and I'm not involved with his investigation. I have a very limited responsibility: to bring him back to normalcy. Once he's at that point, I take no further responsibility for him."

"But he's—" McElroy stopped, noticing what was written on the report in his hand "—writing goddamn poetry! Is this poetry? It *is* poetry. To you?"

"I said put that down."

He was reading it.

"Chuck, maybe you'd better leave now."

"'I have died, but you are among the living,'" he read aloud. "It is to you, isn't it? It's a goddamn love poem."

"That, a love poem? It's about death and dying, or can't you tell?"

"Don't you see? It's about death—and it's about killing. He's telling you his plans to kill again. It's so damn clear. Why're you protecting him? You in love with him?"

She charged him, snatched away the report, retreated to her side of the sofa.

"Listen! This is not a poem about anyone killing anyone," she explained loudly. "If you knew more about the world than your butt and where it itches, you'd know that this is the poetry of Boris Pasternak, the Russian poet. He wrote *Doctor Zhivago*, a novel about a poet—so he also wrote the poetry of that fictional poet. Mister Talbot did not write this. It's a quotation. This is part of his treatment. I have him write—write about his dreams, his thoughts, his views on everything. I can do that with an intelligent patient like him. That's why he's improving so quickly."

McElroy lowered his head, seething. He had never hit a woman before, though he had come close several times. He had always managed to hit a wall or a door. Once he hit himself—his head—against a door to release his anger. He did not carry his pistol tonight since they were going out to dinner in a nice restaurant. But he could never hit a woman. He had too much respect for—

Bam! Toni fell back on the sofa and McElroy leaped on her, both of them sliding off onto the floor. She held her arms up as he slapped his open palms against her. He boxed her ears trying to get at her face. She pulled up her legs, curling into a ball against his assault.

Out of breath, he got up and stood over her.

"Goddammit, I hated to do that, Toni, but—"

"Get out!" she shrieked.

"I'm sorry, really. I don't know what happened—"

"Get out, I said! I'll call the cops!"

"I am a cop, honey."

"You creep! I'll have my lawyer call you! Now, get out!"

He backed up, not sure what to do, then stuffed into his pants the shirt tail which had come out, and stormed from her condo.

Chapter 6

Nativity

The kid flicked the gray flakes from his Nikes and scanned the horizon, his eyes searching for any sign of the kind of civilization he had known. The plain stretched as far as he could see, and two suns blazed low in the sky, the larger yellow one and the smaller blue one, together casting a green glow over him. He smiled, trying to believe it all.

His new step-father was younger than he expected—and didn't even have a job. Maybe that was good, not being tied to a desk or standing on line at a factory. Of course, that's what his escort had told him: everyone ages slower on this world. On this world. How was he to believe it? Like the video games he had mastered, the Dungeons and Dragons, the sci-fi books he read at school when he did go to school. It was all so much crap, he could hear his teachers telling him. Hah, they were probably wondering where the hell he was right now! *Hey, Teach, I'm not coming to school cuz I'm on another freakin' planet!* That amused him. His grandmother would be worried, though, already being away for more than a year on this world—and who knew how long it had been back on Earth? Set-d'Elous, his escort, said he would call her and explain everything. The main thing was that he was once again with his mother. She looked like she did in the pictures on his grandmother's piano, wearing her high school cap and gown, and fully pregnant belly. Now she wore a royal robe. Was she really the queen of this desert land? And if she was, and he and his new brothers and sisters were princes and princesses, then what the heck was there to do to pass the time here?

Jason, his step-father, came over and sat beside him on the steps of the wagon.

"You need a hobby, son."

"Do you have to call me that?"

"But you are my son now."

"Yeah, well, I don't feel like it."

"Give it some time."

The kid glanced around, as if looking for something.

"Got any arcades? Any McDonald's? There ain't even any normal kids here. They all talk funny. And they—I mean, the ones that're outside the palace, not my brothers and sisters—they're all so weird."

"If you'd gone to another country on Earth, you'd feel the same way."

"Yeah, that's another thing." The kid shook his head and began poking in the sand. "How can I really, like, believe this is some other whole planet?"

His step-father raised his arm, pointed into the sky, and the boy's eyes followed until they met the brilliant light from the two suns.

"Okay, you're right. Another planet. Not Earth."

"We're about a hundred-ten light-years from Earth...as the crow flies."

"But what's there to do around this place? I can't spend the rest of my life digging up these marbles every day, and wearing all these Arab clothes. I mean, it really looks nerdy. It doesn't go with my Nikes."

"Well, son—and I'm going to keep calling you that until it feels right—this is what we do. These 'marbles' are the source of our family wealth. Think of them as desert pearls. People up north pay fabulous sums for them. Not too bad if you have to live in the desert, huh? You have to learn the family business."

"Business? I thought we're royalty, don't have to work."

The man extended his hand, filled with several orange *gealan*. Curious, the boy picked one out of his step-father's hand, examining it. Glass marbles. But not glass, something else. And the glistening colors when held up to the sunlight transfixed him. The effect was hypnotic. He held it away from his eye and rolled it in his hand, balanced yet strangely heavy.

"Well, we don't really, but it helps to collect some of these for a rainy day—"

"No rainy days here."

He returned the marble to his step-father's hand.

"Up north there's always rain," was his father's reply as he returned to his work, dropping his knees to the sand. "We don't want to raid the national treasury every time we want to take a trip somewhere, do we? It wouldn't be good. We aren't Rouê. Yet we're the rulers. That means some of our people might not like us. It's conceivable that one day we'll be asked to leave. In the meantime, it helps to be as benevolent as we can, so they will enjoy having us here."

Chucker threw himself off the wagon, landing like a cat on the sand.

"Man, even the king's gotta work. Makes me wanna run away—only I ain't got no place to run away to. I'd even settle for a trip into town—I mean a real town, somewhere normal." He watched his father kneeling in the sand, digging with a trowel like a kid himself. "Ya know, maybe I could like go somewhere, just to see what the places look like here. Ya know? I could just, like, go around and see things."

His father regarded him, hidden in the glow of the two suns. He shielded his eyes.

"I had planned something like that for us. But you're not ready for such a trip." He saw the mask on his son's face, not the triangular clay mask the Rouê used out on the desert but the mask of his inner secret. More explanation was needed; the boy still did not trust him. "You haven't kept up in your lessons, have you? You can't travel through Zissekap and be speaking English. They'll think you're weird—to use your word. How much of the language have you learned? I never hear you speaking any."

The boy laughed, threw some sand out into the void.

"Why? Are you, like, some kinda expert? If I talked some Ghoupallêan to you, would you understand it?"

The man stood up from his work, hands on his hips.

"Try me."

"Are you like for real, man?"

"*Ju naxem-durren emai Pazar-ga nex* man," he spoke in a falsely angry tone.

The boy grinned, realizing he understood.

"That's something about 'you're the father.'"

"Not bad. I said, 'You can call me 'Father,' not 'man.'"

"Okay, okay, I promise to study. Geez, just like a real father and son." The thought hit him that he was now experiencing something of which a few of his schoolmates had some direct knowledge: parental authority. But Jason was not his real father. "Where is my real father, anyway?" he spoke suddenly, digging in the sand with the toe of his shoe. "I never saw him, not even a picture."

This time the man did not look up, or slow in his work. Maybe he did not care, the boy thought.

"You'll probably never find him," his father said at last, still not regarding him. "Forget about him. You don't want to spend the effort to find a jerk like that."

"He must be a jerk. How about that Michael Fenning? Is he the jerk who hurt my mom?"

"I never met him but, from what your mother tells me, he was a bit of an asshole. She thinks he was an all right guy at times, but in the end he turned into a real jerk. Her words."

He tried to get up, fell back on his butt and patted his belly. The kid came over and helped his step-father up. Then the boy grew sullen, began kicking the sand once more as his step-father gathered up the cloth holding the precious *gealan*.

"Am I ever gonna have any friends here?"

"You'll make friends, if you try," Jason told him, carefully wrapping each *gealan* ball in soft fabric for transporting. "And if you learned to speak their language."

The boy watched him intently, beginning to understand the value of *gealan*, seeing how they were easily scratched and made worthless, seeing how his father took great pains to protect them.

"Hey, do you think we could take a trip—like you said before—up north. It doesn't matter, really—I mean where— well, as long as it's cooler. And, also...I kinda had an idea. Maybe you think it's weird or something, but I wanna meet Michael Fenning and see what kinda jerk he is. If Mom was so hung up on him.... Yeah, I know you probably hate his guts, but I just wanna meet somebody Mom knew back then. He was kinda like a father to me when he was dating Mom. I kinda remember a guy coming over to take Mom out. Tall...blond...dressed like a disco freak...very friendly, I mean, *too* friendly—at least with me."

"You're talking about the father of O'Ro'ma'le, you know. Your sister wouldn't like hearing that. If it were not for O'Ro'ma'le being conceived, none of us would be here now."

"Well, O'Ro'ma'le is an awright kid, I guess—if I gotta have a sister. But I can't see that Michael Fenning as her old man. I really wanna meet him. Then I wanna punch his lights out. Really deck the jerk for doing what he did to Mom. Screwed up her life, made her come here. Screwed up my life, too, not having Mom around to look after me, make me do homework and go to school and stuff, ya know. Look what kinda kid I turned out to be!"

Jason closed the small wooden box containing the *gealan* and locked it, slid it under the seat out of sight, and turned to his step-son.

"That's not what I had in mind when I planned our trip. This is the Roûê custom, this father and son traveling. Call it a Youth Trek, if you will. It's for the father and son to spend time together, you know, so the father can pass on to the son all the family knowledge. It's a time for the son to become a man, for the father to guide the son to manhood."

"Sounds kinda weird to me."

"True, you're not my biological son but you're still my son, so that's all the more reason we need to go on this trip together. Another handful of good *gealan*—let's try over at Yvo-Tharii; this place is empty—and we'll be off on our Youth Trek. Then we'll be father and son for real, and I'll teach you about this planet, and how to live here if you want to live. I'm talking about not dying, not being killed—living. I'll give you a Roûê name, if you like. When we're finished, and you know all that I can teach you, then you will be your own man. Then you can do whatever you want to do: be the king, search for Michael, go back to Earth, or find some nice lady here to have a family with. It's your choice—but not until we finish this journey."

"Will you help me find him?"

"Michael? I wouldn't know where to begin. He was in Lyas about twenty years ago—that's where Set used to live. Michael was undergoing some kind of medical treatment. Set-d'Elous arranged it—just like he brought your mother here to have her baby. Then Michael decided to wander off. Haven't heard anything since, and Set won't tell me any more. He probably doesn't care about Michael, the way the guy ripped him off. I wouldn't blame him. All the more reason not to look for him."

"I'll find him, somehow, somewhere, someday, then—"

"Bold talk from a sixteen year-old who can't speak the language or read a map."

"I'm gonna do it!"

"Then I guess I'll have to help you, so you don't get lost and wind up in jail. We've got to set a goal anyway, some destination. I have no desire to find one Michael Fenning, alias former IRS paper-shuffling scoundrel, but we can start off in that direction."

"Thanks, Dad."

"That's the first step of this Youth Trek—acknowledging who's who. You pass the first test with flying colors."

He helped his son up onto the wagon, and took the control bars of the dune buggy-like vehicle he had invented, stepped on the pedal to allow the cactus-juice fuel to flow into the combustion chamber, lit the ignition unit and the machine roared to life. He pulled back on the left switch and they rolled forward across the sand.

"The next step," the boy's step-father said, "is to bear the hardships that are inevitably ahead."

Sebastian cradled her face in his hands, rubbed the purple mark with his thumb.

"Does it still hurt?"

She shook her head.

"It looks a lot better," said the patient.

Toni almost cried, wrapping her arms tighter around his shoulders: "I'm glad there's at least one good man in the world."

"Who?" he asked, stroking her curly black locks.

"You know we can't continue making love every session. Every time we run the risk of being caught. Neither of us wants that."

"Then get me out of here so we may continue unabated."

She thought of McElroy's words and wondered if her patient and lover really was acting simply to make her believe he was sane. Feeling his heart beating against her chest, she tried to sense irregularity caused by the stress of telling a lie. None. He was good at neutralizing stress readings. She knew he would ace any polygraph test, but could he pass the review board next month?

And if he did, would she ever see him again? Or see him only in the newspaper?

She kissed his cheek, not sure if it was sincere this time.

"What are you thinking?" she asked, the two of them still tightly embraced on the couch in her office.

"Me? Nothing."

"Maybe you're wondering what the good doctor is thinking about. I was thinking about your review board and, if you pass, where you would go and what you would do out in the world again."

"Is that it? You're worried."

"Not worried, concerned."

"Concerned if I'll pass?"

"Concerned if I'll ever see you again once you leave."

He was silent and that unsettled her. She began tearing her hot flesh off his, peeling their bodies apart.

"Aren't you going to answer?" she asked.

"Of course I'll see you." He smiled. "Let's make a date. One month after my last day here, seven in the evening, in front of the Nichols Fountain on the Plaza. Then we'll have dinner at Santa Fe. Or, since you're French, we can go to La Mediterranée. After dinner, we can go dancing, or we could go back to your place for a nightcap. Or take in a show—"

"Why one month after?"

Again he was silent. Her eyes turned inward in a vivid

searching of her soul, waiting for the words she expected to hear.

"I'll need time to get settled again, find a place to stay, get some decent clothes. All of my things are gone, you know, after the police confiscated them and their warehouse burned to the ground. I needed new stuff anyway."

She sighed, sitting up, feeling naked as she reached for her bra.

"And after that evening?"

"After? You mean right after, or days and weeks after?"

"Days and weeks."

"I'll travel."

"Where to?"

"Here and there. I need to see the world again. To get in touch with reality, so to speak. Maybe you can join me. Can you get some time off?"

"How much time?"

"At least a year."

She held her smile, but he quickly saw how it decayed. That did not matter. Sure, he could fall in love with her, if all the obstacles in his life were removed. It might be possible and he would be saved from the guilt of a convenient affair.

"We'll see about that later," he said with a grin. "After our dinner."

"But before dessert. Promise me there will be dessert."

Chapter 7

Death by Example

The boat slipped into deeper waters and turned north. He knew it would hug the coast until they neared the port of Selauê, then turn west to return him to his island.

He had accomplished his mission, reuniting mother and child, introducing step-father to step-son, and all was right with the world. As long as he did not dwell on the details. His efforts had greatly exhausted him, yet the stress he still felt was more than the sum of what he had done. A mere mortal would have died with the exertion, he mused as he stood at the bow of the ship, taking the sea spray welcomely in his face. He remembered another time when he similarly took the chilly sea wind in his face as he crossed the Tebbi Sea on a previous mission to rescue Gina.

At his private paradise, there on barren, volcanic-scarred Little Biznuik Island, he could rest. He could return to his pastimes—and the realization that he called them 'pastimes' led him to ponder what it was that he wanted to do with his life. It would be satisfactory to mull around on a desert isle if he were an old man who had done great things and spread much wisdom. It would be quite acceptable to live out his remaining days in solitude, write his memoirs, receive occasional awestruck guests. But he was still young—perpetually so, it seemed.

They docked in Selauê overnight and he stayed in town as they refitted the ship for the next leg of the journey.

Selauê was his adopted hometown, the place where he wished he'd been born. It was the place he'd come to call home and much of his life on Ghoupallesz had been spent there. Selauê recalled for him Paris without the Eiffel Tower. Actually, Selauê had three towers of similar ironwork structure, one in the business district, one north of the district, and one along the waterfront. The many lush parks, landscaped cobblestone boulevards, great universities with spire-topped buildings, and the quaint backwater district with its old gray or red brickfront townhouses where he had lived with Zaura and their children— ah! he held images of them in his heart like a portrait of his family kept in his wallet. And the vast highland expanse which dominated the eastern district was crowned by the great walled fortress. All the fortresses in Sekuate were shaped as eight-pointed stars. The star represented the four independent Ghoupalle city-states of the north and the four independent Rouê kingdoms of the south which had united to form the nation of Sekuate in Ghoupalle year 1167.

The city of Selauê, however, was also a city-state in ancient times (GP 207-739) and then its own republic (GP 739-1041) before union with the Seas government to form the nation of Sekuate North (GP 1041-1167). Through the centuries, Selauê had remained the continent's seat of learning. For him, the search for knowledge, the resolution of problems, the idealization of better ways to do things and the collection of data were more than hobbies. Learning was what made him get up in the morning and what drove him through his days. In another time and another place he would be called a professional student; now his title of *Mexas* gave him the time to learn. He had studied at the Selauê Academy. Taught there, too.

He smiled as he walked the autumn streets of Selauê and gazed at places familiar and others that once were familiar but had become ravaged almost beyond recognition by the wars. It was a perverse curiosity which held his attention, regarding every bullet hole and every crumbled building. He was not living there when the city was attacked toward the end of the wars, but he should have been. Everywhere he turned were signs of the wars. And signs of Sekuate's defeat. He had read about it in a history book his son had written after that period of history. His son had given him the book as a gift.

He thought back pleasantly:

Returning from an unstimulating life on Earth, he had found himself caught up in the final phase of the war. The Sekuatean invasion of Tebbicousimankalê was at hand and after being pushed back into military service, he had lived the campaign as though reading a book. He carried the book with him and consulted it daily for news of which battle they would lose and which they would win. He noticed, however, that nothing he might do to change the outcome of events ever made a difference.

Of course, all of the trouble began with the revolution, followed by the civil war between rebels and those loyal to the *Mexas* of Sekuate. After the commanders of two army corps gave their support to the rebels, the installation of the five-member Gangus Council as the new government was assured. Their quick rise on a wave of popular support emboldened them to threaten neighboring countries with the expanded military might of what became the Sekuatean Empire. And when they finally met a foe that would not back down, the Great War against the Northern Megan Alliance was initiated by Sekuate's invasion of the kingdom of Bezua-hü.

All manner of marvelous military machines and special strategies were used and the region was nearly conquered save for one small but devastating error: greed. In their excited dash to overrun the nation of Tebbicousimankalê—the most powerful nation of the Northern Megan Alliance—they allowed the Tebbi armies to fall back and wait out the severe winter while hired warriors from Zetinê held the Sekuatean army in check, bogged down in the snowfields. He lived through that winter of 1533. Then, as spring spread over the northern city of Siaa, the Tebbi forces broke the siege and drove the scattering battalions of Sekuate to the southeast, back across the subcontinent.

The surrender at Milipour was not the end, though. The forces of the *Nog-Megank-Ulsinyn* moved to liberate the nations of northern Zissekap, then those of southern Zissekap, and finally they invaded the Sekuatean Empire, cutting it into quarters. The occupation lasted eight years and during that time the Sekuatean army was outlawed, then reorganized as a defensive force. What remained of the Gangus Council were the grandchildren of its five founders: brother Metour and sister Mourta, who were publicly executed in front of their palace—in the same great square from which they had blessed their loyal legions.

He was not there for most of it. His Ghoupalle wife, Zaura-Matousz, was ill in the autumn of 1481 when he took his regiment to put down the rebellion in nearby Kamtan district. When her condition deteriorated, he was granted leave to be with her on her death-bed. His unit went on to fight the rebels in Manioug and Yiexe districts southeast of Selauê. That was the beginning of the revolution, he knew in hindsight. When Zaura died, he was destroyed and returned to Earth to languish in his grief, trying desperately to forget everything about his life on Ghoupallesz.

A job at the IRS service center was not the answer, he quickly realized, pausing at the corner of one of his favorite parks near where he and Zaura had lived. He chose a bench and sat, gazing at unfamiliar constellations and thinking of war.

The war was at its peak in 1531 when curiosity about his offspring pulled him back again. He learned that one son, whom he had seen graduate with honors from the Selauê Academy years before, was now a general, had campaigned through Arêsz and Feasfend on behalf of the Gangus government. He knew what his son would write in that history book some day. So, in the guise of a wise old ascetic, he had persuaded his son to take the family away from Selauê.

Later, he was recognized by military officials on the streets of Selauê and pressed into service, made to take up his old command with the 102d cavalry regiment. He soon found himself part of the massive invasion force under the supreme command of *Berron* Tomak-Brounadar—who once upon a time had been a mischievous cadet assigned to his regiment. Ah, the lessons he had unwittingly imparted to the young man!

Then came the invasion of the vast northern continent, Tebbicousimankalê, and the battles across the lower and upper peninsulas, and the siege of Siaa during the endless winter. He had been there, freezing with his men, men he had trained, had fought alongside. He could not abandon them, even when they were forced to retreat and after weeks of struggle found themselves backed against the sea with the Tebbi army surrounding them. He used his own *gealan* wealth to buy ships to transport his men off that rocky coast and take them back to their homes.

For that merciful indiscretion, he was banished from history. He did not care. He was an Earthling, anyway, and owed no allegiance to them.

Instead, he had returned once more, somewhat gladly, to Earth, to his squeaky old chair behind the government-issue gun-metal gray desk set in the corner of the section, near the other graveyard-shift tax examiners at the Internal Revenue Service processing center. Even there, he could not find peace. He wished to forget everything. In time, the visions in his head were pounding to get out, and he knew that he was being called to duty once more. It was Gina, his long-lost love, who needed his help.

He smiled, remembering it all, then got up and crossed through the park where he and Zaura had been paraded on their wedding day, heading to his next stop on the nostalgia tour.

After he and Gina had gone separate ways following their very first adventure through the interdimensional doorway to Ghoupallesz, they seemed to take turns rescuing each other from fate and misfortune. By now, he was far ahead in the tally, and she was calling him for yet another favor. She had married a Tebbi official who became the prime minister prior to the war, and she became a willing hostage to the ambassador of neighboring Zetinê in order to secure a treaty. The Zetin warriors would fight alongside the Tebbi army, their eternal enemies, against the invading Sekuate forces. When the war was ended, the Zetin would regain territory that had been in dispute for centuries and the Tebbi hostage would be returned. However, the war ended and the treaty was broken by the Tebbi—they would not return control of the land—and so Gina continued to be held in the castle of the Zetin ambassador. It was left for Gina's high school sweetheart, Sebastian Talbot (a.k.a. Set-d'Elous), and a band of retired soldiers from his former 102d regiment to rescue her—and dozens of slaves also held in the castle.

Gina was grateful, of course. They settled in the city of Kipzon, where she bore him a child. Then she left without warning or excuse, taking the baby with her, traveling into a new life, a new identity. That was her custom: to move on before the familiar became the sentimental, to always leave before life became too dull. Considering they both were Voyagers, he had expected they would stay together forever. After over thirty 'lives' lived in many places using many names, her habits were set. She did as she always did, and simply left.

She would return, of course, somewhere, at some date.

He had acquired a history book which made reference to her presence on a certain date and in a specific place, and he intended to intercept her. The rendezvous was in Aivana in the latter part of 1574. He knew no other details about her trip; only that her stop in Aivana was noteworthy enough to be included in a history book. She was called an assassin. That initially puzzled him, but he was not concerned with technical details.

Gazing up at the street lamp at his new destination, he saw tiny dots of rain dropping through its light. As he watched, he could feel anger running out of his fingertips. He stared up at the townhouses, and lingered on the gray brick building which had been his home some one hundred years earlier. He and Zaura and their youngest children had lived there.

The breeze picked up, blew chilly, and he moved on, finding his way over to the military academy where he once taught. That was a pleasant time for him. He looked for the moon, forgetting that on Ghoupallesz no moon lit the night. He was left alone in the dark with his secrets.

He hailed a carriage, his mind full of film clips of his life with Zaura, their newlywed life on Karluk Island, his disappearance and her mourning him, then her remarriage, his return, their flight, her brother's pursuit—

Distraught once more, he had returned to Earth, to the IRS job, and kept to himself. Later, Gina came and took him back to Ghoupallesz to attend the ceremony uniting Gina's son with a young woman who, he was surprised to see, was his daughter.

And there was Zaura! It was 1474. Reunited, he and Zaura had stayed together to the end of her life, with his whole military career and three more children, up to the second day of the month of Gouo in the year 1481—

Satisfied to take a brief pause in Selauê on his way back to his barren island, he regarded the gloomy façade of the same hospital where Zaura had died—as the carriage master waited patiently for payment, the *Jêpe* snorting impatiently in the wet night air. The building still stood, its official name changed to reflect its peacetime use.

If only he had done something, he cursed, his breath frosty. What he could have done, he never understood. Only that she had died so young, at seventy—like a forty-year-old woman on Earth. If she had lived, he would have moved them away from Selauê to avoid the wars. He would have had another child with her. And Zaura would have grown old and gray with him—or not, since he aged at the same rate at which his Earth body was set.

When tears ran down his cheeks—or was it rain?—he adjusted the collar of his jacket and hailed another carriage, then headed to the inn where he was staying.

Stripping off his clothes and dropping onto the *qala*, he sighed and counted the time until he boarded the ship to continue to his island.

Chapter 8

Inner Storms

The light was fading outside with the approaching storm, and the candles had yet to be lit. Deep in the twilight room they sat within each other's aura. She lay against him on the couch—he felt her weight, lithe though she was—and he became pressed into a dream about another time he was likewise positioned. The woman was Gina, his long-lost love. He hated that phrase, yet every time he thought of her it came into his head. What else to call her? He pondered different titles, decided none fit her better.

He lifted his hand from the small of Toni's back and scratched his nose, thinking.

"When I was shot, I felt the bullet." His voice was heavy, weary, echoing the deep, rolling thunder overhead, "It felt like a butter knife sliding through my flesh. Slowly. I actually felt it enter me, millimeter by millimeter—and, no, I wasn't on drugs."

The doctor smiled quickly. "Your hindsight gives you extraordinary latitude in the memory of your perceptions." Her chin rested against his chest as she gazed at him. "I'm sure you do indeed remember it that way."

"I would change that way," he responded, "if I could. And the vision."

"Do you mean the vision of your old girlfriend?"

"I mean Gina, but she was not an old girlfriend; she was much more. More like a soul mate, eternal best friends. Is it even possible to have such a cosmic twin of the opposite sex while still being completely in love with one's own spouse? Never mind. But that vision, or whatever it was when I was shot and dying, whatever it is we don't have the vocabulary for, it disturbs me even now. I know it was real, that she was there telling me something. She *did* tell me something, and I can never forget it."

Toni pushed herself up so she could see his face.

"It shocked you that much?"

"I wouldn't say shocked," he chuckled. "It was more like a flash of insight. I suddenly could see everything."

"Everything? Your life passing in front of you? That sort of thing?"

"No, it was my future I saw," he said. "They said I sat up in the middle of the operation. Just sat straight up. I looked around and saw I was being operated on, and it looked rather serious. I saw all the blood and my guts were opened up and strangers' hands were in there fiddling with my organs."

The doctor nodded. "That sounds like the Temporal Exit experience." Thinking, she gave a violent shake of her head, shooing away the locks of hair falling into her face. "I wrote about it in my journal article, where a person who is on his death-bed realizes that death is near. Some people have reported that they looked down and saw themselves being operated on and knew they were going to die. They were already outside the body—their soul was—looking down on themselves."

"Maybe it was like that, but I stayed on the table. And one nurse—I heard her say something."

"Could she have been someone whom you thought was Gina?"

"No, Gina was before that, before I sat up. Gina was the angel escorting me into the white light. The nurse said something like 'I thought he was a goner.' I remember that word 'goner.' Then someone else said, 'He just came back to life like he had unfinished business.' I remember laughing at that."

"Laughing? When you were in surgery?"

"That's the best time. I really needed to laugh."

She avoided his eyes, taking his face in her hands and holding it in place so he could not think of anything but the words she was going to speak. She lowered her nose until it touched his, their eyes point blank.

"You feel now that you should have laughed then. You certainly did not laugh during an operation. What about all the tubes down your throat?"

"I laughed. I'm certain of it. But what I remember most is what Gina said to me."

Toni sighed. "Before you sat up?"

"It was exactly like I had always heard it would be. You know, people who come back from the dead and tell what they saw— people like me, who were dead on the table for a few moments and come back to life."

"Do you think that's what happened to you?"

"I never believed I was dying, or that I would not wake up. Gina came to me, in that white light, like an angel. She said, 'Are you coming?' I just said, 'Where?' I kept asking, 'Where?'"

Toni pried herself off his body, swung herself to a sitting position on the edge of the couch. Brushing back her hair, she felt the coolness of the air, and the spot of warmth where his hip supported her lower back. It was as if death itself had entered the room, and a flash of terror swept through her.

"Death is always weird," she said. "That's why people are so fascinated by it. I can see the way your mind works, by the way you talk about your near-death experience."

He sat up, braced on his elbow, his hand reaching out to caress her back.

"Toni, don't you think it's a little strange for us to be doing the dirty deed and keep talking psychology at the same time?"

She moved away, toward the edge, balancing herself there like a mountain climber on a precipice. Her voice was the coarse rockface and the grunting of rappellers scaling the cliff as she turned to him.

"Two things, Sebastian, *dear*. First: this is not 'doing the dirty deed.' It's part of the therapy, a vital part of your rehabilitation. Second: there's no reason why we can't double up two tasks in the same period of time. If I were charging you by the hour, it would be a bargain, but in your case the state's paying the bill."

He lost his smile. "Let me tell you what Gina said."

"You've done that before," she growled, looking at him.

"I didn't tell you everything, because I knew how you'd analyze it."

"You're not supposed to hold anything back from me." She sighed. "I'm surprised you don't trust me."

"If I didn't hold anything back, you'd call it premature pontification and put a big, black mark on my file. Because you call me an 'educated patient' and give me special treatment, I'm entitled to use my own judgment as to what I tell you."

"Enough." She went to her desk, grabbed her panty. "What did she say?"

He watched her pull on her hosiery, resisting the urge to help. He noticed her formality, as if she were drawing a shield between her reason and his fantasy. Their sessions were beginning to be the same: sex for producing trust, then dressing to hide true feelings and provide cover for their sins.

"I was talking to her," he said, "but she kept trying to persuade me, saying, 'You can see your wife again, and your sons and daughters, and your grandchildren.' I took that to mean they had all died. 'They're all here waiting for you,' she said. I couldn't understand what she meant by that. Oh, I knew about the heavenly liturgy, but the words had a double meaning. Maybe she meant I could be with them again in heaven because we were all dead. But I took it differently. I took it to mean I could be with them again in life."

She stepped over to him, dropping his shorts into his lap and turning for him to zip up her dress.

"She said that's what I've always wanted: to be with my family again. Because of the regrets I had about missing so many years of their lives. I missed all of their childhoods. I missed a big ten-year chunk of time with Zaura, too. Then, when I found her again, she died so young. Gina said those lost years could be lived again."

"Wait a minute," Toni cried, throwing up her arms and spinning around. "Are you talking about your wife? Of course you are. Your wife, Linda? You were married to her for a couple years, no children. That wife?"

"No...." he said, suddenly guarded. "Linda was murdered. Check your notes."

"I thought so. You're rambling again about your fantasy world family. I told you not to dwell on that; it's not good for your rehabilitation. You've got to deal with reality. How can I pronounce you rehabilitated with one of these stories of yours always popping out?"

He jumped up, the band on his shorts snapping back dangerously.

"Then I'm crazy—like they said when I first arrived." He righted his shorts. "Listen to me! I'm not telling you some 'fantasy world story'—as you keep calling it. I'm telling you what my near-death vision was. That's all. You can analyze it all you want. Where was I?"

She shot his hospital pajamas at him. He caught them and continued:

"She said, 'Anything is possible.' So I asked her—just to be clear—'I can return to the past?' That's what came out. She was saying one thing and I was hearing something different. I kept asking, 'So I have the power to change the present by going back and doing something differently?' She never would answer me directly. She kept saying, 'Anything is possible.' And 'Are you ready to go?' So finally I told her, 'Why should I go with you if I have the chance to make things right with my family—with the whole world?' She didn't have an answer for that. She said she was leaving and I was losing my chance to go with her, but I knew I was doing the right thing. When the light was going out, I got a little scared but I had to do what I had to do. Then I awoke, ready to take care of my 'unfinished business.'"

He took a breath. The chill in the room engulfed him and he quickly put on his pajamas. He waited for the inevitable comments from his doctor. She leaned against the desk.

"All right, I've heard you," she said. "I think I understand. I still believe it's the same road we've gone down many times before." She straightened herself, then smoothed the hem of her navy blue dress, felt his eyes following her fingers. "Sebastian, it's only your subconscious desire to change the events that happened. It's quite common. People want to have another chance at something. In that respect, you're normal—maybe more than most. But you can't. No one can. It's plain impossible to go back in time and change history. It makes for some great movies, but it can't be done. No one has yet invented a time machine, and unless your mechanical pal, Mister Aronstein, can whip up something, you are grounded in this time zone. Therefore, you have to live with what you've got. You have to learn to live with the consequences of events we cannot change."

She looked so great in that outfit he hated to disagree.

"But it can be changed," he dared rebut. "I don't have any time machine, but I know it can be done. Toni, you have to believe me—and help me. There's so much at stake. If you could prevent a war, wouldn't you go back to kill someone? even if that person was a child? How about your parents? Wouldn't you do anything you could to keep them from getting into their car that night in Paris and being blown up by the terrorists? You could not do nothing. You'd at least call out and say, 'Dad, let's stay home tonight.'"

She slapped the desk hard.

"I'm not going to stay up all night debating time travel with you and arguing about how to change history! There's enough misery in this world without some crazy idiot trying to change things. I'm tired of this conjecture. I've got to get out of this office, get a good night's sleep, and maybe in the morning none of this will make sense!"

Chapter 9

Requiem

The ship set sail before dawn, and after a night drinking *skual* with his old comrade in arms, Samot-Angêron, now a retired general. The rocking of the sea as the ship left Selauê bay for deeper waters quickly took its toll on the chief cargo: *Mexas* Set-d'Elous. Resting in his bunk below deck, he held his stomach. It was only after they were far out into the Bær Sea's current that the ship became steady and their passenger came out to examine the sunshine. With the fresh sea breeze on his face, he could live again.

Until the words of the previous night returned to him.

"Are you mad?" the old general had exclaimed, though it sounded more polite in the Ghoupallêan words.

It was no secret to the general that the man before him was from another planet—"Greetings, Off-worlder! Have you come to torture me with your jokes?"—a fact known to him, having served the Prince of Aivana before retiring to his hometown of Selauê. He was one of perhaps a dozen Ghoupalle people who knew and believed that he and his fellow Voyagers were from that mysterious world which Ghoupalle legend ascribed as Hell. In times past he had served under the command of Set-d'Elous, cavalry captain, back during the invasion of Tebbicousimankalê, and earlier as a young lieutenant, the communications officer of the 102d regiment at the Selauê garrison. It always amazed the general how the man who was his senior when they first met maintained his youthful appearance; now the general could be mistaken for his grandfather.

"I'm not mad," Set-d'Elous retorted. "It can be done, I know. But it's such a precise and delicate matter that I'm afraid to attempt it alone. If I'm wrong, whatever the consequences might be is beyond my ability to calculate. I need your advice, and your expertise, *Kanê* Angêron."

Calling him by the equivalent of 'sir' impressed the old soldier.

Angêron rubbed his bewhiskered chin as he always did when faced with a difficult decision.

"You are the oldest friend I have on Ghoupallesz," the *Mexas* continued, "the only living Ghoupalle who knows my secrets. It is also your people who would be affected by such a mission, and they alone would suffer the results."

"Then I advise you not to do it."

"Have you thought of the benefits your people would have if we succeed?"

"That does not matter."

They were quiet for a while, then the general spoke up, cleared his throat, knowing he had a lot to say: "I must recall for you, *Kanê*, one adventure in which you thought to do a great deed, yet failed. You told me of it. Although we have been through many adventures before, it alone stays in my mind to torment me in my advanced age."

"What is it?"

Set-d'Elous smiled as the old general spoke of events long forgotten. A woman came to Set-d'Elous for a special mission: her mother was captured and needed rescue. Why him? He happened to be her grandfather; the young woman's grandmother was a Voyager named Renée—

"A mistake I once made," muttered Set-d'Elous.

Angêron continued, explaining how the airship crashed among the high mountains of Hikbok, on the Mazonnarox plateau, and everyone was taken prisoner by the nomadic Jêvon people.

Set-d'Elous hung his head, let it rest on his chest for a moment, then looked up, his face red. Angêron knew him not to weep easily.

"Yes, I remember," the *Mexas* sighed. "I took my men to the Mazonnarox. We arrived on the plain, waited until night, then rushed their campsite. Only the chief had a tent, and his warriors slept outside in concentric circles. Inside was the chief and his retinue, his harem, his slaves. I was able to enter the tent and free Batü. In the next moment the camp came alive and it was all we could do to escape ourselves. We regrouped out of range of the warriors—but not out of sight of them—and we saw that in the fighting they had recaptured Batü."

The general clasped his shoulder.

"Yes, and there was nothing you could do."

"There was!"

"No, *Kanê*, there was no possibility."

"The Jêvon warriors taunted us, tied the woman to a post where we could watch them torture her. Several times we charged the camp to reclaim the woman and each time they fought us. I had the power to choose to leave and save my men or continue trying to attack and save the woman."

"There was a choice, but I did not think of it."

"We cannot think of everything in this universe, *Kanê*," said General Angêron.

"But—"

"There was nothing that could be done that night on the Mazonnarox. You and you alone had a power to use. But that power was a shackle upon you. If you had been weak, you would have succeeded. Jêvon stared at you—indeed, glared defiantly at you. As you watched the woman suffer, you did what only you had the power to do."

Set-d'Elous sighed, and felt that it was his breath which moved the clouds across the sky, which caused the trees to bend and kites to fly—then remembered that he was far from a god.

"I killed her."

"You killed her."

"I raised my rifle and put a bullet into her forehead."

"She died instantly and her suffering ended. Perhaps she would have lived on in agony for hours or days—the Jêvon are skilled at torturing. You stopped that. You halted their perverse pleasure. You halted the woman's suffering. You had mercy for her, yet you did not think that way...then, or now."

"Why now? The result was the same, whether or not it was a merciful act."

"Because you have never forgiven yourself for it."

"Do I deserve forgiveness?"

The general chuckled.

"Does anyone deserve forgiveness? I've forgiven myself for atrocities committed in Tebbicousimankalê in the name of the Empire; no one else would forgive me. No, *Kanê*, 'deserve' is not a word we can easily use. That's a religious question, and since I'm a soldier and not a priest, it is not for me to say. However, listen to me now and accept these words. You took twenty men to the Mazonnarox and all but four died trying to rescue one person, who also in the end died."

The *skual* bottle was empty—again. They moved the eight bottles, four to each side of the table, and sat back in their chairs. The general glanced around for his daughter to bring another one but everyone had long ago gone to bed leaving the two old soldiers alone. It was a time of solitude and solemnity, when hearts could speak more freely than could mouths.

"I want to change that," Set-d'Elous spoke up. His voice was clear but lowered, full of intensity despite his drink. He leaned forward, stared across the table into the general's weary eyes. "And more, if I can. I want to make things the way they should be, the way Fate and the seven gods and nine goddesses have decreed—or, how they should have decreed."

Leaning against the ship's railing, he remembered how the general had thrown his arms up in frustration.

"Are you mad?"

"No, I'm only a little crazy. It comes and goes." He had chuckled uneasily. "I don't believe the gods plan to make people miserable. It just happens, like accidents. The gods aren't perfect, either, you know. I'm not a god, but I can do it. I can change these things, Samot. If you'll help me, I can undo the suffering of many. I can make the right decisions and do the right thing. And I will be able to be with Zaura once more—and she won't die this time. I'll see that the wars will never happen here in Sekuate. And I won't have to travel so far away to climb mountains and face gruesome travails just to do a simple mercy killing. There won't be a need anymore for mercy killings!"

✳ ✸ ✳

Chuck McElroy grinned. *Mercy killing, huh?* The detective paused at those final, handwritten words. Now there was an idea, he pondered. He flipped the page and saw another essay assigned by Talbot's doctor. He wanted to laugh, reading more about the criminal's fantasy world. Story after story, the endless diatribes on the where and how of an alien existence. There were no clues, as he'd hoped to find, only fantasy stuff. This was only the second folder he'd checked. There were a lot more on the shelving by the door.

He looked up, noticed the time. Almost an hour had passed since he had entered her private office.

It had been empty when he knocked, but then he had not knocked very loudly. He had stepped inside, taking in the huge desk in front of the windows overlooking the hospital's evening lawn. Between him and the desk, the long antique sofa sat perpendicularly with a low coffee table before it. On the walls, as expected, were her diplomas and certificates, on her desk family photos: no husband, no kids, parents. To the sides were high bookcases packed with medical volumes and stacks of Manila folders. The folders were her patient notes, the growing surplus from her stuffed file cabinets. He had gone over to the shelf marked 'T' but did not find Talbot's folder.

Then he saw it on her desk. The fact that it was still there past office hours had sparked his jealousy. She was here working overtime on the bastard's file!

He opened another one.

```
Subject displays symptoms of paranoid-
schizophrenia, accompanied by delusions of
grandeur, martyr complex, & other minor
mental afflictions.
```

McElroy read on down the first page. He thought he knew what the words meant. They all meant 'crazy'!

85

He flipped through several pages of handwritten notes, then stopped.

```
Subject has continuing fantasy episodes
involving same set of characters & same
locations, all being--in patient's own words--
on a planet called Ghoupallesz (according to
patient, it's meaning is "Paradise of the
Gods" in local language). Consistent with
documented incidences of patient's belief that
he is capable of interacting with, & having
responsibility for well-being of inhabitants
of fantasy world.
```

The detective grunted. It was interesting to read about the bastard in scientific terms. Made him sound crazier.

"May I help you?" the hard-edged woman's voice hit him in the back as he stood in front of the desk.

He knew it was the doctor, even before he turned, so he measured his steps and timed his moves.

"What the hell are you doing here?" she growled, coming up to him. "I thought I told you we were finished, or didn't I make myself clear?"

McElroy spun around and the fire in his eyes made her step back.

"I came to clear things up with you," he said.

"What things? We're finished, I said."

"You called my supervisor, didn't you?"

She tried to examine his intentions from his face and his voice, but her own heartbeats had shifted into stress mode so it was impossible.

"Yes, I called. What did you expect? You can't go around hitting whoever you feel like hitting. That's not the way the world works."

"Bullshit. More people go around hitting each other than don't, I'm sure."

"Not here. Certainly not in my own home. I think that's enough. We understand each other, don't we?"

He sat down Talbot's folder, straightened his posture. Toni prepared herself for violence, but he only adjusted his tie and smoothed his sports coat lapel.

"I came over to apologize."

"Really? You?"

"My captain thought I should."

"*You* didn't think you should?"

"That's not the question. I am apologizing. You want it on videotape to prove it?"

She crossed her arms over her chest.

"Sergeant McElroy, why in the world were you ever interested in me? I mean, you and I have absolutely nothing in common."

He grinned, maybe a friendly style, maybe an evil one.

"We do have something in common: Sebastian Talbot. And although I think you're a fine looking woman, and smart to boot, I have to confess I was hoping to get a few bits of info out of you. But you didn't say anything wrong, so you got nothing to worry about."

"I'd say *you* have nothing to worry about. I knew you were trying to learn more about him. I had a strong feeling from the start."

"Then why did you keep going out with me?"

She shook her head slowly.

"I don't know. Maybe because I don't go out with anyone. Your hours and mine seemed to fit, so I thought 'why not?' So why are you so interested in Mister Talbot? I mean, besides him being your case—and considering the case is closed. Your captain told me."

His calm seemed to melt and she watched him struggling to hold himself together.

"Because, Miss Franck, that bastard killed my wife—er, my *ex*-wife. She was one of his victims. I can't never rest until he's punished."

"He's been sent here, Chuck."

His face wadded into putty and turned red.

"I'm sorry about your ex-wife. I didn't know. You should have told me before."

"You should have asked! You're the shrink."

"Chuck, how could I ask you something I had no reason to ask about? That's not being fair. I can see it's really upsetting you, though." She took his arm, tried to lead him to the sofa. "Why don't you sit down and we can talk about it."

He grabbed her arm and twisted her down on the sofa.

"Why don't you sit down here! We don't need to talk about me. I'm not the crazy person here. We need to talk about *him*. He's the one who murdered people in cold blood. He's the subject of my investigation."

"I'm his doctor," Toni insisted, wrenching her arm away from his grasp. "I can only tell details of his treatment in court."

"I already read some of the crap he wrote, you wrote. What a bunch of bullshit, honey. The bastard's obviously handing you a line and you are biting it big time. Have you even *read* this stuff he writes? About going to other planets, and trying to rescue some woman, putting her out of her misery, calling it a mercy killing? On some other planet—and you believe it?"

"It's not a matter of what I believe," she explained, but was not fully convinced herself. "What matters is that he believes it. If you'd been able to follow his case as I have—thank goodness you're a detective, not a psychologist—you'd see all of the parallels between his stories and his real life activities. However, that's privileged material. You aren't allowed to read these private files, you know."

"Yeah, and I know he's full of shit."

"You're full of shit yourself, sergeant, and I'm not shy about saying it. I'm not his judge and jury like you want to be. I'm his doctor. My job is to return him to normalcy, to bring back his sanity. I'm not concerned with his guilt or innocence—except how the details of his case affect his treatment."

"He killed six people and one of them was my ex-wife, Tammy Sue Tucker."

She stepped back, mouth agape.

"I see, Chuck. Now I understand why you're so unnerved by my association with him."

"We had a kid—a boy—but she started fooling around with some guy at work named Michael. He's another victim. They were out together that night."

"Oh, I'm sorry. I'm sorry for her death. However, as your own report states, none of the bodies were ever found."

"What's that suppose to mean? Other serial killers have eaten their victims to get rid of the bodies. He could have done that, you know."

"Actually, he's quite gentle. And a gentleman, too." She started to get up but he pushed her down again. "I'll show you something he wrote and you'll understand."

"I don't need to read any more bullshit. I'm already convinced he's insane, but that shouldn't excuse him. These crazy psychos can kill just as well as any sane person. They should be judged on what they really do, not what they were thinking about when they pulled the trigger. Killing is killing and there's no excuse good enough to get off the charge. Either he did it or he didn't do it. No middle ground. The judge and jury only have to decide if he's the one who did it, then execute the sucker!"

"He still maintains that he didn't kill anyone. He says he took them to this 'other planet' that you're so upset about."

"That's just his psycho reasoning—like he's saying 'I'm gonna send you to Hell.' Well, Hell's not a real place—but I wish it was for him."

She tried to stand up again but was held down.

"Chuck, let me go. I'm gonna show you something that will convince you."

"I said I don't need to see any more."

"You don't understand, Chuck. There's a direct relationship between his fantasy life and the events in his real life. When his wife was killed by one of his students, back when he taught high school, he fantasized that she died from cancer. He couldn't accept that her death was preventable, that he could have stopped the student. Saying she had cancer gave him an excuse. It shifted the blame off his shoulders. He likes to feel guilt. That's his psychological profile. He wanted her death to be unpreventable: he *could* have stopped the student from killing her, he could *not* have stopped the cancer. Don't you see? Those events of last year correspond perfectly to the fantasies he's written down...in that file...on my desk...over there...."

She slowly got up, sensing McElroy's attitude softening, and went to her desk. Opening the folder, she studied one page for a moment before continuing.

"You see, any extreme confusion or trauma sets him off into his fantasy world. He's stuck there until...until his mind grows tired of it. Or until there's another trauma. That's what I've discovered...and what you law enforcement types could never comprehend. Yes, he is crazy, as you put it. He has a genuine right to receive psychiatric treatment."

McElroy shook his head, not accepting, not believing.

"That's bullcrap."

"Then let me show you another file—" and she started across the carpet to the shelving on the wall but McElroy grabbed at her as she shouldered past him. She tripped. He caught her and rolled her onto the sofa, down on her back.

"I don't need to read anymore of his fantasy stuff."

"Chuck, get off me."

After a long glare, he gave up and rolled off her, standing beside the sofa.

"You haven't had the training to understand a man like Sebastian," she said, getting up and straightening her dress.

"Like Sebastian?" McElroy mocked. "What, you're on a first name basis?"

"You're completely missing the point," said the doctor, standing. "This is a very fragile man. He lives on the edge of reality. What he sees is not always what is there. This balance is difficult for him to maintain...as you can well imagine."

"So, the guy's crazy. We already knew that."

She turned to face the detective. "You don't know how crazy he is—if he is."

"What do you mean, 'if he is'?"

"Well, I don't know. Sometimes, I mean, he—he's so sane it's creepy."

"Creepy? Is that one of your psychiatric terms?"

"No, but...." She could not find the exact place in her heart where her feelings belonged. "Let me tell you, even though you know I shouldn't, that I was ready to sign papers stating he is now normal, but every day he—it's just hit and miss—"

"Another psychiatric term?"

"No, Chuck."

He went to her, reading the file over her shoulder, then gently slipped it out of her hands as she stepped away from the desk, trying to remove herself from his proximity.

"He'll be going along fine, as sane and normal as anyone, not even playing the absent-minded professor or the eccentric academic that he might actually be, and then suddenly he says something, something quite off-hand, something that's just like a jack-hammer through a window pane. It's as if all my careful, patient work with him is thoroughly shattered. I don't know what to do; I have never had any case like his."

"So don't sign the papers," McElroy suggested, and put down the file. "That's what you should do: don't sign. If he's as 'normal' as you say, he'll kill again as soon as he's out."

"I wish I could be as certain about it as you seem to be."

The detective stood before her, and for once he really seemed sincere, she saw.

"The judge said he was insane. You say he's insane. I damn sure as hell call him insane. So don't sign the papers. This is a paradise compared to where he should be doing time, but it's better than letting him go free."

"That's what you want?" Toni asked, and crossed her arms over her chest again, seeing his eyes going there. "To be sure he stays here. Is that why you're here tonight?"

He shook his head, hesitantly, as if he were not sure what his reasons were, deciding that the motive she had offered to him might do.

"No, not exactly. I came to apologize, and maybe take you out to dinner, and—"

"I have to finish a report due tomorrow before I go home tonight."

"A report on him?"

"Well...yes, it is. For the Board."

His hands went to his hips, angry.

"He's that important to you?"

"It's my job, Chuck. I write reports about all of my cases."

She moved around the sofa, back to her desk, keeping the furniture between herself and McElroy.

"You're always talking to him, listening to him. I don't even get your smile. That bastard is here to be punished, you know. And he sees more of you than I do. You don't even return my calls. You don't talk to me. You don't listen. Why can't you ever listen to me?"

He intercepted her in front of her desk. She held her ground.

"I *was* listening to you," Toni responded.

"No, dammit!" He pressed against her, took her wrists in his two hands. "You did not listen to me. You keep talking about that psycho murderer. You never stop talking about him. Are you in love with him or something?"

"Chuck, I've had enough of this."

"You're always talking about him, but when I ask you any questions—like, it's my frickin' job, too—you never answer. You say it's your goddamn doctor-patient privilege. Well, what *other* privileges does this damn patient of yours have, huh?"

"I can understand why she's your ex-."

She watched in horror as his face burned crimson.

"What's that suppose to mean?" he spoke, anger held back by sheer willpower.

"It means, Chuck, that maybe it's time for you to leave." She spoke calmly, smoothing her nerves and straightening her pride. "I've got a lot of work to do."

The heartbeats were loud in Toni's head as she held herself firmly in place, her back to the desk, thinking of the alarm button on the underside that was out of reach unless she was sitting in her chair on the other side. She hoped she would not need it; she had handled rougher patients than McElroy.

She expected it yet was still slow to react when he came at her. His arms were out as if to grab her, possibly strangle her. She tried to dodge his bear-hug and slip around to the back of her desk but he caught her and jostled her back and forth within the ring formed by his thick arms, tightening around her. She needed to get to the alarm button—if she could get free from him.

"Let me go, Chuck!"

He relaxed, smiling, playing with her.

"You like games? You play games like this with him?"

"It isn't a game!" She tried to break free of his arms, then dropped down to climb out from under them.

McElroy saw her attempting to get free and in his hurry to regain control of her, he grabbed at her and his big bear arms became bulldozers. Instead of clutching her lithe body, he was driving her head-first into the edge of the hard oak desk, into the protruding rim running along its front. There was a cracking sound and he knew something had gone wrong. He was only trying to tease her. He had no intention of...*that*.

Stepping back, he let her body slide limply away from the desk and drop onto the floor, blood oozing down the wood, dripping upon the carpet.

He stared down at her, crumpled at his feet. He stared as a professional, already examining the scene of the crime. Here was a body, a victim. There was a struggle. She knew her assailant. She died from a blow to the head by a dull instrument: a desk. She died instantly—

He threw himself to the carpet, bending over her face, blood running out of her temple, rough edge of bone shifted upward through the meaty mess. His ear to her heart, his fingers to her nose then to her throat, he sensed some life still in her. *What have I done?* He glared at her, holding her hand, found it limp in his. *What the hell's happening?*

Maybe it was only a concussion, he thought. She might yet live with immediate medical attention. And after she recovered? She might remember who had pushed her head-first into the desk. Maybe her neck was broken. Better not touch her. *Fingerprints!*

"Shit!" he cursed loudly, punching the floor.

The carpet was becoming stained around him and all he could do was stare at her and make himself feel what he was supposed to feel. Maybe he had been doing his job too long, had lost his objectivity, could no longer feel anything. He slammed his fist into the desk, right where her head had met the oak, and let out a series of deep sighs as if to temper himself for the hassle to come.

"I didn't mean to, I really didn't."

He thought what to do next. Suddenly recalling that he had a plan, he sniffled away his emotions.

He regarded the woman—not as a doctor, not a Ph.D.—just a woman: too young, too thin, too saintly, not a woman he wanted to know intimately. Crumpled on the floor that way, her legs were unceremoniously spread apart. Her hose was torn as if by cat claws and her pink panties were in plain view. Lacey, delicate, feminine, a narrow mesh in the right place. He reached down and slid them off and stuffed them into his jacket pocket.

It was no perverse act. He often examined bodies; that was his job. He looked for motives. Every crime had a motive. A sex crime worked here. He could kill two birds, no pun intended—no, one bird and one crazy bastard—with a single act. *Ah, then it really was a plan!* Just as Talbot wrote in his report: it was a mercy killing. He put the doc out of her misery, and with that, put her out of his own misery. Or it was just an unfortunate accident—which it *was*, he knew, staring at the corner of the desk. But why face hell because he was at the location of some accident? Unfortunate, yes. He'd rather have dated her, not be cleaning up after an accident.

That was part one of his plan, he sighed. Hopping up onto the desk, he pulled out his pack of cigarettes and lit one, smoking it slowly as he pondered part two.

Chapter 10

Environmentally-Friendly Escapism

The dream ended before it was becoming interesting, but he guessed it was due to his visitor. Sebastian sat up on his bed.

"You don't know me but...well, you might say I'm a friend. You can decide later."

It was a man's voice but none he recognized as one of the orderlies.

"So listen up. I'm only gonna say this once: Get. Outta. Here."

He could barely see in the dark, only small hallway emergency lights illuminating the figure at his door.

"Who are you?" he asked the stranger.

"What, you need a written invitation?" the stocky male silhouette barked. "Get out of here."

"What do you mean? Go where?"

The man pulled a set of keys out of his pants pocket and dangled them in the air, making them jingle.

"Here's some keys. They go to a yellow Camaro outside. It's yours. Now go."

The patient stood, sensing danger, adrenaline flowing.

"Who the hell're you and what're you doing interrupting me at this late hour? I need my beauty sleep."

The man shifted his stance. "Are you stupid? You don't need to know everything. Just get outta here. Go! Can't you figure it out? Drive all night, drive all day, I don't give a shit. Just drive away. Cuz if I find you, I'm gonna kill you."

"Why are you doing this?"

The stranger laughed.

"Are you looking a gift horse in the mouth?"

"No. More like a gift horse's ass."

"You stupid bastard!" The beefy detective came into the room then, pistol drawn, and ordered the patient out.

In the light, they saw each other. Everything became clear to him as he measured the resolve of the cop with the gun. He was being set free, whether or not any court authority approved it. The thought sailed past him that Toni had signed the papers and his case was being rushed through. Yet why would they release him in the middle of the night? And give him a car to drive home?

"Now go!" the cop commanded, giving him a shove through the doorway. "Just keep going. If you even look back, I'll shoot."

So he took the keyring offered and stepped lightly down the corridor, dressed in his state hospital pajamas, the shadows dancing on the walls resembling the flickering images of some tangent he had once passed through.

Outside, the stars greeted him and the moon shown upon his getaway car. He climbed inside and started the ignition, checked the rear-view mirror as he backed out of the parking space. The cop was standing just inside the double doors, watching him turn the car through the lot and head out the gate.

The PSYCHO3 license plate was the last thing the detective saw before he pulled the alarm switch on the wall beside him, in that instant contemplating that such a license plate meant there were at least two other PSYCHOs out there.

The dashboard clock showed twenty past midnight as he pulled off the road by the entrance to the quarry. Sebastian ignored the red and yellow signs proclaiming the area off limits due to radioactivity. If it were true, there would have been more security than the wire cow fence and chain-link gate.

The gravel drive up the hill to the quarry was overgrown with weeds, and at the top a pair of black and white striped sawhorses, still strung with tattered yellow police tape, blocked his path. He climbed over the sawhorses, by habit not wanting to show that anyone had been there, and strode to the center of his private stage. Beyond the entrance, in the arena of the quarry, lay bits and pieces of his various scientific paraphernalia, trampled in the final shoot-out, torn down in their investigation, blown away by the weather. He hoped he had time to find the right point in the frosty air that hovered over the dusty clay chips. It was there, he knew, somewhere. He scanned the beige limestone rocks and fixed his bearing by the outcroppings and dents in the stone, by the marks of the jackhammers years before.

He wasn't sure what the man calling himself a policeman was doing letting him go. And in Toni's car. He discovered it was hers the first time he stopped under a street light, saw the picture of her and her cat on the dashboard, then the jogging suit with her name on it in the front passenger seat. Then it occurred to him that he was being freed so he could be chased. It did not matter who the man was, though he claimed to be a detective, because there were no places to go where he would be safe—except to pass through the tangent. He had to tear the curtain once more to escape.

In hospital pajamas and barefoot, he was chilled by the autumn evening. He turned the corner through the short canyon to the wide central basin where he and his high school sweetheart and fellow Voyager, Gina, had first found the opening to the other world—

Suddenly, the radioactivity signs suddenly made sense.

There, literally floating in the center of the stone arena, encircled by cliffs, was a strange apparition which danced and flowed at random before him. In the darkness it seemed like a curtain, nearly invisible but faintly traced by scattered moonlight, waving in the breeze. His first thought was that a weather balloon had fallen there, torn apart and flapping. But it was not, he quickly determined. He fell to the ground in surprise, regarding the phenomenon.

The night they had achieved their breakthrough, a tiny spot of light had grown and then split apart to form a hole, literally a hole in the air, through which appeared another dimension, another world. Even on many later passages through the doorway, he had to carefully locate it and pry it open with his will and his fingertips, and then only enough to slip himself through before it flowed back together and closed. Now, however, that hole was big enough to drive a couple of elephants through. It swam in the air before him, as open and wide and inviting as any funhouse entrance. It pulsed like a massive heart and shifted its shape like the dancing ring of some cowboy's twirling lasso, constantly and with no pattern.

The sound of the car door shutting down the hillside came to his mind before it struck his ears. He knew someone would come, and he did not expect to hear sirens. This was a lone hunter, he knew, and he waited for the man to come walking up the gravel road.

Meanwhile, he stared through the opening—he did not know what to call it now: tangent, doorway, the tear in the curtain, the grand entrance to the other world. It was night there also, on the other side, he saw—as easy as gazing at a motion picture screen at a drive-in theater. The hillside was familiar to him, and the ridge beyond, his homeland.

He stepped forward, a few inches at a time, slow paces, cautious movements. The opening wavered at his approach, as if sensing deception. He held himself motionless. For once, for the first time since he and Gina had stepped through the unknown gateway, he was fearful. He could not go back, but he could not go forward.

"Hey!" came the expected call.

He refused to face McElroy. The detective shouted again, gave an order which they both knew the fugitive would have to ignore. Then he took one more step toward the opening, and suddenly felt its strange magnetic pull. It seemed as if only at that moment the detective saw it.

"What the...hell...is...that?" McElroy exclaimed.

Then the detective was ordering him not to take another step, reciting the tired words he had memorized from so many action thrillers.

"Why did you let me go if you just wanted to catch me again?" he asked McElroy, turning his face back toward the oscillating phenomenon.

"That's exactly why. I *wanted* to catch you!"

"What do you mean? You want to get the glory?"

"I'm not interested in glory. Only in satisfaction. I want the satisfaction of killing you."

"You could've shot me back there, at the hospital."

"Too many people around. An escaping criminal is a better target. Any judge in the country would thank me for what I'm about to do. And the way you crushed Toni's skull against her desk and left her for dead, driving off in her car, with me close behind—hell, I won't be just some hero, I'll be the goddamn police chief!"

"What did you say? Toni's *dead*?"

McElroy seemed to enjoy the expression of horror on the fugitive's face. "You should know. Who else could have done it? Why, the way you've been hanging around her office after hours, of course it's gotta be you. Seemed like a good way to do the doc in, huh?"

"I—I never touched her!"

"It had to be you, Talbot."

"Who's the insane one here?"

The detective held up the pistol.

"This is the same place you took out all those cops two years back, huh? Why'd you come back *here*? The first place we'd look for you."

"Because it's my way home."

"Your...*what*?"

"I live beyond that gaping...whatever it is. It wasn't so big last time. I don't know what's happened."

McElroy shook his head, not believing what he saw, but not caring what it was so long as it did not cheat him out of his execution opportunity.

"A goddamn tornado's what it is!"

"No, it's...my escape route."

And he dove through the opening, landing roughly on the soft clay soil on the other side. A bullet was flying past him as he sat up. The opening was too big, and he was not protected by its fluctuating power surges which previously had been like a transparent shield against any intrusions from outside. Now enlarged, it had thinned too much to hold back the bullets issuing from the detective's pistol.

"You can't escape from me, bastard!" McElroy shouted, charging for the wavering tangent, pistol up.

The borders of the tangent began collapsing, swirling like an eddy in ever-tightening circles, just as the detective arrived at its jelly-textured surface. He held up, examined the thickening mass, saw his prey through it. His fingers went to the transparent substance and it had the resistance of water in a swimming pool as he pressed his hand through it. Then, seeing the bastard starting away from him on the other side, he pushed himself forward and felt his chunky body being sucked through the mass like a fly through gelatin. He could move his arms and legs inside it, and he gazed back slowly—the only speed at which he could move—and wished he had called for backup.

Then he was falling, spit out of the slick-slimy membrane like a bad apple, and crashed head first in the soil, his body shaking with electricity.

Chuck McElroy opened his eyes and watched the sun rising through the opening—the sun that shone in Earth's skies. An hour had passed and dawn was melting over the horizon. The sunlight was filtered by the weird material that—that—he couldn't describe it, but he understood what sperm must feel like passing through a cervix.

He stood up, glancing around for any sign of his prey, found a line of tracks in the sand. He took one last look back, at the quarry then started off after the escapee.

Trudging up a slope, he noticed the sand was flaky, like soap, and almost melted in his hands if he rubbed it between his fingers. Ahead of him a band of yellow light was spreading across the world, and he wondered where this endless plain was on a map. He could not remember such a land feature. There were no deserts in Missouri.

"Okay, you jerk!" Sebastian Talbot called as he grabbed McElroy by the shoulders just as the detective mounted the crest of the ridge. Talbot threw him down, knocking the pistol out of his hand.

The detective scrambled to his feet and took a swing at the pajama-clothed man, who ducked and punched back into the cop's gut. The big man dropped to the sand and the man who was home at last swung his bare foot out to strike McElroy's chin. The detective swung backwards like an earthquake-shaken building, then crashed face first into the sand.

Catching his breath, Talbot sighted the pistol and went to collect it. There were only two bullets left in it and he quickly fired them off into the sky. With a long sigh of satisfaction, he returned to the detective as he was reviving.

"Now we're even," Talbot cried out. "Actually, *I'm* ahead, because this is my home. I know the rules here, the way things are done, the language and customs, all that's necessary for survival. You, on the other hand, are in some really deep shit. You haven't a clue what kind of a place you're in now."

"Isn't this Missouri?"

"I believe the line goes: 'I don't think we're in *Kansas* anymore.'"

The detective turned his head, taking in the barren horizon that surrounded him.

"Lost in a lost world, eh?" Talbot chuckled at the detective's bewilderment.

He stood and bent over to help McElroy up. The cop begrudgingly accepted his hand, pulled himself to a weak standing position. He swayed there, regarding the growing dawn and the bland landscape: nothing as far as he could see, only the same soap-flake soil, gray and dull with distant patches of reddish-brown slopes and ridges like a desert, and the endless sky, the endless green sky.

McElroy sighed, starting to believe.

Talbot turned him around, away from the sunrise.

"You can go back that way. Just follow our tracks. When you get to the tangent, just dive through it like you did to get on this side. If it doesn't work at first, keep trying. You've got no choice; you must go back. You're out of your element here."

The cop staggered, slipped down the sandy slope a step, recovered drunkenly, faced Talbot.

"What're you talking about? I came to get you...and bring you back."

"How are you going to do that? You can't. Not here. Not now."

"You crazy bastard. You're gonna die. Right here, right now. I'm gonna kill you. For screwing around with Toni—messing with her head like that. For killing my wife. You gotta pay for your crimes...you bastard!"

His voice was weakening, as though he did not believe his own threats, gazing at the world around him, noticing the two suns, a larger yellow one and a small blue one.

"I didn't kill anybody," said Talbot, taking the crest of the ridge and surveying his domain like a rancher. "That's the truth. I've been trying to tell everyone that, but nobody will believe me because there are no bodies. Well, I'll tell you, Mister Detective: they're here, all of them. The bodies are here—alive! Last time I checked, Michael Fenning was a playboy in the city of Lyas, gambling and whoring his life away. Tammy Sue Tucker was living in the capital city of Aivana, married to the King. And—"

"Tammy? You mean...? Hey, she's my wife!"

"Your wife?"

"Yeah, we were married for a couple of years...then got divorced. Had a kid...named Chuck, I think. Named after me."

"If you're divorced then there's no reason to go looking for her. So back you go.... Back to the little planet you call home."

"But, I have to—"

"And on this world you should address me by my professional name: Set-d'Elous. Don't ever call me 'bastard' again, do you hear me? I own this world."

"Yeah, I hear ya—*bastard!*" McElroy sifted the soapflake sand through his fingers. "Set? What kinda name's that? S-E-T, right? Just like Sebastian Ellis Talbot, huh? Clever."

"Now get out of here! I'm only going to say it once." Set-d'Elous threw his arms up to shoo the detective away. "If I see you after dawn tomorrow, I'll kill you. Understand?"

"Where's my gun?"

"It's over there, empty. Go back the way you came and everything'll be fine. Forget me. Forget this whole crazy adventure. And if you see any guys riding *oñacha*, you'd better get down in the sand and hide."

"What's that? Ongachee?"

"Something like a cross between a camel and a giraffe, what the Rouê ride out in the desert."

"Roo-ay?"

"The nomads who live out here."

"Out here? Where the hell are we?"

He stalked away, laughing, leaving the bewildered detective kneeling in the sand, just as the two suns broke over the horizon and blasted him with yellow and blue light.

A voice trailed in the wind, mocking him: "We're in the Dream Land now."

* ❋ *

The IRS Service Center in Kansas City was a wide, single-floor building of vast rooms, filled with columns, shelving, boxes of files on carts, and rows of desks and computers. The mind-numbing work was made worse by the environment: paper dust in unventilated rooms, radiation burning off of the computers, billowing cigarette smoke, sugar-coated fat-laden salt-sprinkled junk food in vending machines, rust-tinted water from drinking fountains, and poor fluorescent lighting, surly security guards, arrogant managers, disgruntled workers, pompous administrators, long hours, low pay, and the physical strain upon necks, shoulders, hands, wrists, and the eye-popping hours staring at the tiny green numbers on the computer screens and people's scrawled handwriting trying to make sense of their mistakes—

"No wonder he went crazy," said Cassie Dorfman sitting at the messy table in the south canteen for her midnight lunch break.

Priscilla, her lunchmate, looked up curiously from her microwaved lasagna leftovers.

"You say something, girl?"

Cassie was silent, staring into another world.

"Girl, you look like you seen a ghost."

"I just had a weird feeling," said Cassie, "like...I dunno, like I knew something was gonna happen, ya know, before it really happens. What's that called?"

"Hell, I dunno. Predictin' the future, I guess."

"I just had a thought...about him."

"Him? Who him? What you talkin' about?"

"Him. The Perfesser. Talbot the Terminator."

"Shhh! Y'ain't s'posed to talk about that no more."

"I wasn't. It just, like, popped into my head. Like I was seein' him on TV. He was running, in pajamas, chased by some fat man in a suit."

"That's crazy. What you been smokin'?"

"I know it's crazy, but...."

"Forget it and finish your lunch."

Cassie took a bite of the bologna sandwich, chewed slowly as her eyes stared through space. She swallowed, reached for her diet Pepsi, gulped it down.

"He's escaped," she muttered.

"What?" Priscilla shook her head, double chin jiggling. "He's locked up behind ten thousand bars and a hundred mean-ass guards with big-ass guns. Don't get freaked. You're safe, girl."

"No, he escaped from there. I saw it. I mean, I *felt* it, like, a feeling—damn, what's that word? Premonition? Is that it? Like right this minute, right *now*. I felt him escaping. It's been more than a year now—I'd almost forgotten it."

"You crazy, girl."

"So was he. I gotta go tell the others, warn them."

"They're gonna call ya crazy, too! Shit, he use ta sit next to me. Ta think I knew 'im. Then he went an' killed all them people. He was too creepy, that's for sure."

Cassie jumped up and tossed her food away.

"Wait, girl!" Priscilla called after her.

She was off, walking determinedly through the maze of desks and walls of shelving, back to the section of the tax examiner department where she had once gone every break and lunch time to see her ex-boyfriend, Michael Fenning—who only a few weeks before his untimely death became friends with the quiet, reflective man they had all called the Professor. After the killings, she could not venture into that department, could not look at his desk—no worker used it. At least that girl Michael was hung up on, Tammy Tucker, was killed with him, thought Cassie. She never liked Tammy. She couldn't understand why

Michael liked her.

Her heart was pounding as she passed through the doorway and up the ramp of the raised floor, nearing the haunted section. Everyone was at lunch when she arrived, except a new woman who occupied the desk next to where he had sat. He used to face the wall, sitting his desk in the corner, all the better to concentrate on his work, he always said. Now they knew he had been plotting the murders of his co-workers that night out at an abandoned quarry.

The new woman, fifty-ish and stout, blue-gray hair, folds of belly falling out over her polyester slacks, had turned the desk back to face the others. But Cassie knew it was his desk by the chipped paint on the front top drawer, revealing the dull gray Government Issue metal desk.

"Where's Kate?" she asked the woman.

No reply—only sign language from the woman's hand.

Cassie made a disgusted face and turned to leave.

Kate, the department's comptroller, was in the west canteen laughing with Joyce, the manager of the section, and two others Cassie did not know.

She looked up, smiled. "Hey, Cass."

Cassie scanned the others as they fell silent.

"He escaped," she announced.

Jaws dropped. Eyes widened. Hearts stopped.

They all knew who she was talking about and at that moment a death-knell seemed to sound among them. Kate asked how she knew. Not in the newspaper, in her head, Cassie told them. They started to grin but Kate caught them, made them respect Cassie's thoughts.

"You've been having a lot of these premonitions lately," Kate said to reassure her. "It's just the season, maybe the anniversary of his arrest, huh."

"Two years of this shit." Joyce shook her head. "I don't see why they can't just fry the guy so we can all rest easy."

Cassie insisted she was right and so they marched out to Kate's van to listen to the radio. Just to humor Cassie, she said. Kate flipped the dial again...again. Then a station with breaking news—

"No kidding!" Joyce exclaimed.

It was as if Cassie had told the reporter exactly what to say. He was telling about the escaped criminal, how he was at large, how he broke out of the mental hospital, how he killed his doctor by bashing her head, how he stole her car and drove into the night. And they named names: Sebastian Talbot, also known as The Professor because he had once been a teacher.

Kate shut the radio off, their hearts were pumping hard.

"Well, ya know he was in that coma for about six months after the cops shot him," Kate said. "He was put in that institution cuz the judge ruled he was insane. He underwent therapy for a year there, had a lady psychiatrist."

"No threat there," Sandy spoke up from the back seat. "I went out with him a few times." She laughed, boasting of it. "He's just a cold fish."

"He could be charming, I remember," Kate offered.

"He wasn't interested in women," said Sandy, always enjoying the chance to talk about the maniac she loved to hate. "I don't mean he was like a homo or nothing, just that he was always like busy with more important stuff, ya know—that's what he always said. One time we went out, we was, like, gonna—I *thought* we was gonna—ya know, screw around, but he was, well, like he had something more important to do. So I, like, went home."

"Hey, we all lost friends cuz of him," Kate summarized. "Michael and Tammy. Fat Ken—okay, he wasn't nobody's friend, but he was still one of us, a third-shifter. And Alison from the mail room, and Donna Mae. And Wilma—we baby-sit each others' kids. Listen to me. We can't let our feelings keep getting messed up. We gotta get over it."

"You're right," said Sandy. "Since he didn't get the chair, we should go out and get him."

They were all surprised because they had thought she, being the only one to date him, would be one of his few supporters.

"We don't know where he is, do we?" Cassie asked.

"Don't they always return to the scene of the crime?" Kate offered.

"He ain't that dumb."

PART TWO

Every man will fall; though born a man,
he proudly presumes to be a superman.

Sophocles

Chapter 12

Incarnations, Incantations

And so he lived in wholesome goodness with his once-and-future bride: he pretending to be her new lover, she welcoming a man she pretended was her old lover. His journey of a thousand suns was nearly complete, though he could not have known it then. Her journey of a thousand nights was about to begin, just as she had long imagined yet feared. Together their mutually-constructed illusion served them well enough [...] until the future dangerously happened.

—from *Tarag-d'Er Pazar* (*"Tales of my Father"*)
by Metour-d'Elous, 1562; translated by
Sebastian E. Talbot

Light streamed in through the curtains, marking his face until he wrenched his eyes open. He could not move, held down by the imposing peacefulness of his surroundings. Still, he sensed something was askew in this perfect picture. He forced himself up and caught sight of a woman in the bed beside him.

She was turned away from him so he could not see her face, but her full, luscious, golden hair made him think of Gina, his long-lost love. He leaned over to kiss her shoulder but sensed her waking and fell back against his pillow. He waited for her to roll over. The woman was not Gina.

"Who are you?" he asked first in English, followed a beat later in Ghoupallêan.

She faced him, struggling herself against the oppressive morning calm.

Wiping her eyes, she lurched forward, pressing her lips against his cheek.

He repeated his question and she only smiled, but with another utterance from him she realized he was serious.

The woman sat back in the bed—the hammock-like *qala*, suspended from the ceiling by four cables—and a fat tear slipped down her cheek and ran to the end of her chin. He saw it and knew he had said something offensive. His hand went to her shoulder but she shook it off.

"*Emai-g'er epouz*," she replied. "*Es ava-mærod zu shi'lev kejê.*"

Somehow he had known to speak Ghoupallêan when he awoke, but his words felt strange. Her reply in the same language settled awkwardly on his ears. That meant he was in the right place, maybe only at the wrong time. 'I'm your wife; we've been married for seven years,' she had said.

He sighed, not remembering anything. He accepted that this lady was similar to his Ghoupalle wife, Zaura-Matousz. The resemblance was striking. He calculated the time. If they had married in 1444, as he originally had done, then seven years later, as she had just stated, would be 1451. That meant it was only four years from when he, as his original self, would return from Earth to continue his life with her—to the end of her life in 1481. He developed a headache calculating it all.

She turned to him, tears dried but face still red. It was her: Zaura!

"*Possi-de-grex ez Ju vizâren qam emai, epouz*," she spoke softly yet with determination.

'Such a cruel joke you play with me, husband,' he translated in his head—as she continued, telling him if he ever made her weep again, she might never stop weeping. Her eyes held his attention as he ran her words through his mind.

Then he grabbed her and hugged her tightly as if holding her back from the edge of a high cliff from which she had threatened to throw herself.

"*E zu-ji amalen, epouz*," he cried. 'I love you, wife.'

* * *

When he was dressed in his khaki uniform, his dutiful wife of seven Ghoupalle years took a polishing cloth to his brass buttons as he straightened his crimson peaked cap. Then he left their gray brickfront townhouse and stepped through the dew-freshened streets to the greetings of neighbors and street folk alike. They knew him, accepted him: the cavalry captain with the lovely wife and wonderful children.

He did not become lost. His legs carried him to his destination, though he did not know quite where that was. By his uniform and the sword at his side he guessed it must be the Selauê Garrison. Yet he dared not believe that he was still employed there. If there was some special assignment today, he felt no confidence he could command the 102d cavalry regiment.

The guards at the gate saluted him—he carried the rank of *Serpan*—and one guard escorted him across the vast compound to the headquarters of the battalion commander, Aroun-de-Sotos. That name conjured for him the image of a younger man with whom he had fought in a later war—far into the future. This *Merzel* Aroun-de-Sotos was the father. No, he was not in the snowfields of Tebbicousimankalê in 1533; rather, he was in his hometown of Selauê. It was 1457 and he had always commanded the 102d *Jêpedor-regêlad*. He had always taught classes in military history and cavalry tactics at the Selauê Academy. And Zaura had always been his wife. Everything was as it always had been, and always would be. In this loop of time.

Merzel de-Sotos was not in when they arrived, so he continued on to his own building.

The lieutenants reported to him, the sergeant-major told him the training schedule, and he sent them all away. From the privacy of his office he watched his men saddling their *Jêpe*—the ugly donkey-like beasts they rode into battle: three-toed, long-eared, grayish dewlap tied up for combat, brown-striped throat against the dull reddish coat, too slow for a frontal charge but a sturdy pack animal. He recognized some men by sight, others by their behavior. The similarity both pleased him and surprised

111

him. From his office, he breathed in the scents of leather, steel, and the pungency of the *Jêpe* outside.

Sitting on the cushion gracing the deck raised along the back wall, which he and all commanders were offered, he saw the portrait of his dear golden-haired Zaura on the wall before him, a stoic reminder he had nailed there sometime in the past, a reminder of his reason for existing.

He let out a grand sigh that he feared would draw the concern of his staff outside the door.

It worked.

His grin could not be sent away when the *Karrond* arrived to reply to something he had suggested on an earlier day, a day he did not remember and could not imagine.

His aide informed him the colonel had come to see him.

"*Kanê!*" he spoke as he saluted. 'Sir!'

Ah, the years shooting past him at the speed of light!

Back in Ghoupalle year 1445, after a year of marriage, a weekend on Earth had cost him ten years on Ghoupallesz, thanks to shifting tangents. So he wandered the planet in search of his Ghoupalle wife, Zaura, found her married to another man, Tolour-Frêdin, with whom she had a son. That was in 1455. He and Zaura had spent some time together while her second husband of eight years was away—

And yet, she had told him just this morning that he had been married to her for seven years. He was certain she meant seven continuous, uninterrupted years. And now it was 1457. He checked the calendar on the wall—

So...there had been no Tolour-Frêdin? No son named Samot? If it were true, he contemplated, then with his return now Zaura would never have met Tolour, would never have lived in Sairel as a bored housewife. Thus, he and Zaura would have had no reason to run away, taking the children with them, fleeing all the way to the city of Milipour in the far north. They would never have fled from her enraged elder brother, Rasek, who vowed to kill him, and he would never have had to kill Rasek in their confrontation the day after he had sent Zaura and the children back to Sairel—

He caught the closing words of the colonel's report as his mind slipped back to the present: his superior officer standing before him, discussing something about which he had no knowledge or recollection. The colonel seemed impressed with his idea, however, whatever it might be. He nodded, grinning—

One thing was clear to him: he had changed history, his personal history, at least. It was as if he had never left his dear wife alone on Karluk Island in the northern sea after the birth of their first child. She had not mistaken the ship which sank in the storm that night for the ship he was on. He had not drowned. They had been married for seven years! She said so! He had replaced Tolour-Frêdin, stepping into her life before she could marry him—

The colonel asked him why he was grinning like an idiot when the matter being discussed was his idea—which the colonel was turning down as unworkable.

Serpan Set-d'Elous lost his expression of delight and promised to revise his proposal for the next training cycle. If he could remember what the idea was.

His aide showed the colonel out and Set-d'Elous retired to his office, chastising himself for his lack of concentration, then cheering himself for his successful bending of history. Sitting on the bench, he gazed at the portrait of Zaura.

After a moment, he called his orderly to run an errand for him. He wanted him to go to a certain address and inquire about the health of one Rasek, eldest son of the family Matousz, whose younger sister was his wife. Then his aide was to go to the great Archives and look up the biography of one Tolour-Frêdin of Sairel, a merchant in *moussalaganê*, a cactus used in an herbal potion. He was to report back as soon as possible. The adjutant would write him an off-post pass.

He remembered being back in the palace in Aivana—that is, back in the future, in Ghoupalle year 1575 or 1576, he forgot which—dining with his friend, Jason—after Queen Tammy's Earth-born son, Chucker, had been brought to her and the boy's new step-father was, after almost two years in Aivana, finally preparing to take the boy away on his Youth Trek. He had teased

Jason about whether he could keep up with the boy or not. Jason had over the years put on quite a bit of weight. The jokes continued until Jason, quite perturbed, suggested he should go back through the tangent to Earth and return at a different angle so as to reverse time and lose the weight.

Time travel? He was intrigued, even as he listened to Jason's complaints.

The subject had just come up between the third entrée and the first dessert and he could not avoid ceasing on it. His interdimensional voyaging colleague pounced on the idea even harder than he had pounced on the grilled *zurrek* with *fez-yvo* sauce.

"What's all this talk about time travel?" Jason exclaimed, bits of *zurrek* falling from his greasy lips. "There's no such thing. I can't lose weight that way, and you sure can't change history by going back and doing something different. If you could, everybody'd be doing it."

Jason swallowed, washed it down with a swig of *gor*.

"Time is linear—it goes in a straight line—and even if you do a loop-de-loop and go back to the past, it's still the same straight line, like a tape or ribbon that you have merely twisted around your finger. It's straight but you've bent it. That's all. You can't cross over from one part of the ribbon to the next part of the ribbon. It doesn't work."

Jason paused to take another mouthful of the *zurrek*, so succulent when it was grilled the way they did it in Aivana. When he was satisfied, he picked up the conversation as though he had not just put away another plate of the big four-legged bird.

"Everyone's fate is just that: Fate. I don't mean that our destiny is pre-arranged...mmm, like a page in some cosmic calendar. I mean, it just happens that way. Nothing can change it. If you change your routine at random so you're out shopping when an airplane crashes into your house, when you otherwise would be napping on the living room sofa, then that's what happens. It wasn't planned by any God of Fate, and it wasn't anything that you specifically did that made it happen or not happen. It just *is*. The changes you make *are* your fate. Changing your fate is part of your fate. It's just some mind game. It's the stuff of movies."

Being the *Mexas*, Sebastian could indulge his host's wild ravings, but this was different. Jason was on to something. Besides, Jason was more than his host; indeed, being Tammy's husband now, the palace belonged as much to him as it did to her. More importantly, he wanted his childhood friend's advice. And assurance. So he put on his salesman's face and began selling him an idea.

"So all of these events that just happen.... Are they so predetermined that part of the predetermination is we don't think about them being events that are predetermined?"

He waited for his colleague to reply, but Jason was still contemplating the words, or the next dessert.

"Look at what happens to people in the world. Things like earthquakes, and that airplane crashing into my house—do they just happen, as you say, or are they actually accidents? That's what the word means: it's something that happens without anyone expecting it. We say 'it's just an accident,' right? Well, suppose that someone somewhere in some distant time zone has done something by design or *by accident* which causes that airplane to dive into my house. There's no reason—no *logical* reason why that airplane should crash, or that it should crash into *my* house instead of an empty field. And there's no particular reason that I should decide that particular morning to alter my routine and go out shopping instead of taking my nap. It's an *accident*, like you say. It's not planned, it's an *accident*. That is why we call them 'accidents.'"

Jason was nodding, either understanding or simply to acknowledge he was listening, since his mouth was full of the next course, something creamy, peach-colored.

"You see," the *Mexas* continued, finished with his meal, "accidents are caused by something unexpected, unplanned. They just happen, as you say. But they must have *some* cause and the only such thing that can *be* a cause is some action by another thing or person. Every action has an opposite, equal reaction, they say. You've studied that a little, haven't you?"

Jason wiped the *dupoi* from his lips, nodding his head.

"Doesn't matter," the *Mexas* continued. "You understand, right? What about in time? If it were possible, then one mere extra blink of my eye sometime in the past may catch someone's attention, and taking their attention away for one extra millisecond may cause them to not hear what their friend was saying, such as, 'Watch out for that airplane about to crash on us!' You see, anything could be an instigator of some reaction that assumes itself in another time as what we call an accident."

Jason cleared his pallet with a *ghot* wafer and motioned for the servants to remove the dishes he had emptied. He belched loudly, not an Aivana custom but one of his own. A nearby maiden brought a cloth to wipe his crumb-spotted face, like a mother and her dirty little boy. Once cleaned, he returned to their discussion:

"You're saying that every time someone has an accident it's actually someone's responsibility in some past time?"

"No, there's no responsibility," the *Mexas* replied. "I'm saying there are no accidents. Things just happen, as you say. Those are *your* words. By design or accident these things happen. But something still *causes* them to happen. Now, suppose that if someone who *knew* something bad was going to happen had the power—and by 'power' I mean they had the knowledge and ability as well as the will or desire to assert themselves against whatever inconvenience might be involved to perform the act, not 'power' like with magic—if someone had the power to do something that would result in that future bad thing not happening and went ahead and did it...? That person would be a hero. I mean, if he prevented the bad event, right? He'd be a hero."

Jason thought for a moment, let out gas, grinned.

"So you want to be a hero? Is that it?" Jason asked. "I thought you did that already. Why do you want to be a hero *again*?"

"Not me. I've had enough of that. Too many close calls at hero-dom. Accidents are what I'm talking about. And the power to change them. It's not some theoretical debate. It's real."

"You *are* talking some theoretical debate—because it can't be done."

A maiden brought a new bottle of something, and Jason grabbed it to scan the dark blue liquid inside.

"It's wishful thinking, like prayers or flipping a coin into a fountain," said Jason. "The power of will cannot change the straight line of fate—and I use the word 'fate' loosely for your benefit; be aware—" he popped the cap on the bottle, spilling some of its contents over the fine saffron robe that stretched over his belly—"be aware that I'm not attaching it to any mystic or religious ritual or dogma. By 'fate' I mean 'whatever happens to us now, whatever will happen to us in the future, or whatever has already happened to us in the past'...regardless of *how* or *why* it happens."

"Happenstance, eh?"

He poured the drink into the silver chalice of the *Mexas*, then filled his own vessel: the old white ceramic mug made in Taiwan, inscribed with 'World's Greatest Grease Monkey' that he had rescued from the garage where he once worked.

"All right," he grunted. "Does that satisfy you for now?"

They raised their drinks and clinked them, but only Jason sampled it.

The *Mexas* sighed, set his drink down on the table. "Here all theory ends and reality begins."

Jason finished the mug, reached for the bottle. "What are you talking about?"

"It can be done."

Jason took up his full mug in both hands. "Only in your dreams."

The *Mexas* chuckled, like he had a secret deep inside that he desperately wanted to tell but could not bring himself to share. He began the diversion:

"Perhaps, but also in reality. There's no machine that can do it, no magic formula, no" [*air quotes*] "cosmic doorway to another time. But there is a doorway to another *place*, as you know. We've used it more than a few times. And that *place* can be entered at different angles or at different points in a three-dimensional grid. We've already proven that if we pass through the tangent at a slightly varied point we can arrive at a different location on Ghoupallesz. This doorway exists as a phenomenon of nature, of the universe—whether it's a blessing or a curse. If we also pass through one point at different angles, meaning— well, exactly what the word 'angles' means, dammit: degrees or inclines—then we can achieve a similar result. As well as arriving in a new place we can arrive in a new *time* in a familiar place. Before, it's always been done *by accident*—we land where we land and we take our chances."

"Some scientist you are, talking that way about chance," said Jason. He patted his belly, decided it was not full. "Hey, that *zurrek* was pretty damn good, wasn't it? We could have them bring some more, if you want."

"No thanks."

"How about some more *dupoi*? That was good, too. Not too salty, just right."

The *Mexas* waved him off.

"You remember the time I was off by a hundred or so Ghoupalle years and got stuck fighting with the Jisilikan army in Foixe? Then we stormed the enemy bunker at Arrêgon and I became one of them damn heroes you love to hate? That was chance—or fate, or destiny, or merely blind luck, or a legitimate miscalculation. If we *knew* where a certain point in that three-dimensional grid was, the point which would lead us to Place X at Time Y, then we could go there, to that place and that *time*, as easily as we walk through a curtain—or as easily as you put away your Thanksgiving dinner, *zurrek* and cranberry sauce and all: a bit of polite resistance, then freedom...in a new world."

"And what would you do there?" Jason yawned, feeling the food working its magic. "And could you get back?"

"That's not the question we should be focusing on at this early stage."

"*We...*? How about just *you*? I'm ready for a nap."

The *Mexas* slapped Jason's big belly.

"You don't believe it; therefore, we need to confirm the phenomenon to you. Then we'll go on to ask and answer other questions. In the end, perhaps we will be able to do some good, something like prevent a war that killed millions of people. Or find a cure to a fatal disease before anyone could ever contract it. We could do that, if we had a little scientific luck—and if we're very, very good. I mean, extremely good."

Jason belched once more, nodding.

The next day the *Mexas* had bid the royal family farewell and left for his lonely island of Little Biznuik.

A few days after returning, while deep in the basin of the dormant volcano there, among the igneous rocks and tiny tufts of virgin grass sprouting through the black, caked soil, he had paused to survey the caldera. He was determined to find the tangent he believed must exist there. The Ghoupalle race was said to have come from this desolate island in the middle of the Bær Sea in ancient times, crossing over to the mainland. And yet the island was too small to hold such a large gathering of settlers and conquerors. No sign of any civilization had been found on the island. It was considered haunted and generally left alone; his presence there was proof of that! They must have come through another tangent, he guessed. They may have come from yet another world somewhere across the galaxy. Finding that tangent might open up his whole plan to correct the history he had already lived. He measured the area, examined it inch by inch, analyzed rock and soil samples, studied the limited flora and fauna. Step by step, he physically felt for the invisible resistance which signaled a tangent's presence.

The afternoon was long and the sun warm on his back. Gradually it clouded over and bathed him in the greenish haze of dusk. He paused and sat on one of the larger rocks. He breathed in the acidic gases which vented occasionally from the soil. He regarded the high rim of the caldera above him, and scanned the wide basin below, the shadows of the jagged rocks momentarily alarming him.

He sat there, watching the blue-green ten-legged ant-like things crossing the ground at his feet, watching their labor, feeling the weight upon their backs of the long grass blades and petty crumbs of food from his lunch pack. How they struggled! Did they know they lived on a desert island? Did they somehow fathom that it was only the remnants of his lunch which provided their sustenance? Would they starve when he left?

He pondered them for a while.

Then he raised his foot—slowly—and wondered what possible moral consequence he might suffer were he to smash them all. A grin spread across his face. What would happen to him if he destroyed them—and would he feel guilt for his purposeless gesture? He glared at the boiling emerald clouds above him, defiantly, even arrogantly, although he did not bother to shake his fist at the sky this time. That would have been futile. Catching himself, he pondered his madness.

119

In the end, he smashed half of them and let the other half go freely about their business, deciding that the gods would have a moral dilemma of their own when they decided his fate: he had killed, yet he had also been merciful, and somewhere in the middle was the road he knew he must take. The good acts he was prepared to commit in the future, should his plans succeed, would surely weigh the balance in his favor.

His stomach growled, startling a seabird...

The crumbly soil felt pleasant against his naked back...

The sea breeze spoke to him, told him a bawdy joke...

The next week, sometime in early afternoon, working on the south side among the more active gas vents, he had felt it, first with his bare backside, then with his hands. It resisted him and so he played with it. Eventually, the air parted for him with some effort, and beyond lay another land, a new world: brown, green, blue, and yellow, somehow familiar, somehow foreboding, as yet uninhabited by his imagination. He had smiled—

And opened his eyes again in 1457, caught napping in his garrison office, the snorting of *Jêpe* outside the windows....

Chapter 13

Future Confessions

The captain nearly fell off his bunk in the rustic office he called home, having momentarily dozed off on the hard wooden plank. With the recollection of his talk with Jason still on his mind, the memories of his first meeting with Zaura-Matousz crept into his consciousness.

He stretched and stood, yawned and glanced outside through the tiny window, saw the afternoon dragging on, the sky darkening in its green hue as dusk was floating in on emerald clouds. It was a rare day for him to hide away in his office, but this was no ordinary day, he felt. He had the premonition that it was special from the moment he first awoke.

Though he had lived with Zaura for seven years, he did not know her. Yes, she was the same Zaura he had married previously, but there was a much different rapport between them now than he had expected. In fact, he remembered the words she uttered in her soft mezzo-soprano Ghoupallêan upon their first meeting:

"You have the appearance of a man I once knew." It took all of his power to hold back his knowing grin.

When he returned through the tangent to Ghoupallesz in the year 1449—he had been aiming for 1446, the year he supposedly had been lost at sea—he found his adopted world intact and almost as perfect as he had left it. He stopped first to get his bearings at the Selauê Archive, a repository of obsessively collected information from around the world, especially anything happening in Sekuate. He saw that his official record in the Selauê Archive had a blue square around a red circle, indicating unconfirmed death.

"No, Zaura, I wasn't drowned that night when the ship went down; I was swept to shore in Zetinê and held captive by the Zetin for three years." That was what he had planned to say. She would pull him into her tight embrace, tears of joy streaming down her cheeks. The years he had been away from her would become only a bad dream.

Springtime was the right season for a reunion...

The door bore the mark of the Matousz family...

He had followed her to a neighborhood market...

"Excuse me," he had spoken, "could you hand me a bag for these fruits?"

Two pairs of eyes met, recognized each other...

And the weeks that followed rolled out like a carpet...

Sitting in his office, he cleared his throat, spoke aloud in a gentle baritone, in English so that his office personnel would not be able to understand him even if they could hear him. It was a quirk of his, thinking aloud when in private as a means of separating a single focused line of reasoning from the general ocean of babble washing around inside his head.

He blew words into the air like smoke rings, watched them drift and sink as he said them.

"You could never understand, Zaura, my dear. I wanted you so much that I crossed the dimensions, braved the police on Earth and all my cynical friends on Ghoupallesz. I returned to you. I only wanted to pick up where I left off, to live with you the rest of your days."

He paused, forgetting that he had no dictation machine at his disposal. He allowed his thoughts to roam, to graze in the meadow, to trek homeward along a well-beaten path through the idyllic forest, along the brook, and on to the farmhouse where he knew a feast had been prepared for his arrival. He sat down at the dinner table in his daydream but instead of whispering a prayer of thanks for the food, he caught a thought trying to escape down his throat and he forced it out through his mouth:

"And you died so young, too. I want to find a cure...."

The quiet knock on the door was followed quickly by the sheepish countenance of his aide, inquiring if he needed any assistance. Evidently, he had been heard. The captain shook his head, smiled, and waved the young man out, continuing his monologue before the door had been closed tightly.

"I regret all the troubles you've had because you have known me. That's the reason everything I do now is aimed at alleviating those troubles. That's the reason I have come back to you to live again those missed years."

He listened to the echo. The words sounded insincere, but he pressed on with his confession.

"And you did marry me. Again. But it was not quite the same man who left Karluk Isle that you married this time...."

The door opened once more and his Second entered; a vice-commander had that right.

"*Kassera aven-kal, Kanê?*" Aroun-Qalanou asked. 'Are you well, sir?'

"*Kassera aven,*" came his formal reply, followed by a casual wave to come in and sit down. 'I'm fine.'

When young, just-promoted *Serpan* Qalanou had made himself comfortable on the *batê*, a kind of hammock strung over an open box, the senior captain continued in his accented Ghoupallêan: "Do you remember when I first came here to the Selauê Garrison?"

"Yes, sir," Qalanou replied.

"Remember my first day as commander of the hundred-second regiment?"

"Yes, sir—in a general way."

"Did you think me a foreigner from the first moment?"

"Sir, it is not my place to remark upon your personal—"

"Did you think I was a foreigner?"

"You *are* a foreigner, sir."

"On that day, did you think I was a foreigner?"

"No, sir, I did not. Not until later."

"Later?"

"In the evening—when I was speaking with the other lieutenants. One of them asked me if you were a foreigner."

"Which of them asked that question?"

"It was *Landor* Sartanou, sir."

"Did he say why he believed me to be a foreigner? What gave it away?"

"I recall he said it was the way you walked—not like a man who had been riding *Jêpe*. My memory is faulty on this, sir. I told him a walk could not show you to be a foreigner, only someone not accustomed to a cavalry regiment."

"Thanks. Anything else?"

"You did not speak to us that day, so I could not hear your speech. Also, you are—sir, I am embarrassed to note it—you are of shorter stature than many of us. Yet you do seem to be spryer than—"

"Thanks."

That was honest, he decided. The average Ghoupalle adult male was a head taller than him, a hand broader at the shoulders, a dozen seconds faster in a sprint, a meter farther in a leap. He could not change that. The lighter gravity due to the planet's smaller mass and the higher oxygen content of the air helped him keep up.

The senior *Serpan* stared at the junior *Serpan* for some time, as though trying to burn a hole through his skull with the power of his vision. The junior fidgeted.

"Sir, is there anything else that you require at this time?"

He grinned—his big, foreign grin—and shook his weary head once more, slowly.

"I must confess a secret to someone, and it should be to you who serves as my Second. As vice-commander, you are pledged to keep my secrets."

The younger *Serpan* stood in protest but was put back in his place by his commander's casual gesture: his little finger pointing back to the seat.

"You have known me for almost seven years, since you were the rank of *Landor*. And you have also met my spouse on several occasions. It was not long before then that I met my spouse, Zaura-Matousz. That is why I asked you about my foreign appearance. Now comes my secret: My secret is that my spouse does not know who I am."

Qalanou appeared consternated.

"Give me free rein to explain," the commander said, throwing up his hand to halt any utterance. "She agreed to make a marriage union with me because I reminded her of her first husband. I have the appearance of that gentleman, she said, and I have seen lightning-box pictures of him. That previous gentleman left her when she was recovering from the birth of their child. He was lost when his ship sank in a storm. She has mourned him ever since—even now, in our seventh year. She will not give me all her heart because she reserves a portion for him."

"Sir, why should she give you her heart? It seems a useless sacrifice."

He realized he had spoken literally, translating directly from English to Ghoupallêan.

"That is an expression in my country. It means to express affection for someone."

"Ah! I apologize."

"I knew she would always think of the first husband. At first I was willing to allow it because of the affection I have for her. But now—"

"Sir, should I truly be your confessor?"

"You should and you are!"

He paced the room, feeling the heavy gaze of Qalanou.

"Now it has reached a point when I cannot hold back my secret any longer. Once I tell it, I do not know what I should do. That is for you and your advice to decide. Understand?"

Qalanou nodded reluctantly.

"It is simply this: I am *not* the man with whom she happened to enter a marriage union in 1449 but actually the *same* man who left her in 1445 and allowed her to believe he had drowned. She has believed the lie these seven years, believed that I am a separate and different man who only resembles her first husband. The truth is I *am* her first husband. It is complicated. Suffice to say, I had thought she would come to love me for myself, as her second husband, yet she refuses to give up the obsession with her former spouse—who was and is, ironically, actually me."

Qalanou chuckled, repressed it as best he could.

"Is it a joke?"

"I apologize, sir. It was not the secret I expected."

"Ah-hah!"

"Sir, you do not have a problem in this instance. If you tell her that you are the same man as before, then she will be overcome with joy to know your return is a safe one."

The captain pointed a stern finger at his Second.

"She will kill me for my dishonesty."

Qalanou folded his smile away, then nodded.

The cold silence was filled by melancholy sighs. The cannon shot marking the end of the training day did not disturb them. Nor did the wheezing of the troop of *Jêpe* tied up outside his window while one of their riders dropped off a scrolled message tube to the regimental sergeant-major. Then his bashful aide again entered, this time with a bottle of *gor* and two mugs.

Qalanou poured for his captain.

"It would be best, sir, to continue to play as an actor."

They drank down their first mugs.

"If I do that, she will continue to mourn me, in my own house, in my presence. I do not believe I can continue to live in my own funeral chamber any longer. I must tell her—even if it means that her hatred might ignite."

He wanted to tell Qalanou the rest of his secret—that he was from planet Earth—but he knew that the Ghoupalle man would not understand. It was not easy to explain how he'd wanted to return before she could mourn him for too long—so he could then step into his previous life as his true self. Or how he would have to leave her again in a year so he would not interfere with the previous timeline. Or that the letters of introduction, streamers of valor stars, and embroidered certificates of merit from the Queen of Fenula were fakes. Oh, yes, the queen was real and she had actually given them to him, but Queen Jinetta was previously his high school sweetheart, and his fellow interdimensional voyager Gina Parton, who had been lucky to marry a prince, who eventually became a king, thus making her the queen.

And yet, with all his apparent good fortune—rank and privilege, loving wife, impressive home, a few adventures, a few amusements—he knew that in a few years there would come a revolution, followed by civil war. The rebels who would come to power in the capital would rule the nation recklessly, building an arrogant, swaggering empire, waging relentless war with neighboring states. They would fall when their enemies united and fought back, leaving Sekuate in ruins—and generations of his family along with it. He could move the family away but he knew he could not account for the subsequent generations. In a few years war would wipe out his country, his family, his life—

That is what I must change.

"How long can I go on playing this confusing game?"

His Second had no answer for him. Their talk ended with the finishing of the bottle of *gor* and the drunken singing of the Sekuate national anthem in triple meter. Their aides outside chuckled at the performance of the two old farts.

In his drunken state, his mind burst wide open and all the ugly, sordid history of his wild meanderings lay brutally clear before his tired eyes. He began again to speak his story—it seemed more real to him when he spoke aloud—then dismissed his wide-eyed Second who seemed shocked at his captain's mind-bending story.

"You have the appearance of a man I once knew," Zaura had said when he sat down at the table with her in the tavern after meeting in the market.

"It's strange, isn't it?" he had responded. "You have the appearance of a woman I once knew."

Their dinner was barely touched as they shared their life stories, and they remarked on the similarities. He needed to interject several discrepancies to keep his act believable. It was enough that they had the appearance of each others' old spouses. That was what had led them into the *qala*.

The sex they had, however, did not have the intensity he recalled from their early days together, and he suspected the power of her aura was already in decline. Being an Earth man, the effects of her natural *senzenaxii* powers on him were much greater than those of the average Ghoupalle. He knew that such a defect would not matter to him now, on this second trip, nor in this ten-year life to which he had returned. He was with his once and future spouse, his beloved Zaura-Matousz, from that sentimental night of reunion onward, no matter what problems might develop later from his illusion or from her sympathetic charms.

They registered their marriage at the Selauê Archive six Ghoupalle months later, thus preventing her from remeeting Sairel businessman Tolour-Frêdin, an old *senzenaxii* client, the next year. That was the first step, he knew.

The next step was to enjoy. Simply enjoy.

Chapter 14

Autumn Aura

It was harvest season in the northern districts of Sekuate in Ghoupalle year 1457. Around the city of Sorêg, bands of marauders were going from farm to farm demanding food and whatever else they could get from frightened country folk. Sekuate had no national or district police, so units of the army were regularly called upon to maintain order and deal with such local matters as harvest season marauders. The units involved rotated each year; since this was Sorêg district, they always came from the 2d *Coræsz* garrison in Selauê.

Serpan Set-d'Elous saluted his colonel, *Karrond* Sonel-Timê, as he accepted the usual rolled parchment of mission orders before the assembled troops of the 5t *Treskand*, which included those of his own 102d *Regêlad*. He had the honor of acting-commander by virtue of his immediate superior's absence. *Merzel* Aroun-de-Sotos was attending the birth of his first child, a son who would be named after his father, a son who would one day accompany Set-d'Elous on the Sekuatean army's campaigns into the snow fields of Tebbicousimankalê—in another incarnation of himself: agèd cavalry commander and all-around vagabond.

Now, however, his unit was ordered up to Sorêg to patrol the country roads and arrest any marauders, bandits, and scoundrels they might encounter, and, if necessary to maintain order, they were authorized to execute criminals.

Set-d'Elous was reluctant to be so far away from Zaura at this crucial time. He had just spilled his guts to his Second, revealed his great secret, and could not leave the matter suspended for the two months they would be in the field. And they were to be sent immediately with no time to notify their families. Messengers would be sent to the families of each officer; the line soldiers lived in the barracks.

The sky was crystal clear and they made good time, taking the road to Kamtan, where they camped for the night. A cavalry unit traveled much slower than the electric coach—especially slow with the finicky *Jêpe* they rode, unreliable and stubborn but the only creature available on Ghoupallesz to press into service as a beast of burden.

The third day of the month of Ahok brought an overcast sky and the threat of rain. The green droplets floated down upon them as they passed through the small farm towns lining the road to Sorêg. They camped overnight twice more, and arrived at the city of Sorêg late the next afternoon.

After his introduction to the *Boiar*, the city's mayor, the commander deployed his four *Saxêrad* and gave instructions to the officers how their troops should cover the area between the city and the foothills of the mountains.

They caught a band of twelve brigands, searched thirty farms for others who may have been hiding, took one farmer into custody for killing a bandit who had been caught stealing harvested crops. The vegetables grown in that locale were mostly the yam-like *habl* and *koriñ*, a plant that produced five or more long green bean-like appendages. The common grain there was *qink*, a reddish wheat. The few farmers who raised livestock had small herds of the pony-sized three-horned cattle called *krañ* while those with piglet-like *lorg* usually had less than thirty. No farm was worked by more than one family, so they were easy targets. The third day they shot two bandits trying to escape across a barren field with one *lorg* under each arm. Another actually tried pulling a *krañ* on a rope, but the horned beast resisted until the soldiers could get to him.

In the following days they patrolled the rural roads by *Jêpe*, taking wide, leisurely circuits around the farm villages. More than a few times the captain had to scold the new recruits, chiding them to remember to wrap the dewlap of the *Jêpe* so it would not become tangled in the brush. The thin, veiny skin hanging from the tropical beast's throat was easily hurt, causing the animal to refuse work. Part of every cavalry soldier's accessories was the hooded scarf for their mounts to wear, slipped over the long rabbit ears and wrapped to cradle the dewlap against the beast's thick neck.

As they went along their many designated patrol routes, most farmers waved cheerfully at them. Those who did not were suspect; they were either marauders or citizens who opposed the lavish lifestyle of the *Mexas* down in the capital. Sometimes a farm family would provide a warm drink for the patrols. In the northwestern quarter, many of the fields had already been cleared, the cool summer having brought an early autumn with less-than average harvest. That made their task more difficult: marauders would also have less food and be more desperate.

For eight days none were spotted. Then news came of the murder of an entire farm family to the west of Sorêg. A full force of soldiers combed the forests and searched in and under and behind everything but did not find anything to lead them in pursuit. The fourth squadron was in the vicinity of the band's next attack and was able to capture ten of the twenty marauders. Two were killed as they fled. The remaining prisoners were taken into Sorêg, for the district magistrate there to deal with them. In the end they were ordered to be executed.

It was the custom for such public executions to be carried out by the resident military force, but Set-d'Elous, captain of the task force, was hesitant to allow his men to kill outside of war. It was a weakness he had, being from a foreign land where war and hardship were less common—or so it was rumored. He ordered the act performed when the city *Boiar* threatened to send a message to the garrison in Selauê concerning the matter. So early the next morning the ten marauders, seven men and three women, were stood up in the town square and his soldiers, chosen by lottery, stood before them and fired their AT-6 guns. The orange molten-metal blasts from the stubby-barreled rifles burned through the marauders' chests, darkening the old plaster wall behind them. The *Boiar* nodded approvingly from his balcony, believing the public punishment would send a clear message to other marauders.

The captain brooded in the hotel room he shared with his vice-commander. In this incarnation, *Serpan* Set-d'Elous had served seven years in the garrison but had never seen combat, the closest action being the annual patrol missions and the war games played each spring in the countryside east of Selauê. It was not good for a soldier to be a pacifist, he mused, sitting on the edge of his bunk. If he stood and walked to the window he could see the wall with ten black stains on it, and he would feel nauseous. Somehow it was not the bandits' fault, he wanted to believe. In a different society, on another world, their plight would be met with sympathy and assistance. The marauders were the hill people who did not or could not grow crops in their rocky environment. It was a tradition, from perhaps a thousand years before, to come down from the hills every autumn.

He was awakened by *Serpan* Qalanou at dawn, before he realized that he had slept the night through.

By noon they had covered the road west to Qoxe and north to Rêfan without incident. All the people they passed had proper papers. They stopped at the crossroads outside Sorêg-Lend, the lakeshore town. The troops dismounted and set up their camp, prepared their meals and ate. The fields around them were turned over, the crops harvested, the dirt dull and almost black. A line of trees broke the fields in both directions, high enough that they obscured the afternoon suns as they slipped between the clouds.

Ah, the moody skies of Sorêg! The captain sighed, holding his mug of *gor*, sitting back against his hard saddle, set on the ground as a chair. He had only been to the northern city as part of this patrol duty, and yet he always noticed the gloomy skies. The mountains to the north and east collected clouds which filtered the sunlight in eerie ways. The same sky now, with the clouds that always seemed to hover there, was darker, heavier than it should have been. It played on his spirits.

Ever since the executions of the ten marauders, they had lost their joking manner. It was a real mission, they now understood. They were midway in the assignment of new recruits and thirty-eight had joined the 102d Regêlad. This was the new recruits' first patrol duty. The patrol duty would toughen them, he knew, and they would be ready when war would come—some twenty years down the road, on a day he had already lived.

The captain stretched against his saddle, pulled himself to his feet.

"*E mab' zu darre besh-te z'kûxen toba-de-ganê*," he said with a yawn to drowsy *Landor* Mekmelus sitting nearby. 'I'm going over to those bushes to take a leak,' were his approximate words, trying out the colloquial phrasing his troops used.

The reclining lieutenant fumbled to get up. Not only had the captain addressed him directly, but the captain was stalking off on his own, away from the campsite. That was rule number one: never leave the commander alone. The lieutenant called two *brevet* to follow their captain across the dirt field, over to the line of trees.

"*Serpan, güpen spad-se*," the lieutenant called after his captain. 'Draw your sword.'

"I will when I get there," he shouted back in English, his voice full of cynicism. The worried lieutenant had meant the blade at his side.

Posed against the bushes doing his business, he heard hurried footsteps approaching from behind, caught a whiff of the musty, unbathed soldiers, and bent his head back to see the two *brevet*—new privates whose names he had yet to learn—running toward him over the uneven ground and stumbling miserably.

"*Santor-se*," he ordered them. 'Go back.'

They were too scared of not obeying to disagree with the lieutenant's command and stood in the middle of the field, half way between each order-giver.

When the captain gestured at them to return to the campsite and saw them take their first step in that direction, he resumed his relief. Then, just as quickly, he saw there was someone in the bushes before him—on the opposite side. He watched, deciding it was a girl.

She was dressed in a silky *sabêl*, a kind of tan-and-blue striped pantaloons, with a long frilly beige *uêsk*, a kind of half-cape made from *maothai* fiber, hanging around her shoulders and falling limply to her hips, covering a short, tight-fitting white blouse. It gave her the appearance of wearing a harem costume. It was common dress for Danid women. Most marauders were of Danid heritage.

She had not noticed him. As he refastened his trousers, he observed her. She gazed up at the sky, out across the lake, and back to a sheaf of papers on her lap. She sat on a large flat stone and scanned the lake often.

He drew his sword and glanced back for the two *brevet* who had finally returned to the campsite. They had left him, as he ordered. Now was the time for them to accompany him, he thought. Never mind! Through the bushes he went and the girl was not startled as he expected.

It was something in the breeze he felt first, a fragrance or a feeling which he could not identify. He regarded the girl: her short hair was a bushel of dark curls, her neck white and graciously curved, and her face when she studied him was a pale hue not of sickliness but of purity. She had the features of the Danid in her heart-shaped face, the short impish nose and smoothly carved cheeks, dark eyes drawn with bushy brows, and the gently pursed lips. Her small body was lithe but he knew it would be strong under the command of her will. Her crossed legs held her papers and a certain vitality seemed to pulse beneath the folds of her pantaloons.

"*Ghou ben masai, Kanê?*" she asked him. Her voice was rich in feeling but light in pitch, like a whisper with a full chest of power behind it. 'You are lost, sir?'

He lowered his sword momentarily—and if she had intended harm she could have killed him then—before raising it at the threat implied in her quick eyes. It was nothing that he saw, yet he struggled to grasp the thought that flashed through his mind.

"What are you doing here?" he found himself asking her in gruff Ghoupallêan.

The girl was not shy, nor was she frightened by an officer of the *Coræsz*. She was required to respond quickly, completely, courteously, and truthfully.

"I have come to this place, as I do most days, to compose poetry," she sang to him without any music but what played in her heart.

"Poetry?" he asked, far from an answer he expected.

"I write *harrê*."

He nodded his understanding.

"Do you have your papers?" he asked her.

She raised the sheaf from her lap, offering the pages.

"No, your citizenship papers!"

Her eyes held his face, caressed his cheeks before she looked away to fumble with her pantaloons. Her deft fingers slid her ballooning pant leg up over her knee, revealing the small purse strapped to her thigh. She released it and opened the flap, found the folded certificate of citizenship he wanted and extended her arm to him. He took it, brushing her fingertips as he did—not intentionally, but as she let go of the paper—

"*Kassera avenk, Kanê?*" came a deep Ghoupallêan voice behind them and he saw that a *sargan* had brought two *zevron* with him to check on their commander.

"*Om-da*," he said, glancing at her folded certificate. 'Fine.'

The sergeant asked whether or not she was alone as he directed the corporals into defensive position with a quick shift of his eyes.

"*Gul ben bisep?*" the captain asked. 'You are alone?'

Something which seemed like her version of a genuine smile passed across her lips then was immediately lost.

"*El ben essan bisep,*" she said. 'I am always alone.'

It was a statement of deep meaning and he felt it in her aura—something wild, full of undirected passion, or a cry for help, a plea for friendship which shot through his veins like a drug.

He stepped back from her, handing the folded paper to the sergeant, who continued what quickly was becoming a routine set of interrogation questions.

The captain listened to her answers, then ordered the others away, declaring that she was of no concern to them. There was no way that the girl was a bandit. She was young enough to be a student, and spending her time beside the lake on an autumn afternoon was no crime. It was not against the law to daydream either, he noted, and told the sergeant. Rebuked, the three of them left.

"May I see your poetry?" he asked gently.

Her face changed colors, a healthy glow. She offered one page, its corners slowly fluttering in the breeze, as he first hesitated then took it from her hand. There was history in her touch.

"We must be sure there is no subversion in your poetic expression," he told her, adding a wink to reassure her that he was not about to arrest her for her opinions.

"Is love a subversion?" she asked.

He scanned the words, feeling the movements of her hand as she had earlier scrawled the loopy characters, the sensations still there on the parchment. Not only was he reading her words, feeling her thoughts, in the poem, but he was reliving the tiny manipulations of the stylus as she had written the words. They were not political subversion. Love, being a four-letter word (five in Ghoupallêan), did not dirty a poem written in any language.

"Who is this for?" he asked.

She made a sound like a tiny, repressed chuckle, and her movements were precise yet fluid as she arose, the stone where she had sat falling away with the crystalline lake further back, *she* completely filling the world in front of him.

"There is a student," she spoke in her velvety voice. "He studies science. Yet he pursues me every day. He has not caught me, and I will never let him. So I come here to hide."

"A student? What is your school?"

"I belong to Sorêg University."

She meant the small provincial institution where mostly city workers were trained for clerk positions. It was not a place for poets to learn their craft—nor for political rebels to gain an audience.

"Sir, I must leave now, if I may be excused."

He did not immediately hear her, lost as he was in the confusing, transfixing text.

...the death-like skies above are my canopy,/ the fertile earth below can be my bed,/ And the one who joins me there can never be a harvester,/ Only a planter...

It was a kind of poem called Sênal-*harrê*, named for the ancient poet who first wrote the odd-metered form. He knew that fact only because of helping his daughter with her literature homework—last month, in Selauê. It felt as though it had all happened in another life. The poem he now held in his hand he knew in its completed version from a visit in 1530 on another trip, at the height of the Gangus Council reign. It was not a great poem, even in its final form, yet, with the new government's popularity, her poetry was widely assigned in schools. Today, however, he was in the autumn of 1457, well before the revolution. He had memorized the poem quite unintentionally by endless repetition as his daughter learned to recite it.

...the way earth is hoed, and seed is sown,/ And never to see its ripening...

"I've read this before," he mumbled in English, staring at the words.

She asked him what he'd said and only then did he come out of his trance.

"When did you write this?" he asked in Ghoupallêan.

Benign puzzlement splashed haphazardly over her face.

"Today, sir."

His expression went blank.

"It is not finished, sir."

"Of course it isn't."

He turned away from her, holding the beige parchment in his hand, and his fingers crumpled it without thought. He had read the poem before, a text about the power of a woman over a man when he is shackled by the throes of love. He was no judge of poetry; once in power all of her poetry was read, the good and bad. He realized who the woman was. That meek poetess had written other poems which were not innocent portraits of amorous relationships but harsh and direct political declarations.

He opened the folded certificate once more, and saw her name printed in red letters across the top—

BASURA-KANOUN 66701-5459002-33

—and regarded her once more: the face he had seen in countless official portraits and news bulletin sketches was the young, melancholy face before him now.

The Basura-Kanoun he knew from the resources in the Selauê Archives painted her as some kind of dragon-lady or witch-woman, the evil goddess whose supporters had done terrible acts in her name. And yet, he pondered, everyone is young and innocent at least once in their lives.

- BIRTH 1432-SHAE-16 STUDENT SORÊG-UNIVERSITY RANK-3
- FATHER SAROUN-KANOUN, BEING GHOUPALLE, OF CITY SORÊG
- MOTHER IPA-DOXE, BEING DANID, OF TOWN VISSE

His heart beat faster and he tried to calm himself before she could sense anything was amiss. The words were there on the paper before him and his hands were shaking with the urge to act. He commanded himself to be steady, wishing his men were still there—even though he did not want them to see him in his moment of weakness.

His eyes shifted beyond the edge of the certificate, down to the whiteness of her feet against the gray stone.

The limp paper slipped casually from his nervous fingers and floated down to the reddish grasses sprouting at the base of the stone. He automatically bent to retrieve it and found that she also moved to catch the certificate before it could touch the moist grass. Their knees bumped as they lowered themselves, their hands going for the certificate simultaneously, their cheeks brushing for a heartbeat.

"*Pakê-se*," he whispered. 'I'm sorry.'

It was not an intentional whisper; he was simply out of breath. Suddenly, the world was spinning around his head. That was all the breath he could muster.

"Will you come tomorrow?" she was saying.

His fingers felt for the certificate, found it, and offered it to her fingers, all out of sight. Her eyes leaned against his, and when she announced she could feel his heart beating, he believed her. He could feel hers beating, too.

"You are Basura-Kanoun," he said, not quite a statement and not fully a question.

"My father gave me the name," she replied.

"You're father is a carpenter."

She took his hand in hers, cupping it like a live animal, a fragile pet. For Danid people it was a gesture of sublimation, a disarming act that signaled complete honesty.

"Yes, sir."

"Your mother is your father's second wife," he continued as though reciting something he once had to memorize. "His first wife died without giving him children, so he was old when he married your mother, and he has since died."

"Yes, it is true, sir. How do you know about my family?"

"The student who pursues you at school," he said, ready to check her expression when he spoke his next words, "his name is Diert-Gangus."

"Yes! You can see inside my head!"

His other hand clasped hers and with their four hands interlocked they stood together, never more apart than the modest projection her bosom allowed, never turning their eyes away from each other.

"You will be a great poet," he spoke solemnly. "Children will study your writing."

"Who are you?" she asked.

Lowering his eyes, he felt faint.

"You don't need to know me. I'm just a soldier. I'll die someday in a battle and be quickly forgotten. You don't need to remember my name."

He tore away from her.

"*Kanê! Dajê!*" she called. 'Sir! Please!'

He broke through the bushes, taking long strides across the dirt field, seeing his troops preparing their *Jêpe* for the afternoon patrol.

"*Kanê!*"

He refused to look back.

"*Læforen il alandaot-kal?*" she called after him, wanting him to return tomorrow.

He continued on, shaking with fear at what he was thinking: he should not hesitate to drive his sword through her. Laying to rest the girl—this charming peasant student, this daydreaming poetess who would one day become the queen of the rebels who would overthrow the government of *Mexas* Tomodon-Sarrêban—was an act that would save millions of lives. He could do it in a flash. If only she did not so closely resemble his psychiatrist, Dr. Toni Franck.

Chapter 15

Socio-Economics

The morning breeze brought strange, ghostly words to him: "Are you ill, sir?"

It was *Serpan* Qalanou come to raise the commander at the break of dawn. However, it had been a sleepless night for him, his head full of the images of Earth. Atop the bunk in his room at the inn in Sorêg, he found the picture of Zaura that was burned in his mind the day he sailed away from her and Karluk Island hovered in the chill around him. Not even three *ræl* blankets could keep him warm. And the snoring of Qalanou only reminded him of the ship's long horn blasts in the depths of the storm on that voyage.

He opened his eyes, focused, saw Qalanou register surprise on his face.

"You must be ill, sir," Qalanou said. "Your face is so pale."

He tried to sit up but Qalanou pressed him back. There was no explanation, but it was not uncommon for a foreigner to be stricken with what was called 'northern sickness.' Of course, he would, in coming years, survive the snow fields of Tebbicousimankalê while the acclimated Ghoupalle soldiers around him fell like sacks of dung. Even so, Qalanou insisted he stay in bed and promised to follow the patrol patterns designated the previous evening by the captain, searching the region north of the city and up to the edge of the foothills.

The captain nodded faintly, pulled the blankets tighter around himself.

He was not really ill, not in the usual sense. It was more like a hangover, but he had not been drinking. As familiarity came to him he recognized his ailment as the effect of too much *senzenaxii*, too much psychic stimulation from a *senzenor's* potent aura. It had been so long for him to experience it that he felt completely abused by the girl at the lake.

It was the same with Zaura when they were young: overwhelming at first, but he learned to take it and she learned to restrain it until the effect was optimal for both of them. Her powers had declined with age and childbirth; he no longer took any special precautions such as drinking *tal-ganê* before sex. It became less of a strain on his body as their time together lengthened. But the exposure to such a raw, passionate aura like the girl had was similar to diving into a whiskey barrel for an alcoholic.

He felt light-headed, weak, emotionally drained, as though the orgy at the lake had been physical.

The maid brought a breakfast ordered by Qalanou, and two *brevet* were stationed outside his door to wait on him further. He was strong enough by that mid-morning meal to partake of the *tabli*, *uli*, and *sebal* set before him—standard Ghoupalle morning meal: fruit, chips, and dip. The bottle of *gor* was particularly effective and he felt refreshed—enough to leave the premises without his escort, causing great concern for the two young soldiers he ordered to stay at the inn.

A cool wind swept the lake, tossing the waters into rippling waves. The trees which had hidden them the day before now bent with the wind, the long, gray, leathery *hurraqir* leaves dipping, brushing the ground. The slab of stone where she had stood was wet from a morning shower. When he dismounted, she came into view, like an angel emerging from the clouds— and for an endless heartbeat he wondered if he were really in heaven and not just on another planet.

Without words, they came together and he inhaled her aura like fresh air, feeling her emotions as surely as if her delicate fingers were clawing up his spine to get to his brain. Their eyes met but at the last moment he held back from kissing her—

realizing that it was her will that had told him to do it and not his own heart. He knew he had to be careful, had to know when a thought was truly his and when it was merely planted in his mind.

"I have almost finished my poem," she spoke, as though she knew he would be interested in her progress.

He smiled, just then remembering the soft Danid accent in her Ghoupallêan speech the previous day. He allowed the precious time it took for her to open her sheaf of papers and hand it to him. The seven pages were neatly copied in her elegant script, wide margins around them, blank lines between stanzas. He read it from the first line to the last that she had written and tried to recall if this was the final version he had seen in the literature book.

"And the conclusion?" he asked, to which she grinned, gesturing with a nod of her head to go with her along the shore.

"I will need your assistance," she said.

Stepping lightly among the reeds, they outlined the shore of the lake. And with a wave of her hand over the waters the winds died and the waves flattened. The clouds, too, parted for her, those moody green clouds of Sorêg which haunted him. She took his hand, curling her fingers around his thumb in Ghoupalle fashion, as they reached a point of land extending out into the lake. There they found an old boat and used it to go out to the thickly wooded island in the center of the lake. Pulling the boat up between two rocks, they drifted back into the trees, hidden from the world. They sat there among the bushes in the meadow, playing with autumn flowers.

When the sun slipped behind the clouds once more, they returned to the boat and stole back across the dark waters. The grasses were cool, and walking barefoot with his boots slung over his shoulder, she laughed hesitantly at a joke he made. Her countenance was poetic, and her words were a song. The drug which she emitted fully saturated him. He knew the situation was now hopeless.

The spot where they had first met was the spot where they parted.

She asked him again if he would return the next day, to which his head forced him to decline but his heart screamed its desire.

Then, under the waving boughs above, Basura-Kanoun rose against his chest and pressed her lips to his forehead, pausing to run her tongue down to the tip of his nose. His hand automatically went to wipe away the wetness but stopped. He understood the custom: it was an overture to sex. But it was not the right time, he knew, checking the sky for the hour. He was long overdue.

She watched him stand and pull on his boots, studied the slinging of his scabbard around his waist. She noticed the eight-pointed star patches on his shoulders, the rank of a *Serpan*. A surge of guilt must have swept over her then for she shuddered like she was engulfed in an arctic gale. She had been cavorting with the enemy: if he in the uniform of the *Coræsz* was not the enemy of the folk with whom she shared a way of life, then who could be? She was not one to spout politics—and she told him so—but she had heard about the events of the past week when she returned to school. The talk of the soldiers riding down the poor people from the hills made her want to write a eulogy for them.

"How can you attack innocent civilians?" she asked him. "We should help the forest people instead of turning them away—or worse, cutting them down because they come in search of food for the winter."

His hand routinely went to the hilt of his sword.

"It is the law," he replied crisply. He knew what she meant, and he could identify with their plight. "It's my job," he added, more for himself than her.

"They only want food," she said. "From the northern hills they come every autumn, only seeking food to sustain them through the cold season."

He knew she was right. There was no charity here.

"I agree." He tried to smile. "I am not a soldier because I enjoy hurting people, or killing." He gazed into her eyes, then looked away. "I am a soldier because I believe in maintaining order. That is the best way to ensure an environment where happiness can be made for all of us. When some people have no thoughts of the pleasures of others, it is the soldier's job to segregate those people from the population. It is not for me to decide what actions to take. My commanders give me orders. Higher powers decide for or against those who interfere with people's pursuit of happiness. I am not allowed to decide their fate, only act to be their fate."

He mounted his *Jêpe* quickly, before he could take back his words, but he sensed her tears among the rustling of the trees as he rode away.

* * *

The words slapped him hard across both cheeks: "Is that your only reason, to give you more time with your precious Zaura-Matousz?"

He sighed, wiped the sweat from his forehead as he sat up on the bunk—as his friend Jason's words rang in his ears just as though he were standing right beside him, shouting. Shaking off the dream, he lay back, and listened to Qalanou's snoring.

He nodded his head in reply, then knew that it was a lie.

It was all a lie.

He left Aivana, in Ghoupalle year 1571, to travel back through the tangent to Earth and then, seventeen minutes later, re-enter it at a different angle. He arrived back in Ghoupalle year 1449. Before that switch, he and Jason had one of their many heated discussions over a lavish dinner. Despite all their discourses and debates, all the joking around and their cruel teasing back and forth, one thing stood out whenever he tried to forget everything. That was Jason's words: *Is that your only reason?*

Of course that was his only reason! He told Jason about going to all the trouble, physical as well as emotional, to return to Zaura in that way: it had to be the reason. The only reason. He could not understand what Jason was suggesting, but in the chill of the midnight room in Sorêg, he suddenly saw it clearly. It was a power trip. That's what Jason had meant. Sure, he enjoyed coming and going at will between two worlds and different time zones. That was something only a god could do, yet *he* did it—and enjoyed doing it. Yes, he had the idea of venturing to Ghoupallesz and re-doing his life—as everyone wanted to do at some time, he mused. Now it was his self-appointed challenge. It would also affect Zaura's life, already fully lived with and without him.

However, there was more—and knowing he could not now return to sleep, he pulled himself off the bunk and got dressed for a late walk. He really did want to change history, as much for his own entertainment as for the good of the people. Which one was foremost never really mattered so long as he proved he could do it. Proved to whom? To Jason, for one. It was like a bet. Also to his long-lost love Gina.

Her words came to him with the night breeze: Gina had long ago given him the name 'Set' because it was the name of an ancient god, and he—indeed, *they*—were becoming god-like. Of course, he would humbly and totally deny it with every breath— except to those poor, wretched Earthlings at the IRS service center. Certainly he was better than them. It seemed being a god was simply a matter of perspective. To a flea, the mangy mutt is a god.

He stared up at the moon. Only after a long gaze did he realize that it was not the moon of his native Earth but merely a lighted window high on the wall of a building in the next block.

Now that he was here in the past, or one version of the past, and the student-poet Basura-Kanoun was known to him, what could he do to affect history in any meaningful way? He sighed, as though he had known the moment for decision-making would come eventually and was resigning himself to meeting it head-on. He knew more than everyone around him. He had seen the future, had lived it. Now he was back where it all began. There she was: queen of the rebels! And he was the king of conformists—at least, long ago.

He walked the streets, pondering his twin lives, until he came to the town square.

Stopping before the wall stained with the splatters of execution, he sucked in the cool air, stuffed his hands in the pockets of his greatcoat, and studied the twisted angles of the crude abstractions. Through a different pair of eyes, the splatters might be called art, he mused. Modern art! Human art, he sighed. There would be more of that. He knew the time would come when every town from Sorêg in the north to Erê in the south would have its own martyr's wall.

In his pocket his hand felt the metal key to his room at the inn, felt it weighing heavily there. He let loose a loud exhale, blowing his own path through the gelatin of night air. If only it were the key to the door standing firmly shut before him now. He could so easily walk through it!

❄ ❄ ❄

He was getting used to hearing words in the wind: "*Serpan-se, jui-kal?*"

The voice that called to him seemed only the wind at first, but when he felt the hand on his arm, he knew it was her. 'Captain, is that you?' she had said, using the private, familiar form of 'you' in a public setting, daringly impolite as linguistic customs went.

He spun around.

"What a cold day to be out," he accosted her.

"Yet here we are," she sang, warming his spirit.

His hands, once again in his warm pockets, clenched the key to his room at the inn. His foggy breath hid his face.

"You remind me of someone," he said as she drew alongside him, "someone I once knew." He meant it to be a compliment, an opening.

"Were you in love with her?" she asked; in Ghoupallêan her words were borderline rude.

He managed a grin then, embarrassed. They turned away from the road, worried about being seen. He took her arm and led her into the shadows of the trees.

"I've made a terrible error," he said as they walked. He held the branches of a bush so she could proceed into the woods. "And I must correct it before I leave."

"Tell me the error and I shall help you correct it," she said as she wiped a stray leaf from his shoulder, then another.

Again he smiled, not knowing how to speak to her.

"It is complicated," he said.

They found a fallen log to sit upon.

"I know of someone who will commit a crime," he said. "However, I am confused by the circumstances. Shall I arrest that person now, or wait until the crime is committed?"

Basura took his arm tightly, concerned.

"Can you arrest a person before he has acted?"

He regarded her face in the dim light, her large eyes, her small nose. "No, of course not."

"Then do not arrest the person."

He thought for a moment, but she continued:

"Are you speaking of the woman you once knew? You were in love with her. And she hurt you? Now you plan to arrest her as revenge?"

"No, it's not like that."

"Tell me the story."

"There is no story to tell." He felt her eyes penetrating him, felt her stare folding back layers of his skin, pushing aside muscle and bone, exposing his soul. His heart was clasped. His breathing became shallow. "The only story is that the woman was my dearest friend since our youth. We had many adventures together—this is what I cannot reveal to you—but in the end, when I believed we would finally be together forever, I awoke one morning to find she had disappeared."

"You must feel great sadness," his guest whispered, laying her head against his shoulder.

He felt perplexed that she would be so comfortable in his presence that she did not hesitate to do such an obviously inappropriate act, even when shaded by the trees. Was she calculating? He had to be careful—

Careful? Why am I even here? With her? Do I have a plan?

"Of course she hurt you," the girl spoke, shaking him from his thoughts. "I feel it in your breath. And you think I resemble her? Do you think I will hurt you?"

A sigh escaped. "I don't know what to think."

They sat for a while in silence, her head against his shoulder. He wondered if his thoughts were open to her mind, even as he tried desperately to think of baseball.

Finally, she took his hand in hers.

"You are not a warrior, not like those others," she told him— probably she meant it to be a compliment, he thought.

"What if the crime will be murder?" he countered. "To arrest that person before the act will save a life."

"To arrest that person before the act is prejudgment." He noted her word choice: *âhifaxii*—having the double meaning of 'marking an enemy' as well as 'to judge before evidence is presented.'

"What of the life saved?"

"What of the criminal before the crime?"

"Lives saved is more important."

"Prejudgment is more serious."

"More serious than death?" He shook his head, suddenly in control of his senses again. "Prejudgment is no crime itself. Murder is!"

She gave his arm a squeeze, stopping him.

"Of whom are you speaking?"

He started off and she ran to him, repeated her question, grabbing at his arm.

"The someone of whom you remind me."

He was surprised she laughed, but he turned to face her, deciding whether or not to take her in his arms, choosing to keep his hands in his pockets. The key was still there.

"You can never understand."

She laughed again, a pleasant song which cradled his heart softly.

"Should I follow that person, wait for the first instance of criminal activity, and then try to prevent the act once the act begins, and if thus unable, then to arrest that person? Would that satisfy your sense of justice?"

She smiled, her breath clouding her face, and nodded.

"You should follow that person." Her face was solemn, almost as if knowing where his line of reasoning was leading, "and wait until that person attempts a crime, and then you should step in to prevent the crime, and arrest that person if it is appropriate at that moment—"

"That is what you think?"

She nodded, hesitantly at first, and her aura shifted its grip on his soul. "And it should not be for vengeance."

"The murder?"

"The arrest."

He guessed she knew what was going to happen next. She was the criminal about to commit the crime, he the dutiful policeman waiting to step in to prevent it at the last possible instant. To act too soon would be immoral. Too late, equally unfortunate.

So be it, he spoke to himself, I'll follow you—

She stood, her dress unsettled against her body, leaves on her shoulders, in her hair, her face pale and rosy and determined and calm, her hands at her sides awaiting a task, her torso straight and strong but somehow weak and in need of a firm embrace, wanting someone or something to make her feel alive, truly alive like never before, like never again.

"Timing is everything," he whispered in English, turning his back to her and marching off to his *Jêpe*, tethered in the empty *qinnet* field.

Chapter 16

Beauty's Beast

To his eyes, the campus of Sorêg university resembled some old institution in a European city, ancient brown-bricked buildings adorned with decorative ornaments around doorways and windows, tall columns and lofty buttresses, stained-glass windows and the ever-creeping white ivy on the walls, impressive banners and colorful flags, harried students in dark blue robes and peaked red caps, professors in green jerkins with tasseled yellow collars—and the random *pugua*, a popular reddish fox-like pet that fit easily in a student's book bag and looked so cute with its bewhiskered snout protruding out of the bag and its bulging golden eyes staring everywhere, a study buddy caught in the woods of eastern Sekuate or available for purchase in pet shops in the larger cities, such as Buiskê—

"There you go!" he muttered in breathless frustration, finally snatching the *pugua* by the scruff of its neck and hoisting it up into the air and over to the young lady standing in tears at the escape of her pet.

"*Dara, dara, dara,*" the girl sang in delight, thanking him. She seemed a little embarrassed. It was fortunate the kindly old gentleman had been there to block her pet's escape. And yet he was so quick for an old man, leaping and pouncing and finally corralling the little animal in his steady hands! She bowed in thanks, her blue robe brushing the pavement of the main walk.

He waved her away, suggesting she hurry on to class. After all, he was once a professor at the prestigious Selauê Academy—though no one here was the wiser. He couched himself in civilian garb, less than fashionable garb, at that. He had the look of a man down on his luck—which might be somewhat true, he mused—yes, a man who was searching for something, possibly hidden in a book in the university's modest library.

He entered the main building, saw the ancient ornate walls of plaster and the larger than life gray stone statues of famous graduates, famous lecturers, famous headmasters, and a couple of local politicians. In just a few years, five more statues would be placed in the wide corridor, he knew, statues of the gang of five, the [ahem] Council of Five, a. k. a. the Gangus Council. The white and blue tiled floor echoed the clicks of hard-soled shoes as students hurried to and fro. Out one door came a high-ranking professor dressed in the green jerkin but with a crimson collar and yellow streamers down his back, challenging the passing students to study as hard as they were running, no doubt late for classes, calling after them in equal amounts of disdain and amusement.

The high-ranking professor caught sight of the old man in the corridor. The two men waved at each other. The professor seemed curious at the stranger's presence. The stranger seemed cautious at the professor's attention. But it was not the time of the revolution nor the rise of the Council, not a time of watching what one said, of being aware of one's public behavior. No, it was still a free time in Sekuate. So he laughed, nodding his head, as though he was similarly amused by the professor's boisterous challenge to his wayward students.

"*Bañson-ke?*" he asked the professor, inquiring about the library.

The professor pointed to the nearby intersection, gesturing to turn down a side corridor.

"*Dara, Kalmonê,*" he replied, thanking the professor. As he stepped away, he added something about once being a professor himself.

He did not go to the library. Instead, he kept to the corridors, spying into the classrooms, peeping through the tiny windows in the doors, searching for someone. He had met the girl already.

This afternoon was devoted to tracking down a certain young man, awkward in his height, ungainly, shy in most encounters, but with a seething fire beneath his soul; yes, a match could spark him to violence. But a few gentle words spoken from a kind girl would ease his fury, set him in balance once more.

Between two statues hung a large calligraphic display and he paused to read it. It seemed to be a poem, one that dared to rhyme in the final two lines of each stanza. It concerned the admonition to study hard but to play hard, too. Both sides of a coin, it seemed, were needed to make the coin a coin. Nice words, good message for the students. He was beginning to feel professorial again, almost hearing Brahms' German university music in his head, forgetting that he was actually on another planet than where Brahms had lived and composed. There was a similar composer on Ghoupallesz, certainly, and someday when he had the time he would track down some good examples of Ghoupallean music. He knew some folk songs from his time on Karluk Isle in the northern sea—

BASURA-KANOUN was the name he saw at the bottom of the poem, followed by her student identification number. Someone had scribbled a few words of encouragement on the bottom of the parchment.

He caught his breath, glanced in each direction for spies, saw none.

It was beginning, he sighed. Was the scribbled note from that young man Diert-Gangus? He could only wonder. He knew the image of that person only as a mature man but he could never pick him out of a crowd of students at the university. He had to try, so he wandered up and down corridors, pausing to listen at every classroom until he heard a lecture on politics. He stopped and leaned against the opposite wall, the door across the corridor half-open, the lecturer's baritone firm and melodic, passionate yet controlled, insipid yet compelling.

He followed the lecture through the establishment of the Sarrêban monarchy's fifth Economic Committee and came to understand the connections between family quirks and the kingdom's economic policies in that era. Particular attention was given to the plight of the Danid people in northern Sekuate. The lecturer's voice rose higher, louder. He moved slightly to be able to see into the classroom, not a good view but enough that he determined the lecturer could have some Danid blood. A question was asked by a student: "What protests were arranged to counter the policy?" The lecturer answered calmly and quietly, and he could not hear clearly. Soon the lecturer was back on track and at full voice.

After the class was dismissed, the corridor was full of students again. He waited and watched as the young men exited the classroom, their blue robes billowing like kites in a breeze, red caps in hands, books in slings over their shoulders, chatting about the next class, the girls they had to meet after the close of the school day, the evening jobs, the family back home, the hunger or thirst or need for rest. He was not sure which of them was Diert-Gangus.

"*Etusz* Diert-Gangus," he grunted, addressing someone in the crowded corridor by the title of 'Student,' as was the custom.

Three young men turned toward him, probably just in response to his voice. Ahead in the corridor, however, he saw a tall young man turn his head back at him, eyes searching for the caller as other students streamed past him, jostling him. The young man had a thin moustache, bushy eyebrows, a visible scar on his forehead, dark straight hair brushed back on his head, a countenance full of frustration. Gazing a moment longer for whoever had called him, the student resumed his walk, shoulders bumping, merging into the crowd and disappearing.

A letter had come from his wife in Selauê. It had been tossed upon his *qala* in the room at the inn. He recognized Zaura's handwriting, and though the news inside was unimportant, the sight of her marks on the parchment and the scent of her upon the pages made him forget the past few days.

Yet as he read of her daily diversions, the antics of their daughter, the gossip of officers' wives, he found himself remembering the poem on the wall in the university, the words somehow sticking in his head, speaking to him in the voice of Basura-Kanoun, with her pauses and intonation, her accent, her wispy soprano—

"*Kassera aven-kal, Kanê?*" *Serpan* Qalanou, his Second, asked. 'Are you well, sir?'

"*Kasser'ven,*" came his mumbled reply. 'I'm well.'

His Second referred to the letter. No trouble at home? Nothing urgent?

He divulged the latest playtime mischief of his daughter, a few bawdy comments about the Ladies Society members, and the sudden change in the weather. A storm had blown in from the Bær Sea and made a mess; the storm was proceeding inland and losing strength as it rose in elevation toward Sorêg. Only a gentle rain for them; that storm was a week past now.

"And the previous curiosity about which you spoke so surreptitiously?" asked Qalanou in polite Ghoupallêan, his voice lowered.

"You mean the silly questions I asked before leaving on our mission here?"

"Yes, Sir—that."

"I've been too busy to concern myself with my domestic matters," he said.

"Of course. You're engaged in your duties."

"And that is all I am doing in Sorêg!"

The captain seemed irritated, had snapped at him for perhaps only the third time in their working relationship.

"I apologize, Sir, if I am presumptuous."

The captain waved him out, not looking up. When he heard the door catch, he stood and went to the window, watched his Second walking out, across the town square, and over to where a few soldiers were grooming their *Jêpe*.

The letter from Zaura actually described her latest bout with the illness she seemed to be encountering more often these days. He knew what it was from his previous life with her, yet he believed that in his return he might be able to prevent her suffering. She would eventually die from the illness, he knew, if history continued on its present course. Having children seemed to hasten the illness, quicken the pain, and so during these ten years he was living with her he avoided trying to have children. He had only returned to step in and fill those years he had missed with her—

"Before—previous—another life—the first time...."

There were no words for time manipulation that made sense, that kept it straight.

"If I've come back to right wrongs," he spoke to the ghost in the mirror. He continued silently: *then I should actually do something, not just live with her, pretending to be some man who resembles her husband.* He thought of the disease for a while. "Yet, I'm no doctor. What can *I* do? She will still die. She will always die."

He turned from the window, feeling a draft and grabbed his uniform jacket. With the jacket on and buttoned, he felt different. He felt confident. He was a man of purpose, a man who could do many things, not just be a passive observer of whatever was taking place. He could take action.

I miss her, he sighed.

What he missed, he admitted, was the way she had been when they first met. *That* Zaura was the woman he missed. That was the truth. He could not explain to her how such time shifts were unpredictable.

"Close enough," he muttered in the room's chill, catching sight of himself in the mirror, his uniform looking new and crisp, martial and glorious.

He would have to leave someday soon, he knew. That would allow her to welcome his original self back after a couple more years. They would continue their relationship *as they had already lived it*. He twisted his face at the irony. Yes, continue the relationship he already had with her, right up to the point where she would die, on the eve of the revolution—

Close enough.

He would need to leave Zaura. In his original timeline, he would find her again at the wedding of their daughter, Aisa, to Gina's son, Sartan, a few years hence. That was a glorious reunion, he recalled, though it was yet in the future. He chuckled, wiped his brow as though he had just gotten away with something despicable. By returning when he did, she had skipped the marriage to Tolour-Frêdin and did not have a son, and she did not meet the ever-returning Set-d'Elous again at her home in Sairel and run away with him north to the city of Milipour. They did not, therefore, draw the wrath of her eldest brother, Rasek, who thus had no reason to pursue them to Milipour. He had avoided that confrontation and, thus, the death of Rasek. There was no Milipour in this version of their relationship. Her brother still lived. Yet she did not have the son she had named Samot—nor their own son, Set-junior, who would have been born on Keruk 25 in 1456.

It was not going to happen since he had intervened to keep Zaura from meeting Tolour-Frêdin. He glanced at the date of his orders, tacked to the wall with other official documents. Here in the autumn of 1457, he had missed his son's birthday. So had Zaura. Things had already changed, he understood. He *had* changed history. Yet he was the only person who seemed to notice.

No, he sighed, he did not miss Milipour—the city where the remnants of the Sekuatean army would surrender to the Northern Megan Alliance in 1534—

"It is time to go."

He studied his face in the mirror, not recognizing himself— until Qalanou returned for him, telling him the patrol was waiting.

It was not a dream, he decided, yet there he was: standing naked on the rim of the caldera on Little Biznuik Island, as he had many times before. He routinely removed his clothes to more easily sense the energy vortices, continuing his investigation of the tangent grid he believed must exist there. Usually, he did not mind an occasional breeze or the blazing sun or the nosy ant-like creatures scurrying about, he being careful to avoid stepping on them, especially with his bare feet, dirty toenails and all—

And there she was, in the flesh, similarly unclothed, her short, curly black hair bobbing in the breeze, her figure untanned and a little unsexy. He waited for her to smile, to acknowledge him, but she did not move. He stared for a while, not sure whether she was real or part of his dream. He thought of pinching himself but decided it was childish, a nod towards doubt. He needed to be confident.

Still, there she was: Dr. Toni Franck.

He shrugged his shoulders, extended his arms, surprised but happy.

"What are you doing here?" he called.

She did not reply, continued gazing at him from the distant rim.

Perhaps she was a mirage, he considered. He waved at her and expected her to wave in return but she did not, so he started walking toward her, his feet slipping in the loose soil and ash, the wind picking up as he approached her. Maybe a hundred steps to reach her, he calculated, then hurried, trying to get to her before she disappeared. She stood still, waiting patiently.

As he reached her she looked better. Except her breasts seemed smaller, nipples larger, darker, and the delightful pooch of belly below her navel was gone. He decided it was just a matter of time, that she had aged naturally.

"How did you get here?" he asked, a bit out of breath. "I thought you didn't believe this place was real. And look at you! Here you are, visiting me on this desert isle far away from anywhere, a haunted place no one ever visits, three days from Selauê. You must have been to my house—" he glanced back over his shoulder as though he could actually see his house on the opposite coast—"and seen the note that I was out on the east ridge today." He thought it strange that he would leave a note in case some stranger happened to visit his island but shrugged it off. "I guess there's not really anywhere else on this isle I'm likely to be if I'm not at home." He laughed. "And you? You look great. As always. But you must be tired, sailing out here, then hiking all the way here. With no clothes, either. Not a scratch or blemish. Quite beautiful, Toni. Now, what can I do for you?"

She smiled, innocently, like some swooning slave girl to the god she adored, and it was the first real movement he detected from her.

"So why have you come all this way?" he asked. He wanted to give her a friendly hug but thought better of it. She seemed sad. "Well, it's certainly a major inconvenience coming here. You must have some words of wisdom to impart to me. Is that it? Or you just wanted to see me again after all this time...after you died."

Suddenly the sky looked different, shades of gold rather than green, and he gazed past her at the world beyond, the sea a shiny amber, the air flecked with silver sparkles, white birds scattering like snowflakes. He felt the wind turn icy, something that never happened on the isle. He longed for clothes but squatted below the top of the rim to escape the worst of the wind. He settled himself against the soil and looked up to relocate her but found her squatting beside him. After a while they stood, like two mimes playing the mirror game.

"Talk to me, Toni." He smiled sincerely, welcomely. "Why are you here?"

She moved, rather like a granite statue come to life, not stiffly but with fluidity, yet so...slowly...stepping toward him—up to him, her arms rising, encircling his chest, her hands pressing against his shoulder blades, her chest touching his chest, her head turned to the side, her chin resting against his collarbone, her breath tickling his skin. Her embrace was warm and soft, like a summer raincloud enveloping him.

"Why are you here?" she seemed to ask him. The words sounded like they came through her voice, but it was not quite the same.

"That's what I'm asking you. Why are you here?"

He hesitated, then carefully wrapped his arms around her shoulders, afraid she would not be real and that the touch of his flesh to hers would make her evaporate. Once he had placed his arms safely around her shoulders and felt relieved that she was real, he held her tighter.

"Why are you here?" she repeated, a faint echo slipping into the caldera below. Her lips moved yet they seemed out of sync with the words he was hearing.

He smiled, willing to play along.

"I'm looking for a doorway to another dimension," he announced, expecting her to express words of disbelief. "It's somewhere in this caldera. I found one not long ago, by accident, and now I'm looking for more. They are easier to locate if I can feel them with my skin. I might never find it if I backed into it fully clothed. Sure, I never expected anyone else to be here, so it never mattered before. It's an on-going project, highly experimental, but with a lot of potential rewards. How about you?"

She continued embracing him, her breath unusually hot against his skin.

"You are searching for an escape," her voice seemed to speak.

Maybe it was the wind....

"An escape?" he asked. "From what?"

"From your life."

Her voice was not the same as before. It was flatter, duller, like a recording of her voice. It had to be her, though. His arms continued to hold her. He would not give up believing she was really with him.

"I've missed you, Toni," he whispered, melancholy.

She nodded, keeping her head against his shoulder.

"Me, too," she seemed to speak.

He wasn't sure if it was in his ears or in his mind.

"How did you get here?" he asked.

"You brought me here."

"I did?"

He thought for a moment, retracing his behavior during the past several days. Nope. He didn't do anything. He was sure of it. That fact was not important. He wanted to know the reason for her visit. After all, she had come all the way from Earth to give him this hug.

"Okay, but *why* did I bring you here?"

"To love you," her voice seemed to answer.

He thought for a moment.

"Well, I love you, too," he responded, then realized the fat yellow sun was winking at him and the smaller blue sun was frowning, disappointed, on the far horizon.

He released his grip on her shoulders, stepped back a toenail's thickness to separate them, a tape-pulling *shrywpt* sounding between their bodies.

"What I mean is, I do have feelings for you, of course, strong feelings. It's always a complicated matter discussing love while embracing a nude woman. I might be biased. I may not be accurate. Right, Toni?—or, should I keep calling you 'doctor'? You have to admit it can be tricky. Perhaps you recall all I told you about my high school sweetheart, Gina, and how I like to call her the Love of my Life? And I discussed in great detail my relationship with Zaura-Matousz, my Ghoupalle wife. You wanted to know details of our sex life. You told me it was perfectly all right to have a soul mate, a kind of kindred spirit as you described it, and also a wife—one with whom I would create a mutually satisfying, highly functional socio-economic partnership. We agreed that it would be ideal if they could be the same person. I remember our talks. But that's philosophy, not science. And you're a scientist, aren't you? At least, that's the impression I got every time I visited your office. However, you seemed to always have an aversion to discussing my dreams, as though they were not real. Maybe they weren't. Maybe I was merely entertained by your reactions to what you believed were nothing but fictions. Who knows? Maybe you figured it all out and have come here to tell me off. Well, I guess I'm as ready as ever to hear your rebuttal. I am also completely honest when I say I enjoyed our sessions. As a matter of fact, a few times I think you enjoyed it, too. But, well, out here is not the best place for us to pick up where we left off. Besides, it's getting late. Let's go back to the house and clean up, have a good dinner, then play some music, get in the mood, and, well, we can just see what develops. I promised we'd get together once I was out of the, uh, *hospital*, let's call it. And I got out—long story, of course. Anyway, I'm completely healed. Really. Nothing for you or anyone to worry about. Good job you did with me, doc. In fact, I—"

She placed two fingers against his mouth to silence him. He thought it was cute and grinned like a little boy.

"Then why are you doing all this?" she asked a little too dramatically.

He thought for a moment, reviewing what he had just said and coming to no satisfactory answer.

"Doing what?" He remained puzzled. "I invited you back to my house. There's not much else to do, nowhere else to go, on this island."

"You know there can be only one," she spoke, her words breathy yet strong.

He stared at her. His eyes glanced down at her breasts.

"One what?"

"You must choose." Her expression was serious.

He smiled nevertheless, thinking she was telling a joke.

"Choose what?"

"Me—"

"You?"

"—or Basura-Kanoun."

Chapter 17

Coupling

He realized that it would be the same every night. And every morning. He would awaken in a sweat, exhausted as though he had run a few *radit* yet feeling somehow energized in such a way that he had to burn it off as soon as possible. He would stumble from the bunk, grab for a bedpost which was not there in the room, and reach for clothes which were hung in a wardrobe rather than tossed over the back of a chair. He would see the streetlamps outside, or the faint glow of the coming dawn, and he would know that he was not back home on Little Biznuik Island, nor home with Zaura in Selauê, nor home on Earth in his small apartment near the IRS service center, nor home with Gina in Kipzon or anywhere else they perhaps had been together, nor home in the cozy bedroom in the old house of his youth, nor home in any previous life. He was here in Sorêg.

He rubbed his forehead, then his temples. He took the crumpled towel from the nightstand and wiped his face. Then he stood up in the darkness, ignoring Qalanou's mild snoring, and stripped off his sweaty nightshirt. He pulled on his one civilian outfit and quietly slipped out of the inn, past the sleeping night clerk, and out into the foggy streets. He walked hurriedly over to the stables where the regiment kept their *Jêpe*. He signed out a mare and rode off before the stablekeeper could call up an escort for him.

The blue sun would soon be rising behind the horizon, the yellow one not long after; the fog would make their green light bleed across the landscape.

He trotted along the silent country road toward the lake. No bird cried out, no rustle of wind in the trees. When he arrived, almost by instinct, he tied the *Jêpe* to a tree and moved cautiously toward the line of trees that hid the lake and its grassy shore. He stepped through the woods and found the spot where he had previously met the young woman from the university. Suddenly, he felt he was on a wild chase, in hot pursuit of a nightmare that had snorted once too many times while he slept—

That's all it was, a bad dream, nothing more. It's always just a dream.

With a deep inhale he gazed up at the vault of stars. The air was moist and heavy. He was filled with a sense of doom. Something was not right and he could not decide if that something lay within his mind or existed outside of him.

"*Ëm afaserend jumas moctar-santoren,*" came a whisper as light as a feather drawn over his cheek.

He spun in place, fully awake, fully alert, and saw a shadow emerging from the dark wood he had just passed through.

"*Fan-se?*" he snapped, his hand going automatically for the sword at his hip but finding that he had brought no weapons with him on this midnight ride. He stepped back, bracing himself for an attack.

"*Ëm afaserend jumas moctar-santoren,*" the feminine voice repeated, then added: "*Kanê.*"

He ran her words through his head a few times: 'I knew you would want to return.'

Yet, he could not believe *she* would be out here by this lake in the silent hours before dawn. It was too far from the town and it was during the curfew period. She was not allowed here. He was allowed, as captain of the patrol, but it would seem strange to be here alone, without an escort, and with no particular business. It would be even worse for him to be discovered with her. It would appear as though he had arranged this rendezvous with a student. His military career would be ruined. And what would his dear wife Zaura think?

"You must go," he told her in firm yet calm Ghoupallêan, keeping his voice low so he would not be heard by the spies he imagined hiding in the darkness.

Instead, she rushed to him, throwing her arms around him, digging her face into his chest. They fell awkwardly to the ground and she continued to hold him as he struggled to free himself, fearing an attack by her unseen companions.

"You came to me!" She was giddy, like her trick had worked. Perhaps it had. "I called you and you came."

He breathed deeply, relaxing in her embrace. Perhaps it was not a trap, though she had the idea it was. He asked if she had been invading his dreams and she denied it, asking how such a thing could be done. He didn't know. She insisted there was no magic, no potion, no formula, only a wish in her mind.

"It is a puzzlement," she said, dropping beside him in the cold grass. She pulled the edge of his greatcoat over herself, turning him toward her. "I felt a force pulling me here for a reason I did not know. I resisted it for a long time yet I could not sleep. So, at last, I surrendered to it and walked the roads to our reunion place. I ran for some time, too. I did not want to be late. I do not know how it happened. Or what the reason must be."

He sensed the truth in her words. "It is strange. I was pulled here, too. I thought you were calling me through magic. Perhaps this force is something neither of us can control. Perhaps it is something beyond our senses."

"Yes! Beyond our senses!" She squeezed him, snuggling against his shoulder.

"We must control our bodies," he spoke seriously.

"Oh, I cannot control my body! Nor my mind! I know I should, yet—"

"We must think clearly, girl! We are fighting against history! We cannot be weak."

"We are not weak. We are connected. I feel it. You feel it. It is the reason we have come together out in the country in the middle of the night—a cold night, too, with our bodies full of heat that must be released. I am ready tonight."

"Ready?"

"We have met for a reason, Sir."

"It was serendipity, not reason."

She took his hand in her two hands and kissed his knuckles one after the next, then moved to kiss his chin. Three more kisses took her across his cheek to his ear and he knew he was done, no longer able to resist her. He should not have ventured out this night. His earlobes were especially vulnerable, the touch of her hot tongue sending electric sparks down his spine.

"It is time to welcome womanhood," she whispered into his ear.

Her hands opened her skirt and he saw in the shadows that she wore no undergarments, no petticoats, as though she had thrown on the skirt in a hurry.

"My body is pulled to you." She sobbed, obviously overcome by the passion of the moment, the rush of hormones.

"It is not your time—"

"I do not know how it can be, yet I must release this feeling."

"That is not the way," he insisted, and tried to sit up. Her arms held him down and he had to jerk his shoulder away from her, separating them.

She moaned loudly, hiding her face in her hands. She mumbled words of embarrassment and apologized for being confused by her feelings, for calling him out in the night. He tried to console her with words, poorly chosen words that did not help. It was the middle of the night, after all, and his Ghoupallêan was not at its best. He laid his arm around her, trying to be parental.

"Worry not, young lady. You will find the right partner," he spoke in English. It seemed just as effective as anything he might say in Ghoupallêan. "You will meet the best man for the job, perhaps another student at the college. He may be tall or short, smart or at least hard-working. Who knows? Now is certainly not the time for you to start a new relationship, and certainly not with me. You need to finish your studies first." He smiled at her though it was too dark for her to see. "Besides, I am much too old for you—I think. Actually, I'm not sure of my age anymore but I know I am older than you. And I'm in the military while you seem to be a member of a passivist camp—for now, anyway. Hah! For now, you are a romantic. You live in your dreams." His words seemed to echo inside his head, as though Gina's spirit was there, dictating to him. "That's not always a bad thing, of course. I understand that because I've been there. I've done that, too, as they say. You may not understand what I'm saying but hopefully the soothing tone of my voice and my solemn words will give you some comfort. Perhaps my words will impress upon you also that I am serious and care about you. I mean, I—I don't want you to get hurt, either by me or by anyone you meet in the future. What I'm saying isn't nearly as important as—"

She was trying to see his eyes in the dark, then took his face in her hands and stared hard. With their noses touching they could see each other's eyes well enough and in that instant his heart skipped three beats then ripped off a violent string of twenty-nine pulses, as though his heart were rebooting itself—

He fainted in her grasp and awoke later only when the morning's emerald sunlight first struck his face through the trees. She was gone, he immediately saw, sitting up with effort. He pondered whether or not she had really been there with him.

I wandered out here in the middle of the night, he thought, standing on weak legs and turning to survey the landscape. Nobody was in sight, which was good. *Just a bad dream and a case of sleepwalking*—he saw the *Jêpe* tethered nearby—*sleepriding?* He was probably not the first to do it. Anyway, he decided, a good story needed to be invented by the time he rode innocently into town. No doubt Qalanou was sending out patrols already, searching for him. And he was in civilian clothes!

In his pocket was a folded note, he discovered as he went to untie the *Jêpe*'s reigns. He opened it and read the lilting handwriting, a poem which ran from edge to edge on the small half-sheet of parchment.

"*Læfor E-zu il Lok-se*," he read aloud, easier to decipher her poetic language that way, hearing its meter and diction. "*Læfor-ga læfor E-zu il aissan-se,/ Dem bûgen-da Lok-ga—/ Læfor E-zu, Læforen il zerren-da sañia-de-aissan.*"

He did not smile at her loving gesture, instead took it as a warning to be careful. What was she doing? She was acting crazy, going crazy, and pulling him down with her!

'Come to me in the night'?

This would become evidence, he considered.

'Come to me in the silence of the dark night—come to me,

Come in the silence of dream'?

What was she saying?

He continued to the end, reading more of the same ideas and nocturnal imagery. The final two lines were an offer of intimacy, he guessed. The poem was definitely not political, unless love and sex and parting were political acts. Perhaps they were, perhaps they soon would be—when she and her friends took power. He had felt that power, felt his mind being turned, felt his soul squeezed, his heart twisted—

He wadded up the parchment when he reached the end, as though destroying evidence. Then he opened it again and re-read the poem. This time he recognized the lines he had seen previously in a book. That is, in Ghoupalle year 1499.

In the future.

At that breath, he understood what was possible in this new world to which he dared return. In the laws of physics, every reaction had an opposite and equal reaction. So it was the previous night. His vulnerability had drawn her power. Her strength had sought his weakness. Like gravity. Like yin and yang. Like positive and negative energy. In all of Sorêg district, there was no one who was more able to be affected by her power than him. That was how they were drawn to each other. How many more nights could he resist? He knew then how urgently he needed to leave this place, to return home to Selauê before he made a mistake—before he could do the right thing.

"It's me," Toni Franck had said, or seemed to say. Maybe it was all in his mind. He could not be sure now. "Me...or that *Etusz Basura-Kanoun*...who resembles me so much that you fantasize about making love to her!" There on the rim of that caldera, her words had continued inside his head even though he heard nothing more spoken.

And then Basura appeared...

As the suns settled below the horizon, Toni had walked with him along the caldera's rim and after a while they went hand in hand back to his house. He thought they would make love. Yet when he stepped into the shower, pausing to invite her to join him and she politely refusing, he sensed that she might somehow be gone when he stepped out of the shower and, as tends to happen in dreams, or at least in his kind of dreams, he found that he was correct. He called out for her and went from room to room searching for her. By dawn, he accepted the situation. He dressed and lit a fire in the fireplace, made coffee, and sat in his lounging chair, watching the clouds drift past.

*　❋　*

Serpan Aroun-Qalanou had never spoken to him as harshly as he did upon the senior captain's return to the inn at mid-day. The young captain's voice was full of fire and brimstone and the conspiracy theories that occupied him. Patrols had been sent out looking for him, and one even ventured over to the lake area, which the senior captain had been known to favor. Qalanou dared suggest that he was not living up to his duties, perhaps giving up his time to be with a woman!

"And you're dressed as a civilian!" Qalanou exclaimed. A military officer never wore civilian clothes in public unless he was ashamed to be a member of the *Coræsz*. Qalanou complained that he was also putting the regiment at risk. They might be disciplined for not fulfilling their mission.

"You don't know of what you speak!" he barked, waving Qalanou to silence.

He nodded in the direction of the inn, their makeshift headquarters. The younger captain immediately nodded and together they retreated to their room.

"It is a conspiracy, as you suspect," the senior captain said once they had closed the door of the room and secured it. "That was the reason for my absence." He watched for a sign, a look of understanding, a willingness to hear more. More of what? He did not know, yet he believed he could weave an interesting story nevertheless. Then they both would know it.

"You must understand," he grunted impatiently, holding his voice down, "that what I know is bigger than our simple mission to patrol the roads during harvest season."

Qalanou fell silent, waiting for more explanation.

"I, too, have heard of a conspiracy, as you suspect," the Captain continued. "There are always conspiracies in places the military occupies. I have knowledge of a conspiracy here in

Sorêg district. I am in a position to investigate it while under the cover of a normal regimental patrol mission. To ascertain its validity, I was required to dress and act as an ordinary townsperson and mingle with other civilians."

"The result of your mingling?" Qalanou seemed skeptical.

"I learned the conspiracy is true."

"What is it?" Qalanou was still not convinced.

"Only last night did I become certain of its existence. I met with an informant. I have done a lot to gain her confidence. I pretended to be infatuated with her, to let her fall in love with me. Ho! Strange as it seems, I can be charming when my government wishes me to be. I gained her trust and she revealed many details of the conspiracy. Now I know it is real."

They instinctively glanced about the room, though they were alone. In a few years there would be spies at every window, door, and street corner, but not now. Probably not now. Qalanou moved to close the window, though they were on an upper floor. The captain continued in a softer voice.

"It is this: a group of students from the university and some of the townspeople are planning a disturbance. They hope to start a revolt. The disturbance will seek to limit our operations and provide some passages for the hill folk to obtain winter stores. The conspirators want us to be in the wrong place when the hill folk come. They will use lookout people to coordinate their raids. University students are supportive of the raids, and say the hill folk are being discriminated against by the government. They dislike the military here and would enjoy embarrassing us, making us appear as fools who cannot maintain order in a country district."

"How many conspirators are there? Can we just arrest them?"

"I do not know how many will participate. I think it may take dozens to coordinate their efforts. Perhaps some will pretend to be raiders to draw the attention of the patrols so the real raiders may take what they wish from the farms. This is what my informant has told me. I could give you the names of two of the leaders, both university students, but I believe that were we to act prematurely, we could find ourselves running around like fools anyway and they would still achieve their goal."

"There are too many to arrest?"

"I do not have a list of names. There are too many. If we arrest a few, the others will know that we are aware of the conspiracy. Since we cannot get all of them at once, we must be patient and watchful. The patrols should continue as scheduled, the routes identical as before, and we will maintain readiness."

"You are the captain, so I will accept your plan. However, I must tell you that I have begun a report concerning your effectiveness on this—"

He stopped. Aroun-Qalanou, careful officer that he was, faintly recalled the senior captain's dual appointment in the Strategic Command, a covert operations unit of which few people had any direct knowledge. Fewer people believed it actually existed. There was a mission in Aivana, a Sekuate protectorate, he had heard about: removing one leader in favor of another who would be more willing to support Sekuate. His captain had been part of that operation.

"I finally see the whole picture, Sir," Qalanou continued with a wide grin. "You assisted in the Aivana mission a few years ago— forgive me, Sir, for mentioning it but, yes, I do know it, yet I thought it mere boast—and so they rewarded you with a command of your own. It makes sense now. In that way, you are close at hand and remain at their service for any other special missions, such as the present one!"

That Qalanou's captain was here in Sorêg on a separate mission made this ordinary patrolling business suddenly more interesting, even dangerous. Something big was going to happen and he would get to be a part of it.

"Ah! I understand now the reason for our regiment's deployment here in the north," Qalanou's face was suddenly brighter, his voice excited. "It is all a plan to bring you here to investigate this rebellion. No one would suspect your true mission under the disguise of a normal autumn patrol duty. It's brilliant!"

The senior captain drew a smirk, felt a pang of guilt for allowing his Second to believe a convenient lie. He was simply following orders, leading the regiment to Sorêg and supervising the patrols. He had never expected to meet an interesting young woman. He also had not expected that the woman would be attracted to him or he to her—

"Sir, are you well?"

He realized he must have turned pale as he entertained that thought.

"I'm fine," he responded, feeling cold. "You are correct in my dual mission. I shouldn't have involved you, shouldn't have told you. Such knowledge could require you to do things you are not prepared to do, or have no wish to do, acts beyond the scope of our patrol mission. Still, you do not know everything. You may yet be protected from liability or indiscretion. The time remains critical, *Serpan* Qalanou, so you should not be too curious."

"Yes, Sir. I understand."

After his investigation, he knew what he must do. He saw that the youth, Diert-Gangus, was an ineffectual bumpkin who would only be transformed into a political firebrand by the love of a dreamy young woman, Basura-Kanoun. The power lay with her, the *senzenaxii* power never noted in history books. It was not so much her poetry that moved the young man and his circle of friends as the invisible power of her aura, the psychic energy she did not yet recognize or know how to control, the energy he could not resist or avoid.

He felt it calling to him at that moment, a casual pull, as though she were standing beside him, taking his arm in her hand and ushering him into her soul.

"Sir, you seem ill again," Qalanou remarked at the pause. "I am beginning to understand that the northland does not agree with you. For a man from southern climes, this duty must be harsh. Yet, cheer up, for the mission soon will be done. We will put down the rebellion straightaway and be on the road home. Life will continue as it always has, with joy in our families and discipline in the regiment."

Chapter 18

Conspiracy Theory

By the time he got himself up—and slowly, stiffly stepped to the window to see why the sky appeared brighter than usual, and stood in his rumpled gray nightshirt gazing out through the curtains at the dusting of snow across the distant mountains and the city's rooftops—Qalanou was returning from the dawn patrol, brushing flakes of snow from his shoulders and arms, once more in good cheer.

"We have been here for thirty-six days," he snorted. "Now the first snow has fallen! I am happy that our mission is soon to end. The wagons have been loaded and produce and livestock sent safely to market. The country folk are secure on their farms and the hill folk are back to the hills for the winter. Our work is done! Thank the four winds and my itchy crotch! We won't come up in rotation again for five years."

The senior captain, scratching his backside and yawning, turned and smiled.

"It has been a long time coming, these final few days of duty. Come, *Serpan* Qalanou, let us secure the countryside one more time, then drink the night away."

After the Captain dressed in his khaki and crimson patrol uniform, the two of them went downstairs and out into the town square, stamping their boots in the new-fallen snow. The regiment was happy at the change of weather, a sign that their mission was almost done. The previous days had seen their spirits steadily drop but discipline remained high.

The Captain led them ceremoniously out of the city as small groups of townsfolk gathered and cheered or jeered at them. Once out the gates, *Serpan* Qalanou divided the squads and assigned routes. Groups of *Jepêdor* rode out in eight directions for the day's patrols. The senior captain was on hand to receive their salutes as they trotted passed him and he, in turn, saluted back at them until his arm grew heavy. He saluted his colleague, too, and Qalanou returned the salute. Then he waved at the last squad and turned his mount toward the town, the inn, and his freshly made bunk, unused during the night. The senior captain would stand in charge on this last patrol day. Three or four days of packing would follow, then the several-days march back to the garrison in Selauê, where hugs and kisses from family members or a welcome feast for the uncoupled troops awaited.

Escorted by four *Jepêdor* as usual, he started on his own patrol, leading the squad down the road toward the lake. The skies were gray, the clouds snow-laden, yet on the horizon, between the overcast and the mountain ridge a point of greenish light shone through. He sighed at the way the skies continually changed in Sorêg district. It made him feel a little melancholy—

We won't come up in rotation for five years, Qalanou had reminded him.

He stopped his *Jêpe* there in the road and sent the patrol squad ahead. His escort halted with him, keeping him boxed in, one guard at each corner. They silently waited as their commander seemed to be thinking deeply of something, perhaps the march home, or the reunion with his wife, or he was lost in thought about the welfare of his men, the reward they might earn for a job well-done, or ribbons for their effort, possibly a promotion for one or two of them, or more likely he was figuring out the dinner menu.

In five years all will be lost!

The year would be 1462 then. Basura-Kanoun would have given in to the demands of the increasingly bold Diert-Gangus and they would secretly marry late in 1458, before graduation, and solidify their political ambition. The first meeting of what they would call the Gangus Political Society would be in a grove behind the university in 1459 and the two of them would graduate in 1460. By 1462, membership in their club would be more than two hundred, and by 1463 a booklet authored by Basura, Diert, and fellow leader Rasek-Tifloh would be published in Selauê, a work which would highlight their political ideology and would draw disgruntled citizens to their cause. In 1465, Basura and Diert would have a son they would name Kag, while Diert worked to affect political change in Sorêg by becoming a member of the town council. And in the month of Nomat in 1466 the first armed conflict would occur in the Sorêg town square as Diert-Gangus is physically removed from the town hall following a speech against the Sarrêban government, an action requiring the local militia to step in, unable to wait for a regiment from Selauê. That would be the start.

He knew it all because he had lived through it. Actually, he had never paid much attention to the news of passing days back then, preferring to keep to his duties at the garrison and tend to his ailing wife, Zaura. Soon he knew what was happening—they all did: armies clashed and the government fell. He understood how the events unfolded. His notes were eventually included in the history book written by his son, Set-*jousta*—

No—wait! Little Set was never born—because I returned to Zaura this time and we did not run away from Sairel. We never made love that night before I sent them back to Sairel in order for me to deal with Rasek.

He gazed up at the sky, searching for answers in the snowflakes flittering on the breeze.

I have no son?

He wondered at that moment whether or not he was dreaming this pause on the road outside Sorêg on this late autumn morning.

No son, no history book?

He felt ill; time-sick. His body was feeling the stress of being in two different time zones at once.

We haven't made a child during this visit of mine.

They had Aisa, the daughter born on Karluk Isle. But no others; he did not want to worsen Zaura's health. Besides, when his original self would arrive in a couple of years to continue with Zaura, they would have more children—as they had already done *in his memories.* Yet he would not be there to witness it.

I just want her to live a long life.

He stared at the tree lines ahead and to each side, the fields barren from the road to the trees, to get his bearings, then glanced at his escort.

"*Alanze,*" he ordered, erroneously choosing the word for moving back in time rather than in space. *Furank*ian-slip, he mused. Perhaps he did want to go back in time. Instead, he wanted to return to the inn and figure things out. "*Kauzu!*" he barked at his escorts. He saw their puzzled faces and realized he had told them to 'back up,' to move away from him. They did, much to his chagrin. He winced in frustration. "*Santor,*" he corrected himself, ordering them to go back whence they came. Not quite right, he thought, and shouted "*Santoren!*" His escort slowly nodded their understanding and turned their *Jêpe,* but he still felt it necessary to get it right once and for all, so he said, "*Santor-pen!*"—a more accurate expression for going back to one's point of origin. The four escorts turned smartly as a quartet and trotted away.

He checked the treeline again, then returned his gaze to the departing escorts.

Hmmm. No protest? No insistence that the captain never be left alone when out in the field?

They did not even look back at him. Probably they were finally disgusted at having to take so many stupid orders from a foreigner—*from an insane, foreign captain!*

And yet, something was not as it should have been. The world around him had turned into an odd dream. He felt a strange vulnerability surrounding him there on the barren moors, alone on the road, and it seeped down to his bones.

Today's escort must be in on it. He felt cold and shivered as he glanced about, searching the distant treelines for hidden marauders.

Perfect! The last day of patrol and I'm left alone for an ambush! They've been waiting for the right moment. What planning! What patience!

"Bring it on!" he snapped and his mount jerked.

He urged the animal forward, to the right, moving off the road and across the trail that led between two barren fields, toward the woods growing at the end of the fields. There was a pull, like gravity, which drew him in that direction.

He dismounted and led the *Jêpe* into the woods, tied it out of sight, and waited.

With a deep inhale he gazed up at the drifting clouds and saw one that, with a moment to consider it, seemed to resemble his psychiatrist, Dr. Toni Franck.

The breeze curled around him, trying to avoid him...

The trees encircled him, like arms welcoming him home, inviting him into the temple...

"You have returned."

The voice drifted through his ears long before he saw her hidden among the trees. Only then did she step into full view. Her skirt and jacket matched, a rich dark blue with gold trim at the cuffs, neckline, and down the front, streaked with embroidery in red, green, and white, of flowers and garlands. A wide belt of linked silver rings settled low on her hips. From inside her jacket a white blouse sprouted at her neck. Her dark, curly hair was tied up with a red ribbon, allowing him to see her ears clearly: slightly pointed, elven. She had taken off her shoes, as always, and set them on the grass. As she walked, the dim light alternately striped her and hid her, passing under the trees, still bearing their long, gray, leathery leaves.

He smiled but he did not know why. He raised his hand in greeting and she swept her hand up to her jacket, undid its buttons, and fingered her blouse. She opened the blouse and showed him her left breast, pale as milk.

"I knew you would return," she spoke with measured breath, stepping against him and pressing her cheek to his shoulder. Her behavior seemed to be a ritual. "We have much to discuss." Her hand gathered his hand and placed it beneath her breast, made him cup it, showed him how she wanted him to caress it. She smiled at him. "Your pain calls me. I want to calm you. I want to make you whole. I want to shield you from pain—"

He held his other hand to her mouth, wanting to silence her. "I don't want anything. I don't need anything. And don't worry, nobody is hurting me."

She pulled his hand away from her mouth abruptly.

177

"Perhaps you are hurting yourself."

He restrained a chuckle, moving the edge of her blouse to cover her breast, and dropped his hand.

"I can sense that you hurt inside," she said. "The pain you feel has continued for so long that you believe it is normal. It is not normal. It remains inside you. It causes you to decay. There is nothing anyone could do to prevent it. Such pain begins in childhood. Do you recall what you told me about Gina?"

He fell back, noticing he was unable to breathe easily.

"How do you know about Gina?"

"You told me, the first time we met, that you mourned for a loved one."

"I meant Zaura, my wife. Or maybe..."

"Do you remember your childhood? When your mother left you?"

"No, I don't." He really did not recall any story like that.

"You cannot remember because you were too young. Yet, deep inside, you remember it. There is a spot inside your head where that picture was burned."

He grew bold, doubting her. "Tell me what I'm supposed to remember."

"When you were an infant," she continued, like a trained psychiatrist with years of experience, "you were left with another woman. You were put in a crib on the second level, and the woman returned to her own children. You would cry and demand attention and the woman ignored you. Both your mother and a substitute mother abandoned you at the time you should have learned it was safe to be apart from your mother, that she would return. This continued for many months."

"Months?" He pondered the idea.

"Your mother did not know—not until she came early one day and saw the truth. After that, you were cared for by an aunt, yet you always have that pain stuck inside: the pain of abandonment. You cried and got no comfort. You repeat that pain each time someone important in your life leaves you. Each time you are abandoned you feel that pain again."

"But...how?" He had to find the answer. "I don't believe you, Toni."

"My name is Basura," she replied. "Because you are my

intimate friend, you may call me Basii from now on. After we copulate you may call me Bai when we are alone."

His head was swimming, unaware of where he was or *when* he was. He was sixteen again. He was thirty-seven. He was sixty-eight. He was three months old. Simultaneously. His vision blurred. His skin felt hot, began peeling from his ribs. His groin was stimulated, excited. The woman standing before him was seductive, sensuous, and knew everything about him. She knew what he would think tomorrow, and yet he could not believe her. He could, however, unite with her—as she seemed to be expecting him to do.

"Think of Gina," she said. "Remember how she abandoned you in Kipzon," this young woman continued, casually undressing both of them. "Others have abandoned you, so you learned to never get close. Think of Zaura. You expected she would soon abandon you so you left first, from Karluk Isle. You always expect to be abandoned by those you love. You seek one special person who will not abandon you. That is the reason you came here today, the reason we are meeting—not because I have dreamed of you, or wished for you, or called you with magic potions and long chants, not because I welcome you into my body and mind, but because you know I will not abandon you."

He waited, afraid to move, wondering when he would be struck down by her rebel cohort hiding in the shadows.

"Do you hear me?" she asked, seeing him entranced.

He gazed at her, met her eyes, felt reassurance.

"I will not abandon you," she spoke.

He stared at her, his mouth probably agape.

"I will not abandon you," she repeated. "Do not abandon me."

Suddenly, the two of them were standing together, awkwardly undressed, talking softly among the trees. They embraced and his heart fell into rhythm with hers.

How did she know about his childhood? What power did she have? Could she read his mind, read the deepest memories which he himself had long ago forgotten?

"I know," she said, "because I am your mother, your daughter, your sister, your lover. I am also you."

He stepped back, breaking away from her, yet he felt he was

standing in the same position.

She reached out and took his hands in hers, pulling him close again.

"And you, dear Sebastian, are also me."

Sebastian? His name on Ghoupallesz was Set-d'Elous. *Serpan d'Elous!* Didn't she know?

The ticking of an entire clockshop filled his ears...

The woman's arms rose and her clothing was carried away by the wind...

Basura-Kanoun or me, Toni demanded...

He was on his back in the grass, the woman atop him. Her hands were hot against his cheeks as she held his face between her slender fingers, balancing it like an egg, feeling the egg within her launching into the stream of time. Her skin was moist, the fabric of her skirt covering their lower bodies.

He could not catch his breath until she spoke.

"No one will ever hurt you again," she whispered.

She ran her fingers through his hair, uncomfortably similar to how his mother had done it when he was five years old.

"You are safe with me. I feel your weakness. I strengthen you. We belong together."

He had never discussed his weakness with her, whatever it was. The translation inside his head was imperfect. He tried to think back, to rewind her words while he tried following what she was saying, but some sensation was overwhelming him, a sensation of blackness, some shadowy presence, slowly filling him from deep in his core, spreading outward to fill the limits of his skin. He felt it taking charge, as though he was no longer in command but following the instructions of a stranger.

"I must be leaving you," he spoke quietly yet intensely, trying to break free.

"You must not leave your safe place," she responded. "If you leave, people will hurt you. You are a fragile person, so beautiful, so miserable."

He tried to push her off but she grabbed his ears and held his face close, pushing her lips against his. Her tongue slipped deep into his mouth. All of his muscles tensed then relaxed, his body weakening.

"You will finish soon," she said, her voice tinged with a dark tone that seemed to portend the future. She rolled them over as one, he now on top, cradled in the crevasse of her thighs. "You must finish what you began."

He did as he was commanded and found a bit more energy, only then wondering why he was now inside her.

"I must be leaving you," the captain repeated in a weaker voice, strained through his exertion, pushing deep inside as her fingers dug into his back, holding him in place. He heard the accent in his Ghoupallêan voice slipping away. "Forever this time. It has to be. We cannot continue—"

She reached up and squeezed his face tightly, almost as punishment.

"I—we—can't continue—"

She noticed he was tired and rolled them over again so she was on top, sitting over his hips.

"We must finish it."

She let her delicate weight press against him, settling his body deeper into the thick grass at the edge of the lapping lakeshore. She sat atop him, her hips pushing down, rising, pressing down, drawing him upward, within her.

"You will be the father and I will be the mother." Her breaths were shallow as her body shook violently. When the spasms subsided, she exhaled loudly. "We have met. The season of planting. Growing inside me."

He was catching his breath, letting the world return to normal.

"What—are you—talking about?" he asked, sucking air.

With a smile almost stretching from ear to ear, her white teeth caught the filtered sunlight. She drew in a breath and held it, gazing into his eyes, then let it out ever so slowly, sending her exhalation into his nostrils.

"It is a biological activity," she said.

"Making love?" He smiled, strangely satisfied. "Some say it's an art, not a science."

"Creation is science, not art."

He laughed uncomfortably. "Your poetry is art."

She kissed his eyelids, an intimate gesture.

Parting, she whispered, "We have created a beautiful thing. It is not art. It is science. You and I have met inside my universe, part of each of us has grasped the other. Now we are whole."

"You can't know," he clamored. "Not yet. It's too soon. It takes two weeks before you can know. Unless you have one of those blue stick devices easily purchased from a drug store or grocery. And they don't make them here."

"I feel the child attaching.... Growing.... Dividing.... Growing..... Dividing—"

"You feel it? Or you *want* to feel it?"

"I have always felt my internal processes."

He grinned, embarrassed. He shook his head, denying the inevitable.

"I can't be the father—"

She put her finger to his lips. In retaliation, he rolled them over, setting her on her back again in the cold grass.

"Sir, you took the gift I offered," she said with a grunt. A lone tear ran down her cheek. "Now you must remain with me. Forever."

He felt control returning, his breathing back to normal, regaining strength. It seemed her aura diminished once their mating was done. She was weaker now. He could make his own decisions.

"Forever is a long time," he whispered in English. He continued in English, thinking aloud more to convince himself than to inform her: "That's not how it is supposed to be. You and I are not the couple. You and I have no history. We cannot become history. You and I are not supposed to be together. I'm only here to...to stop you. I'm supposed to keep you from starting a war, from destroying the nation, from killing millions. That is what will happen. If I don't stop you. If you go on...living."

His desperate eyes swept across her innocent face, saw an ephemeral sorrow there, and suddenly noticed the glow of piety, the glistening of her sweet perspiration. He counted the dewy bubbles of saliva spotting her lips, ignorant of his words. She seemed to be unaware of what had happened, as though she, too, had been caught up in some force neither of them could resist or control. He imagined a kind of Danid heat that drove her to dominate him until she got from him what nature demanded she get. He had been vulnerable also, and yet as his reason returned to him he remembered the future. He tried to see the face of the older woman, the Basura-Kanoun of the palace balcony, sending troops off to war, a model of elegant beauty—even when she stood as a gray statue of evil in town squares across the empire. He tried to see that woman whose affection had pushed an awkward hot-tempered youth from a rural college to birth a rebellion that leads an empire to ruin.

He cleared his head.

"I cannot stay with you," he said in solemn Ghoupallêan, meaning it. "Not now, and certainly not forever."

Her eyes closed peacefully, opened after a moment.

He smiled as sincerely as he could but he knew that she knew it was fake.

"As I said, forever is a long time."

"Foreba iza lawn tayim," she mumbled, repeating his English.

"Yes, forever." He looked away. "Forever. *Ouranii*."

"*Ouranii?*" she asked, puzzled.

He switched to English; it all made more sense in his own language.

"The only way to change the history I have lived through is to change it all with you. At this place. Here. Now. I'm so sorry for my actions...but millions of people will thank me in the morning."

He did not grin. Instead, he visited that dark place deep within him where primal instinct takes over, to the core of primeval soup where swims the single invincible cell that decides everything. And as he did so, he remembered the sensations he had felt as he had gone deep within her body and touched her soul. To take her love, knowing he would kill her, made him no better than a criminal himself. To give her his love, knowing he would kill her, made the act ironic. And yet he held Fate to blame: that he had stumbled upon this angelic sorceress at this precise time and place, that she had captured his heart even as he plotted to stop hers, and on through the days of meeting when everything had fallen into place so effortlessly— so perfectly innocent, he knew it had to be right, it *was* right, it had to be, he had to do it, to make the world right, no matter what he did now in this bucolic meadow beside this mirroring lake, late in autumn, whatever he did to save the world and make him a hero. So he would do it without hesitation, without guilt, his hand stretching across the grass, hand on the hilt, the sword out of its scabbard, the blade glistening in his hand, in a ray of sunlight, the tip sharp and clean then slick and red, quickly wiped on the grass, replaced in the scabbard, hidden from the world, and the words *Would you kill your son?* trickling from her mouth, hovering in the air before dropping into the grass like a fistful of feathers, to the soil, and suddenly he saw the small, limp body of a young poetess, now looking so much like his psychiatrist, Dr. Toni Franck, perfect face and figure etched in the swaying grasses, caressed by the breeze, dreaming of love instead of the rebellious future, sensing conception and announcing to him their success even as his fingers formed her pale lips into a winsome smile, his warm hands gathering her slender wrists across her chest as though in prayer, as though calling the gods to sustain her karma and hearing more words, words like *There is no karma on Ghoupallesz* drifting past his ears, and deciding to let the bouquet of flocculent clouds overhead be her funeral flowers, hearing the final faint words repeating over and over and over: *Why are you doing this? I thought you loved me....*

He made a pillow of his blood-stained uniform jacket for her head, then he stood, gazing down at his destiny, an icy wind on his face as a kind of unyielding truth, knowing he could never return to 1457. *Serpan* Qalanou would see the results of the Captain's attempt to put down a rebellion and instinctively know what to do, how to interpret the signs, what to say. Nothing would ever be the same.

The break room at the IRS Service Center was busier than usual, a flood of desperate people grabbing midnight snacks from the vending machines, chatting at the tables, five minutes of downtime, then back to work again.

Cassie remained, her eyes transfixed on the television hanging from the ceiling.

"Come on, girl, time to go," said bottle-blond Bethany in the blue pantsuit.

Cassie *shhh*ed her, kept her attention on the television. Bethany waved goodbye.

A couple seasonal employees waltzed in, young women dressed more for a nightclub, thinking they owned the place.

"That new guy is so cute, gotta find out if he's married—"

"Shhhh!" Cassie cut them off, pointing at the TV.

"What's up?" one girl asked, thinking it might be important, like another Space Shuttle exploding.

"It's him," Cassie mumbled.

"Who?"

"*Him.*"

She could not believe what she was hearing from the TV.

The two women looked at each other, shrugged their shoulders and began laughing at her.

Cassie stood up, stunned, alone in the room. She started out of the break room, returning to her section, excited to share the news.

Joyce was giving instructions to everyone about the new project. She paused as Cassie arrived. They all glared at her for interrupting them, for slacking off.

"Sorry," Cassie muttered, and took her seat.

Fifteen minutes later, Joyce started assigning tasks. She stopped at Cassie.

"Don't you know what time break's over? You were twenty minutes late. I have to dock you some this time."

"I was watching the news!" she snapped. "It was about *him!*"

Joyce narrowed her eyes. "*Him?* What happened?"

A couple others leaned in to hear the news.

"Well, you know how he escaped from that mental hospital, right?" Cassie could barely contain herself. "Well, this evening his psychiatrist woke up from her coma. Yep, she's alive! They thought she was gonna be asleep forever but she done woke up. They said she just sat up and asked where her son was. She said she had a son with *him.*"

"Of course, she's gone crazy being in a coma like that."

"She's lost her mind."

"Plain retarded now, after that kick in the head, poor woman."

Cassie waved her hands to quiet them. "There's more."

They fell silent, waiting. Any news about their former colleague, the serial killer Sebastian Talbot, was certainly worth stopping production.

"Tell us!" Sandy barked, the only one who actually had a date with him.

"They also said—'in a related story,' ya know—about Tammy's husband, the cop? So, like, they never found him, right? Or his body. They said on TV the police s'pected he kidnapped him, Tammy's husband—"

"His name's Chuck," Priscilla chimed in.

"Okay, Chuck. Jeez! So they was thinking *he* killed Chuck, like he made him help him escape—"

"Slow down," said Joyce. She waved others over. "Start again, Cassie."

"As I said, the guy on TV said the police cleared Chuck being a suspect in that doctor's death. Course she didn't die, anyway, and she woke up. Seems okay, too. But since they can't find him, they think that Chuck guy, Tammy's ex, he was killed by Sebastian Talbot. Hey, it's been long enough."

"So they think he's dead now?"

"Guess so."

"So they think *he* killed Chuck?"

"Looks that way."

"And he's charged with killing his doctor, too?"

"Don't know," said Cassie, "but as long as he stays gone we can relax!"

Joyce chuckled uneasily. "As long as he's gone, can we *please* get back to work?"

PART THREE

Salousz-de-logæo hañofen sernon ulef-se.

(The voyage of the mind takes a million years.)

—old Ghoupalle saying

Chapter 19

Three Fathers, One Son

The screams from the foreigner amused them, so the twelve Rouê men took turns jabbing their victim with a fire-seared lance. The way the man was spread naked on the dead tree made it easy to attack his ribs—playfully. They did not wish to kill him outright; that would end their entertainment too quickly. The broad-chested man they found in the desert, was easily subdued with ropes and nets, then tied to a rock as they discussed what to do with him. The strange women they occasionally captured in the desert proved valuable but what price could a well-muscled laborer fetch? They placed wagers on the profit they might make. In the end, they determined he would be too much trouble to care for, keeping him fit, to present him at the Typeg market.

So the leader of the nomadic band took a lance and jabbed the man in the ribs, releasing an ear-shattering scream that echoed across the dunes. The Rouê laughed, showing their toothless mouths. Several jabs latter the blood flowed steadily across the man's body but he had long tired of screaming.

"I keep tellin' ya: I don't know nothin' about nothing!" the man grunted.

The Rouê chuckled. The leader stood and strode over to their entertainment.

"*O'gul'lue'he me're'de l'ha u'fale'de?*" he asked, and the victim shook his head absently.

It was clear he did not understand the Roûe language.

The leader repeated the question in broken Ghoupallêan but their captive did not answer.

The man was breathing heavily, with difficulty. It was too painful to take a sufficient breath, too agonizing to move his ribcage.

"Damn you all to hell!" he then roared, fighting the pain.

The Roûe leader took the tone to be defiant and slapped the man's face with the barbed-knuckled glove of his riding hand, ripping skin from the man's cheek.

"I don't know where the hell I am," the victim groaned, trying to get out his dying words, "I just wanna go home. I only came to find my wife. Tammy Sue Tucker's her name." He held his breath, then exploded in rage: "Tammy Sue! Tammy Sue, where are you?"

He shouted to the sky until his breath ran out.

The Roûe watched him, puzzled at his demonstration. The leader bent low over the man's face, studying the shape of his nose and cheeks, the color of his eyes.

"*He'ilo'ye Alebafe?*" he asked. "*Tami'su'o? Tami'su'o?*"

"Yes—yes—yes," Chuck McElroy sighed, "Tammy Sue—she's my wife. Was.... She's here—on this planet. Okay, I admit, it's another planet—like Talbot said. I'm on another freakin' world. She's somewhere here. Tammy Sue—"

"*Tami'su'o! He'ilo'ye Alebafe!*" The leader glanced at his band: their faces were grim.

"Okay, Alebafe," Chuck McElroy agreed. "Whatever. Alebafe. Alebafe."

He didn't care what they were saying. None of it made sense anyway, but if they insisted he say 'Alebafe' instead of 'Tammy Sue,' he would comply. Anything to halt the torture, anything to save his life, little knowing *Alebafe* was the Roûe name their king had chosen for the woman Chuck knew as Tammy Sue. He did not understand why they untied him, why they bandaged his wounds, why they offered him their water and something he took to be food though he could not make himself eat it, and why they threw a golden cloak over his shoulders and packed him up on their *oñacha* and headed quickly toward the setting sun.

They pointed and gleefully announced that ahead was his destiny: *Alebafe!*

＊ ❋ ＊

"You see, Chucker," spoke Jason Aronstein, the laid-back regent of Aivana, to his step-son, the offspring of his wife, Queen Alebafe, also known as Tammy Sue Tucker in private, "a little bit of culture never hurt anyone. Not really. Call it opera, if you want, but it's really more than that. It's history, it's culture, it's literature, it's spectacle, farce, comedy and tragedy all rolled into one big happy musical experience. I'm impressed they still perform it here in 1574 instead of giving in to cheap, popular entertainments. Just because it takes a full three days to get through it shouldn't make you wait so long for the next show, eh?"

Chucker, the teenager, gave a teenage retort. He was not yet convinced of this man's right to be his step-father, much less take him across the continent on something called a Youth Trek. They had been gone almost three years and Chucker was still waiting for Jason to prove himself worthy. Meanwhile, he missed his mother, the Queen of Aivana.

"Come on, it wasn't that bad," Jason laughed.

They stepped from the outdoor theater grounds, colorful streamers flapping in the tepid air, and waved down a golden carriage to take them back to the inn where they had been staying. The inn served as a base from which they could explore the surrounding towns in search of Michael Fenning. They were hot on his trail, sighting to sighting, rumor to rumor, angry woman to angry woman. Michael had left a clear trail of deceit and heartbreak everywhere he went.

"The last story, you might remember," Jason continued when they were stepping out of the carriage in front of the inn, "took place in Jisilika, up north, and I can tell you the story first-hand; well, second-hand is more correct. That dude who brought you here, Set-d'Elous? He lived through the war. There were no catchy tunes back then, only death and destruction. He was trying to find his girlfriend, Gina, and he miscalculated the shift of the tangents. Easy mistake, you know. He arrived at the wrong time, in the wrong place, yet he made the best of it. There's a lesson for you, young man. Make lemonade! Out of lemons. You get that? If life gives you lemons? Anyway—"

They went inside and the youth sat on the chair and the man threw himself on the *qala* with a weary sigh. Jason was looking thinner already, Chucker noticed, with all of the traveling and strange foods, the sheer exercise of being away from the palace, the constant worry (though he was good at hiding it) all seemed to contribute to his diminishing girth.

"Anyway, that's where he met this Ghoupalle woman—Aisa, I think her name was. Not the Aisa that's his daughter, obviously. So he was made part of the Jisilikan army there, fighting in Foixe—we'll visit there soon—and his squadron charged an enemy bunker at Arrêgon and he became a hero! You don't know him like I do but hero is *not* what he is. But there he was: wrong place, wrong time, damn hero. Go figure. He called it fate or destiny—yet fate never thought we could cross between dimensions, eh? That was when we realized we could visit different times and places just by entering the next dimension at different points. That starts getting into serious math—I know your mother says you have trouble with it and she's paid a tutor to help but you blew it off. Shame on you! Anyway, we had to become mathematicians so we could come and go as we wanted."

"So...?"

"So, he goes back and finds himself in another place, another time, meets another Ghoupalle woman named Zaura, who's— well, she had powers like...for making people healthy, or that's how he always explained it to me. So he—"

"You're not going to tell me his story again, are you?"

"No, I'm telling you the short version."

"Get to the point, if there is one."

"There is a point! You're just like him. Like Set! Whose son are you, anyway?"

"I'm the queen's son. Prince Chuck R. Tucker!"

"Right, and I'm married to the queen."

Chucker grinned. "I got half-brothers and half-sisters from you and Mom."

"Are you okay with that?" asked Jason. "Maybe you're still adapting to the idea."

"Adapting? How should I know? That was like two planets ago! I don't even know how long I've been here. How old am I now? Can I drink beer yet?"

Jason laughed, caught off-guard. "If you really want some, I suppose it would be okay."

"But how old am I really?"

"The year's four hundred and eight days long and each day is about thirty-two hours. You do the math, son."

"Son? Stop teasing me."

"In absolute time, a year here is like a year-and-a-half on Earth—"

"So I'm about six years older than when Set brought me here."

"It's only been four years on this world. Not much difference. But if you factor in the shifting tangents, a whole decade could have passed back home as you pulled lint out of your bellybutton the whole first year you were getting acclimated in Aivana. If you went back now, you might find everyone you knew was older than you."

"So I should stay here? Is that what you're saying?"

"You don't like it here?"

"It's not that. I—I miss some things from back home."

"You mean back in Aivana?"

"No. Back in Kansas City. On Earth. You know, third rock from the sun?"

"I've heard of it. Bad reputation. Anyhow, this is your home, at least for now."

The boy stared at the floor, then the ceiling, then back at his step-dad.

"So now I'm on another planet looking for the guy who messed up Mom's life. Is that the point of this story?"

"The point to this story is: Why are we here?"

Jason sat up, caught his breath, then stood. It was getting dark outside, seven shades of green fading below the horizon.

"That's one reason I took you to see the show," said Jason. "The battle scene in that opera should've made an impression on you. War is not fun. Especially for the soldiers down there doing the fighting. Set was there—and other times, other places, always fighting. I was there, too. Right there in the middle of the fighting. Remember the invasion of Tebbicousimankalê, the winter siege of Siaa? He was there. So was I. It was hell. I want you to remember that. No war is good. Oh, somebody might gain some land or get some cool souvenirs, but the price is always too high for both sides. So we want to prevent it—all of them."

"Okay, I get it. No war. Bad, war, bad. Go to your room."

"No, you don't get *all* of it. He had a family with that Zaura woman. They were destroyed by the wars. One son was a general, another was a—"

"Their fault, then."

"Right now, your godfather is trying to prevent that war from ever starting."

Chucker glanced out the window, impatiently waiting for Jason to tell more.

"How?" he finally asked.

"Thanks for asking. Let me tell you. We have the benefit of looking back through the dimensional gaps and seeing what did happen and how it started. We can pinpoint exactly the moment when an idea is planted in the mind of a certain person to start a chain reaction that leads to political intrigue, revolution, conquest, war and death for millions of people. He is trying to stop that. He is trying to keep his family alive."

Chucker stood and went to the window, stared out at the rooftops of Feasfend and the blue, forested hills embracing the city at this late summer's sunset. The day seemed like life, coming to an end against its will. He sighed.

"I get it," said Chucker. "But while he's saving *his* family, I'm wondering: where is *my* family?"

Jason went to him at the window, hung his arm across Chucker's shoulders and for once it was not shaken off.

"You have a mother and father, a step-father, godfather, a dozen half- and step-siblings, a handful of friends, and several classmates, tutors, play companions, and assorted pets. I'm not saying that's enough, but perhaps for now it's plenty. When your Youth Trek ends—when we reach our destination and can head home—you will take your place at your mother's side. When your Youth Trek ends, you will be ready to start your own family."

Chucker stepped away from Jason. "You mean I have to get married?"

Jason laughed, returned to the *qala*. He sat on it with a great sigh.

"If you can find the right partner, someone who can stand you!"

"Maybe—"

"By then, let us hope Set's infernal work has made the world a better place to raise a family. Anybody's family." He smiled at the sunset, then at Chucker. "Then we can all go home."

❋ ❋ ❋

The band of Rouê nomads had traveled for two days under the blazing suns, the yellow by day and the blue most of the night, over the dunes and along the dry ravines, measuring the distance by the accumulation of heartbeats. Finally they stopped in an oasis, beside a small pool of brackish water the color of blood that seemed to be draining away even as they hurriedly gathered as much as they could in the clay jars they brought down from the backs of the *oñacha*.

Sitting around the small fire, cooking strings of *falu*, they seemed to be considering his fate again, one then another gesturing toward him. He grew concerned as he lay quietly on the dirty straw mat the youngest one gave him.

Chuck feared to speak as he watched them bickering. The leader jumped up angrily, pointing at him. Suddenly, the others rose and Chuck thought there might be a fight. Instead, they all gathered around him, saw he was awake. They were not smiling.

One of the men dropped to a knee and lifted the cloth covering Chuck's chest. The Rouê spoke among themselves. The man poked his finger with its sharpened, pointed nail at the wound in Chuck's side. Another tossed a leather pouch against Chuck's chest and the kneeling man opened it and retrieved some tools. Chuck saw the tools: a long curved needle and some thread. He felt liquid against his skin and realized he was bleeding again. These men—*Roo-ay*, he had figured out—were going to stitch his wound. One of them had speared him in the ribs and now another was going to sew it up!

They shoved a stick between his teeth and held his head as the needle went through his skin twenty times. They poured some liquid from a clay bottle over the wound and it burned intensely, more painful than the sewing. They gave him a sip of the liquid and he knew it was some kind of alcohol. He dared not breathe deeply.

Chuck rested as the Roué returned to dinner, speaking in calm voices. He soon fell asleep—or passed out.

Later, he awoke to the roaring of a storm. The Roué were shouting at each other, trying frantically to pack up the camp, the *oñacha* pulling wildly against their tethers and resisting the loading of supplies on their backs. The wind was ferocious, drumming loudly in his ears and spinning the dust and sand into a thick brown soup.

He was helpless there on the mat.

"Don't leave me here!" he cried out but no one seemed to hear him. He shouted again, trying to be louder.

One Roué turned. It was the one who'd sewn his wound. That Roué came to him and brought a dirty golden cloth. He knelt at Chuck's feet and began wrapping his legs in the cloth. The cloth seemed to extend forever, unwrapping from a rod as it was wrapped tightly around his hips, then belly, then chest. The Roué stumbled from the force of the wind, falling against him, and the third time it happened, Chuck saw a stubby knife fall from the Roué's belt. Not noticing it, the Roué continued wrapping him up, as a mummy, until only his eyes were uncovered.

Chuck could not move but held the knife secretly beneath the wrapped cloth along his inner thigh.

Two others came over and lifted him and carried him to the awaiting *oñacha*. They considered him valuable now, he surmised. As long as he uttered the sacred word *Alebafe*, they would take care of him. Now they needed to remove him from the path of the storm.

Atop the *oñacha* he could see the storm: a towering brown mountain of sand and dirt was moving toward them. He instinctively knew if it reached them, given the thickness of the dirty air around them, they would all suffocate. The Roué knew what to do. They covered themselves with every cloth available, placed hoods over the heads of the *oñacha*, and lead them hurriedly away.

The dark gray morning left Jason's senses dulled and the pea-colored snow tossed randomly by the wind did little to raise his spirits. Winter was coming on.

"Now that we've cleared Jisilika," he said to his step-son, "we can move on to Gotanka. Lots of sordid dens of iniquity there—especially that rat hole of Peror. What a damn, dirty city! You can't spit there without hitting someone with moral turpitude!"

The boy was silent in the seat beside his step-father as the KOHAX chugged along the river, a steep cliff rising on the opposite side of the track.

Jason cleared his throat. "I spent some time there during the war," he said, adding a sigh. He stared at the boy, growing into a man during the years they had been traveling together in search of Michael Fenning. "Don't worry, we'll find him."

They watched the scenery pass by for a while, first the tall trees with their gray, leathery leaves, then the farmlands full of the red grain bowed over and nearing harvest, then a small town perched along the riverbank.

Chucker thought about their journey, following the trail of Michael Fenning. It was not a pretty trail and they often lost the scent. They had yet to find him, but Chucker had managed to bond with his step-father. Jason saw Chucker's transformation over three Ghoupalle years and calculated he must be eighteen by Earth years.

For Chucker, the time that had passed only served to intensify his thoughts and feelings about the man who ruined his mother's life. It was clear to Chucker what kind of man Michael was. In a small town south of Feasfend—he forgot the name already—they found an inn where Michael had stayed. Jason sent Chucker up the stairs, all eight flights of them to the top apartment. His knock was answered by an elderly woman, her hair down to her knees, bent as she was. *Did someone by the name of Michael Fenning live here?* he asked the woman in his improving Ghoupallêan. He had to repeat the question, adjusting his Ghoupallêan accent until the woman could understand him. She invited him in to tell the tale—the sordid adventure, his step-father would call it.

"Not here," Chucker said to Jason as he descended the stairs.

"How long ago did he leave?" Jason asked from the wagon.

"About two years ago. Seems he left a debt here, just like last time. About three month's rent and some payment for damage. And a pregnant daughter of the landlord."

Chucker climbed into the wagon. Jason grabbed the reins of the *Jêpe* and they started off.

"She killed herself when he left," said Chucker.

Typical scenario, they were beginning to learn. Michael's disease had gradually festered, leaving him more infirm each time he attempt sex. His partners knew his affliction—not contagious—and tried to comfort him. That always seemed to lead to some kind of amorous relationship. He still could be charming, it seemed, when he was not in pain. He took various drugs to numb the pain, especially more *moussalaganê*, the same drug that had, in his initial overdose, caused the affliction.

"And what exactly is his, what you call, 'affliction'?" Chucker had asked.

"I suppose you are old enough to hear the details," Jason had sighed. "It is caused by an extreme overdose of a local drug: the juice of the *moussala* plant that grows in southern Sekuate and Aivana. Unfortunately, the effects on an Earth man are rather frightful. A Ghoupalle man will feel excitement and find his sexual performance enhanced. The Earth man, sadly, will find his performance enhanced, yes, but to the point where he can no longer return to his normal, uh, shall we say, his normal dimensions."

"Huh?"

"To put it bluntly, the penis remains engorged, in fact, it remains enlarged permanently."

"I hear that's what guys want. They got drugs for that back on Earth, don't they?"

"Yes, but the effect here is different. The engorgement continues—forever. As I've guessed from our encounters with those he's left behind, he continues to take the *moussalaganê* to ease the pain of engorgement. Such a pity."

Chucker was finally understanding. In the three years of traveling, he was adapting to this new world, learning its customs and culture, its language and its ways of thinking. He no longer thought the two suns were odd. He no longer thought the people around him were idiots and dorks, nerds, geeks, sluts, or fags. They were just people, all trying to get by each day. He was the son of a queen—though he tried not to let the chip on his shoulder grow any larger; eventually, it fell off on its own and was lost in the dust of some dirt road in the Feasfend countryside.

"The old woman said he was heading to Peror, where he heard of a new cure."

"Then we should head there, too," said Jason.

Chucker was silent as the KOHAX ran along the mighty Peror River. He was thinking of what he would do to Michael Fenning when they finally caught up to him. He hoped the man would not die of his disease before he could confront him. He would make Michael look into his eyes and understand the hell he had caused for his mother and him. That she was now a queen and had an easy life did not matter to him; his crimes had been committed on Earth.

Soon they came to the border. The KOHAX stopped and all the passengers exited and stood in line to have their travel papers checked.

"You are from Aivana?" the customs agent asked Jason.

"Yes, we are. Both of us. This is my son."

"Step-son," Chucker added in English.

"Occupation?"

"Administrator."

"Of...?"

"The government."

"Are you honest?"

"Yes, I am in charge of finances, you might say. Chief Financial Officer."

The customs agent looked him over.

"Of course, I'm in traveling clothes, not my daily business attire."

The customs agent nodded. "What is your business in Gotanka?"

"Tourism."

"Skullduggery," Chucker muttered in English with a snicker, then looked away when the customs agent stared at him for any clue of moral turpitude.

"Never mind him," said Jason in Ghoupallêan, adding a laugh. "You know how these youth are. Never follow the rules of polite society. I've tried to train him but his mother lets him get away with everything."

The customs agent smiled, amused, and offered a few details of his own parenthood.

Their travel documents were stamped and they joined the other passengers boarding the KOHAX for the final leg of the trip to Peror.

"Skullduggery?" Jason laughed. He sat back in his seat. "Where'd you learn a tenth-grade word like that?"

"Your friend uses it a lot," Chucker responded after a moment's thought. "Set uses it to describe what you and him do on this world. How you both use your *ahem* 'special talents' to get whatever you want."

Jason rubbed his chin, a gesture more of drama than habit. "I suppose he's right."

When the wind had stopped, he opened his tightly shut eyes and found the suns low on the horizon. He also saw he was buried in the sand up to his face. With a little squirming he managed to pull his hand, caught beneath his wrappings, the hand with the knife, up to his chest, and he began cutting through the cloth. The tightness of the cloth prevented sand from entering his wounds, he discovered.

With his hands free, he clawed his way up and out of the sand. It was too loose for him to stand up but on his hands and knees he could survey the surrounding area. He found no sign of his escorts nor their animals.

Before the light could fade, he realized, he had better mark the right direction to go. Yet each direction seemed the same to him, all equally unknown, equally brown.

He checked his sewn wound—it had stopped bleeding.

He saw a clay jug which he assumed would have water in it, lying at the bottom of the depression, so he stumbled down the dune to get it. His foot hit a rock that protruded through the sand and that stopped him. A stream of sand swept downward beside him and landed in what suddenly appeared to be a patch of quicksand. He picked up a loose rock and tossed it down to the flat area below, striking the jug, and watched it sink into the sand.

All around him the dune walls rose and he wondered how he could now climb up. But he had to, so he turned himself over on his belly and dug in, as deep as his hands and feet could reach into the sand, searching for solid ground. He moved like a turtle up the side of the dune, each motion sending new streams of sand downward.

A voice called to him from above but he knew it was not God asking him what he had done to deserve this fate.

He lifted his eyes to the top of the dune and saw one of the Rouê standing there, covered in wrapped cloth. It was the young one. A metal hook attached to a rope was tossed down to him and he grabbed it with one hand as he maintained his balance with the other.

He pulled gently on the rope, testing it. The Rouê waved at him to climb up. He hesitated, not sure which fate would be better to face: continued captivity or drowning in quicksand on another planet, far from family and friends. Left to contemplate his misery midway up the slope, he decided it did not matter. He gazed up at the sky, the blue sun and the yellow sun side by side in this season. He knew he was a long way from home. Who would miss him? Who would care? His hand loosened around the rope, ready to accept the quicksand.

Immediately the Rouê jerked on the end of the rope and the hook caught Chuck under the ribs, and hand by hand the Rouê pulled him up the slope dead-weight.

When he opened his eyes, Chuck was not in heaven, nor in hell, but at the top of the dune looking down. When he rolled over onto his back he found himself gazing up at the almost toothless grin of the young Rouê who had sewn up his spear wound, the Rouê whom he dubbed the 'good one.'

The hook had pierced his skin but had not gone farther, locked as it was between his ribs. He was used to pain now and laughed it off. The Rouê checked the wound, spit on it.

Chuck did not know the fate of the others but was content to listen to his new friend talk on and on about whatever was so interesting. As he listened, he watched the Rouê cleaning him off, brushing sand from his skin, checking every nook and wiping away the dirt. When the Rouê was satisfied, he pointed between Chuck's thighs and made a remark.

Chuck smiled, embarrassed. There was little he could do, being naked out in the desert, depending on this local guy to show him the way...somewhere.

They found one of the *oñacha* wandering not far off and roped it. Chuck ran naked after the animal, chased it back in the direction of the Good One. A few pieces of equipment and a box of food were still strapped on the beast. They set off in the direction the Good One seemed instinctively to know. He had to trust the Rouê.

Chuck rode the animal for a while, then thought better to try walking, to show he was not an invalid. The night grew dark, both suns setting, and the Good One kept to a steady pace, pulling the *oñacha* and Chuck with him.

By dawn they could see a village ahead.

Jason waved away the irritating *yüp*, a green-yellow flying insect with barbed feet, as he stood beside the carriage, watching the boy slowly come down the three external flights of stairs of the beige, plastered country inn.

"He's close," said Chucker, "but not this one."

"Where then?"

He held up a slip of paper. "This address. A few blocks from here."

They rode away and merged with the traffic on the lanes, just two Earth men visiting an old friend in the dirty west end of

Peror, up the slopes from the snaking brown river, a district of warehouses and the rough hovels where workers lived and played, a perfect location for someone of Michael Fenning's ilk.

"Your Ghoupallêan must be improving for you to get that kind of information out of her," said Jason.

"Desperate times call for desperate measures," spoke the young man, emotionless.

"And you've taken up books."

"Not exactly."

"You're serious this time, aren't you?"

"I've always been serious," Chucker replied. "I just never knew about what."

"Until now."

"Until now," Chucker responded, looking away.

When they arrived in front of the white plaster building, they checked the address. It was correct. The building was a kind of hospital, one for the poor and destitute to be treated by volunteer members of an ancient religious order, a place where only the most decrepit would go.

"He must be in his final days," muttered Jason.

Chucker jumped down, staring at the hospice.

"I hope."

✳ ✸ ✳

When the two travelers entered the village, everyone they passed stopped and gazed with curiosity at them. A Rouê outlander was not so rare. The desert-crossing traders often passed through the village on their way to or from the larger towns. Some stopped overnight; most, however, could not endure a night on a *qala* and so they tended to crowd together on the outer rim of the village, back to back in the sand.

What caught the villagers' attention was the fact the young Rouê had only a single *oñacha* in tow. The Rouê also had a man. It was not just any man—not another Rouê or even a Ghoupalle—but a naked man. Perhaps the creature was a prize to be bartered in the next town, perhaps a slave to be sold. Yet what an amazing creature! The creature had a golden-brown mane growing from its face, and the hair on top of the head was long and tangled. The creature was shorter than the Roué leading him yet more muscled, stockier, and clearly wounded. They could see the wound in the side of the ribs that had been sewn up. They could see the other cuts and knew the creature had been tortured—but most understood it was often necessary for getting a slave to obey. This one seemed to be in complete obedience and submission, walking calmly through the village, naked from feet to head, burnt by the sun, yet with a strangely defiant air about it.

They stopped at a café and the Roué tied up the *oñacha* and the man, and went inside. The *oñacha* looked around and then focused its eyes on the ground in front of where it stood, content to gaze at the dirt. The man also looked around, though more slyly, and kept his head lowered so as to not arouse curiosity. Eventually, the man sat down in the dirt, legs crossed, back hunched.

Children soon gathered around the man, studying him. One dared to toss a pebble at the man and they laughed as the man swung wildly in the air. Then the man jumped up and growled at them. They knew it was trying to scare them away, yet being tethered to the post it could do nothing but endure the taunts of the Roué children. Finally a woman appeared to shoo the children away.

"*Ho'!*" the woman cried out, observing the naked man.

Chuck was ready to tear himself from the tether and attack if need be. There was nothing more he could lose.

"*Fe'a'lo l'pare he' le'le o'jelo'po?*" the woman asked him, her voice lowered.

Chuck just stared at her. She was draped in long, flowing clothes of various shades of brown; she did not seem to be someone of high rank. The wealthy wore colorful clothing, he had observed. This woman covered her head with an amber cloth, held it pinched around her face. Her skin was dark, he noted, thinking like a policeman: African-American female, five foot six, brown eyes, medium build, fifty-five to sixty years—

"*Hela' o'po,*" said the woman but he did not understand.

The Good One had cautioned him with gestures that he should act as the Roué's slave when they entered the town. At least, that's what Chuck thought, so he submitted to having the rope around his neck and walking passively behind the *oñacha*. As for clothing, he had none any longer. Now this female was staring at him, speaking to him, and he feared for his life if he should speak in response. No doubt some Rouê men would spear him like some shish-kebab were he to raise his eyes to the woman—

"You—from—Earth?" the woman asked in hushed, halting English.

He looked up at her, entirely out of surprise.

She cleared her throat. "Nod yer head—if you from—Earth."

He nodded his head.

"Thought so." She cleared her throat again, as though she was clearing it of the Rouê words she had learned to speak long ago. "Me, too."

He looked up again. Their eyes met—briefly. Then they both knew he should look away and he did.

"I been here long time," the woman said, "an' I never saw no one from Earth 'til you."

"I—I'm Chuck," he grunted. "I'm a cop. I was—"

"A cop? You far from home now!"

"I know. I was chasing a guy and—and I ended up in this desert."

"And the Rouê caught ya. Just like me. I work as a nanny now."

"I'm trying to find my ex. Ex-wife. Her name's Tammy Sue Tucker."

"Tammy Sue?"

"Yeah. They seem to call her *Alebafe* here."

"*Tami'su'o! He'ilo'ye Alebafe*?" she almost gasped. She glanced around, then spoke in hushed tone: "She da queen here. She married da king an' he died an' now she da queen of Aivana."

"Tammy's a queen?"

"Yessir, but you best be nice to her or these Rouê'll kill you. Don't disrespect da queen. Tammy Sue is *Tami'su'o*. That's how they say her name. Rouê name is *Alebafe*. This is Aivana. She lives in da capital city. It's called Aivana, too."

"Thank you." He let out a sigh, feeling some relief but not understanding why. "What's your name? How'd you get here?"

"Me? I'm *He'o*—been long time. I mean, my real name's DeeAnn. From Philly. That's Pennsylvania. Shit, long, long time ago. Just a teenager. One Sunday I was visiting out in Amish country and—shit, now look at me, old 'nuf ta be a granny. Hey, the words—English words! They still in my head!"

She was ecstatic, jumping up in delight. Some passersby called to her, evidently asking her to calm down. She rambled on, though, dancing around him.

A tall, muscular Rouê man came up to her and grabbed her arm. She wrestled out of his grasp but he caught her again, knocking her to the ground. Chuck wanted to get up and punch the Rouê but he knew to stay hunched, stay out of trouble. The noise attracted a crowd. Just another foreign servant gone crazy, nothing to see here, folks!

"Good luck living in Aivana," DeeAnn grunted from her position on the ground, held there by the Rouê man.

Three Rouê men helped the first one pull the nanny to her feet and escort her away. A moment later his own Rouê burst out of the store, followed by a Rouê woman who pointed at Chuck, then at the nanny being led away, and back at him, chattering away in their sing-songy language.

The Good One grinned down at him and chuckled. He untied his charges and led them away, first the useful beast, the *oñacha*, then the useless creature, the man. Children pursued them at a distance and lobbed stones at the foreign slave as they left the village.

Chapter 20

The Child is Father of the Man

Inside the hospice, two yellow robed nurses confronted the young man, stopped him from simply waltzing through the corridors and with sharp words asked him his business.

"*E ben serzen Maixel-Fenenk,*" he spoke. 'I'm looking for Michael Fenning.'

They questioned him about his business. He took their attitude as indication they knew something of the patient's history. He considered other men might have attempted to confront the playboy, perhaps threatened violence, so the nurses were wary of anyone who asked for him.

First, he needed to know the man was in the building.

"*E ben mur zäf,*" he said to their stern faces. 'I'm his son.'

The nurses seemed shocked. This Michael Fenning could not have a son, they no doubt had decided when they admitted him. No wonder he had no one to care for him in his forlorn condition.

Chucker asked to be shown to the room where the man was being treated. His rough, slangy Ghoupallêan alerted the nurses that he certainly was no academy kid. The young man might even be a bit simple in the head. Genetics, one of them muttered. A sad case: like father, like son.

They got his meaning, however, and one waved him to follow. The other watched them walk away, still suspicious, then decided it would be prudent to inform a staff physician the next of kin had finally shown up.

The corridor on the fourth floor was suddenly filled with an icy breeze and Chucker shivered when he stood at the doorway where they stopped. The attendant pulled back the folding panel and in the darkness he could make out the silhouette of a figure reclined on a simple bed. It was not the *qala* most people slept on, nothing hanging from the ceiling in a basic clinic like this. The bed was wooden, hammered together as needed then burned when a patient died. This patient would soon die, he surmised. Even the once-white sheet was plain, like a burial shroud.

He smiled his thanks to the attendant and jutted his chin down the hallway, suggesting the attendant could leave,. The attendant made some remark Chucker could not understand, then gave a *hummph!* and turned to go.

Entering the dark room, Chucker became acquainted with the scent of death: the odor of dying flesh, a pungent, nauseating smell that made him pause and consider whether he wanted to go further.

"Man, how can you let yourself get so bad?" he spoke.

Something in the bed stirred and Chucker reached for the oil lamp sitting in a recessed niche in the side wall.

"*Fan?*" came a faint response in raspy Ghoupallêan.

Chucker's hand turned up the lamp, the circle of light spreading only to the patient's shoulders. Far enough, he decided.

"You don't even know where you are," Chucker grunted, "do you?"

"*Fan-se?*" Grumbling, throat-clearing. "Huh?"

Chucker stepped to the foot of the bed, studying the patient in the dim light. The dirty white sheet covered the feet, the cloth dropping almost to the floor. Brown, red, green, and yellow stains spotted the cloth. His eyes moved up the legs to the hips. Then he noticed the raised lump between the legs. He stared, not surprised but curious. He knew the consequences of overdosing on *moussalaganê*, and he knew of Michael Fenning's abuse of the liquid. He still could not believe what he saw.

Atop the sheet rested two bony arms, skin red and scaly,

dotted with black-headed pustules. The arms were covered in sores that leaked yellow pus. The ammonia odor of the pus stung his nostrils. Although he had been informed about the disease, he was not prepared for what he saw. *Obophæ*, or simply 'the pox', caused boils that burst and spread pus which, as it ran over healthy skin, had the effect of acid, burning into the skin. Eventually the body became riddled with burrows, often exposing inner organs. In the final stages the organs themselves became filled with boils and burned deeper into the surrounding tissue. Not a good way to die—or to live even a few final months.

"You're Michael?" he asked with a steady voice, something a detective might utter when arriving to check out a domestic disturbance in some middle-class suburb.

The mass on the bed jerked as if responding to an electrical charge, then became motionless again. Perhaps the man could not pull himself up, so weakened by disease, thought Chucker.

He held his hand over his nose as he stepped alongside the low bed, moving from the light into the shadows. He could see the head was bald except for a few long strands of gray hair hanging on here and there, the scalp sporting a half-dozen red pustules, swelling toward eruption. The man's face was turned away as Chucker watched the chest rise and fall. He made himself reach out with his left hand and touch the squarish lump beneath the sheet, what should be the man's shoulder—

"*Famê?*" the man grunted, initiating a hacking cough that shook the entire bed for a few *pii*, then fell silent.

"I said, are you Michael?" he spoke in English.

Suddenly the sheet ruffled upward as the body beneath it shook through a spasm. The sheet settled in a different position, revealing the bare chest and scrawny shoulder of the patient. His face was visible now, too, and Chucker turned away in horror. He glanced back, turned away a moment, then snuck another peek. Even in the dark portion of the room, Chucker could see the scattering of pustules, several of them oozing yellowish pus. And the face! The skin was pulled back so tightly from age, from disease, from hard living, the patient seemed a skeleton. The mouth seemed to have no teeth, sockets pulled back around the closed eyes—eyelids not closing fully—and the pimply cheeks sunken while the nose was swollen, bright red, flinging remnants of pus with every exhale. The throat was wasted away, down to the inner tubes and bones. The skin on the shoulder and chest was like paper, a minefield with many exploded blisters and the stains of dried pus.

Chucker held his breath.

"Are you Michael?" he asked again through his hand. "*Plaerense* English?"

The half-agape mouth of the patient came to life, seemed to choke on the mucus collected there, and let loose a single grunted word: "En—glish."

The patient's eyes opened, stared up at the canopy over the bed a moment, then rolled slowly downward to fall upon the face of the youth standing beside the bed. There was no look of recognition.

"Michael Fenning?" Chucker asked, sounding like a cop ready to arrest.

A long silence. A period of motionless.

"Me," the patient muttered. The hand attempted to rise to tap the chest but could not and fell against the sheet.

"Great," said Chucker. It seemed the patient was unable to carry on a conversation and he had a lot to say. He expected to get answers, too. "Do you know where you are?" No response. "Do you even know who you are?" No answer, blinking eyes. "Do you know what's happened to you?" He stared, waiting for a sign, any sign of understanding. "Do you know who I am? Can you guess why I am here?"

A deep throttle, cough, spray of spittle from the mouth as the patient spoke: "You."

Chucker smiled, not in delight but in something akin to finding an extra dollar in his wallet.

"You know me?" He was ready to lecture, felt the words building in his gut. "Well, in case you can't quite place me—give me a good look, will you? In case you can't figure me out—I said look at me! I'm Chuck R. Tucker. I'm Tammy's son. You know Tammy? I've grown up. I'm not some stupid kid you can stand in the corner or send to my room while you work on my mom. I'm a man now. I'm not sure what my age is on this world but I feel like I'm maybe twenty-two, but probably about eighteen in

Earth years. That's right—in *Earth* years. You dig that? Because we ain't on Earth no more!"

He had to catch his breath, exhaled and carefully inhaled with his sleeve pressed against his nose.

"Talk to me!" Chucker watched the patient studying him. "*Plaeren-ga!* Say something—anything. Remember English? Are you so wasted now you don't know anything? Speak—"

An ugly growl emanated from the open mouth, a clearing of years of deceit, of lies, of unspoken words, then: "You—can't be—here—"

"Well, how about that! You can talk. And believe it or not, I *am* here, so don't go telling me I can't be here cuz I sure as hell *am* here—"

"Go—away—"

"I am not going away! I've been looking for you for three years, so I'm not gonna leave now that I found you. You can bet your next fix on that. Me and my step-dad, we've come from Aivana, all the way up here to Peror looking for you. For three years. Looking for Michael Fenning. You should be ashamed of yourself, man! You should just kill yourself and save everyone the trouble!"

"Go away—get out—"

"I bet it's hard to think what to say to the kid whose mom you messed with. But don't worry. I got lots of time. I can sit here and watch you die, minute by minute. What's a few *peth* or *pii* to me, huh? I enjoy seeing your pimples pop."

"You don't—understand—"

"What don't I understand? What? That you got—?"

"It's—contagious—"

Chucker stepped back to the foot of the bed.

"This crap is contagious? Then why didn't the nurses stop me, or make me wear some suit? You're just making it up to get me to leave. You always were a phony."

The patient shook his head slowly, then tried to sit up. At the height of his effort, just a few inches off the crusty mattress, he spit up a greenish fluid that ran down his chin and dripped upon his chest. With the effort, he crashed back on the mattress.

"That's disgusting!" Chucker took a step back.

"Told you—to go." Coughing. "Save yourself."

"Save myself? I'm not the one who completely pissed away two lives, one on Earth and one here. You had another chance here, as I hear from my step-dad. You had the chance to make things right for yourself and for my mom. My step-dad's friend, Set-d'Elous, brought you and her here to fix you. Instead, you just kept going on with the drugs. You can only blame yourself, Michael! That *moussalaganê* is tough stuff. But you kept taking it. Doesn't work so nicely on Earthlings, ya know."

He glanced at the pathetic figure beneath the stained sheet.

"And now you got the pox. How long you had it? How many you pass it to before you even knew you had it? How many killed themselves when they found out? How many tried to kill you when they found out? You are exactly where you should be: dying of an ugly, painful disease away from family and friends, no money or medicine, on some far away planet. You are so alone now! You could not be more alone. In fact, I think it's time for me to go. I can't stand your stinky disease—and your poxy face makes me sick! Seeing you like this is enough. I think I've got my closure. Have a nice life, however many days you got left! See ya round, sucker!"

"*Aisê! Aisê!*" a man's voice snapped, calling for silence.

Chucker's way was blocked by a stern man wearing a red and yellow cap and matching striped apron, the uniform of a physician, who warned him in a quiet voice to maintain a restful environment.

"I'm leaving anyway," Chuck snorted, not bothering to repeat it in Ghoupallêan.

The physician left the room, waited in the corridor as if to escort him out.

As he turned to exit, holding his breath, a raspy voice called after him: "Don't go—Chuck—please—"

No longer did they make their way across the open desert. Instead, they could now follow a road, the Good One leading the *oñacha* with the naked man tethered to the beast's tail. Though they moved along a road, every stone, rock, pebble, shard, chip, grain of mineral taxed the man's bare feet. Soon they were bleeding and he moaned in agony.

When his moaning prompted the Good One to stop, the young Roué retrieved some rags from the pack on the *oñacha*'s back and tied them around the man's feet. He looked over the badly sunburnt flesh of the man, now a dark crimson, the color of blood, but in many places blistered and peeling, exposing pink underlayers that would quickly turn oven-red under the two suns. The Good One pulled off his own cloak and laid it gently around the shoulders of the man—which prompted a mad shrieking from the man, leaping up and shaking off the cloth. His flesh was too tender for the soft fabric.

The Good One took a gourd-bottle from the pack and squeezed out some thick yellow ointment and began dabbing it to the worst patches of raw skin. At first the man would shriek, then, understanding it was medicine, held his breath and gritted his teeth through it.

Soon after they started down the road again the suns were setting, so they stopped for the night. The Good One erected a lean-to, lashed to the starboard legs of the *oñacha*, trained not to move. He slept inside while the man lay stretched across the stones, rocks, pebbles, shards, chips, and grains of minerals that littered the landscape, both on and off the road. Exhausted by the journey, he fell into a troubled sleep and turned throughout the night, awaking before dawn with his body bruised and sore from his bed.

The journey continued and after half a day they found themselves approaching a city. The Good One pointed ahead but all Chucker could see was a volcanic cone rising from the flat plain. As the Good One explained through strange words and clever gestures, the wide mountain held in its vast basin a deep green lake and a large island which seemed to float on the waters, a garden paradise amidst the desert, protected from the harsh desert by the high lip of the crater: the city of Yvo.

The Good One watched the man not comprehending the description of the peak in the distance, and grinned. They were almost home. The Good One pointed to the mountain and then tapped his chest. The Good One's home, Chuck guessed. Maybe that was also where Tammy lived.

And for delivering this man to the Queen of Aivana, the Good One must dream of the vast rewards that would be showered upon him for rescuing and returning to her a valued slave. Perhaps he was a bodyguard, or a mercenary. Look at his musculature! His jawline! His eyes! This man was someone of worth to the queen! And he, the nephew of a lowly Rouê merchant from the southern hills, had such a prize to deliver! And now he is reduced to a ragged shell, stripped and humiliated, flesh torn, spirit crushed. He would have to bring the slave back to good health before he could present it to the queen.

Chuck stared out at the world he never believed existed, imagined how good it would feel to awaken from this dream. He studied the twenty shades of brown that striped the flat, rock-strewn plain stretching to the horizon in each direction. All that broke the plain was the mountain far ahead. The road seemed to extend straight to that peak. It seemed farther into the wilderness, not closer to a city. And what good was civilization anyway? He knew how a man was treated by the Rouê. How could his ex- be a queen? How would she treat him? Would she seek revenge on him? Or would she be delighted to learn of all of the hardships he had endured to find her?

The Rouê jerked the end of the rope that was looped lazily around the man's neck. Time to get up and start the journey again. The mountain was still several days' walk—according to the number of fingers the Good One held up.

Chucker watched a mature pustule burst on the patient's chest, saw the greenish-yellow pus seep from the open wound, studied how the acidic fluid bubbled, burning into the healthy skin around the pustule, soon to make new pustules. The patient scream, shaking violently against the mattress. Chucker wanted to leave. He wanted to be fourteen again and know nothing of this world. But he wanted to hear Michael's poor excuse for an apology, an explanation, a reason for messing up his life and his mother's.

The living corpse had once been a lively youth who had quickly realized his talent: charming women—his mother, aunts, sisters, nieces, cousins, girls next door, classmates, teachers, shoppers, women in parks, at laundries, police women, neighbors, co-workers, an auto mechanic, the mothers and sisters and aunts of girlfriends, and others. But his talent was eventually overcome by his age and he fought hard to continue his playboy ways, using lines and behavior that now seemed silly. His efforts seemed to work, however, on one lady, co-worker Tammy Sue Tucker. She seemed to dig him, and she laughed at his jokes, thought he was handsome, even sexy, and dared to spend some time with him in his car after work at the IRS service center. That led to a few visits to a cheap motel, and one weekend in her house—the house she shared with her husband, the cop, who was away on a training exercise for the Missouri National Guard. After that, she swore the affair had to end, that she was going to stay with her husband, even though he was abusive, slapping her once in a while, shouting at her for just about everything she did, calling her stupid, a stupid whore, a skinny bitch, comparing her to the perfect women in his magazines. Michael had listened to her and she'd liked that. And she rewarded him with that weekend in bed. He tried to seduce her away from the cop, not quite sure if he genuinely liked her enough to want to marry her or he was just hoping to keep the affair going.

"I think I loved her," the patient muttered, staring at the ceiling. Chucker leaned in to hear more clearly, "or maybe I loved how she made me feel. You know, feel young again. Sexy. Worthwhile. Okay, she was skinny, had those big teeth, and was dumb as a doorknob—"

"Hey!"

"Sorry. But what I'm trying to say is even the way she was, I was hooked on her."

And then came the night he talked her into breaking into the Professor's apartment. Sure, it was a bad idea. They had suspected the man Chucker knew better as Set-d'Elous was a fugitive from justice, maybe in a government witness protection program, or he was just some weird psychopathic pervert. They wanted to check him out, purely for their entertainment during the slow season at the IRS service center. After Michael got in through an open window and let Tammy inside through the door, they started looking around and found some strange brown juice and thought it was refreshing, like old lemonade; they drank it all down, not realizing what it was: *moussalaganê*, the elixir of love from a distant world. On fire by the drug, they could not stop what they were doing, they were compelled to start and could not stop, right there on the kitchen floor in the Professor's apartment. That's where he found them later. The Professor could not easily separate them, not until they lay in complete exhaustion, their bodies spent.

"That's when she got pregnant," the patient confessed, "but it was an accident. The drug made us do it and then we couldn't stop it."

"I heard this part before," said Chucker. "Set explained it all. But what happened after he brought you and my mom here? I thought you were supposed to get treatment?"

"I did." He coughed. He coughed out his left lung, then tucked it back inside his chest. After the discomfort faded, he continued: "I did start treatment."

However, he quickly grew tired of the daily exercise of the countering-drug injections into his vital organ. He liked the way the nurses teased him, how they responded to his naïve ways, his lack of language proficiency, his uncouth manner, his sly grin, and not least of all the engorgement. It did not take long for him to seduce his nurses, leaving two pregnant and the others disappointed when he ran away before dawn one autumn morning. He'd learned enough of the language and customs to get by on his own. He also had money in his pocket from the nurses, and from an old man he helped along a country road one night. He found himself in a gambling den later and won. He made enemies and continued to run, continued to gamble, continued to meet and seduce the females he encountered along the way to...?

"I didn't know where I was going," he said, "just going away, away, farther away, always just ahead of somebody chasing me."

"Didn't you realize stopping the treatment would doom you to an early, painful death?"

"I knew, but...but that wasn't all."

"No?"

"No. I stopped treatment but I kept taking *moussalaganê*."

"But why?"

"Why not?"

The ladies liked him that way. He was a kind of a legend, a celebrity, and he could not walk away from that narcissistic glory. Before long he was spending his gambling winnings on the drug, taking it daily to keep up his enhancement, to maintain his readiness to engage in various sordid pleasures. It did not matter to him that what he saw attached was discolored, swollen, often painfully so, and he found he needed the *moussalaganê* just to ease the pain. He became less and less able to meet the challenges that his charming persona could set up. The ladies laughed at him rather than fall for him. His partners were gradually drawn from the lower ranks, from women worse off than him. He also kept running, hiding, and continually begged for food, drink, shelter, and another sip of *moussalaganê*. This time the sips of the sour fruity brown liquid were to stave off insanity.

"They found me in a garbage heap, digging for food."

"That's dramatic," Chucker responded with a sneer.

"It's true!"

"And here you are, at the mercy of the Sisters of Perpetual Pain."

"I have my own pain." And to prove it to the youth he again attempted to cough. "See? I can't even cough. Not like I need to to clear my throat."

Chucker gazed at him. "What you got is what you deserve, man."

The patient gasped for breath, chest heaving with effort.

"I get that you hate me." He looked up, searching for the youth's eyes. When he found them, he grinned. "I want to ask you something." Raspy cough. "I want to ask a favor—"

"I don't care what you want!"

"Please—"

"I listened to your story, like you wanted. That's enough of a favor."

"No, I—I told you cuz I want you to know—about everything—before I die."

217

Chucker frowned. He slowly shook his head and turned to leave. "Goodbye."

"One more thing," the patient called out.

"No more. It's done. I'm satisfied now."

"Help me—"

"I just wanted to find you and tell you what a...how you messed up my mom's life, and...what I think of you! I wanted to see you, look in your eyes, when I kill you. I just wanted to find you and kill you, man, for all the shit you done to us. But now I see I was cheated of all that. Nature's already done to you what I wanted to do. You may live a day or a year more, but right now, I'm satisfied. I'm satisfied you'll die the death you deserve. Painful. Humiliating. And slow."

"But—Chuck—"

The patient erupted in a coughing fit. The youth saw veins rupture along his ribs, dark patches growing where blood seeped. A pustule under the patient's chin burst and fresh yellow-green pus spotted the collar.

Chucker waited, watching.

"I guess I feel sorry for you a little. It can't be easy being you. How did you manage to put up with yourself so long? And on two worlds!"

"I need you to—"

"We all need something. But nobody needs you, not now, not ever. It's finally time for saying all of those meaningful goodbyes, Michael. Adios! See you in Hell—or whatever they have here. Maybe the devil here is a bottle of *moussalaganê* and a harem you can't touch. Maybe it's—"

The patient's arm rose into the air, like a salute.

"Yeah...?" said Chucker. "Final words?"

Their eyes met, lingered. There was history between them they both seemed to know. Still, when two people find each other on another planet, there is a certain custom, a particular hospitality that seems more instinct than ritual. Pausing, eyes to eyes, a vibration of empathy wavered across the room.

The youth felt the words in his mind before he heard the words stumble from the patient's decrepit mouth: "I want you to end this."

The room was silent. Outside the singing of *tixou* filled the silence, matching the beating of faint hearts up and down the corridor of the clinic. There was a languid, watery peace out there. Somewhere. Inside the clinic, a dry, cracked death awaited, counting the clocks and calendars, marking time in heartbeats.

"What are you talking about?" asked Chucker.

The patient lowered his arm, which now seemed to have been involuntarily raised, frozen in place by the stiffening of the body.

"Please—stop this pain. Please—end it."

Chucker felt like smiling but did not know why. Instead, he formed a scowl, a wince of disgust.

"You should have asked me a few years ago. Then I would gladly say 'yes.' But now? I'm not sure. It seems you will die soon anyway."

The patient grimaced as pain shot through his body. When it passed, he gathered his breath: "I told you my story—because I want you to know—I ain't a bad person."

Chucker nodded.

"Yeah, I got that. Michael's all right. Let's all give a cheer for Michael!"

"Listen to me." He tried to sit up, fell back.

Chucker glared at the patient, wanting so much to pull from his belt the XG-48, Zetin army standard issue pistol given to him by Set-d'Elous upon the commencement of his Youth Trek.

Youth Trek? No, it was a Search for Michael Trek.

He steadied his breathing, eyes fixed on his target, denying the target was human—

"I'm ready," spoke the patient. "You can kill me now."

Chuck looked up when he felt the rope around his neck slacken. He turned and gazed at the landscape behind him, saw only the rusty horizon and the amber sky. Ahead he saw the Good One standing at the head of the *oñacha*, one hand petting the muzzle of the beast. Chuck heard talking and saw the road, as meager as it was across the flat desert, was intersected a short distance ahead by another barely visible road. More importantly, what he noticed when the Good One called to him was that another caravan was about to cross their path.

There were three *oñacha* driven by two Roûê, Chuck saw. Behind the *oñacha* was a line of pedestrians, maybe a dozen. He squinted. They were different sizes, some clothed, some less so. All hung their heads as if in shame. He didn't know what to expect, wondering if there was any custom about two caravans meeting in the desert. He thought he'd seen something on TV a few years ago. Something about hospitality in the desert, even to your enemy.

The Good One was right in front of him when Chuck next looked ahead, startling him. But he knew his place and bowed his head. He listened patiently as the Good One tried to explain something, speaking slowly but in excited tones, enunciating each syllable as though the Earth man would understand. He seemed concerned, even fearful. Chuck just nodded. He did not have a good feeling and his body felt the pumping of adrenaline.

He gazed up at the endless sky, cloudless and pure.

"Dear God," whispered Chuck, then wondered where those words burst forth from. "I've never been a good church-goer," he continued, the words falling like precious drops of moisture he was sacrificing at the height of the desert afternoon. He didn't know who was speaking. It seemed like someone else.

The new caravan was approaching. The Roûê waved and called to each other, seemed friendly, happy to find someone else on this desert road.

The Roûê sitting atop the lead *oñacha* jumped down, landing on his feet like a cat, and waved his caravan to a halt several steps from where the Good One went out to greet them.

Chuck measured the distance. *Not too far from the beast*, he thought, willing his warning to penetrate the mind of his master. The only weapon the Good One had was a knife strapped to the saddle and a broken lance.

The caravan came alongside them, slowing to a stop like a freight train. The broad chests of the *oñacha*s were beating outward, drawing breath. They must have been in the desert a long time, thought Chuck, becoming some kind of expert. Probably they were only asking each other about water, accommodation, destination, sights seen and other travelers encountered. Chuck watched the conversation while sensing the movements of the line of slaves and the other Rouê who was now behind him. Without appearing suspicious, he slowly cranked his head slightly back and glimpsed what he could.

There were only two Rouê: the first on foot speaking to the Good One and the second sitting atop the trailing animal. Between them was the line of merchandise, strung out like pearls on a necklace, ropes encircling their necks—as he also had. He was naked and he saw the caravan's wares mostly were, too. But something was wrong with the picture.

The Rouê leader's voice rose, agitated momentarily, and Chuck turned to watch them. The two Rouê were holding up their hands, each time with different fingers extended, like sign language. Or counting. Were they making a deal?

He squinted to see the Rouê's face, especially the eyes. He knew eyes never lied.

The Good One waved both hands, calming the other down, it seemed. They chatted on and Chuck turned back to examine the merchandise in the other caravan.

They were not all naked. The clothes that hung on them were rags—rags that were not of the kind of material Rouê typically wore. One slave's outfit resembled what Chuck would call a tanktop with shorts. The slave was barefoot. They all were—and some of them had pools of blood forming on the ground where they stood. He looked closer at the tallest one whose shirt seemed to display some logo or design. If only he could turn to his left more without drawing any suspicion, then he would be able to make out what it said.

He glanced back at the Good One and the leader of the caravan. They were laughing over some shared anecdote. The Good One's laughter did not seem natural.

Chuck returned his attention to the slaves, daring to step a few inches to the side. He could almost make out the shirt's words. Not words, but a number—84.

A basketball jersey?

He stared hard at the two slaves lined up after 84. Their shirts also matched, though they were too ripped to reveal any number. The tall one was African-American, dark bronze skin, age 20 to 25, slender, tattoos on upper arm and calf. The next one was White, early 20s, dirty red hair, once pale complexion now a deep red, skin blistered and severely peeling. The next a Latino, short-cropped hair, wide nose, an earring or other jewelry once had hung from his ear but now was a bloody mess of dangling earlobe. He saw an older human in what once was a brown work coverall, now reduced to rags, something a pilot might wear, but the man's face had empty eye sockets and lines of dried blood down his face. There was a woman—he guessed it was a woman by the breasts, but couldn't be sure—maybe Indian, as in Pakistani, as in Hindu, one of them—so dusty and bloody that he was disgusted at the sight of her. None of them were human any longer. Whatever had happened to bring them to this world, to reduce them to automatons trudging aimlessly over the burnished landscape—whatever had taken their spirits away, they were no longer human.

His eyes went down the line. Human. Human. Human. Human. Frogman—

The last being was a squat figure with no neck, a flat upturned face and an extremely wide mouth. Its arms were longer than its legs and the fingers seemed to end with suction pads. It too was naked and the green-gray leathery skin was marked with welts and cuts. A creature from another world? He was a creature from another world, too. He did not belong here. None of them did. Especially the frogman, toadman, whatever it was! He was in some kind of hell he could never have imagined, forced from the swamp to the desert—

The Rouê atop the last *oñacha* jumped down suddenly and Chuck glanced quickly back in the direction of the Good One. He and the first Rouê were walking toward him.

"God, if you can hear me," Chuck muttered, "if you can hear me way over here on this other planet, please just let me live through today."

The Good One gave him a command and when he did not understand, several fingers were thrush into his mouth, pulling his jaw down, his lips stretched wide, and the leader of the other caravan examined his teeth. Satisfied, the leader's attention went down his chest, pausing to point at and remark on the wound in his ribs. The Good One winked slyly at him, then spun him around and the examination continued. The leader's voice was serious as he probed the man's anus, while the Good One's voice was lighthearted, artificially playful. Perhaps the leader wanted to make a deal but the Good One did not want to sell him.

Apparently satisfied, they stepped away and Chuck breathed deeply, readying himself for whatever might happen next. He felt stronger, despite his ordeal through the desert. His adrenaline was filling him with the old Chuck, the football runningback, the Tae Kwon Do blackbelt, the wrestler, the sharpshooter, the third baseman and clean-up hitter—

He saw movement in the corner of his eye and turned his head just in time to see the other Rouê retrieve a long lance strapped to the side of the last *oñacha*. It was maybe fifteen feet long and had a bronze spearhead with a useful barb on the back side. Perfect for fishing *gaung* out of a sandpit from the top of an *oñacha*, thought Chuck. He had witnessed such a scene before the storm. He remembered how the lance was used, imagined how it *could* be used—

The Good One was not happy, he could see. The caravan leader was speaking loudly, threateningly. Something was wrong. Something was about to be more wrong. The Good One wouldn't sell his last remaining slave, Chuck guessed, so these two were set to take him by force. They thought they could do it, too. He saw their intent, recognized the moment before action, the thought building into behavior. He felt it in himself, too.

If only I had my .45—or a shotgun—

Chuck planted his feet for balance, ready to spring in either direction, as the second Rouê from the caravan extended the long lance toward him, the bronze metal point close to his chest, holding him hostage.

The Good One had let his noose lay slack against his shoulders, loose enough he could slip it off in one quick twist of his head and shoulder—

With a quick spin of his body, ducking below the point of the lance, Chuck grabbed the shaft of the lance with both hands and stabbed the bladepoint harmlessly into the red ground.

The second Rouê was surprised—especially when Chuck slammed the lance shaft back at the Rouê, into his mouth with the butt end—three times—until the Rouê released his grip on the lance to tend to his broken teeth.

The caravan leader, seeing the attack, quickly produced a short curved knife from the folds of his robes and struck it forward into the Good One's abdomen, then turned to charge the crazed slave.

Chuck swung the lance around like a long ladder to the side of a burning house, cutting the air. Like a pendulum, the swinging shaft slapped the caravan leader in the middle of his back, pushing him hard to the ground. The Good One was knocked down, too, out of the way. Chuck swung the lance around again and again, full circles of angry staff and bitter blade, striking the Rouê caravan leader as he tried to rise to his feet, striking one of his *oñachas*, striking the line of slaves, cutting their ropes, cutting the miserable beasts they had become, striking the frogman, striking the ground, the stones, the red dirt, striking a vulture-like flying reptile that had come down to dine, striking the Rouê caravan leader again as he attempted to pull himself up to a knee, striking the second Rouê of the caravan as he rushed at the whirling madman of vengeance, striking the caravan leader again, his head bowed in pain, severing that ugly head, slapping that head into the dirt, striking the other *oñacha* of the caravan, striking the line of slaves again as they remained dumbly in place, striking pieces of meat, the line of meat, the line of anger and rage and violence and vengeance and murder and frustration and pity and mercy and madness—

He held his ground, chest heaving, arms tightly gripping the lance, surveying the damage for four heartbeats.

Then Chuck raised the lance, flipped it around, repositioning it in his hands, point-first and in two lightning-quick thrusts opened a neat hole in the throat of the second Rouê just recovering his balance. Chuck spun around and planted the point of the lance in the caravan leader's chest, lifting the Rouê a few inches off the ground and dropping him into the dirt. He thrust the barbed point into the Rouê's abdomen again and again until it was pulp.

Chuck saw the crippled slaves in the caravan, squirming silently, pitifully, mindlessly, and he stepped toward them and with the lance firmly in his moral grip, he struck each one fatally, mercifully, through their hearts, ending their pain, ending their humiliation, ending their lives.

Exhausted, Chuck dropped to the sand, staring at the line of fallen slaves, the wounded *oñachas*, the two dead Roué, the endless red desert, the two suns melting on the horizon, the amber sky, the red dirt, the Good One lying silently beside the road—

The Good One!

Rushing to the Roué's side, Chuck saw the ugly belly wound from the caravan leader's knife. He saw blood pooling there. The Good One had tried to save him, had held out as long as he could against the two slave merchants. But the Good One was no warrior. It was Chuck who had to take action. His rage had overwhelmed him.

Blood leaked from the belly cut—red like his own blood.

Chuck pulled away the robe and examined the wound. He worked up some saliva and spit it into the wound, then pushed down on it with his two hands as the Good One exhaled from the pressure. Chuck held his hands in place for a few minutes. He felt the hand of the Good One on his arm. He glanced at the Good One's pain-struck face.

"You can't die," Chuck spoke in the only language he knew. "You hafta stay alive. You hafta get me home. I need to get home. Home! Gotta get home!"

"*Ho'm...ho'm.*" The Good One smiled weakly. "*Alebafe, Alebafe, Alebafe'la?*"

"Yes, Alebafe," Chuck responded.

He kept one hand on the wound and the other hand clasped the free hand of the Good One. Their eyes met. The Good One recognized Chuck was trying to help. There was forgiveness in his eyes, understanding, thankfulness. Chuck gazed back at this strange person with whose life his had become entwined, the one who had stitched his wounds. The Good One motioned for the sewing pack on the saddle of the *oñacha*.

"I will stitch up your wound," said Chuck.

Tears filled Chuck's eyes, some dropping down upon the chest of the Good One. Chuck felt embarrassment. Then he dug his arm under the Good One's shoulders and pulled him close, chest to chest, embracing him, and let go all of the tears he had been saving during the past many years.

Chapter 21

The Fragrance of Time

"It's a lot like oranges," said the weary traveler, "you know: the pure sweetness, fruity and delicious. Like that."

"You mean like *pomora*?" his companion responded.

"If you must use a local equivalent!" the traveler snapped back. He had left Ghoupalle year 1457 through the tangent near Lyas and returned to 1574 for *this*? Not the reception he'd expected. He took a deep breath. "But, yes—like that. It's full of life, of beauty, of goodness. It's optimistic. It's the smell of good fortune. That's the fragrance of time."

The room had grown dark by that hour, in that latitude, in that season of the new future. Set-d'Elous forced himself to smile as he sat back across the large marble-like table from his old friend, the now-much-less-rotund Jason, loyal spouse of Queen Tammy of Aivana, dabbler in various mechanical contraptions, inventor of modern conveniences. Construction of the first elevator on Ghoupallesz was underway—discussed in technical terms through appetizer and first entrée.

Then he began the tale of his adventures in the previous century, their conversational English a secret language to the staff serving them. However, the lavish dinner seemed less delicious this time, he decided. His stomach was in knots, his heart beating strangely.

"So I left her there. And *I* left there," he continued, decorating the truth to make it prettier. "I left Zaura there, too, of course, again wondering about my fate. Yes, you and your debates about Fate! Your words have been messing with my head for years now." He wanted to light a pipe then, felt it fit the scene but instead he pretended to blow smoke rings into the evening air, watching them curl with the woody scent of the undercooked *zurrek* set between them. "I had to." He watched the imaginary smoke rings fade away. "Once she was dead, there was no way I could stay there, maybe be accused of her death—"

"Her murder!" the king snorted, mouth full of food.

He ignored the implications, reached for another long red stick of *lug* and licked it once to remove the grease before biting off the chewy tip. He refused to let Jason be his conscience this time. Next time, perhaps. He was still deciding whether to forgive him for the last time Jason acted as his conscience, what, ten years ago?

"They saw us together, her and me. Some of my men knew we'd met. If I were still there, I might be arrested and end up in prison—at least questioned about it. What would Zaura think about that? Her husband—her *new* husband—consumed in a public scandal, and she, my dear wife, surrounded by public scorn. Her husband, a man of some notoriety in the neighborhood—in the city, too, in the military complex—he just went out and killed some young girl while on duty up in the mountains. How would that look? How would she deal with that?"

"How will you deal with that?" Jason was unusually snide this evening. His friend had actually stopped eating before his plate was cleared.

"So I left."

Set moved some food around on his plate, decided he was finished eating. Either the food was not prepared to his standard or his guilt had changed the taste from savory to sour, from sweet to bitter, then tasteless.

"It was a beautiful day, a sunny afternoon," he continued, shooing away uncomfortable memories of that cold, late autumn day in the wood beside the lake along the road outside the town of Sorêg. "We had been walking through the meadow and she stepped on some thorn on a fallen branch. She fell into the grass like her leg was broken, teasing me, coaxing me to treat her. I examined her foot, pulled out the thorn. She wanted to save it, the thorn. She said, 'Good luck falls upon the person who kisses a wounded foot; will you kiss my wound?' So after cleaning the spot of blood, I kissed her damn foot. I needed the luck, I suppose. I wrapped her foot in my uniform jacket, got her blood on it."

"Quite a gentleman, aren't you? Did you send a bouquet of flowers?"

"Your cynicism is much appreciated, as always."

He glanced around the room, for a moment believing it contained a crowd of onlookers, a silent jury. Perhaps his friend sitting across the table actually knew what had happened yet was playing dumb. Time had passed, certainly. More than a century. Books had been written. History classes had been taught. And yet nothing seemed to have changed. His friend, Jason, the queen's consort, had complained about nothing, so just how much of history had really been changed? He wondered what the present held for him, much less the future. The past was fixed; he could breathe easily. Somewhere scribes were cursing him for forcing them to write new books and alter pamphlets.

Set-d'Elous elevated his voice to make his case clearer: "Then, since we were already there in the grass, we decided to make love. And she seemed to know what would happen next. I'd already asked her about that same, hypothetical situation, and she agreed with me. She essentially gave me permission to intervene."

"Were you speaking in Ghoupallêan? How could she understand what you intended? How can you read a person's heart and mind like that?" Jason wiped his mouth with the back of his hand. "And which of you really decided to, *ahem*, 'make love,' as you say?"

"You're suddenly full of questions! What happened to the jolly inventor we used to love and adore, at least in public?"

"He's going on a diet. A spiritual diet." Jason pulled himself up in his seat, leveled his eyes at his friend. A maid came over and wiped his mouth with a cloth, then retreated to the margins of the room. "I'm finally losing my appetite, I guess. You and your conspiracies! What will you think of next? A doorway to another world? Leading a pilgrimage—oh, yes, some diaspora to Earth? *Hmmph!* Dreamer! You once thought you were a god—we all did, I guess. But I settled for being this. You know, taking Chucker on his Youth Trek was about the best thing I ever did. It made me realize I'm interested in coming and going as I please, not being royalty and having to *do* things. How about you? You're bored, so you get into trouble! Go back to your island and leave the world alone! You could've stayed there, safe and happy, perhaps insane. Now you've gone too far: killing at random because you think you'll change the whole damn world. Who thinks like that? Who has that kind of vision or foresight? You? Only a god would see everything with that vast scope and then act on it! Ah, yes! Send a precisely targeted bolt of lightning down to strike the inflated head of Set-d'Elous: take him out for the good of the planet. Is that what you're trying to imitate?"

After the angry words echoed out the window, the silence expanded to fill the space between the planet and the blue and yellow suns. He dared not burst it but the room was full of pins and needles. They stared at each other for a while. Officially, they were waiting for the third dessert.

Jason waved off the serving maidens; no more food tonight.

"Afterwards, I started to return to town," Set-d'Elous spoke at last, "but then a thought stopped me. Yes, I felt guilt, but I had to stay on track, keep thinking of the greater good, the long-term goal, the righteousness of my actions. If I were to remain there and were caught then the plan would be all for naught. That wasn't the plot I sought—pardon the rhyming! Could I argue in court that I was doing it to save all of them from the disastrous future I had already lived through? They wouldn't believe me. The only way to finish it was for me to leave. Absolutely vanish—as I did before. So I decided, right then—right there sitting atop my *Jêpe*, just before I was about to enter the town, gather the regiment, and march back home—I realized that I could never return to the garrison, could not even continue my life with Zaura. Not that I wanted to get away from Zaura, you understand. Sure, the previous me was due to remeet her soon anyway. I think that was at Aisa's wedding, hmm? I still had another couple of years I could spend with her. I was just doing what I was required to do by Fate."

"Fate! You talk about Fate like it's some old grammar teacher ready to snap your hands with a wooden ruler!"

"Fate isn't a person. It's a force." He gestured wildly in the air, drawing an image of Mrs. Fate somewhere in the shadows. "Me leaving that time zone is part of the plan. All right, perhaps me leaving is always the plan, wherever I go—people just want me to leave. But I *am* doing the right thing here! Besides, now that I managed to change history, everything will go well for Zaura and our entire family. I'll be returning to her as the previous me, so we'll be together again. I know it's confusing but try to follow. Making this small change means no war, no death and destruction. That's what I want for them. I could always return to her later, I thought, having missed less than a year. That's what I'm doing now: returning to pick up where I left off. Soon I'll be on my way—the original me, that is—to be reunited with Zaura in Selauê, knowing everything will go smoothly. Back again through the tangent, back to that time zone again. After all, I love the fourteen-hundreds!"

"She's been mourning you all this time," said Jason with a dark tone. "You want her to go through that anguish again? Leaving her on Karluk and then leaving her again from Sorêg? How cruel can you be?"

"Everything will work out!"

"Are you worth it to her? You have this presumption that she, an alien woman—and don't lecture me on who's really the alien here—you think she will care enough about you to mourn you every time you vanish, then welcome you back whenever you happen to return, like some king without a crown, a muse without a lyre, a *Jêpe* without a dewlap?"

"You should cut back on the hookah. Your words are overwhelming you—"

"Words! They're just figments of my imagination. Sentences will kill us all if we let them. Tie them up! And whole paragraphs? Well, I don't *think* so—"

"So I returned to the body—in the grass beside the lake—and I stained my uniform jacket with more of her blood. I repositioned her body as though she had been attacked—as though *we* were attacked and she was killed immediately and I

231

stumbled off somewhere, or was taken hostage. My body was never found, yet my bloodied jacket would have been found and they'd start searching for my body, search for my attacker. The regiment would accept my demise and search for my killer, all the while—"

"All the while here you are, a hundred years in the future, sitting pretty at my dinner table in Aivana!" Jason snorted, amused, disgusted, distraught. "Once again you're overstaying my hospitality. How delightfully mad! How adolescent of you!"

"It will work! It will work, dammit!" He shook his head, struggling to believe his own words. "Original Me will return soon, before the next month begins, and Zaura will welcome him back. She'll be surprised, of course, but delighted to see him again. I'll say I was kidnapped, held for a while, but I escaped. I'm in good health, spent some time recovering, which extended my stay too long. What's it been, five months here? Just a couple of weeks for me back on Earth—though more than a year's passed since my last visit. Maybe this moment in time is too soon to see any change in history, but it's too long to let Zaura mourn me. I need to get back to her. As the story I'll tell her goes, even in my captivity I never wavered, never forgot her, always kept her in my heart and mind, always planning to return to her, desiring her—always! And she will believe me. She must." He stared at Jason's sullen eyes. "'Aren't I clever!'—I know that's what you are thinking. Well, there is cleverness to it, to any plot, any scheme, no matter what we eat. Say, what's in this *ummm* food, anyway? The *zurrek* tastes funny this time. Decaying flesh in the heat of the Aivana autumn, I suppose. And we ate it anyway."

He let out a wild belch, unable to restrain it, and almost fell over in his chair. Recovering, he sat through a risqué performance of Jason's belching and belly scratching, then continued:

"So I managed to escape and now I'm finally able to return to my one true love—as the triumphant, repentant, heroic warrior: loving husband, faithful soldier to the end. They'll write songs about me. Myths will be born. Then we live our lives free of the war and its ravages. All of us. Everyone. I have changed history from horrible to around average with possibilities for perfection. I am a hero. Accept that."

"You're not a hero, you're a fool." Jason struggled to climb out of his chair, two attendants rushing over to assist. "I advise you to be very careful. If my life changes for the worse because of your arrogance, you won't be invited to dinner anymore."

"Fair enough." He stood up with effort, patted his belly, and smiled. He brushed crumbs from his jacket. "I'll have to find a library and check things out. Or, better yet, I'll return to the Archives in Selauê and read all about it."

"Better wear a disguise, then," his host grunted.

"Yes, your royal high-ass!"

Jason waved a hand, shooing him away.

"And, by the way," he said, hiding the urge to quibble over semantics again, "those folks who moved into your house? They painted it forest green with white trim. Not a bad look. And they planted a new tree in the front yard. And it looks like they have another kid on the way. Thought you'd want to know. It's business as usual back on Earth. Oh!—they've got a TV channel that shows music videos all day and night. Nothing but music videos! Called 'Music Television,' or something like that. You'd like it. And my old house, the family home? Well, it doesn't exist any longer. It's been bulldozed—with the others on that street— to make room for a shopping center. Seems like a whole 'nother life."

"It was," sighed Jason Aronstein. "We all know you were never born."

He snickered. "So I'll never die!"

In the morning he made his way north, dragging his guilt like a fully-loaded footlocker. He hated the facts of the case, and he could only find peace by reciting the mantra he had composed in the hours after the killing: *Everything will work out for the greater good*.

When he arrived in Selauê, the city appeared as it always had, bathed in perpetual spring, an early morning shower glistening on the streets when he stepped off the KOHAX from Aivana. He had stopped over for a night in Lyas, just for old times' sake, to once again walk the neighborhood that now seemed so distant, unchanged and unvarnished. He vowed to return someday with Zaura and buy the apartment block where they had first met, and set up their children there. Then, boarding the KOHAX, he continued north. He watched passively as the KOHAX moved sluggishly through industrialized Seas, through its impoverished quarters, through the grime and the garbage, and then broke into the bucolic countryside, the golden fields of *juñi* on the left stretching to a coast he knew existed over the low hills, lime-green fields of young *ular* and *shirrom* on the right spreading to the distant mountains parading the horizon. Finally, they pulled under the cosmopolitan skyline of Selauê, his adopted home, a few blocks from the main gate of the Selauê garrison.

He walked out of the station wearing civilian clothing, not looking around, not wanting to set eyes on anyone who might know him. By the calendar, he was returning only a few years after he had been murdered along with that female student from Sorêg University. The scandal had not been forgotten, it seemed. He saw old posters of the girl on a wall, worn by the wind and rain but still begging for information on her killer. Being noticed could make him newsworthy again.

So he went straight to a style shop and had his hair combed and tinted, then braided. A long braided moustache of dark gray with crimson highlights was applied (the new "Zetin warlord" look, he was told), and his fingernails were painted navy blue, as was the fashion trend he overheard someone on the KOHAX insist. "Only laborers refuse to paint their fingernails!" the woman had sneered. It was part of the decadence rampant in those years, something the Gangus council would soon rail against to incite the masses. Next door he changed into fresh clothes he purchased: a brown *kitl* over a pale yellow *boêr* with a crimson *them-boêr* around his waist. His high-waisted *burk*, which buttoned down the front, was also brown and was made of *olpar*. No one would recognize him when he stepped out onto the street.

As was his custom, he went next to the Archives to catch up on the news. Digging through a stack of news bulletins, he found the article he was searching for: a report of the search for a missing cavalry captain in the area around Sorêg. He slipped the page out of its cover and stepped to the back corner of the room, behind the shelves, afraid someone would recognize him from the portrait of the missing captain at the head of the article. The sepia print did not do him justice, though he rather liked the imposing portrait that was drawn.

Only the third time reading through the text did it make sense to him. When the regiment had returned to the garrison without him, his vice-commander, *Serpan* Qalanou, was forced to report the loss to the garrison commander. The loss of a regimental captain on a simple patrol mission was a bizarre event and thus a serious matter. Two fresh regiments were dispatched to Sorêg and began a more systematic search, going house to house, rounding up citizens, harassing the Danid minority, combing the woods for bandits, examining every square *tiv* for any clues, questioning every person within two or three *radit* of every spot the captain had stepped, whether on foot or by *Jêpe*. He was presumed murdered, or kidnapped and killed later, and they would not rest until the attackers had been found and executed. He regretted the people of Sorêg were subjected to such harsh treatment when he had not actually been killed, but it was *for the greater good*.

His heart beat a little faster as he realized that what had happened in Sorêg as they searched for him was just a small preview of the terror that would spread across the nation under the Gangus reign.

And now...?

He looked up, checking the noise of new arrivals at the tables near the shelves where he read. Nobody of note. So he retrieved other issues, scanning them for articles following the crime. The focus seemed to turn to a college student, Diert-Gangus, a young man who had often been seen with the other victim, Basura-Kanoun. He had been arrested and underwent interrogation at the hands of the regiment's best disciplinarian. The result was, as expected, a denial of the crime. More interrogation, more denial. A month went by. Eventually, he was tossed out on the street, broken and bitter but free. In those days, one could not bring a lawsuit for police brutality, so he disappeared quietly, rumored to be headed toward Selauê, to seek a fresh identity and start a new life.

The search went on a little longer before they were ordered back to the garrison. There were no other suspects. The case was closed, still a mystery. The town turned out to mourn the girl and a sample of her poetry was printed and distributed in the region. Included was her last poem, lines left unfinished when she was struck down by her attacker, the parchment still in her hand when her body was found beside the lake. It became her symbol, her words a rallying cry, a memorial, a famous quote school children would recite. Meanwhile, no one had any interest in what had become of the captain, representing as he did the cruelty of the soldiers who had destroyed the town.

Later Diert-Gangus was seen in Selauê visiting an uncle. The army continued to spy on him, following his every move. Not only had he been beaten and accused of murder but he languished under the cloud of sorrow for the one he had lost, the object of his obsession: Basura-Kanoun.

Set-d'Elous choked up behind the shelving, feeling the misery he had caused.

"Someone sabotaged that army officer and the girl he was meeting," said a rough, raspy Ghoupallêan voice.

When he looked up, it was an old man in gray coveralls, the uniform of an ex-prisoner—perhaps the only clothing he owned now.

"I heard them say he was in a love-bond with the girl," the man continued. "They believe her jealous boyfriend, her schoolmate, killed them. What was his name? No matter. I feel for the widow. I lost my missus, too. They thought I killed her, sent me away but I was pardoned and now I'm back, looking for the real killer. You better stay clean, young man, or the police will pull you inside for whatever crime needs a scapegoat! Mind your step down the avenues!"

The old man left the aisle, slinking from shelving to shelving as though he were back in prison, watching for attackers, for police, for shadows.

And the widow...?

He knew the procedure. His vice-commander, Aroun-Qalanou, would report the loss to the garrison commander, Rogar-Omlen—promoted to 2d *Coræsz* commander in a few years. Omlen would have summoned Zaura to the garrison. An aide would have been provided to assist her with completion of the papers needed to receive the pension of her deceased spouse and make arrangements for various aspects of her life. Knowing Zaura as he thought he did, she would have sobbed and possibly collapsed at the news. He imagined she would be taken to the garrison infirmary and treated for a weak heart. She would have explained it was not a weak heart but her diminishing *senzenaxii* powers, the result of bearing children with her husband, that caused her to lose her composure, to always feel faint. Then she would rise from the bed and step out into the compound to take her place beside the widow's monument, touching its eight-pointed star, breathing a prayer to a dead soldier, and then, when her heart had grown strong enough, lift her head high and stride across the courtyard, accept her memorial gifts, and turn out the gate, down the avenue, up the side street to her home and in through the door to a secret place where she could be alone with her future, a time and place represented by a simple document. She was now eligible for the widow's pension and supplements, plus special consideration in almost every public action. When the wars came, he remembered, such special consideration would be repealed because too many were needy, too many widows overwhelmed the system, too many widows walked the streets.

"I sincerely believed this man would be a good replacement for the spouse I previously lost," the war widow spoke in measured Ghoupallêan. Beneath her crimson veil, she sat beside the pension counselor. "He resembled my first spouse, both in face and body, and in the way his words came from his mouth, the look in his eyes when he saw me, the touch of his hands on my body—it all was the same. He even had the same name, as though it was fate."

"Then why do you doubt?" asked the counselor, an older woman dressed in the khaki and crimson uniform of official service.

Dressed in dirty, well-worn clothing, he sat in a nearby chair, appearing to wait his turn but actually spying on Zaura-Matousz. The Ghoupallêan words he overheard were stilted and overly polite, as befit the status of a war widow. Was she an ex-wife because he had killed himself in Sorêg, or was she still his wife? He knew that in a couple years his original self would be returning to her—the earlier Set-d'Elous, the one who had already lived with her, loved her, and watched her die as the wars were beginning. This was just cosmetic, he told himself, a chance to check that she would be all right until he and she would be reunited.

His ears had become acute since his return, though his long hair remained swept back into ragged braids. He resembled a war veteran, a beggar, a vagabond, not a decorated captain of a cavalry regiment.

"Every man who takes me as spouse soon dies," she said. A heartbeat later she burst into sobs requiring the counselor to hand her a towel. "He comes and goes and I never know his fate until the garrison calls me."

"What shall you do now, dear widow?"

Zaura looked up, eyes red and wet. "I was a *senzenaxii* before I met my first spouse. Since then, I have used my talents only for him. And his replacement. Yet now they are diminished. I cannot return to that occupation. That is a reason I could not sense my second spouse—part of him was like my first spouse, part was new, different, confusing, a strange signature in his aura, as though he were only a mirror image of the man and not the true man. That frustrated both of us. For me, I wanted him to be my first spouse, yet number two remained dulled by my memories of number one and though number two tried to honor me with his care and love, he could not close that gap between my heart and my hands."

"I understand your confusion, yet you seem to have a sensitive nature. Could you become a counselor such as me? It is a worthy occupation. The uniform is easy to care for, simplifies one's life, does it not?"

He stood then and the others in the waiting room stared at him. He feigned weakness and stumbled out, no one following, no one assisting, no one caring.

Down the cobblestone streets he went as a light rain fell, spotting the stones, green clouds rolling overhead, smothering him. Strangers watched him trudge toward the wharfs. The sailors wondered if he sought a job onboard. One asked and he waved off the sailor.

The rain grew thicker, and thunder banged his ears, streaks of lightning cutting across the sky, the roar of time filling his head. He knew what he had done. He had changed history—yet he had to wait years and years to see what effect it would bring. That feat was impossible, he suddenly realized with a snap of a ship's mast near him. Sailors scrambled to untangle the ropes and steady the fallen post. The world was collapsing around him, and only he knew it.

The years he had spent with Zaura after their reunion in Sairel—and his later reappearance in Selauê as a captain of the garrison—could not be lived again. He had kept her from marrying Tolour-Frêdin. There was no son, Samot-Frêdin, born. She would not need to endure the death of Tolour, bitten by the poisonous *ghu*, a spider as big as a man's head.

He sighed with regret.

On the wrinkled, torn calendar he carried in his jacket pocket like a good luck charm were the printed dates: the first time he lived through Ghoupalle history—Tolour-Frêdin had died in 1462 and Zaura and the children had returned to Selauê, leaving the desert city of Sairel forever. Then he had been brought by Gina back to Ghoupallesz to see his daughter Aisa's wedding to Gina's son, Sartan. There, he had been reunited with Zaura and they were married soon after. A new child arrived in the next year.

"And the rest is history," he muttered, ignoring the ceasing of the rain, the drenching of his clothes, his dirty but once-fashionable *burk*, and the sudden appearance of rays of green sunlight between the clouds. Had the storm passed by or had he entered a fresh tangent and emerged dry on the opposite side of history, a new calendar curled up in his hand? He breathed deeply. "Now she's a war widow on pension. And the war hasn't even begun."

A shadow fell over him. "There won't be any war."

At first he thought it was his alter ego, his doppelganger, a past-time self come to talk him out of suicide. But it was not. He looked up and saw a man staring down at him, the black silhouette somehow unmenacing.

"You speak English?" he asked the stranger in English.

"*Famê-ke*? *Famê* Ingloosz-*se*?" the shadow responded.

The words were all in Ghoupallêan; he had merely translated them into English in his head. He knew he was still sane and continued in Ghoupallêan, using a rough country tone that fit a man of his appearance. Only moments before, he was soaked by a rainstorm on the wharf in Selauê harbor yet now amazingly dry, waiting for the future and feeling a twinge of hunger for crusty bread and creamy butter, perhaps a spicy sausage and a slice of cheese on the side, and iced tea. Lots of iced tea.

"Why do you say there won't be any war?" he asked the stranger.

The shadows shifted, and the sunlight was momentarily blinding as the man sat down on the wooden planks beside the captain.

"No war as long as Sarrêban stays in power," the stranger replied, alluding to the monarchy, a passive family business content to let the bureaucrats run everything. The military offered a counterbalance to official incompetence and rampant corruption. "I don't wish for war, yet the people cry out for justice in all corners of the land. In the end there will be war, yet not as long as Sarrêban remains in power. In their comfort and luxury they have no will to change, not a finger to lift toward justice. I have seen their kind of justice from close!"

He looked over the man, tattered clothes like himself, soaked and forlorn. They were two of society's rejects. Only, he was an expatriate from another world, someone who could come and go as he pleased, someone with a steady job on the graveyard shift at the local Internal Revenue Service Center, someone who might have a wife and 2.4 kids, a 401(k) plan, and a late-model minivan. He studied the image in his mind, then dismissed it. That was not him. Somehow, sitting in once-again wet clothes beneath the green sky, he felt empathy with this stranger.

"Tell me your story," he spoke finally.

Through the curls of smoke from a clay pipe the stranger wove his tale of desperation: from a simple boyhood in the bucolic forests of Sorêg disrupted by the accidental death of his father by soldiers on patrol and the death a few years later of his mother while gardening, mistaken for a scavenger and cut down by saber, to the life of a state-sponsored student at Sorêg University, focusing on politics with the goal of gaining entry into the local government, all the better to affect change in policy and do away with the annual patrols, with the interference of Selauê, with the controlling claws of Seas—ah! the crops of Sorêg set upon the dining tables of so many administrators in that southern capitol, the meat of Sorêg livestock slathering the dinner plates of so many bureaucrats while peasants dug roots and made do with the hooves and tails of the same beasts that were shipped off to the starving cities, praying for a heavy rain to muddy the roads and halt the train of wagons removing their wealth week by week, year by year, as all the while the youth ran thin and dumb in the streets.

In his third year of study at the university he had met a young woman, another student beginning a satisfying journey through the state's curriculum, blissfully unaware of the true condition of the economy and the laws which permitted the wanton destruction of their Danid way of life. Her name was Basura and she wrote poetry beside the lake, sitting in the thick grasses binding the shore, writing verse which set aside the worries of the world for him one stanza at a time. Sometimes, she would read aloud to him, the two of them side by side in the grass, beneath the shading branches of the trees, the suns warming them, the breeze cooling them, the bird calls reminding them they were one with nature, far away from urban noise and urban grunge and urban terrorism. Then one day she announced she had met a captain of the *Coræsz*, straight up from the Selauê garrison, an educated man who knew something of poetry and appreciated her talent. From that day, she went forth to meet him and returned only in spirit.

The regiment detained him and beat him until he would confess to an act he had not committed, would never consider committing, not given the pure innocence of the victim. Innocence! he laughed. The medic determined she had started a child, and they guessed he was the father. He, a student, would fear fatherhood prior to graduation so it was a motive for murder, to shield something that would ruin his scholarship, something that would bring scandal. So he endured the abuse for weeks, well past the time when it was no longer possible to pull out of him the words he refused to surrender—until it was solely for the amusement of the guards, until they grew weary of him and had him thrown out, bloody and ravaged. Having no school ties following the ordeal, having no family, no occupation, no money to his name nor beast to carry him, he had walked the road down to Selauê seeking justice by his own hand.

The courts were full of guards, he was not surprised to discover, and fearing another vacation in the local garrison he relented and wandered the streets to invent a new plan. That brought him to the wharf, where most vagabonds ended their wanderings, staring out across the harbor at the sea, the swaying green waves soothing: the complaisance of contemplation assuaged all manner of horrors, swept away the past, occasionally encouraged the future, made the present something like a statue that could be examined from all sides, could be walked around, could be frozen in time, a moment in time—

"Gina said that, once upon a time," he muttered despite the stranger's never-ending tale—and he saw it suddenly: the shift of time, the appeal to perfection he had wished for.

History had changed, indeed! Beside him was a man named Diert-Gangus who once was inspired to pursue a curriculum of justice at Sorêg University, a course which would lead him to form a group of students to lead a revolt that would eventually topple the monarchy and set themselves up as the new government: the Council of Five.

"The least I can do is buy you a drink," he spoke up in Ghoupallêan.

They clasped thumbs in agreement and stepped down the wharf. There were many taverns in the area and the second one they found was open to them. The first had refused them entry even after he showed a handful of coins to pay for their drinks. It was the clothing, he knew. And perhaps their smell. So, before they could finish their first drinks, others more easily offended came over to persuade them to remove themselves from the establishment or risk a beating. His companion had enough of that activity and hurried out, and he followed in sympathy.

"I'll need to get you some decent clothes," he announced, pointing toward the shopping district, "so they don't think you're a rebel or terrorist."

"How could I, ragged as I am, ever be mistaken for a rebel or terrorist?" Gangus grunted and stared up at the overcast sky. "True terrorists are clothed in clean, pressed uniforms. Yet no one sees that." He kicked at some dirt on the street, willing it to fly into the gutter. "People see with two eyes, do they not?"

"That Zetin high priest DNT'O-KRA' had three, you know." He chuckled to himself, then added in English, "But he was still so blind."

Chapter 22

Agoraphobia

Escaping from the Selauê of 1460, he did the loopty-loop and returned to 1574 and his desert isle, there to sleep for forty days and nights....

The next afternoon a ship appeared on the horizon and he watched it make its way toward the wharf far below the clifftop house. He estimated it would take another hour to cross the remaining stretch of water so he continued setting up his easel and painting materials. He would appear as a dedicated landscapist for whoever visited him. Painting was an eccentric hobby suitable for his location. Nobody seemed to appreciate that his real business was searching for useful tangents on the island; that could only be the work of a madman.

Through the telescope he saw the colors of the ship's hull: the crimson and powder blue of Selauê, the ship sailed by most visitors to his island. The flag was Selauan, thus an official boat likely bearing official passengers and the usual compliment of crew. There were times when he wished that Aivana and Selauê had never signed a pact of economic cooperation. That made every visit an official one.

Protocol required that crew members remain aboard the ship or on the wharf and not come up to the house. Once the ship docked, he knew there would be a knock on his door after the forty-minute climb up the hairpin trail. No one just happened to visit, no salesmen, no census takers, no wayward strangers asking directions, no soccer moms with broken-down cars asking to use the phone, no street preachers offering to save his soul. It had to be important, so he stepped into the shower and was out and wrapped in a towel well before the knock arrived. He pulled on his fuchsia smock, set his raspberry beret at a suitable angle atop his head, twirled the imaginary moustache, struck a pose and waited.

Soon he heard the visitors' raspy huffing and puffing outside the front door.

"Come in," he called out in casual Ghoupallêan when the knock finally came. He added under his breath, "If you dare," and chuckled.

The door swung open and five men stood there. Four were in uniform, the khaki and crimson of the Selauê military, powder blue caps and epaulets for the naval division. The fifth, the youngest, was wearing blue jeans and a black t-shirt emblazoned with a logo of the Moody Blues, a relic of some rock concert in the late '70s. He was the only visitor not breathing hard from the climb. Instead, the young man looked angry, ready to pounce.

"And you are...?" he asked them, maintaining his pose, brush held aloft, ready to strike the canvas with the first stroke. He decided green would be good.

The ranking uniform, wearing bright yellow chevrons crossing the blue epaulets, stepped forward and greeted him, swinging his peaked cap off his head, bowing stiffly, apologizing for the intrusion and introducing himself and his colleagues. The last of them was the young man, who stepped forward, brusquely cutting off the official introduction—

"He knows me!" the youth impatiently growled in Ghoupallêan with an American accent, glaring at the master of the house.

The ranking uniform was alarmed, moved to hold the youth back.

"You remember me, don't you?" the youth asked in English.

The painter stared a moment, waved off the uniforms.

"You're Chucker, aren't you? Tammy's son. My, how you've grown!"

The youth turned back to his escort. *"Guls dur-parten!"* he growled at them, ordering them to leave but in a rather sarcastic way, making clear with his pronoun usage that they were all inferior to him. Then the youth gave further instructions: they were to wait on the ship until the next morning; if he did not join them by mid-morning, they were to sail back to Selauê and be relieved of their duty.

The commodore nodded his understanding and ushered the others out the door.

"Little rough with them, weren't you?" suggested the host. "What'd they ever do to you?"

"That's not it, Set—or whatever your real name is. Sebastian? You don't look like any Sebastian I ever met. Don't look like a Set, neither."

"Pissed off, are we?" the painter laughed. He set down his brush on the lip of the easel. No painting today, it seemed. It was time to tell a story, instead. Or listen to one.

"If that's the right word for it."

"Relax. Have a seat." He gestured to the wrap-around sofa with the wide view of the sea.

"I came here, all this way," said Chucker as he examined the sofa sections and chose one that seemed firm enough and with a good view. He dropped himself onto it. "Because I can't stand it anymore, can't stand the whole damn thing you and your cronies've got going on here! So I came here to get answers since nobody else'll give me any, none that makes any sense!"

"Calm down." He stepped into the kitchen. "You must be thirsty. *Oxo-ganê?*"

"Water will do. Pure water. If you got any."

"I have everything," he mumbled, scanning the cabinets for a suitable bottle.

He tossed an unopened Aquafina bottle to Chucker who acted surprised.

Set smiled. The truth was simple enough. The island was riddled with tangents, some convenient to convenience stores in Colorado and Connecticut and Calcutta and Cologne and Canberra. He thought there was one that led to Cairo but he had less interest now in finding it, while the Calgary tangent was proving elusive.

Chucker wanted to ask how it was possible but his host cut him off. He demanded that Chucker catch him up on the news from home, from life in Aivana.

All Chucker could say was that his mother was happy and showed no signs of wanting to go home. She continued to move further in the direction of traditional Aivana fashions every year, filling her wardrobe with the light-bending pantaloons and tiny, open vests and filmy blouses—like any harem girl might wear, according to Chucker. He described her in a way that suggested to Set the heroine of that old TV show *I Dream of Jeanie*. Chucker did not like his mother dressing that way, showing off her belly, no matter how big the ruby or diamond or sapphire or *têxodi* was she put in her navel. The populace seemed to notice her gradual transformation into one of them, or into a mocking figurine of Roûê royalty. He felt uncomfortable at official audiences.

His step-dad, on the other hand, was always engaged with some invention. Now he was planning to build a magnificent arch of some kind—like they have in St. Louis. He'd seen pictures of it back when he was in school. In St. Louis, it commemorated the opening of the West. In Aivana, it was to be a memorial to the king who rescued Tammy from Agani Island and subsequently married her, quite a charitable act given that she was visibly pregnant. The arch was supposed to placate the citizenry.

So, yes, the people of Aivana were becoming impatient with the rule of his mom and her husband, two foreigners running quickly through the treasury. There were rumors of plots but Tammy always dismissed them, refusing to believe anyone had anything bad to think of her and her gentle ways. Besides, her blond hair was legendary. It was the feature her late husband admired most. It was always prominently displayed whenever she went out in public or held audience. She fancied herself as some kind of Helen of Troy, whose beauty was the envy of all. Her countenance, with the lustrous blond curls prominently displayed, graced the money of the kingdom and all official correspondence stamps. And Jason's great arch would make them proud and show the world what the kingdom of Aivana could do.

It was hopeless trying to talk sense into them. They could not hear him. It was almost as though the world had changed, everything in it had changed somehow. Except for him. He didn't know where he was or what he was supposed to do. As for the rest of them, Set included, they obviously had been on Ghoupallesz much too long.

"Some of us have been, 'tis true," said Set smugly with a barely visible wink.

He sat across from Chucker, sipped the *gané* and gazed casually out the window: a bright, sunny day, just able to see the prow of the ship jutting out beyond the brown cliff.

"So how long are you staying?" He grinned at Chucker. "I don't mean to be unwelcoming. Surely you were told about me, how I've become eccentric, have strange thoughts, see things that aren't there, make out voices in my head, and generally have a sour disposition toward the world, any world. Hmm? It's mostly correct. On good days, however, I am often—"

"I just want my questions answered!" Chucker exploded, almost desperate. "I hate all the damn run-around. I just want to know things. To know it's real, or not. Then I'll leave. Then I'll get the hell away from this place."

"You don't find my home comfortable?"

"This place means this whole planet."

"Ah, you're resisting a good thing."

"Good thing? You've isolated yourself here like some—like a diseased vagabond hermit. How can you say you need to be here instead of back home on Earth—which *is* your home, after all? You could be crazy anywhere. You could be alone anywhere. So why here?"

He did not take more than a heartbeat to consider his answer: "I'm a god here."

Chucker stared at the man. What was he, forty? forty-five? Hard to tell in this time zone. Yet he had many years of experience, more years on both worlds than he had. But was Set just playing with him or did he know something? But if he were a madman, were any of his answers worth hearing? He stared deeper into his host's eyes, found another world there staring back, of jungles and cliffs, foamy seas and bucolic meadows, icy blue crags and sandy red shores, a city of green glass—

"Are you sure?"

"Pretty sure," responded Set.

They both breathed deeply, ready for a fight.

Then Set mercilessly continued in a voice as bleak as the landscape of his island: "When I'm on this island I'm sure. When I travel to the mainland I need to be careful. In Selauê, for example, I usually wear a disguise so I'm not recognized. Things have changed. I'm safe here because everyone thinks the island is haunted. It's in their legends. So I'm the madman, and nobody bothers me. Except for the curious. And the similarly mad. But that is not very often. And, of course, when I slip back to Earth for supplies. That's always a tricky proposition. A lot could go wrong if I'm not careful. Is that what you're worried about?"

"I don't know."

Chucker shook his head and looked around the room, seeing a room like any family room, any den, in a suburban mansion. Outside would be a curving driveway, out back a swimming pool. Down the street upscale shopping. The reality was a barren landscape, part desert, part sea, part sky. His mind was playing games with his senses.

"I don't know what I'm doing here." Chucker sighed. "I mean, I don't know who I am—here—or anywhere." His eyes sharpened. "You took away my childhood. You said it was like a vacation. Now five years have gone by, or however many they are here. *Here!* Where *is* here? Geez, where are we really? Geez, h-h-how do I get back? Do I wanna go back, or will everything be screwed up? If I go back, I'm an adult but I never learned how to live on Earth."

"You want to go back. Is that it?"

"Yes—no. Maybe. I don't know!"

"It's an easy decision, but there's a ton of related considerations to, umm, consider."

Chucker looked up. "Why did you bring me here?"

"Your mother asked me to bring you. Personal favor. It's not an easy thing, moving back and forth. But I did it for her because she asked me. She said she missed you. She wanted you to join her."

"But *why*?"

"What do you mean *why*? Mothers need their children. Simple."

"I don't think so."

"Oh?"

"I think she wanted me to do something."

"And what's that?"

"I think she had plans for me—"

"All mothers do."

"—for me to do something, something she couldn't do for herself."

"Like what?"

"Like find Michael Fenning."

Set spit out his juice, then frantically wiped it from his smock.

"What?"

"I'm beginning to understand it all. Not all of the pieces are coming together. I need you to fill in the gaps."

"Sure, Chucker. At least, I'll try."

He finished his drink, got up and left the room, saying he needed to change out of his artist garb.

❋ ❋ ❋

Wearing a thread-bare olive-green Bermuda shorts, a coffee-stained beige tanktop from Port Aransas, Texas, and blue flip-flops from K-Mart, he sat comfortably in a vinyl lounger beneath a huge pink parasol on the back deck, the one that faced the black caldera, and listened patiently as Chucker complained about one thing after another. Most of his chatter was about the randomness of his fate and lack of direction among myriad choices. It was the same story, or a similar one, as that which he had told himself long ago. Questions of identity, of purpose, of direction, of *raison-d'être*, the will of God, or everything about the future, the arc of life, the clenched fist of Destiny, the open hand of possibility, and how the consequences of the past play out in the present—the usual stuff.

Watching Chucker ramble on, he noticed how much the youth reminded him of himself, of that precious teenage time when the world was new—when there was only *one* world—and it was in glorious full bloom and he was in the right place at the right time to pick its petals guilt-free. Ah, the summer he and Gina found the tangent! He watched the youth—not that Chucker acted the same manner as he had when he was Chucker's age; only that the youth spoke with the same passion. He recalled that time, one of many, when he had confronted Gina, the love of his life, as he referred to her, trying to persuade her to return with him at the end of their initial adventure through the looking glass of the quarry tangent, and she had given him a dozen reasons to stay but only eleven to return with him. He chose to return, she chose to stay, and though their paths had crossed many times after that, it was at the moment of that first parting, that he had first come to realize the nature of Fate, or Destiny, or the Force, whatever one wished to call it. What was ever truly planned? What was truly random? Where was serendipity in all the minutiae of existence?

"Are you listening?" Chucker asked, a hard edge in his voice.

"Of course," he muttered in reply. Their eyes met. "I am!"

"You seemed to be in some trance, *Doctor* d'Elous."

"No, not a trance. I was admiring you. From afar. From all the way over here in this chair. I was admiring how much you resemble me. Not that I'm suggesting you *should* resemble me. Rather, I see in you the same person I once was. Yes, back when Gina and I first pierced the tangent and emerged unscathed in a brave new world, as it were. I had the same questions, the same complaints as you. I sought answers but there was no one to answer them. We were the first, at least in our circle of Voyagers—we met others eventually, later. But you—you are lucky! You have me to answer your questions."

"My step-dad couldn't."

"He didn't have the same experiences as me. How could he? He had it relatively easy, with everything already explained to him, before he ever went out into the universe."

"You know, he thinks you're insane."

They both paused to listen to their laughter circle around them and plop like pink guano on the deck.

"I probably am," said the man, staring straight into the yellow sun.

"I thought so. But I think my step-dad's insane, too. Keeps busy with his arch plans. Wants to turn Aivana into the land of the Golden Arch. And Mom's always working on some new outfit for her next court audience, pushing the limits of good taste, I think. And me, I think I might be going a little crazy, too."

"Must be genetic, then. Are you worried about that?"

Chucker grunted, shook his head. "I don't want to end up like you."

"Hah! That's what I thought. I mean, that's the thought I've always had: I never wanted to end up like me, either. The way I've ended up—here—now." He rose from the chair with some strain, caught his balance. "I'm not that old. The mirror in the bathroom—the only mirror on the island, I might add—shows me a man in his mid-thirties, but sometimes I feel twice that age. It's something in the air. Or radiation in the soil out on the caldera. I go out there far too often. I feel something affecting me. Perhaps—as you seem to suspect, and fear—I, too, have been here far too long." He stretched in the sunlight. "Ah, glorious! The light of summer, how it bathes my golden skin!"

"You're sunburnt, not golden."

"It's in the eye of the beholder, lad!"

He moved across the deck, robotically, and found the stairs leading down to the rocky soil and the trail heading across the island to the caldera.

"I know I'm at my wit's end living alone upon this barren rock," he muttered. "I can feel the neurons blinking out with every passing day. A day here is like a month back home, right? Feels like it. So I'll be going back soon. I have work to do first. Important work! I need to answer a few questions, and they can only be answered among the rocks and dirt of that caldera. Over there. That one. The big one. See it?"

When he looked at Chucker and saw the youth's puzzled expression, he realized that he had not been pointing to anything and only then did he raise his arm in the direction of the black mound off in the distance.

"See it?"

"Yes, I see it."

"Want to see it up close?"

"Why?"

"To get your questions answered."

"Is that how you do it?" asked Chucker, stepping off the deck.

"Yes, sometimes."

He took a few steps toward the caldera, stopped and looked back. The boy was following him, only he wasn't quite a boy any longer. How much time had passed here? Was he really going insane? *Too many questions!* And never enough answers.

"Today seems a good day to plan tomorrow," said Set-d'Elous with a wave of his hand, "and see what happens, take a good stiff swallow of air, gaze at the back of my head, anything like that, anything at all. Better than being stuck in front of a bad sitcom. Hah! Maybe they'll make a sitcom about you and me. Two guys stuck on another world, making themselves kings. That would be fun. You think?"

They watched the blue and crimson ship set sail back to Selauê, then started out earnestly on their hike.

They ventured back and forth between the house perched on the cliff and the wide caldera where they felt for invisible tangents, even staying overnight at the worksite a few times. No new tangents had been discovered since Chucker joined the operation, but a few moments of each hour were still devoted to questions and answers. Often they were repeats of earlier questions and answers. Clarifications. Chucker was growing tired of the daily routine. He was, however, impressed by the extent to which his host had marked the grid with metal piping and wire and ribbons in a three-dimensional box-like system of lines and intersections that crisscrossed the flat plain and some of the inner slopes of the caldera. It resembled some modern art installation he remembered seeing when he was a kid back on Earth—

Back on Earth! The phrase continued to amuse him. Yet each visit to the caldera was punctuated by the old man's sharp retorts to *Watch your step, Don't go there, Don't touch that* and

Feel the force! He was beginning to hate it all.

On the twenty-first day of Chucker's visit they once again started out for the caldera, packs of supplies hanging from their shoulders as they stepped down from the deck of the house and followed the trail across the volcanic landscape, over a few of the lesser ridges and down into the narrow valley between them that led to a part of the caldera to which he had not yet been.

Suddenly, Set-d'Elous stopped as though walking into a wall and dropped down on his hands and knees, pressing his nose down further toward the black chalky soil.

"What's the matter?" asked Chucker, also stopping and squatting as though they were hiding from enemy snipers on the surrounding ridges.

"Damn ants! These bug-eyed bugs!" his host grunted. "The only indigenous lifeform on this island."

Chucker looked closer and saw the line of insect-things moving with military efficiency across the landscape. He stood.

"So what? They're just ants."

"Ah, you don't understand," the man spoke louder. "They are representative of the powers of the universe, each one of them a cog in the wheel that turns from before the first second of time and will turn after the last second of time. They're not just ants—"

"Whew it stinks out here!" he snorted, at that moment aware of the putrid odor sailing on the breeze, something between the sulfur of hell and the stink of decaying flesh.

The man stood up, still gazing down at the line of ants.

"You don't smell it?" asked Chucker.

"Smell what?"

"It's—"

"Look at these things! I've had run-ins with them before. They always try to steal my lunch."

Chucker saw the man turning to anger.

"Well, sometimes the gods they smile upon you," said the man, raising his foot.

"Stop. Are you going to stomp on them?"

"What? Are you crazy? They'd sooner stomp on me than eat my lunch!"

Chucker grabbed his host's arm, pulled him back from the

line of ants. "What kind of person are you?" He sniffed the air, recoiled in disgust. "Maybe it's the gas leaking. Maybe the gas is making you crazy."

He looked harder and spotted several nearly colorless spouts of gas venting from the soil. The venting was barely visible and rose to the height of his head. He put his hand to his face, covering his nose and mouth.

"Come on, we need to get outta here! There's no wind to clear the gas from this valley. Come on, let's get to higher ground!"

But the older man jerked his arm free and dropped again to his knees. He dug his hands into the black dirt and pulled up two huge handfuls.

"Sometimes the gods smile upon you, my little friends," he sang, his voice full of perverse delight, "but other times, they block your way and sit laughing as they watch you deal with it! Here you go!"

With that, he dropped the dirt down upon the line of ants, forming a new mountain for them to have to find their way around.

Chucker took his arm and pulled him away, dragging him up the slope to where the wind could clear the gas from their nostrils.

"Breathe!" Chucker demanded, slapping the man's face. "Breathe!"

After several minutes of deep breathing, they sat and took in the view of the blue-gray sea stretching out below them.

"Are you okay now?" asked Chucker.

"Yes, I think so." He smiled at Chucker. "Thanks for the slap. I needed that."

"You said the island is haunted, that people go crazy here. I think it's just the gas. It must be poisonous. You spend all your time out here digging in the dirt and breathing in the gas, whatever is in it, and that's affecting your brain. You need to leave this place, Set. You need to get back to society and find something to do. Being a hermit, a crazy one at that, is not any way to endear yourself to anyone. Especially not to Gina."

He snorted, surprised. "Gina? What do you know of her?"

"My step-dad told me all about you and her."

❋ ❋ ❋

Set-d'Elous sat back against the volcanic soil, amused at the playfulness of the yellow sun's light against the distant line of clouds, footsteps across the sky for a pixy or a troop of fireflies.

"The problem with Gina," he began casually, reaching for a stalk of yellow grass emerging from the black dirt and plucking it out, "was the time thing. Eventually it catches up with you and you have to decide where you want to die. That's it. Sorry to make it so blunt, but you need to know." He studied the stalk for a while, as though he could not believe life would ever take root on his island. "You see, when we came through the tangent, that was our first time—if you want to use the sex metaphor. We were teenagers, or barely. I was eighteen, Gina two years older."

The young man smiled, half-amused, half-disgusted. He had been listening to the story of Gina for weeks now, each episode blending with others, each session overlapping with the previous or an explication of an earlier discussion. The man surely was mad. Even so, he could not stop listening. Somewhere in the haystack of crazy ruminations was the golden needle he sought. Not a needle, of course, but a key—one that would unlock tomorrow.

"It was a long haul that first time," the man continued. "We passed through several different worlds and never knew when or how we could get back home. It was frightening—and fascinating. Looking back, however—and I was much too amazed at the time to put it into any kind of scientific perspective—well, that had to be the scariest time of my life. Can you imagine stumbling through an invisible doorway to another world and not knowing how to get back? It's pants-shitting time, my friend! Oh, sure, it happens all the time in those sci-fi movies, what, *Star Wars*, *Star Trek*, Star light star bright whatever I dream tonight—whatever. But imagine—hah, that's the wrong word!—*envision* the experience where you, or any kid, do the same thing: let yourself be sucked through some invisible gelatin and *plop!* there you are in another world. And that's not even considering the physics or biology, the *how's it work?* part of the experience. How is this even happening? Is it something like a wormhole? I heard that term used on an episode of that *Star Trek* show one time when I returned to Earth for visit. Don't believe any of that stuff; those TV shows are just science-fiction, pure make-believe. But, to answer your question, Chucker: no, I don't think this phenomena is any kind of wormhole, just a...umm something else. I don't explain'em, I just use'em. Anyway, the only thing Gina and I could do was keep going, so on we went through several different *tangents*—what we call the interdimensional doorways. So, eventually we found ourselves back in something rather familiar, what we call Ghoupallesz now, our home away from home."

The man began shredding the stalk he'd plucked from the dirt as the youth asked his questions, the usual ones, about how it all works, and the man nodded politely, wearily, as though he had been asked the questions many times before by other wandering youth, already understood everything, and was waiting patiently to give the answers. Then he did:

"I don't know." He laughed and the youth frowned. "Sorry, but I really don't. I know what works for me. That is, I know how to get back and forth, in the right year—or pretty close, hah!—and to know when to leave again. Before I get into too much trouble. Sometimes I prevent trouble. Then I feel good about myself, feel like I deserve something, something special, a treat or reward, like a fine steak dinner or a really good night's sleep. Or my own island—like this one. Remind me later and I'll tell you how I changed history for the good of everyone. That's surely got to be my greatest accomplishment. That's what makes me a god."

The youth held his frown, trying to detect sarcasm in the man's voice yet found none.

"Back to Gina," the man grunted. "She stayed behind when we had the chance to leave. We'd been on Ghoupallesz for a few months. Seemed like enough, so I left. I thought I had more waiting for me on Earth, more opportunities, more dreams to fulfill, than what I could do on Ghoupallesz. Gina picked up the language quickly and was teaching it to me. I still have an accent. But she kept calling me back. Always getting into trouble and expecting me to bail her out. One time, a mutual friend, another so-called Voyager like us named Renée, she gave me a box when

Gina died, some of her belongings. She died of old age. Like a hundred and fifty if she had been on Earth. She chose to stay on Ghoupallesz, so whenever she popped in for a visit it was a physical strain on her, like the cells of her body were about to erupt. She could never stay too long; minutes only. Extreme jet-lag. That's the time thing."

The youth smiled, embarrassed.

"You have to be young to get started with this," Set spoke up after a while. "When I returned, it was still the summer after I graduated from high school. Gina was not interested in returning to college. Heck, I was lucky to get back alive, and in one piece, unhurt, and still sane. I worried about Gina, of course, but life quickly returned to normal. I started college—went on a music scholarship, if you can believe that. However, I stuck to the science classes mostly, trying to understand how all of this business worked, how it was possible."

"And...?"

"None of those classes helped." He sighed. "I could've spent a whole lifetime in grad school, in research labs, devote my whole life to studying those few days abroad. Or I could simply do it again. And again. You see, Chucker, while I was in college, living in the dorm, staying up late studying, I got the itch to explore from time to time. But that tended to get me into trouble from time to time, too. Yep, too curious for my own good. To be a Voyager you have to have a good amount of curiosity—but not too much. When I get too curious I stay too long and I get into trouble. Now I can't go back to Earth, not openly, because I have no friends or allies there. In fact, when I brought your mother here it was...let me think...about 1983. And when I came to get you, it was, I think, about 1986 maybe. I remember it clearly."

"That makes you...what, about forty?"

"I've lost count. Here, I'm ageless." He noticed Chucker inspecting him again, trying to guess his true age. "Back with Gina, our first time, that was August of 1976. After that, I had some other, minor voyages, in the fall, and throughout '77 and '78. Short trips, there and back in a few hours, but several days on Ghoupallesz. They were just for fun—or curiosity—"

"Fun!" Chucker snorted. "Yeah, I get it."

"I'm serious. The time differential was very favorable back

then. So I wanted to figure out how this worked, how it was possible. But I could never get any answer that made sense from a physics or astrological point of view. I did manage to learn something about how it works, how there are different tangents, each leading to different places, even different time periods. And I learned to manipulate them."

"And you did all this while you were going to college?"

"Well, yes. Of course. As best I could." He stared at Chucker, who repressed his laughter. "Even a Voyager needs a good education."

"I suppose so. Don't you think the Socratic method may be more useful for Voyager training?"

"Indeed!"

They laughed.

"So I was taking classes on Earth and once in a while, during a weekend, I would sneak away for a few weeks, just exploring the other dimensions. A few times, Gina visited me, came right into my dorm room or in my family's house. She got me involved in all sorts of nasty business. It became our routine: she'd get into trouble, call me or send someone to get me, and I'd rescue her."

"My step-dad told me some of those. Like when you were in some war in Foixe. Or lived on some island in the northern ocean. And you commanded the whole Sekuatean army in Tebbicousimankalê in 1533—"

"Well, for a week. Then I was relieved of command."

"Still, you've had a shitload of experiences. And you're, what? Forty years old? Something like that."

"And I met a few other Voyagers, too." He cleared his throat, deciding what not to tell. "One of them, that Renée woman, came and got me when Gina finally died. I say 'finally' because she lived many lives on Ghoupallesz. Eventually her body actually reached its end. I got a box of papers, all her notes about everything—history, politics, events, who's who and what's what for the many years of her many lives, plus lists of lovers, husbands, and children, grandchildren, great-grandchildren and so on. I saw some mention of a child she and I would have in what then was going to be my future. It's confusing. We had that child, then Gina left for another new life—took our daughter with her. I returned to Earth. It's all recorded, but she lived them out of sequence. Earth was always the same, time progressing steadily. I knew that when I returned you to your mother, it was the right time, only a few short years before I would be meeting Gina again in Aivana. It's in her diary."

"I see." Chucker's head was bowed, contemplating.

"Then, in 1979, Earth year, I was going for a short research trip but I found a good reason to stay longer. That's when I met Zaura-Matousz—"

"The Love of your Life, as you say!" Chucker exclaimed.

"Yes. Not to be confused with my Long-lost Love, Gina."

"I get it."

And Set-d'Elous talked late into the night about each of his adventures and what he had come to know from such practical experience while maintaining a 4.0 grade-point average in mostly science courses, yet still wrote the neo-Romantic five-movement *Symphony #1 in E minor* as his senior project. He explained to Chucker how the music classes actually helped more with understanding tangents: all about the vibrations implicit in music that affect the tangents: the right vibration loosens the fabric, makes it easier to tear. A good song can make a willing tangent practically fall open at the touch of a probing finger. When he searched the caldera for tangents, he hummed tunes—tunes which had populated his music compositions. He hummed a few of the themes, casually waving his arms like a conductor.

"I get the space shifting," said Chucker, "but I still don't understand the time thing. Like how you can go to different times by going through different tangents. I thought time travel was impossible—except in sci-fi stories."

Set laughed. "Time travel impossible? No. Possible. You see, in the quantum world, light is made up of particles and waves—rather, light can be both particles and waves—and they can travel backwards and forwards through time. Since time and space are one, and therefore since it is possible to travel through space, it is also possible to travel through time. At least as a light particle or light wave. However, one would need quite a massive gravitational force—think of shrinking those two suns up there into something the size of a thumbnail—in order to create a singularity, such as a neutron star or a black hole. Then, the energy force would create a wormhole thing, and a wormhole can link two points in our universe. But not conventionally. I mean, not by bending or warping what we like to call 'spacetime.' If we were able to travel through this wormhole, we could end up anywhere within the universe, or even the other side of it, and at any time throughout spacetime—past, present, or future. Dig? So time travel is indeed possible, in theory, but for us flesh and blood humans, not too likely because of the difficulties in creating wormholes, and then surviving the passage through those wormholes. It could get messy, bloody even."

"Then what about us? What about these invisible doorways you always seem to find?"

"That is a total mystery. As far as I know I am the only one to write about them."

"But you wrote about them in Ghoupallêan!"

"Of course."

"Not English?"

"It's the Ghoupalle people who need to know about it, not the Americans."

"Why them? You want them to be able to infiltrate Earth? That could mess us up."

"You and I will not be there, so nothing to worry about. You and I will be here, most likely, living our lives out in peace and prosperity. And because we arrived with an Earthling cell structure, that is, we came from a slower planet to a faster planet, we will seem to live much longer than the local folks."

"So we live longer here? How old?"

"Our eighty or ninety years would last us about three hundred of these spins on Ghoupallesz. See, we keep the timeline of the place of our birth." He looked away, enjoying the colorful dawn crackling across the seascape. "Doesn't that make sense? Our cells are created on Earth and are wound up in Earth time. When we go to Ghoupallesz we are still living on Earth time biologically. These locals, the Ghoupalles, on the other hand, have their own timescale. They live upwards of a hundred and seventy years—*their* years, their planet's years, orbits, that is. It seems to work out between us, though. We meet them, marry them, we age slowly and they age at the usual speed for them. Soon it's time to move on. That's what Gina did—a lot! Eventually she realized that if she did return to Earth she would 'pop' to her true Earth age and die on the spot. I don't think that would've happened, but back then we believed it."

"I think I understand." Chucker gazed in fascination at the master. "I'm like you: young and wild, ready to experiment, prepared for anything, free and not tied down to anything, no family, no school, no job, no—"

"Eventually, I started working at the Internal Revenue Service's regional service center in Kansas City, and—"

"You met my mom and—"

"The rest is history."

"Yeah, history." Chucker stopped, as though he were catching his breath. "But here you are. Here we both are."

"This is my home now. Look around. I have my island, my house, all of my records and documents. Your step-dad even built me a stereo music player to play my 8-track tapes on. I have everything I need here. I even have something to do each day: exploring this caldera, looking for more tangents. It's a life. Granted, it's not for everyone. I do some reading. I write about my adventures on Ghoupallesz. Not much happens here, I'll admit. I do have interesting visitors once in a while. My psychiatrist visited once not too long time ago. At least I thought she did. What was it, a year? ...maybe two, can't be sure. I seem to be getting old despite myself."

"I don't know what's waiting for me back on Earth," Chucker spoke, just as the Master seemed ready to speak again. "You took me away from there before I even had a chance to learn anything, or make any plans, or live any kind of life. I never had a choice. You took that choice away from me."

"Choices are overrated," the old man snickered, waving the air like they were enveloped in a cloud of smoke. The air quickly cleared in his imagination though he could still smell the burnt umber of his words. "Isn't it better to have one well-defined path? Like these damn ants that always crawl across the island? What good are choices? They only confuse us."

"But *you* chose!"

"Hah! Is that what you think?" He sighed. "The truth? I've never made a decision in my life! Never made a choice.

Everything has been pre-determined for me. By Fate, or by the swirling of neurons in my brain, or the chemical compounds of everything I eat, drink, smoke, or breathe in. I have never made a choice."

"Yes, you have! My step-dad said so."

"What's that?" He shook his head. "Don't believe half the things he tells you—and no more than four-fifths of what he tells you about me."

"He said you made a choice for millions of people here. He said you decided, on your own, what millions of people would do. You gave them no choice. You just did it, fixed it for them. Like you were God."

He closed his eyes, seeing the world within, holding his breath for a moment.

"Like I was God?" he mumbled. "You must be referring to the little incident up in Sorêg. It was a small matter, not anything god-like. I simply met the right person at the right time and removed that person from history in order to prevent a war. That has to be a good deed."

"You don't know that. You don't know what happened."

Set opened his eyes, trained them on the kid. "I checked everything—before, during, and after. Look at the calendar. No war. No revolution. Everything has gone on without mishap. I did not make a choice for millions of people so much as I made a choice for *myself* and by doing so it happened to also *save* those millions of people. So don't lecture me on choices. The Archives in Selauê confirmed that I made the right choice."

"And Michael Fenning?"

Set-d'Elous squinted at Chucker, wondering how his former IRS co-worker fit into the discussion. He expelled a loud sigh.

"What about him? Did you find him?" he asked Chucker. "You thought your mother wanted you brought here to find him and deal with him. Did you?"

Chucker chewed his lip, realizing he did not want to go down that path. "But you brought him here first. That was a choice you made. Him, too. And because he was here, where he wasn't supposed to be, a lot of people got hurt by him."

"That may be true. But the acts were his, not mine. Those women may well have met other unscrupulous cads in the course of their lives. One cannot predict what will happen to them if I had not suggested to Michael that he accompany me to the Dream Land for medical treatment—"

"That's it! Listen to yourself!" Chucker shouted, jumping up. "You cannot predict what'll happen. You just said so!"

"In that case—"

"Everything looks good in the Archives today but what about tomorrow? next year? a hundred years from now? What have you started? Where will it lead?"

"Well, I—"

"It's just like you coming to get me, to bring me back to Mom. Nobody asked *me*! You never said I'd be stuck here for years, maybe never get back. And if I could ever get back what would I do? I don't know anything. I can't do anything. It's all passed me! I have no future there! You took me here and just left me. Now my future's passed. What the hell were you thinking?"

* * *

Two stars twinkled in the western sky as the last of the sunlight blazed sadly from below the horizon. The wind blew steady from the north, bringing a rare chill to the island. Despite the chill, the *Mexas* sat on the front deck, watching the sea blacken with the dusk, sipping the bitter olive-green *yvo-ganê* and taking his time.

"You look sad tonight," remarked Chucker.

The man looked up, then raised the bottle to his lips and took another swig of *ganê*, studying the stars.

"Hey, look, man," said Chucker, "I'm sorry I blew up like that the other day."

The man took another sip, swirled it in his mouth, swallowed slowly.

"I came here to get answers," Chucker continued after a while. He sat down on a wooden chair across from his mentor. "I just want to know what I'm getting into if I stay a member of your club."

The man chuckled, acted as though he were trying to hide his amusement.

"Club?"

The youth wanted to take it back but decided to press on: "I know it's not a club, no membership dues, no rules—except the ones the universe imposes—but think about what you and the others have been doing here."

"I have...."

Chucker expected more, perhaps another lecture, but time was loud so he let it pass.

"What you did was criminal," said Chucker calmly. "Playing God is criminal. You don't know what will happen if you—even if you step on a few annoying ants. You might trigger something truly evil, truly grand, like a giant species of ant bent on the consumption of all human life here—"

"I saw something like that when I was a kid," said the man. "Back on Earth."

The youth shook his head. "On Earth!"

"The movie was called *Them!* Giant ants in the sewers of Los Angeles. Blew them up in the end to keep the queen from flying off and starting colonies across the country."

The youth stood, perturbed, went to the railing to watch the sea. He saw the sky reflected there, and turned, pushed his backside against the rail and tilted his head upward.

They studied the stars a while longer, the new constellations brightening in the night sky, the light of the suns now lost below the horizon.

The breeze blew colder.

"On Earth, spring is coming," said the youth.

"Here winter dawns," the man responded, then lifted the bottle once more and finished off the final portion of *ganê*.

"All I'm saying is that if you are going to go around changing things, there has to be some way of checking that what you change will be good," said Chucker. "I mean, a way to see that everything will work out okay."

"I check the Archives."

"The Archives! In Selauê? It's not infallible. They don't have *your* story right, do they?"

"Infallible? Where'd you learn to talk like that?"

"I read your damn book. You use the word a lot. Especially in the chapter about how you saved the world by killing Basura-

266

Kanoun. That could be a best-seller here. *If* you could ever get it published. But they'd string you up if they found you—"

"That's why I have my island."

"Damn your island!"

"It's a beautiful place. It's—"

A meteor lit the sky, streaking from Zetinê in the north to Aivana in the south, a measure of the journey of Set-d'Elous from ice and snow to desert sands, and a warning, a challenge to the youth.

"Never saw that before," said the man.

"Not even on Earth," the youth added.

They watched until it flamed out below the horizon.

"One of those things hits here, we're all done," Chucker muttered.

"It will happen," Set responded. "It is predicted in the religious texts. I read it in Selauê. The sky will fall and only the few brave Ghoupalles, the righteous or the rich, will survive."

"How?"

"They will escape through a tangent on Little Biznuik Island."

Chucker stared at him. "Here?"

The madman nodded, staring at the horizon. Chucker shifted his gaze to the point where the light had flamed out, then back at his mentor. "And then what happens?"

"We live happily ever after. Somewhere else."

"Good morning," said Chucker in a sullen voice. "Looks like you fell asleep out here. And I'm not the sort to carry you in to the bed."

The man stretched his arms and legs. "I'll survive." He sat up and rubbed his back. He cleared his throat, spit off the deck to the sea far below. "It wouldn't be the first time I fell asleep out here."

Chucker breathed deeply. "We should get going now."

"Going?" The man stood up, shakily, caught his balance and once again stretched his limbs. "Where?"

"I came to get you," said Chucker. "To bring you back to

Aivana. Don't you remember?"

"What're you talking about?" He stepped into the house.

Chucker followed. "You promised to come back with me and talk some sense into my mom and dad."

The man pulled a Dr Pepper bottle out of the fridge, popped the cap, drank.

"Remember?" asked Chucker.

"You never shut up."

"My mom's going crazy dressing like a harem girl and my dad's building this giant arch. You promised to help me get them to stop. In fact, we all need to get out of Aivana before they decide they don't want foreigners ruling—"

"I thought you came here to get all your questions answered."

"Questions?" Chucker shrieked, throwing his arms in the air, waving them as though he was pointing to questions stacked here and there. "What questions?"

"You came here with a bellyful of questions, crying how I took your childhood away, how you don't know anything, you don't know what to do with your life. To answer your questions I showed you my tangents. Then you get me drunk and pretend you came here to bring me back to Aivana. And for what? You want me to do what you need to do for yourself. Talk to them yourself!"

He stomped away, entered the bedroom.

"I may be a fool, but you have not fooled me," he called.

Chucker heard the shower running.

When Set returned, fully dressed in his explorer clothes, Chucker had breakfast ready: eight *sängi* eggs and some leftover *gab* meat. The bluish eggs with their white yolks from the blue-backed seagulls and the orange strips from the large sea snail they caught the day before made a colorful meal. Chucker added a few sprigs of *uark* and *fressel* leaves to add dark green and bright yellow. His mentor would be impressed. His mentor might finally be in the right mood to hear a confession. Four months to work up to this!

As his mentor ate, Chucker thought back to that night, the hour he spent in the room at the clinic, standing beside the bed where Michael Fenning lay. He never told his step-father any of their conversation, or revealed the bastard's fate. He had kept it secret for two years, until he was able to come to this island and confront the man who had brought him to Ghoupallesz.

Set-d'Elous sat back from the breakfast table, contented, complimenting the chef.

"And then what happened?"

"Sorry?" Chucker realized he had been speaking, telling his story.

"After you found the clinic, what happened?"

Chucker froze, then began clearing the dishes from the table. With his back turned, standing at the basin washing the dishes, he could feel a weight about to slide off his shoulders.

"I didn't kill him, if that's what you want to know."

"You didn't?"

The man waited for the next dish to be washed.

"So he was there?"

"Yes."

"Terminal?"

"Very."

"So you just let him rot in his bed?"

He took a cup and filled it with the coffee-like drink Chucker had prepared, added a few drops of Ghoupallean green honey, stirred slowly.

"Well, I suppose that would be more fitting: just let the disease finish him off. That leaves you free of guilt."

Chucker turned. "That's not what happened."

"What, then?"

He watched the youth tightly gripping the plate.

"Did you change history?"

Chucker broke the dish against the side of the basin. "No!"

"Tell me what happened and I won't charge you for the plate."

The youth seemed to be fighting tears. He took a deep breath.

"He killed himself."

Chucker took another deep breath, awaiting a response but getting none.

"Really!" Set snorted after a moment for it to sink in. "That doesn't sound like Michael. But—" He thought for a moment. "— he was probably in a lot of pain."

"I searched for three years. I played it out in my mind a hundred times. What I would say, how he would react. I was ready. When I walked into that room, smelled the stench of his rotting disease, I wanted to leave. But he woke up and we talked. Of course, he was sorry. For everything. I expected that. And he was in pain. He begged me to kill him, put him out of his misery. I thought of doing it, had my hand on the XG pistol. Then I thought a better revenge would be to let the disease continue to rot him. But the pistol was in my hand, fireplug charged, and...."

Set stood up and went to the youth. He faced Chucker, stared into his eyes.

"Is Michael Fenning my father?" asked Chucker.

The words seemed to circle the planet and hover for a while in a storm cloud near the island. The winds picked up.

"Did he say that?" Set shook his head. "Michael Fenning is definitely not your father. If he told you that it's probably his attempt at some connection. Maybe he thought it would keep you from killing him. Or, since he wanted you to kill him, maybe he thought it would push you over the edge and you'd pull the trigger. Who knows?"

The man stepped away, surveyed the sea below.

"Your mother told me your father is a man named Chuck, a policeman. I met him, though the circumstances were—"

"You met him? When?"

"Few years ago. And you look just like him."

"I do?"

The man chuckled. "Well, I'm no judge of masculine beauty but I can say you have the same features as Chuck senior. Your mother will confirm that."

"Tell me how you met him."

"Well, that would be a story for another time. Suffice to say, he does not like me, nor did he appreciate my unique situation. Rather, he vowed to pursue me to the ends of the Earth. Ah, yes! Of Earth. And he followed me to it! He never expected that *at* the end of the Earth there would be a doorway leading to another world."

"What? He followed you here?"

The man laughed, then fell quiet. "He's probably around somewhere. I told him to go back the way he came, but knowing his brand of stubbornness, he probably kept following me. Most likely he ran afoul of the locals who pride themselves in not wasting anything they come upon in the desert. He—"

"You left him out in the desert?"

"Questions!"

Set-d'Elous waved him silent, then stormed out of the room. Chucker followed slowly and saw that his host had stepped into the bedroom and was changing clothes again, something more formal.

"I did not leave him in the desert," the man called back. "I went to the quarry tangent, just as you and I did, and I went through it to the desert. He followed. I told him to go back. He didn't. I went ahead, through the desert, until I wasn't in the desert any longer. He tried to follow me, I'll bet, and inevitably he got lost. I did try to send him back through the tangent. It was right there, no more than a half-mile back. I told him to follow our tracks, but knowing him...."

After a few minutes the man returned with an old K-Mart duffle bag in his hand and began quickly stuffing clothing and other items into it as he went from room to room. When Chucker inquired about his activity, he was told they would shortly be leaving the island. There were things that needed to be done, thoughts corrected, pages rewritten, people convinced, and apologies made, said the man. They had work to do. Hah! Not a Youth Trek but an Adult Trek, something necessary before the youth could advance to full Voyager status.

"Just like that?" asked Chucker. "After all this time you decide it's time to go?"

The man grinned, a little to the evil side. "Yes, just like that. It happens that way on this island." He stood straight and took a breath. "You're right: I've been here too long. Time to see the world. Pack up, dear master Chucker. We're sailing for Aivana!"

Chucker stared at him, puzzled.

"But the ship left months ago. How will you contact them to pick us up?"

He stopped his stuffing. "It's a figure of speech."

"What is?"

"Sailing."

When they were packed, they started off across the flat dusty plain that led to the opposite coast. He had never been that way but he remembered Set saying it was the way to go home, whatever that meant. The man seemed in a hurry, as though he had to catch a train, and the youth struggled to keep up, carrying the larger bag.

It was a brisk hike for more than five *peth*—almost two hours—mostly across the plain but across the occasional rocky gorge or over a sandy ridge, too, feeling strange pressures against his body at regular intervals. They passed through a desert of red cacti that could not have been on the same island, then further, along the shore of a dark, muddy, caustic-fuming lake that seemed to be in a more northern clime than their island—"Better cover your nose," Set-d'Elous suggested—until finally they arrived at a great sandy plain, flat as a sheet of paper. A distant flag waved in a slight breeze. When they reached the spot where the red triangular flag flapped atop a white fiberglass pole, Chucker saw that it was the kind of flag used to mark the holes on a golf course.

"Are we playing golf?"

The man laughed. "No, today we're playing through."

And suddenly, with gentle prodding from an experienced Voyager's sensitive fingers, the air thickened and separated right where the flag stood. Through the gap, Chucker could see the line of sand that formed the high dunes outside of Aivana.

Set-d'Elous held the tangent open like a curtain leading him on-stage and nodded for him to enter. Chucker stepped through, not altogether comfortable with the effort but willing to believe whatever the man told him. Proof was in his eyes now. Set followed him through the tangent and the invisible, gelatinous air closed behind them.

In the distance rose the pennant-topped spires of the great palace in Aivana, all twenty-two of them. And towering over them stood the infamous golden arch, two-thirds finished. The top was under construction, a mountain of scaffolding built beneath the gap. Beyond were the coastal mountains, and further on was the fading, misty line of jagged memories of another time, another place.

Chucker instinctively snorted, realizing his host could have taken him home at any time. He guessed now it would take only about two *peth* more to reach the city—the same time, Chucker calculated, that it would have taken for the decrepit Michael

Fenning to die once he summoned a final reserve of strength to grasp the pistol that Chucker had offered. Before the trigger could be pulled, however, Chucker had fled the room and fled the clinic—in much the same way he had fled the innocence of youth.

Chapter 23

On the Future Not Being What it Used to Be

The rough-hewn man of indeterminate age pleaded his case in the cozy, stifling room. He seemed at first to be seeking them. Then, when brought to the woman, he turned fearful. She quizzed him to determine his authenticity, his true identity, and he spoke rapidly in his defense, desperate for her to believe him.

"You probably don't remember much of those years, but I do," he said in rough Ghoupallêan. "I remember everything! How could anyone forget the snowfields of Tebbicousimankalê? Or that accursèd year? Men living beneath the snow, crawling through snow tunnels, rising up to spot the enemy, scramble away to escape—like snow moles! Men dying in their sleep, already buried! The frostbite, the peg legs when they cut off the frozen ends, footless in the daylight, handless arms! The glassy skin, green veined, eyeballs cracked open! Tongues frozen straight out, teeth broken off, noses cold-rotted down to bare cartilage! And the Zetin skinning the dead for the warmth the human leather could provide! I saw all of it in the snowfields of Tebbicousimankalê! I was there, and I lived through it. Look! I got only eight of my fingers—and six of my toes. The others froze and fell off! I was there! And I've got my orders somewhere here—wait a moment and I'll dig them out of my bag."

"That isn't necessary," the middle-aged woman with dirt-blonde hair spoke firmly in the same language.

He noticed her hair color, a rarity especially in this desert land of black heads.

"I've got it here, somewhere," he said, checking each pocket.

The man looked up, almost daring them to go ahead and make him produce the wrinkled parchment bearing his military orders. He had obviously had a difficult life, looked older than he probably was, but he did not strike anyone as an ex-soldier.

"I only need you to answer one more question," said the woman, and he was happy to listen to her, gaze at her kind face and warm smile.

The man closed his pack, relaxed. "Yes? What is it?"

"Who told you about the snowfields?"

The man choked. "What? I told you I was there. What do you mean?"

"I doubt you were there." She gazed into his bloodshot eyes. "Someone must have told you about it."

"No one told me! I lived it!"

"I don't think so."

The guards took the man by his arms and lifted him from the chair. He cried out that he was not lying.

"Someone must have told you," she said, standing, "because the snowfields never happened."

She walked behind him, leaned close to his ear.

"Surprised?"

He shook his head, insistent to the end.

"I should know: my husband is a historian," she spoke, then laughed. "It is a common myth many older people have. They think they remember hearing of a war in the north, a story told by minstrels, or something they read in one of those fiction books. An interesting tale, certainly, but not history. Not the truth."

She glared at the haggard man, fear in his face.

"There was no war in Tebbicousimankalê. It is not mentioned in any recent history book, so you could not have read about it. And since there were no veterans from this imaginary war, there would be no one to tell you of it. You are quite mistaken. Many people are; it is a kind of mass hysteria. People of a certain age catch it and the syndrome affects the brain in the same way—always a memory of a war that never happened. Never happened! The armies of the Sekuatean Empire never invaded Tebbicousimankalê. Not in 1530, not in any year. It's been nearly fifty years now, and we have yet to find proof. There never was a siege of Siaa, no battle of the snowfields, no Zetin mercenaries, no hasty treaty between arch-enemies Tebbis and Zetin, and no Zetin hostage from the Tebbi *Ghêrata*—thus, no dramatic, last-minute rescue by the notorious Set-d'Elous, and no retreat across the Tebbi peninsula, no surrender in—"

"Set-d'Elous?" the man shrieked. He broke free of the guards' grip. "Him! My Lady, it was him who told me all about the snowfields! It was Set-d'Elous—and *he* lived through it! I swear. He told me he was there. It was all true!"

"You are a silly man. A desperate man who will say anything to save himself."

"No, My Lady! I speak the truth!"

The woman could not fully hide her smirk. What a fool this man was! Invoking the name of her former lover certainly was not the best strategy to impress her.

"Set-d'Elous, as everyone knows," she spoke in the strange, lilting language no one in the hot room could understood, "is just a legend, a rather poor one at that. He is a myth. A mystery wrapped in a tortilla." She chuckled, seeing everyone's reaction to her English words. "Something invented to scare naughty children at night."

Then she continued in perfect Ghoupallêan, the language they all knew and had been using since they first met and formed their group:

"*Gul-se, Set-d'Elous logaën-ke?*" She half-grinned. 'So you know Set-d'Elous?'

"Yes, My Lady."

"How do you know Set-d'Elous?" she asked, gesturing for him to sit.

"Why, why, h-he's my g-grandfather! I sat on his knee many times and he told me of the wars, all about the wars. Then he went away. Like I told you many times, I am Latol-Rog-Matousz, son of Set-Matousz, the Sekuatean general. But I'm here seeking my daughter, Seasö. Yet I remember my father telling me about the snowfields and the war, the winter of 1533, and the Great

War against the Northern Alliance, and the bitter cold retreat. And he told me his father, Set-d'Elous, was the *Berron*, in charge of the whole army, all of the armies—"

"For, like, three days," the woman laughed.

"Yes! Three days! That's what he said!"

"And there never was any Sekuatean general named Set-Matousz. A myth only."

Set-Matousz, she recalled from somewhere, had resigned from the Sekuatean military, retiring to the Ghoupallæssus, where he wrote a fictional account of the wars. The woman shook her head, remembering another Set: Set-d'Elous, from another time, another place—trying to forget the last time they had been together. The year or so in Kipzon after he rescued her from the Zetin high priest Ut'r-Bkann was a time of tension; she had to leave. So she took their daughter and left for a new life in a new time and place. Several of those passed before she found herself with Iadon-Repraxa in Typeg in the autumn of 1571.

And now, three years later, this scruffy mercenary-wannabe pulls Set-d'Elous so easily from her memories!

"He is dead now, I presume," the man sighed. "I have not heard from him for more than forty years, so I—"

"Let him go," said the woman brusquely to the guards. "He's no threat to us." She gave a hand helping him out of the chair. "No help, either. We need someone who is not related to—I mean, someone who will tell no lies."

The guards ushered the man out the door, gave him a small bag of coins, and sent him disappointedly on his way.

The shadows shifted with the afternoon sunlight and the muscular man sitting on a wooden stool in the corner of the adobe house rose like a mushroom cloud and glared at the woman. He crossed his arms, tattoos of flies and black snakes covering his forearms, hideous toothy fish and scaly red lizards adorning his chest and shoulders, balanced by a woman's gentle face drawn upon his belly peeking through his unbuttoned leather vest. He slid the scabbard back on his belt, the handle of his knife poking his rib, and tilted his head to one side, his long narrow black beard neatly braided in Typeg fashion, dark eyes somehow darker.

"So what is the plan now?" he asked the woman gruffly.

She, in the pale green pantaloons and blue vest of Aivana, her breasts pushing tightly against the fabric, golden hair curled atop her head but in the heat starting to slip, turned slowly and struck a defiant pose.

"The plan is the same as it's always been, Iadon-Repraxa."

Teeth almost clenched, she glared back at him: the man she had been with for six years, with whom she had a daughter, Lirêa, with whom she had planned and plotted to make the world right—he was beginning to get on her nerves.

"You doubt our plan?"

He frowned. "I meant, is the timetable the same?"

"There is no reason to delay. The city is ready."

"Yes, Jinetta, the people are ready for change. Big changes. They will thank us for restoring Aivana. It has been long enough these foreign sandcrabs are in charge. And that stupid arch—"

"Be careful!"

"It is a symbol of their oppression. That is the reason we will destroy it, too."

"I rather like it," said Gina. She placed her hand on Iadon's shoulder. "It reminds me of my homeland. There was an arch in the city where I went for university studies"—and she thought of that warm August night when she and that curious, hyper-romantic boy from high school had first found the tear in the tangent that led them to Ghoupallesz. A warm sensation spread outwardly from her heart, a whimsical feeling she had not felt for many years.

Where could he possibly be now? She was willing to entertain the thought even with her jealous lover standing so close.

＊ ❋ ＊

The snow fields of Tebbicousimankalê in 1533 would be frozen in his mind for the rest of his life, Set-d'Elous knew, no matter where he spent that life. He had survived it. Kept all of his toes and fingers, too. He knew he'd been there and he had survived it.

Then why...?

He stared at the wall poster, at the endless names in neat columns, arranged not in alphabetical order or by any other logical pattern. It had to be listed, though.

Sure, it was easy enough to return the boy to his mother, he thought as his eyes ran down each column of names. But once Chucker was sent to school, held captive by his circle of tutors and sentenced to daily studies in preparation for becoming a prince of Aivana, his mentor, the old man on the old island, had little to do.

Dinners with his friend, Jason, were not the same. His friend had lost weight, now watched his diet, and their conversation had turned utilitarian rather than the back-and-forth verbal rumble he had always enjoyed. His friend talked about nothing but the great arch: the arch in Saint Louis, Missouri, on Earth stood 300 feet, but his new arch would stand 400 feet! Jason was quite proud of his engineering ability—until his guest had pointed out that the two rising towers might not quite come together but would be out of alignment. Jason had slapped the dining table, knocking dishes off the edge. The maidens had scrambled to clean up the mess, but Jason, Consort of the Queen, stomped out of the room before dessert could be served.

So Set-d'Elous wandered about the city, visited some parks, hiked to the top of the hills surrounding the city, hills which kept the desert from overwhelming the coastal plain, and gazed out at the sea of sand extending eastward to the distant horizon. There was nothing of interest for him in that direction. Except, perhaps, Gina, his Long-lost Love.

Nothing to do. So he left, took the KOHax to Lyas then Seas, then Selauê, where he finally felt comfortable. Yet not too comfortable. Everything looked the same but did not feel right.

He walked the streets near the garrison, stopped to read the bulletins posted on the reading walls and while scanning the pages overheard a couple of young men discussing the Wiseman of Little Biznuik, a hermit who supposedly knew the future. He thought that was what they said. It could be the breeze and the noise of the traffic on the boulevard which interfered with his hearing. Nobody could visit the island, they continued, because it was forbidden. Nobody would want to go anyway because of the poison gasses.

"Certainly it must be the doorway to hell," said one to the other, using the word *Ur-tha* for hell.

Earth, he silently translated in his head.

"Demons will strike down any visitor," said the other.

"Yet a ship sails for the island every few months."

"There must be a conspiracy involving the island."

"A weapons stockpile perhaps?"

"Savage experiments?"

"Building a secure prison for those rebels, I think."

He knew the truth, of course. A madman lived there. Such a madman must have been exiled there. If nobody would dare go there, then it must be a place of punishment. And he, needing punishment, was the perfect prisoner for the island. He could be safely out of reach, out of the way. It was no different than if he had been locked up in some mental hospital on Earth. Escaping the island was the same as escaping from the asylum—night, a cop, yellow Camaro, a chase, quarry, tangent, desert—

Am I really standing on this boulevard in Selauê so many years after that despicable act up in Sorêg?

He was looking for a sign. Certainly there would be news—news of a war, revolution, police action, disturbance, movement of people, adjustment of boundaries, the raising of armies, manufacture of weaponry, drilling of troops, songs, speeches, shiny uniform buttons and kisses goodbye—

There!

The name appeared out of the mass of text, almost boldfaced to his disbelieving eyes. He stared a moment to be sure he was actually seeing what he thought he was seeing. He glanced back over his shoulder, to the right, to the left, returned his gaze forward. Then he looked around again. He waited until the people nearby had finished reading and walked away. He stared once more, stepped closer, stared harder.

The first name at the top of the first column, the first name of the entire list of tens of thousands of names was his:

SET-D'ELOUS: SERPAN-3.

There was no name before his.

The date of his death, not surprisingly, was the day he had disappeared from Sorêg. It was the same day he had walked so innocently into the woods and met Basura-Kanoun one last time. The day he killed her—the day he *had* to kill her.

His escorts had left him on the road, he recalled. Strange. It was almost as though he was meant to follow through with his plan.

There he was: the first name on the martyr's wall!

When his body was not found, the military operation had commenced. He had managed to watch from behind a hay wagon, dressed in rugged civilian garb, as the soldiers went house to house, knocking on doors, kicking doors open, pulling people out into the street, searching for the killer of *Serpan* Set-d'Elous and the girl from Sorêg university. Rebels had killed the cavalry captain and his lover, and the government had stepped in to restore order, to exact justice, to fight against the fervent nationalism that for several years had been boiling in the taverns and side streets, unseen by officials, hidden to the government until that day.

But there was no war. Nothing pointed to such a grand massing of people and materiel. The Sarrêban family remained in power. They had not even invaded Aivana, had not annexed those marginal territories, a long-held political ambition. All that had occurred was a police action in the northern districts. The Danid were hurt, he guessed from what he read, but there had been no war. No revolution or civil war. And no invasion of the Tebbicousimankalê peninsula, no winter-long siege of Siaa, no snowfields of death—

Had he never been involved in that now? Had those events disappeared even within his own history, in his own life?

He still had the scar from the Zetin warlord's dagger, now had the urge to check it.

Perhaps everything was going to work out fine. Perhaps he had saved those millions of people he did not know and, among them, his own kin, his own flesh and blood, his family: Zaura-Matousz and their sons and daughters, all of their grandchildren, and their grandchildren, and so on, the entire line of his seed.

He smiled, stepping back from the poster, only then breaking his gaze from the first name on the list of those who had died in the cause of freedom.

✳ ❉ ✳

Sunlight breached the windows, filled the sitting room with warm, green light, as the occupant of the adobe flat stood from where he sat on the carpet and went to survey the afternoon city. The laughter of children echoed through the streets, and the occasional bay of a beast or caw of a bird only added to his realization of a new life in a new world. Soon his partner would return and they would sit down and enjoy the dinner he was about to prepare.

Ah, domestic tranquility, sighed Chuck McElroy.

He opened the shutters on the windows and felt the hot breath of the Aivana desert burn his face. He was used to it now. A year in the desert, lead around on a rope, naked like an animal, skin burned to leather, feet blistered and broken, abused slave to a band of nomadic cannibals! Then he met the Good One—who was not like the others. When the situation was most dire, he had saved him; he stitched up the Good One and carried him to civilization.

"Godwin!" he called from the windows, seeing his partner walking quickly down the lane.

"Chi'yok!" called the Roué, trying to pronounce Chuck's name as best he could.

Though each had tried to learn some of the other's language, they had instead taken some Roué and some English and fashioned their own mutually understandable language. The neighbors delighted listening to the strange words wagging between them. And though they were the odd couple, Chuck never had any troubles when he went out to buy food or to conduct other business. He was a source of amusement for the townsfolk, naturally, so no one wished him harm lest they lose their entertainment.

When Godwin arrived in the doorway, Chuck greeted him and they hugged, then each told about his day. Chuck finished preparing the dinner as they chatted and Godwin helped serve it. They ate happily and drank the *gor*, talking until it was time to retire to the *qala* for the night.

The annual festival of something was coming soon in Aivana,

Godwin told him. It was a special time, when the royal family would hold an audience with the people and grant them favors, settle conflicts, and assure everyone of the continued prosperity of the kingdom. They should go, Godwin insisted. After all, that trip was what had saved Chuck from the nomads' wrath. They thought he was something special to the queen, and they would be rewarded for returning him.

Godwin reminded him Aivana was where *Alebafe* lived.

"Si'yo ne'm Tami'su'o," said Godwin. No one but Chuck could decipher what Godwin had said: 'She name Tammy Sue.'

If they left in the morning they could arrive in time, Godwin added.

Chuck tried to explain that he was no longer sure he wanted to meet his ex-wife, not under the circumstances that had brought him to this place. He imagined that encounter: she would ask how he came to be in...what had that psycho dude called it? the Dream Land?...and how he ended up with his Roûê partner. He did not want her to be amused at how her tough ex-husband had changed so much.

On the other hand, it might be fun to see the expression on her face when he stepped into the Great Hall and called to her.

He laughed.

"U'at souf an'ni?" asked Godwin, unsure whether or not he was the butt of the joke. He watched Chuck's face.

"'What's so funny'? Is that what you asked?" asked Chuck with a grin. "I can almost understand you, Godwin."

"Good fo'u Godwin," he chuckled.

"No, say 'Good for me,'" Chuck gently corrected.

"Good fo'e'mi," his partner responded.

After an hour's discussion, they agreed to travel to Aivana to see Alebafe. It had been more than three years, after all. At first he could not bear to have Tammy see him ragged and broken as a slave to Roûê traders. Then he simply did not need her. Sure, he was curious from time to time, but that passed with the business of everyday life. Godwin offered the same arguments and Chuck countered with the same responses. There was no longer a need to see her, no reason to let her see him.

Godwin had a reason to go to Aivana, he said. His family members were gathering there because of the festival and he wished to introduce Chuck to them.

"No kidding," said Chuck, feeling a bit embarrassed.

"Verri verri portan'de," said Godwin.

"Well, if you need to have a family reunion, I suppose I'll go meet the queen."

"Tanx duyu," said Godwin, clapping Chuck's shoulder.

Chuck smiled, but inside he felt something strange, something his police sense would not let go. Godwin spent more and more time away from their home and returned later and later. He was working, he said, always working: working hard to pay for the things he and his foreign friend needed. Chuck felt guilty questioning him, but he could not let it go. If he were a woman, Chuck considered, he might suspect Godwin was spending time with a secret lover.

"It's really quite simple," the tall, dark-skinned Roûe teacher spoke in thickly accented Ghoupallêan, adjusting the fold of his brown robe. "In the north lived the Danid, in the south the Roûe. The line dividing them was south of where the city of Selauê is today. The Roûe were not a desert people then. In fact, our mythology is full of stories of forests and fields and all manner of creatures living in a temperate climate. Take the tales of Anatarka, for example: rich, playful stories of kings and their talking animal colleagues, of sweet dainty princesses and hulking ruthless warriors. The tale of Aisa and Samot and their trek to Kish-a-Tek is a classic example of early Danid-Roûe contact. The life of Tukou-Mê, also. We have studied it. Recall also the voyages of Tyuan-Da."

"And the history of ancient Ilait, how their high plateau home was burnt by a falling comet," Chucker contributed. "The populace fled in four directions to found the major nations of central Zissekap. Danid history! I get it!"

"It is not to be dismissed frivolously. A people's history is their lifeblood."

"I know all of that. Can I go now?"

"Do you know all about the social, economic, and political

considerations that followed the tragedy of Queen Lutui of Rox, whose golden hair was the envy of all the Danid—so much so that a Rouê prince captured her and made her his bride! To stop the war that ensued, she shaved off her golden hair and gave half to each side. And then, amidst this great history, as I've been explaining to you this morning, the Ghoupalle people arrived— from who knows where!—wave after wave, wedging between the Danid and the Rouê kingdoms. At first they merged with the existing population, yet during the course of centuries the number of Danid dwindled. Other Danid were pushed north and therein lay the beginnings of their struggles with the Zetin. The tales of Prince Secour and his uncle, mighty King T'OT, come from this period of history and its related literature. Today, however, the Danid live on the fringes of the civilized areas of Zissekap while the Rouê have been pushed south into the desert, lucky to have access to coastal plains where a few cities could be built. Some of the most desperate Rouê, those living on the high desert, have fallen into barbarism, subsisting on the slave trade, indulging in cannibalism—"

"Okay! Enough already."

Chucker never expected to find himself back in school upon his return to Aivana, but his step-dad insisted he continue to learn what he needed to know in order to be a prince of Aivana.

After a short lunch break, they switched to mathematics and language, which for Rouê were the same subject. Numbers served also as words. A sentence might literally be translated as *five twenty fifteen six thirty-nine fifty-two seven*. It was confusing to Chucker, who complained that learning Ghoupallêan had exhausted all of his brain cells. He was also being tripped up trying to remember to use the base-twenty number system Rouê used instead of the base-ten he learned on Earth. To add to the resistance, Chucker was forced to practice writing the Rouê numbers over and over down long sheets of parchment. He remarked that the lines and dots resembled some childish secret code.

"Sixteen forty-one three ninety-five eight," he sighed in English.

"*U'la'he Rou'e!*" the teacher snapped. 'Speak Rouê!'

"*La'ma'e Rou'e o'pe'do,*" he slowly spoke.

"*Ta'fe!*"

"I am not wrong!" Chucker exclaimed in Ghoupallêan.

The afternoon grew hotter. The air in the room, although open to the palace gardens below, was dry like the desert. He turned in his seat, spied the great arch, rising over the red-tiled rooftops of the city.

He shook his head; he did not want this. He did not want to be in Aivana. And definitely not back in school.

"I just want to break something," he muttered in English.

"*O'ko?*" his teacher asked, perturbed by the youth's lack of diligence.

"I—want—to break—something!" he enunciated for his Rouê teacher.

Where was that Set-d'Elous when he had a gripe? His mentor had returned finally from Selauê but remained in his room, depressed, waiting for some woman named Gina to arrive. Truly sad, thought Chucker, feeling he was on his own now. The visit to the madman's island was too short, and his belly remained on fire, wanting to do something, to make his mark on this world—not study to be a prince.

Then came his literature lesson. He especially did not wish to be reciting, much less memorizing, old Ghoupalle poetry:

> *Memæ-se de Ghêrata-se*
> *Qouthen Emai felujê-zu stæ-zum nessan.*
> *Zil-se tadê-ga ussou-mema rik*
> *Qouthenê Ghoum-ga inda nuk kem—*
> *Hama gen Emai mema-de krañ stæ*
> *Arejex-toba kem,*
> *N'yd il var memar murend*
> *Dath il firn de tüg ana*
> *Va elem biæ tuxen däl-se*
> *Ba kem læforenê Emar pesasz—*

Before he could finish his recitation, the door suddenly flung open and in rushed Set-d'Elous, *Mexas* of Aivana, appointed counsel to Queen Tammy, quite out of breath.

Set-d'Elous gripped the edge of the door, sucking air, a most distraught countenance bearing upon his wizened face, royal robe rumpled from the exercise, wet from the climate, smelly from the effort of his climb up the many stairs of the palace, too hurried to wait for the newly installed automatic lift to return to the ground floor and convey him heavenward to the top of the tower.

"What—is that—poem?" he asked in English, breathing hard.

"I dunno," Chucker laughed, amused at his mentor's appearance. "Some poem about breasts." He regarded his teacher: "Right?"

"*Qa*," the Roûê teacher responded, then bowed low to the *Mexas*, upset that his student had not done likewise.

"I heard—you recit—ing it—across the courtyard."

"Was I in particularly good voice?"

"That poem—it was written—by Basura—Kanoun—"

"Yeah?"

The man, ashen-faced, stared at the youth. Something serious had happened, it seemed. It was more than him rushing down the stairs on one side of the courtyard then bounding up another set of stairs to another tower. The man was not that old.

"What's the matter, Mister d'Elous?"

The Roûê teacher bit his lip at the young man's impolite way of addressing of the *Mexas*.

"*Memæ-se de Ghêrata-se*? That's what you recited?"

"Guess so." Chucker glanced at his teacher, then nodded. "Not good?"

"Basura-Kanoun, she—was the matron—of the Council of Five—the group that—"

"I know, I know," Chucker jumped in to save his mentor's breath. "The group that took over Sekuate and started the wars. All that history crap! You told me about that on the island. Remember? You went on and on for literally weeks, telling me everything I need to know, telling me how you went back through a tangent and 'took care of her,' as you said, so she wouldn't be able to cause any trouble. You removed her from the equation. You told me already. And how you felt guilty for doing it—or, you said so, at least. Whatever. So what's the big deal about a stupid poem?"

Set-d'Elous took a deeper breath, searching for the right words. He waved the teacher out of the room, waited until the door was firmly shut.

"Listen, Chucker," he began, and paused to take another big breath in the stifling room. "It *is* a silly poem—about renouncing the influence of religion in society. 'The Breasts of the Church'? Churches feeding dogma like breasts give milk? Come on! But it's widely known" (another deep breath) "she wrote it *after* the Council of Five took power in 1482—following the revolution. That's after she married Diert-Gangus. I mean, that's after—"

"After you showed her the righteous path?"

"Yes. You could say that."

"After you supposedly killed her?

"Yes. Long, long after."

They stared at each other a moment, as the seasons turned.

"She's not writing and publishing poetry from the grave."

"Okay, then...how?" asked Chucker solemnly.

"Something has changed..." and he paused to think. "And, obviously, something has not."

Chapter 24

Interludium

The crash of an exploding shell slapped Set-d'Elous out of his trance, mounted on the back of a horse-like creature, barely able to breathe, choked by the smoke wafting around him, stomach knotted and heart beating loudly. After a few moments, he regained his awareness, knew where he was: somewhere in the past—or the future—too dangerous to spend time calculating which. But he knew he was in command.

The battle-stained beast he rode was exhausted so he allowed it to walk as they went along the once-beautiful city avenue strewn with the destruction and debris of war. On either side buildings stood broken and battered, steaming, smoking, some with fires still blazing. The air was thick with acrid smoke, the skies above a hideous black and perverse pink—

A scene from Hell, he considered.

He turned and glanced at the trailing line of soldiers, leading their battle-scarred mounts through the debris-narrowed road, what was once a beautiful boulevard full of lush flora but now barren and burning.

How long had the war gone on? It seemed ages, of course, as each year passed and each nation fell.

A lieutenant rode up beside him, concerned about their direction.

"We shall meet up with the fifth brigade at Debrêk," he

explained coldly.

"Debrêk, *Kanê*?" asked the lieutenant.

"You heard what I said!" *Ah!* How he loved the scent of Hell in the morning!

The lieutenant nodded, pointing at the blood splatter on his superior's torn sleeve, wondering if he were in need of medical attention.

"No, I carry pain everywhere I go," he responded.

Then the lieutenant raised his cap and strands of golden hair tumbled down upon the man's shoulders.

"What are you *doing*?" the lieutenant asked, the voice suddenly too feminine.

"I'm conquering!" He snorted. "What does it look like?"

"Is that really necessary?" said the lieutenant who, as he regarded him, turned more and more into the face and persona of his long-lost love, Gina.

He squinted at the lieutenant, seeking recognition.

"Look at yourself now!" he/she accosted him. "You went so dutifully to the year 1574 and waited for me. You got bored in Aivana so you went off to your island—where you promptly went insane. And still you waited for me? You know how it all works: you come and you go; you don't wait. I'm here now, but this is not the end of my life; this is the middle of my life. If you look on a calendar, it seems to be a long time but it really hasn't been. In fact, today might not even exist in another life."

He smiled cynically, rather like a two-faced Janus mask. This messenger was not one of his staff, obviously, but a demon sent to torment him, perhaps because of the destruction his armies had wrought, laying waste whole nations on his narcissistic whim. Demons often came to debate with him and he was patient with their intrusions. It was becoming part of his life.

"This is what was required of me," he spoke calmly, as though answering a journalist's list of officially approved questions. "I am doing what I am supposed to do. You've read the history books. You've seen the martyr's wall. You've spoken with the patrons of war. My task is to lay siege to the nations of Ghoupallesz. One by one. Until we are one. That is what the Council has decreed." He waved his arm in the air. "Look around you—is it not glorious?"

Lieutenant Gina chuckled disdainfully.

"It's true," he continued, gesturing at his dirty uniform, the troops behind him, the destruction around him, and at his minor wounds in the arm and thigh. "I have a mandate to destroy all who oppose us. Hah! Did you not hear me last week when I said 'Now I am become Death, the destroyer of worlds'? It was widely quoted."

"The journals tend to be biased—"

"In fact, wasn't it you who named me 'Set'? More than once you called me the God of Destruction, the bull in the china shop, who always manages to create chaos—one who is, let's say, clumsy. Needlessly destructive. You want me to live up to my moniker. And now—now you regret the seriousness of my nicknaming ceremony."

"There was no ceremony, Sebastian," the lieutenant spoke, "only a quickly scribbled signature on a wrinkled parchment in a cold, dark hallway of an abandoned house in the Missouri countryside: a run-down wreck of a house about to be demolished to make way for a new subdivision. Even now they're clearing the land, burning piles of timber, filling the sky with smoke. Just look out the window. Go on—look!" She snickered. "And you thought it was a palace."

"I knew it was an old abandoned house. I never called it a palace. Bunker, maybe, but never a palace. We were—"

"It was foolish!"

"You're calling me a fool?" he grunted, riding on through the wafting smoke and bitter scents of death and cannon fodder. "What about you? You've been such a saint!"

"Of course not. Saint is not in my pedigree, nor in my fate."

"Ah, then you're no better than me!"

"I've merely made my way as best I could, hiding where needed, asserting myself where I could do some good."

"And now? Are you doing good?"

"Yes." She seemed put-off by his presumption. "I am doing good right now. I have joined a group who call themselves the Revolutionary Council. Our purpose is—"

"Good name! Revolutions are always good."

"We started in Typeg and now we are in Aivana. They're ruled by foreigners and the local people demand justice."

"But you are a foreigner!"

"But I do not seek power. I don't want to rule anyone."

"You just want to create chaos."

"Chaos always settles into order."

"Which explodes into chaos."

"Which settles into order."

"Which—"

He thought of pizza and felt hungry, decided it was not worth further argument. How much longer would they be slow-marching to meet up with the fifth brigade? Not enough time to stop for lunch—

He could not tell what time it was with the smoke obscuring the landscape, the burning cityscape. So he imagined himself astride a large bird, soaring high into the sky, looking down upon the blackened, flaming ruins of the great industrial city his army had razed—that was possible in dreams, he decided, feeling the wind in his face. He imagined himself sailing high through the clouds, into the green sky above, the wind holding him aloft—like a god, like an airborne hero!

"The foreigners who rule in Aivana are my friends," he said, landing the great bird, "and they are well-intended, as most Voyagers seem to be. Aren't you and I well-intended? We never wanted to change anything here. We just wanted to have fun. Until things turned serious. Like now. I'm trying to subdue the planet and you are threatening to hurt my friends who have no idea what we Voyagers can do."

"I wish you would've told me that before," said the woman. She began stuffing her golden locks up into her cap. "The plan has already commenced. It cannot be stopped. If only you had let me know."

He let out a long sigh, shrugging his shoulders, one epaulet ripped and dangling.

"That's why I waited for you in Aivana. I read a book about your group assassinating the royal family—*trying* to assassinate them. Ultimately, you failed. But I knew I could find you there on a certain date. I arrived early, so I decided to wait."

"If you had told me they were from Earth, I could have stopped—"

"Everything seems to depend on timeliness, doesn't it?"

She nodded, looked more like his lieutenant than a moment before.

"Like right now," he spoke up. "I really have no idea why I'm on a *Jêpe* in the middle of this burning city. I'm guessing this uniform means something, but in my head I'm not quite clear just what I've done. Or what I will do next. I think I'm in charge of all this mess. Or, I'm the cause of it. Either way, it's like I'm dreaming all this—"

"Now don't you forget the rules. No waiting," said the lieutenant, voice shifting from Gina's alto to a deeper, martial baritone. "It's still possible to meet in Aivana. Shall we say corner of G-Lane and Alley-47, up the slope past the bridge? Let's meet there a hundred years from now—by the calendar." She chuckled. "Of course, that could be tomorrow in our actual lives."

"Naturally."

"*Êdolex, Kanê-se?*" asked the lieutenant, now a skinny man with a moustache, questioning his use of the word 'naturally.'

He grinned, embarrassed. Gina was nowhere in sight—as it was meant to be.

"A silly expression," he said with a quick glance around. "Sometimes I think I'm going mad, as though a demon were following me. Then I look around at the territory under our control and I think, *Naw!*"

He cleared his throat.

"What is real is real, and what I can see and smell are real. Only my thoughts falter and slide into an abyss of fantasy."

He stared ahead at the burning streets.

"Or into dreams."

The wind picked up then, blew hard against him.

"How can I tell them apart?" he muttered in English.

The lieutenant did not respond, could not fathom the question, so the *Berron* sent him back to the line of troops.

❋ ❋ ❋

Then, just as suddenly, Set-d'Elous was back: standing on the wide veranda of the palace, someone speaking to him of important things. Surveying the city of Aivana, its towers and rooftops, the mountains beyond, the mild green skies and the dusky, spicy scent of *sembour*, he had been thinking of other times, other lives. He had drifted into the future—or the past. He couldn't be sure which. But now he was in the present, he realized, feeling dizzy.

"And if something goes wrong?" asked Chucker. "Then what?"

He had thought it was a fair question, deserving of a fair answer.

Once upon a time, he had explained as magnanimously as possible to his young cohort, he and others like him stood atop the highest peak of the planet and decided that they were gods, or as close as any living thing was likely to be. With handshakes all around and smiles, grins, smirks, knowing or furtive glances, all of them knew what to do. Generations later, their lucky offspring had established themselves as the guardians of everything they surveyed. They no longer lived atop mountains, no longer called themselves gods, never did much to tweak the politics or economy of any society, and rarely even met with others of their kind to discuss the past, present, or future.

Sure, he knew he was borrowing the story from a Roger Zelazny novel he'd read in high school, but he thought it would provide a suitably profound explanation.

And then a child was born—he continued, shifting to a Ghoupalle story he recalled—a child of such beauty that all who gazed upon him were awestruck and vowed that this time, surely this time, something truly good had been created that would surpass all of the twisted perversions of divinity that had snowballed for generations. For surely then—

"Surely then?"

He glared at Chucker, a bit perturbed. "Yes, *surely then* we would be redeemed."

"But it was an illusion?"

"Yes, of course. Reality is an illusion."

The child grew, but failed to address any of the faults of the world, as everyone had hoped. It was the stuff of institutions and prayer. Even on Ghoupallesz. The child was Tukou-Mê, born in a cave near the modern city of Hišar, half Danid and half Rouê, perfect for the job of uniting two peoples. He chose to flee his obligations for a war in Aivana, married a Tigu woman who then bore the legendary mariner Tyuan-Da—and so on. Missed opportunities. In any place where two humans meet there always will be some ruling ideology framing the encounter, an ideology forever based on the grand illusion: the apparent certainty of their competing sensorial interpretations of an unfixable reality.

Waving off another interruption, he explained his journey from the dreary life of a night-shift clerk in the tax office to a god reigning over a good portion of a planet.

"No, no, no," Chucker erupted like a puff from a cigar. "I'm talking about the back-up plan. Plan B. What's the protocol for undoing some insane act that doesn't work out for the best?"

He slapped his hands to his hips.

"Listen, if you expect to be handed over the keys to this planet, you need to show some respect to those who have gone before you."

"I'll show respect when you earn my respect!"

"Oh, yeah?"

"Yeah!"

The fight lasted for almost six *pon*: rough bear hugs and weak punches, a half-hearted kick to the groin that missed and a wayward slap to the shoulder that landed hard on the jaw. After two more *pon* to recover, the combatants agreed to work together.

"If—and I do mean *if*—the results are different than what we expect, then we may need to go on a mission to counteract the instigating event—"

"Speak English, you Ghoupalle wannabe!"

"If we screw up everything, we have to undo it. Back to the act that was done to create the, uh, let's call it the 'new timeline.' We'll need to go back and prevent the change."

"And what if *you* are—you *were*—the instigating factor?" asked Chucker.

"What do you mean by that?"

He finally showed his anger, frowning, crossing his arms over his chest. He was not as good an actor as he had been in his youth—he took the role of Banquo in his high school production of *Macbeth*; he recalled that Gina had played one of the three witches, though rather unconvincingly—

"I mean, *you* can't go back to stop *you* from doing what *you* did back then at that so-called instigating event," said Chucker.

"I can't?"

"Think about it. If you find the right tangent to return to the same time you went to before, when you did what you did, then you would be there looking right at yourself. Are you gonna just say 'Hey, dude, don't do it,' and your other self is gonna say 'Okay, I won't'? All the scientists say that if you meet yourself during time travel that you just go *poof* if you even shake hands, or if you—"

"I get it!"

"So we need other people to go back and stop you—"

"Because I can't stop myself."

"You wouldn't be able to, as the theory goes. You'd be facing down your shoulder angel or devil, talking to yourself, trying to talk yourself into doing something that's plain illogical or unreasonable, or perhaps getting you to stop something that is already in action—"

"And I'd go poof, vanish into thin air!"

"Or slip into a slide zone."

"We need a small army, a select group of mercenaries—"

"People who not only can do the job but don't give a crap about this tangent crap; that is, they don't get freaked out traveling to another world and back again. They just want to do the job, get their reward, and do it all over again."

"Teams of mercenaries that we train to—"

"To go from here back to Earth, then return through a certain tangent you designate—since you know, like, fifteen hundred of them or more—"

"I've documented three-hundred sixty-two," he said, proudly, "maybe another thirty-some are still undergoing testing and confirmation. However, almost ten percent go to other worlds than Earth, which is not helpful—"

"And they find the right place, right time, and take action in whatever way we've planned it, silently, without any distraction, then return to us or go their own way—"

"Never to be seen again once the job is done."

"Where're we ever going to find people like that?"

"Willing to follow our orders?" he asked incredulously.

"And able to do the job. I mean, skilled in the kind of history-twisting skullduggery we're becoming famous for."

"We're becoming famous?" He laughed.

"We will be."

"There must be a lot of men out there who would like this line of work, who won't get freaked out by the circumstances."

"Who won't balk at walking between worlds—"

"Men who are happy just being on some mission, like old Qalanou, my Second—"

"Tough men, cold-hearted men, orphans and bastards, groundless men—"

"Cutthroats and criminals, vagabonds, ne'er-do-wells—"

"Men who would do it *gratis* just for the fun of it—"

"Maybe some women would be needed."

"Maybe."

"Men and women, fanatics, patriots—"

"Who just want to break something," said Chucker, almost growling. "Like me."

Set-d'Elous stared at the sad young man in his princely robes, looking so ungainly and uncomfortable.

"I have to get out of here," Chucker sighed, gesturing at his frilly clothing.

He grinned, embarrassed for his protégé.

"Let me join!" Chucker exclaimed, jumping up. "Let me be one of the team, mercenaries who go on missions, who follow your orders to change history. Give me a mission—please. I have to do something! I can't stand being here! I can't stand being a prince."

Set smiled sympathetically, reflecting a wistful longing for his own youthful adventures. There was something in the younger man's countenance that shone as sincerity. He was no longer a child, not a teenager, and more than a youth. In five years on Ghoupallesz, he had grown perhaps seven or eight Earth years. And his experiences served to create a maturity that Set appreciated.

"Then we should head back to Selauê," he announced. "Recruitment awaits!"

"My bags are packed!"

"Mine aren't." He pointed to the closet. "We can leave in the morning."

"Crack of dawn?"

"I'll try to get up," he said, turning to the dresser and opening a drawer.

Chucker watched the retrieval of clothing.

"What are we gonna call this organization?"

Set-d'Elous looked up. "Why a name? Do we need to set up insurance? a dental plan? tax withholding?"

"Well, since we are dedicated to changing history—"

"And, knock on wood, *un*changing history!"

"So we should call it...'History, Incorporated.'"

Set-d'Elous sighed, thoughtfully rubbing his chin with his hand. "History, Inc.?" He spoke the name a few more times. "It has a ring to it."

Chucker stood and saluted. "To History, Inc.!"

"To History, Inc.!"

"For the finest in historical alterations!"

"For the finest history that can be altered!

PART FOUR

The universe is constantly in flux between absolute chaos and absolute order, yet at any moment it is in perfect balance.

> —from an early philosophical text, *Oskarrê-bañ de Ghoupallea* (The wood-mouse, Kipo, is explaining the nature of the universe to the wandering knight-errant named Ê.); often erroneously attributed to *The Tales of Anatarka*

In all things do Order and Chaos wrestle; at any instant they are bosom buddies.

> —Danid saying, from *Danid-ta Šomüx*, a religious text; quoted in *The Tales of Anatarka*

Chapter 25

HISTORY, INC.

When Death stares him in the face, a man is born again.

—Tomak-Brounadar, *Berron*, Gourran Arumê de
Remulgar de Sekuatê-drouñ, 1533

This time when they arrived at the old house, the Captain wore a trimmed beard, graying at the edges. He stood to welcome them, more solemn than usual. He wore the old uniform of the Selauê army, khaki and crimson, powder blue epaulets, brown leather belt, and saber scabbard dangling at his hip (*sans* saber), tall tan cavalry boots, highly polished. He was ready to ride out to battle, some of them likely thought. He dressed in his uniform when the meeting was serious, in t-shirt and jeans when it was not.

His grim expression was frightening in the yellow glow of the Coleman lantern hanging from the ceiling.

"Thank you for coming here tonight," the Captain spoke in a soft voice, as though he was all talked out practicing his speech. "Welcome back to Earth. I trust the journey was pleasantly uneventful. Now that you are here, however, you will need to excuse the latest suburban sprawl to the west, moving dangerously close to our interdimensional doorway. There is no accounting for taste when chain restaurants and stores sprout across the universe unabated. Can there ever be too many 'unique dining experiences' or ever an instance of 'shopping reinvented'? How presumptuous! And the beloved Blue Ridge Mall, where long ago I went late on Christmas Eve to shop for Christmas presents, where I took my high school sweetheart to see a new motion picture, where my mother bought me a cute little suit for church when I was a boy, where I—. Well, the mall has now been leveled, as you saw, and yet another Wal-Mart has risen in its place. A troubling series of changes, indeed!"

He frowned, not understanding his audience's reaction.

"Forgive my frustration with change. It is quite another kind of change with which we must concern ourselves. You might guess the reason for our gathering since we meet only when there is trouble in the universe. An uneasy situation exists once again on Ghoupallesz. Though much good has been done, there have been a few unacceptable side-effects. So I sent two of our members to investigate. They have returned and are ready to report to us. Gentlemen."

The Captain directed his right hand to indicate the young lanky man, Bax-Tovêz, as his left hand moved to mark the other man, Erzuk-Rêssik, an older, bald man with a braided goatee, dressed in feathered jerkin, so atypical of contemporary fashion in suburban Kansas City.

Both stood, Rêssik motioning Tovêz to speak first:

"In Ghoupalle year 1457, Basura-Kanoun, one of the original members of the Council of Five, was—"

"We know who she is!" grumbled Samot-Fênasz.

Several of the men spit on the floor, having lived through the wars. The woman's image was permanently burned into their minds.

"She was found murdered near her home outside of Sorêg."

"Good riddance, I say!" Ikorr-Gulgê snorted. He stamped his foot.

"Die a thousand deaths!" shouted Poun-Halisz, shaking his fist in the air.

Others likewise responded to the mention of her name.

"Gentlemen," the Captain cut in, "let us deal with the present circumstances and for the moment stay relaxed. Our purpose is to make adjustments to history for the good of all. Of all the good people, that is. That sometimes requires us to think objectively, without prejudice, without bias, and with compassion—even of the enemy whose motives we may not fully appreciate. I have heard the report. Now I wish you to know what I know. Then we shall decide how to act." He turned to Tovêz. "Continue."

The young man cleared his throat, spoke with confidence: "Our Lord, Set-d'Elous, also vanished on that day in that place, leaving the appearance that whosoever had killed Basura-Kanoun had also likely killed or captured the captain. The result of this action was intended to be the prevention of her influence over fellow student Diert-Gangus."

He paused a moment, expecting the team to again need to spit and harangue the name of the Council of Five leader.

"I must spit, *Kanê*," Jurrên-Toulorus finally insisted.

"Go ahead," the Captain acquiesced.

A hearty round of spitting and stamping ensued and just as quickly ended.

"Continue your report," the Captain told Tovêz.

The young man nodded. "We expected the separation of Kanoun and Gangus, preventing their political aspirations from forming. It has been well-documented that Kanoun's poetry influenced Gangus to act against the government. Instead, this influence has been thwarted by—"

"*Thwarted?*" Ikorr-Gulgê sneered.

"It means 'stopped,'" the Captain explained. Turning to Tovêz, "Good use of the word. I see those community college classes are paying off. Keep it up."

"Thank you, sir—er, *Kanê*."

"When we are on Earth—at least here, in Kansas City—it is appropriate to speak in English. When we're on Ghoupallesz, Ghoupallêan will do nicely. Continue."

"What happened next was not fully considered, therefore subsequent actions had the effect—"

"English? Make him speak *English*, not this strange talk!" Jurrên-Toulorus complained, and some of the others agreed.

"Gentlemen, he is using standard English." The Captain sighed. "Very well, continue in Ghoupallêan."

The others gradually understood the implications of the earlier action. Several two-man teams had traced the causal chains of each action through time, entering and re-entering tangents leading to different years and places. They had checked many archives, searched court records, perused hospital lists, and interviewed many people as carefully as they could to prevent further contamination. The report was thorough, compelling the Captain to reward them with lavish praise and handfuls of selected *gealan*, and a special excursion to a Chiefs wild-card playoff game.

The ramifications were disastrous, he learned. Once the original act was performed (Set-d'Elous referred to it, not so incorrectly, as the 'original sin'), the lines of history had indeed changed. Once Basura-Kanoun was "removed" by Set-2, Diert-Gangus naturally became distraught. He was interrogated, then dismissed. He went to drown his sorrows at a tavern in Selauê. There, drunk and belligerent, Diert-Gangus fought and injured a man named Danath-Mekmel, sending him to the hospital. Because Danath was in the hospital he was not free to do what he otherwise would have done.

"There is no way to discern," Bax explained, "if Basura's death had not occurred whether Diert might still have put Danath in the hospital."

"The fact remains," Rêssik jumped in, "that Diert made his way to Selauê to escape his ruined reputation in Sorêg. He was the first one accused of her death."

After that incident in the tavern, Diert-Gangus quickly faded from view and the team only knew of him from other vagabonds who occupied the wharfs. Perhaps he stowed away on a ship, or fell victim to others or to disease. He never became a firebrand speaker or any kind of rebel leader. No record of his life exists after the police report of the tavern fight. He might have been picked up secretly and dispatched in silence simply to make easier the maintenance of order. There was much of that sort of action occurring in the years after the Captain's disappearance.

"The story continues with Danath-Mekmel," said Rêssik.

Because of his hospitalization, Mekmel was unable to attend his first day of employment. He had arrived only the day before to start with a new company. The team traced his path of action: that chance yet unfortunate meeting between Diert and this innocent bystander, Danath, had no effect on any action to disrupt a planet-wide war. However, what resulted was the ruin of the lives of the Captain's family.

A hush fell over the group, all eyes settling on their leader.

"Continue," he spoke, showing no emotion.

At that company office, Rêssik explained, Danath would have met co-worker Urrik-Arounê and three months later would have been introduced to Urrik's sister, Talêa. Because of the fight, however, Danath and Talêa had no opportunity to enter courtship and eventually unite in marriage. With Danath not showing for his first day, the boss called upon a current worker to take the position on a temporary basis. Though not as bright or as diligent as Danath, the young substitute, Sonel-Tarrank, struck up a friendship with Urrik-Arounê and thus he was the one introduced to Talêa.

"If Danath had not been injured fighting Diert," Rêssik spoke, "he would have been there at the appointed time and his life would have progressed comfortably, leading him and the others away from the Captain's family."

As it was, however, Sonel became the father of a son, Omlen-Tarrank. Sonel was not as ambitious as Danath and was not successful, gained no promotions, actually took a pay-cut just to keep his job, and a few years later was downgraded and quietly terminated, causing his wife to leave him, causing him to eventually sit outside taverns begging for the final sips from bottles until nameless rogues dispatched him for the few coins he still had in his pocket. Because of the family's meager fortune, the son went to a neighborhood school rather than an academy. At that school, therefore, Omlen met another boy, Iadon-Toulorus, whose mother, Durria-Toulorus, was currently keeping company with a black-marketer named Gushod-Draka.

"This man," Rêssik explained, "was the husband of Jinetta—"

"You mean Gina," said the Captain.

"Yes, Gina—she of the third mission—an associate of Set-d'Elous who had returned to that time to live."

Gushod-Draka had, only a year before, killed the husband of Durria-Toulorus in order to claim her—though she did not know Gushod was the man who murdered him. The boys, Omlen and Iadon, played together. On a certain day in the next year, they played outside while Gushod was taking a rest with Durria at the Toulorus house. He was disturbed enough by the boys' noise that he rushed out and severely beat the son of his mistress, sending the boy to the hospital. Durria threw out Gushod and he realized at long last the extent of his on-going misery, and went to drown his sorrows at a tavern.

"Furthermore," Tovêz interjected, "Gushod recently had been rejected by his wife—Gina, called Jinetta in that time zone—when she discovered his infidelity."

"Perhaps," Rêssik cut in, "she decided it was time to move on to a new life—as the Captain has speculated."

"Of course," Tovêz continued. "Gushod never told Durria he was married to Gina."

At the tavern, Gushod saw a pretty woman who seemed in distress and offered to help. The woman was a young widow, Aisa-d'Elous, the eldest daughter of Zaura-Matousz and Set-d'Elous, left alone with her two children after her husband, Sartan-Tek, died. Aisa had lost her way through the working-class district of northern Selauê and stopped to ask directions. She was searching for the residence of a schoolmate. Gushod apparently presented a different identity that night than his true character and Aisa was charmed, leading to their courtship during the ensuing months and her unexpected pregnancy and hasty marriage to him early the next year—even though he was not yet formally parted from Gina.

Aisa and Gushod had three children during the course of their ten-year marriage. Gushod, however, was constantly unfaithful and eventually brought disease to Aisa. As a result, Aisa died prematurely, though not before sitting through the scandalous trial of Gushod, when he was eventually accused of murdering Durria-Toulorus after she announced she was going to bear his child. This act occurred shortly after the birth of Aisa's and Gushod's third child. All of Gushod's wicked past then became titillating public knowledge.

"Aisa's marriage with Gushod gave him access to the wealth of the Matousz family," Bax explained. Gushod posed as an expert in banking, even presenting false credentials as a commercial banker with ties to banks in Peror, Manên, and Feasfend. Gushod brought the Matousz and d'Elous families to financial ruin and public scandal through his gambling, his poor investments, and all the lavish spending on hedonistic affairs.

Gushod was also able to seduce Zaura's two younger sisters, Effai and Seasö, causing Effai to become pregnant and Seasö to become infected with disease. The women eventually committed suicide together by jumping from the rooftop. Zaura tried having him arrested. Instead, she fell under his spell; one night Gushod seduced Zaura and, resisting him, he raped her. She was at that time married to the original Set-d'Elous, who was on military duty away from the garrison. Zaura was savagely beaten by Gushod and her face cut, severely disfiguring her. Because the act occurred while Set was away on duty, Zaura chose to commit suicide before he could return and see her and know of the acts.

Therefore, returning from military duty in the north, finding the situation as it was, Set-d'Elous plotted to murder Gushod and pursued him almost to Manioug, where he was captured by district police and subsequently put on trial. At the trial, all the scandals involving the family finances and Gushod's treatment of Aisa were made public. Gushod was conveniently murdered on the way to prison by Set's son, Dunas, who was then himself charged, tried, and sentenced to death, executed several months later.

"There is no further record of that Set-d'Elous or his next action," said Rêssik, "though we presume he returned to Earth."

"All of these events," Tovêz said, "are due to a simple act of justice in 1457."

The members of his organization bowed their heads, not daring to look upon the Captain.

How could anyone hear about the Captain's family, knowing what would happen, and not feel pain? If it were not for a chance meeting between strangers, the Captain's world would still be in balance. The ruin of his family had already occurred and could not be undone. It was too complex. Only by returning to the trigger point, the original act, and preventing that act, could the line be erased. The killing of Basura-Kanoun had opened the door to another line of history.

"*Kanê*, what can we do?" asked Jurrên-Toulorus.

The Captain did not move.

"We traced the starting point of this line," Rêssik spoke, "back to the meeting between Diert-Gangus and Danath-Mekmel at the tavern in Selauê a few months following the death of Basura. It's not clear whether her continuing to live would have prevented Diert from traveling to Selauê—"

"We could stand at the tavern doorway and tell him to keep walking, find another place," offered Ikorr-Gulgê.

"We keep that Danath away from the tavern, let him go to his job," Astân-Omlerra suggested. "A fellow doesn't need to be drinking the night before such an important day."

"If the girl lives, then the bastard stays in Sorêg," said Yvagun-Souvisz. "That's the key."

"It was reported he was tortured to get a confession."

"For killing her and the Captain."

"If she lives, he is happy—"

"And he goes on to give speeches for the overthrow of the Sarrêban government!"

"Snatch him then, amidst his inflammatory speeches! Why kill the girl?"

"She was his inspiration!"

"She was a wilting flower who penned simple verse—"

"No matter its literary worth, it inspired him."

"Burn her notebooks. Take her aside and convince her she has no talent, that she should go into nursing or teach animal husbandry, anything."

"Arrange some scholarship for her at the Selauê Academy!"

Several of them laughed.

"She'd make a great *Jepêdor*!"

"A wonderful *Jêpe*!"

"I'd love to ride *her*!"

"Enough!" shouted the Captain.

"Take out Gushod-Draka the second that Gina leaves him. No one will care what happens to a piece of scum like that."

"I'd take out Gushod before he meets that Gina."

"Give Aisa better directions. Or escort her with armed guards."

"We can remove Gushod anytime and save the Captain's family."

"That sets another line in motion," said Tovêz, "which has equally bad results from a man named Forek-Mimat, regarding Aisa, and later another man, named Samot-Arrêmus, regarding

Zaura, and then—"

"How can you plug a thousand holes with five fingers?"

"Tell Aisa not to get involved with Gushod."

"Basura is the key!"

"Diert-Gangus is the key!"

"Kill them all!"

"Quiet!" the Captain called out.

They waited for his next words, the room growing darker, wind outside lending eerie noises to the old house. Time had stopped.

"Quiet," he repeated, softer.

They listened cautiously. A bell rang somewhere and they froze.

"I think the pizzas are here," said the Captain.

✳ ✺ ✳

When the Captain answered the door, the skinny teenager standing there with a half-dozen boxes in his arms seemed nervous. He craned his neck to look past the man standing in the doorway, trying to see who was inside the old house. The plaster was peeling, the floorboards were bare, and a bunch of rough-looking thugs, some in bizarre clothing, were grumbling among themselves, scary in the Coleman lantern light.

"I thought this was a condemned building," the kid muttered, voice shaking.

"It is," the Captain responded, counting out the cash. "Sorry to say, I've let the place go ever since the missus left me."

He handed over the money, then gathered the boxes from the delivery boy.

"Gee, thanks," said the kid, counting the tip and smiling.

The kid nodded, folded the cash and adjusted his cap, backing off the porch as the Captain closed the door.

"After we eat, we need to come up with a plan. The right plan. The best plan for undoing what has been done. Once that has been achieved, we can finally disband History, Inc."

They sat around the room, spread out on the floor, the house lacking furniture. Not one bite or crumb remained in the assorted boxes. The sounds of munching inside and the crickets outside were all that could be heard.

The Captain finished first, eating the least, and licked his fingertips, then smacked his lips.

"It seems strange, *Kanê*," Erutên-Vigasz spoke, sitting next to the Captain, "that we discuss who to kill over a meal of this round food. Is there meaning to your selection?"

The Captain grinned. "There is always meaning. To everything." He motioned to the box on the floor at their feet. "See that box? It is square, suggesting conformity—rectangularity is hardly seen in nature. There is also restriction, limits. Yet, inside is the pizza: round, suggesting symmetry and order."

Erutên nodded, thoughtfully.

"Why not put a square pizza in a square box?" the Captain continued. "Or a round pizza in a round box? The answer is simple: it is easier to make a square box than a round box. Folding cardboard leans to perpendicularity. To make a box one must work from the outer edges and fold inward. Conversely, it is easier to make a round pizza than a square pizza. The dough of the pizza begins from its center, a swirling ball of dough, then a disk that expands outward evenly as the creator whirls it around its axis. To then stretch out the disk, the circle, to fill the corners of a square pan or a square box requires unnatural action. It is natural, hence universal, for the roundness to remain."

Others were now following the discussion.

"And yet, there, too, is a lesson to be learned! These forces, squareness and roundness, are always working together and working against each other: chaos and order—one is always moving toward and becoming the other, constantly in flux, ever always changing, never fixed or satisfied, always seeking balance. Someday, while in flux, chaos will reach a point halfway to becoming order and at the exact same moment order will reach a point where it is halfway to becoming chaos—and both forces will swirl around each other and become one: neither order nor chaos, neither chaos nor order, but a singularity of multiplicity where all that ever was has been reduced to all that ever will be! Thus, all matter in the universe will become a microscopic dot too small for the smallest microbe to notice in the far corner of its jelly—so much smaller than the germ of a germ of a germ's germ. And then, it could only be a mirror image and not an actual microbe—which would, of course, be contained in that germy dot—*if* all matter were compressed into the shape of a pizza, round not square."

"I see," sighed Erutên. "It is very cosmical, what you say. This world is—how do you say?—interesting. I would like to learn more."

"Well, there's a community college up the road from here."

"A college for the community!" He nodded, thoughtfully.

The Captain grinned, recalling the semester he taught a class at another community college, a class on Futurianism under the cover of the Philosophy department. The twenty students hated him and he was not invited back. He laughed.

"Now, then, *Kanê,*" Erutên continued, "how do you explain these round meats you call *pepperoni* and this melted milk product—*cheese* is the name?—and the deep redness of the sauce, like coagulating blood?"

"That is for another day, my friend. Perhaps they represent the random variables of life. Perhaps not. Perhaps a pizza is just a pizza. For now, it is enough that we understand how the pizza represents in its perfect roundness the cycles of the universe: what goes around, comes around. We are always returning to what we have done before, always coming back to our starting point, doing again what we have done countless times, and we seldom ever realize the repetitiousness of it all."

And with that thought, he stood and addressed them.

"It was a good and glorious idea," said the Captain, "and yet it was poorly executed. I am first to accept blame. Now we need to clean up the mess." *His mess*, he conceded, feeling a pang in his heart. "A plan has been put forth and we must decide many things, then prepare diligently, and act proficiently. We are professionals, are we not? We are professional history-adjusters. 'For the greater good!' Remember our motto."

He rubbed his hands together, perhaps testing them, making sure they were still attached to his arms, his arms attached to his body.

"There may never be another chance, nor a better time, nor

more urgent need to change history—your history, not just mine. It is the history of us all. This time, we must prevent our well-meaning colleague, my foolhardy twin whom we call Set-2, from harming Basura-Kanoun beside the lake near Sorêg. The second order will be to prevent her from encountering either Diert-Gangus or the other members of the Council of Five when the group is in its infancy. There is a place I have in mind where Basura-Kanoun may live out her life in peace and safety, free to compose her poetry yet isolated and separated from the Sekuatean public. It is a beautiful tropic isle. That is an equitable solution, agreed?"

Accepting grunts echoed around the room.

"We will deal with Diert-Gangus in a separate mission. There is still time before he can ignite rebellion. The best thing about mistakes is what we can learn from them."

More begrudging verbalization from the membership.

"We will make it work," the Captain insisted. "We will make it all fit together so neatly, so perfectly...well, we'll do the best we can to make things right. I promise."

A more accepting response, punctuated by muffled applause and a raspy cough.

"I will select teams and assign tasks. Success will require a lot of coordination. We cannot just bull our way through the events of history. No, we will not use the bazooka and the bomb. This time, the scalpel and tweezers will be our tools. Prepare your minds and bodies for a trip through the tangents, to a new time and place, with a new purpose."

Steadier applause, some cries of delight, the raspy cough, and a few whistles. They were excited, ready to act. If only he had the plan ready. If only the pizza quickly decaying in his stomach was not fogging his head. For now, perhaps a good act would be enough to appease them.

"Boots and saddles, men!" the Captain called in English, repeating a line remembered from some Western movie he had seen as a child. using John Wayne's voice.

The mercenaries were puzzled.

"He means get ready," barked the blond-haired young man sitting at the edge of the shadows, silent throughout the meeting. "Get your equipment. Get your minds into gear."

Chucker wore torn jeans and rock concert t-shirt to fit his Earth role. Hardened through five missions, returning to Earth for the eighth time since his arrival on Ghoupallesz, since his Youth Trek, since his Voyager education on Little Biznuik Island and royal protocol lessons in the palace in Aivana, he, Chuck R. Tucker, Jr., was indeed ready to break something.

He stood up from his seat, a wooden crate, and strode to the center of the room.

"We have one hour to get ready," Chucker instructed, taking charge as the Captain retired to prepare the teams. "No time to stand around here dreaming of golden piss-pots and pretty girls eager for love. Let's get moving! Team A, you're with me. Team B, assemble at the rendezvous point. Anyone without an assignment, go home. We'll call when you're needed. Use tangent 47-C, in the northeast quadrant, marked with a yellow flag. You'll have a short hike once you arrive but it'll be autumn so you don't need to worry about the heat. Stay ready in case we need you for a back-up mission."

They grunted their understanding. Then they all spoke the motto: "We do what we have to do, no more, no less. 'History, Inc.—for the finest in historical alterations!'"

"To the future!" Chucker cried out and most repeated his words. "May you all live to be great-great-grandfathers!"

"Or grandmothers," Xâta-Mek, the only female, added.

In absolute silence Sebastian sat in the middle of the room, bare floorboards and raised nail heads, feeling the space enfolding upon him. Somewhere a cricket questioned him, but he refused to answer. He gazed about the room, no longer sure if he had been talking to himself or to a roomful of mercenaries who had sworn to go on yet another mission. Some of them had spoken in response; he decided he had actually led a meeting.

It took more than an hour to usher them out, one by one, or in pairs, clasping hands, slapping shoulders, sharing encouraging words, the smiles of reassurance; they all had lost someone because of the wars. Once everyone had left, he closed the door and turned to face the bare floor, empty pizza boxes, bottles and cans of various beverages, the Coleman lantern's fuel depleted, and let out a long sigh as though he had been holding his breath through the entire meeting.

Dawn was approaching and he needed to leave, too.

"I know what to do," he repeated. "I go back and keep myself from killing her." He listened to how the echo sounded. Did it make sense? Had he actually said it? "But I can't stop myself. Nor can I go and just not do it. My previous self has already done it.'"

He chuckled, pulled himself up to a sitting position.

The members of History, Inc. would have to do it. He could not be involved. This mission had to succeed. He was not so good at compromise. He considered something he had read back on Earth—

"Back on Earth in a previous life," he giggled.

Where am I now?

Sebastian Talbot was unstuck in time again. But there was no slaughterhouse in his future, he knew. Perhaps a private prison would be suitable for him. Perhaps a desert isle where only he would reside, allowing himself to be driven mad by the voices in his head all crying out for justice rather than mercy. He could watch the sea ripple under the wind. He could climb the caldera each morning and return each night, communicating with the ant-like insects he had found there.

Why am I sitting in this old, abandoned house?

He was not immediately certain who put the thought into his head, so he laughed to drive away the paranoia. The laughter rattled the old house.

He turned when a spot of light caught his eye. The windows were boarded up but he could detect the dawn knocking outside the house. It was time to go. Time to vacate the house before the construction crews arrived, ready to tear it down. The new subdivision must go on!

Chaos. And Order, he mused. "They swirl around me like...." He didn't know what.

Outside, he took a deep breath, zipped up his jacket against the morning chill, and made his way out to the road.

He pondered reality as he walked along the country road, veering over to 40 Highway, passing closed bars and trailer parks, hourly motels and convenience stores. He stopped at such a store and purchased a few items for hygiene and hunger.

He watched the traffic increase on the highway, morning rush hour, considering that he might actually be home again, in some weird existentialist way, somehow returned by Fate to a place he had never left. It felt familiar, though the commercial development spreading toward the old house was more than he ever could have anticipated that summer evening long ago when he and Gina snuck up to the quarry and found the tangent. That was about a million years ago.

The teams were assembled when he'd arrived at the quarry to do his trick for them.

"Ignore the flapping of A-1," he said, referring to the huge opening that moved as though caught in a breeze, still too wide to close. "That's the way you all arrived, so do not return that way. Not until you've completed your missions."

He stripped down and moved into the wire grid stretching across the abandoned quarry's central arena, slowly stepping across the wet clay and shallow pool of rainwater, his fingers flexed like cat claws, his body a gracefully fluid mass of certainty. Until he felt it.

"Use this one, Team A: tangent C-8," he instructed.

Then he stood in place as the team went one by one through the invisible opening he had made, each of them squeezed like pieces of fruit through gelatin, popping out on the other side, back on their home world but in another time period, ready to begin their mission.

"Ready," grunted their leader.

"Good luck," Set-d'Elous responded, looking through the tangent opening at the twinkling night sky of another world.

He moved to the left and ran his hand along the horizontal wire to the third intersection, held together with duct tape. Again he paused, sensing the spot millimeter by millimeter. He found it, held it open with his index finger.

"Team B," he called, "use this tangent, K-6."

They stepped in a line toward him.

"Be careful, K-7 is very close—but fifty-nine years off. Don't make any mistake here. Let's not end up in the wrong time zone. If you need another route, try Q-45, but that will take you two years too early and give you almost fifty miles to hike."

Team B's leader nodded, then ducked his head and went first through the opening in the air. The others followed, stepping toe-to-toe gingerly through the limited opening, lifting their feet as though climbing over a fence, disappearing into the night.

Done with his escort service, he heard the crickets calling to him and realized he was now alone in the quarry. The moonlight slid off the yellow limestone walls of the quarry and revealed his nakedness. He took a deep breath, filled his lungs. Then he dressed, thinking of previous times he had visited the quarry in the middle of the night. Sometimes he imagined having memories of other places. Other times he remembered images from a dream or of a brightly lit afternoon in another century. This time, this night, he stood barefoot in a pool of rainwater, the cuffs of his pants wet, trying to concentrate on a spot of truth flickering deep in the cave of his mind, knowing that there, still burning, was the last point of reality in his life. He held his breath so as to not accidently extinguish it.

As the sunrise bathed the world in orange light, he left the quarry and descended the hillside, returning past the old, battered house. He paused a moment to be sure it was the same house, not trusting his memory, staring at it until a car approached. He stepped off the road until the car, a police cruiser, passed by, then he continued.

He walked about two miles, squinting against the brilliant sunrise as he entered the parking lot of a place where he had once stayed about twenty years before, it seemed. He had forgotten the girl's name; she was not Gina. Only one car was parked in front of a door: a late model sedan with rust along the bottom edges of the doors and the tops of the wheel wells, big fuzzy dice dangling from the rear view mirror. A curtain in the window flickered as he got closer. He ignored it, pulling out his key, stepping into the shadows of the eaves of the Greencrest Motel.

Inside, he would shower, then sleep until evening. Sometime after dark, he would make his way home—wherever that might be. Sometime during the next several days the teams would return and report their success. Then he'd be able to go with them back through Tangent A-1 and live happily ever after, everything back in balance.

Until then, he would rest.

Towel wrapped around his hips, skin moist from the shower, he reached for the old newspaper stuffed into the wastebasket by a previous guest, curious what the date was—January 24, 1991, six months old now—and about the latest sports scores, the crazy stock market, any news about the IRS or serial killers still sought by police. Instead, the second page carried a small story about someone who had recently awakened from a coma being reunited with her son.

Chapter 26

Imagined Memories

The sun was warm yet the breeze pleasantly cool on a June afternoon, as the dark-haired woman pulled herself along the veranda of the red-brick apartment complex, her arms grabbing the handles of her forearm crutches, the support she needed to help move her legs. In the future, she might try the elevator, as her new landlady, Mrs. Gompers, suggested. Even one flight of stairs was taxing on her arms and back, lifting her legs up one step at a time.

As it was, the afternoon was not quite warm enough to play in the park, so she and her son returned to their new residence after some shopping.

Mrs. Gompers walked behind her, carrying the little boy in her arms.

"Okay! Down you go, little man," said Mrs. Gompers when they reached the woman's apartment door.

"Thanks," said the tenant. "Hopefully, I won't need these much longer. The therapy is making my legs stronger every day. I should be able to go back to work by the end of the summer."

"That's good," said Mrs. Gompers. "I won't always be here to give your boy a ride up the stairs."

"I know, and I'm sorry. I do appreciate your help."

Mrs. Gompers grinned at the boy. "That's quite all right."

The landlady watched her new tenant open the door and

shake one crutch from her arm, then reach for the doorknob to steady herself.

"So you're going back to work soon, huh?" asked Mrs. Gompers. "No more disability checks. What is it you do?"

"Oh, I thought I put it on the rental form," said the woman, taking the boy by the hand and escorting him inside. "I'm a doctor. Well, I used to be."

"No kidding," said Mrs. Gompers. "So should I call you *Doctor* Franck?"

"I'm not a medical doctor, not like a surgeon or G.P.—"

"Not a G.P., huh?"

"No, I'm a psychiatrist."

Mrs. Gompers' eyes widened. "You're not that lady doctor who was attacked by her patient, are you?"

"No, ma'am," said the tenant, brushing her curly hair back. "I had an accident. Car crash. I was in the hospital for a long time."

"And you got pregnant in the hospital?"

"No, I was already pregnant when they took me to the hospital. Didn't know it at the time, sure. They took him out with a C-section."

"So you didn't feel a thing?"

"Lucky, I guess."

"So who cared for him while you were in the hospital?"

"My cousin's family took care of him." She tussled the boy's brown hair. "But I want to take care of him now. I'm able to be responsible for him now."

The landlady smiled, unconvinced.

"No, really. I'm ready."

Mrs. Gompers glanced down at the boy. "So what do you call this little man?"

"I call him Sebastian," Dr. Franck replied.

"You know," said Mrs. Gompers, "I think that was the name of that serial killer."

"Really?" She turned away, stepping inside the apartment. "It's a common name."

"Odd that it's that killer's name, though," said Mrs. Gompers. "You might want to consider changing it, or using his middle name."

"I'll consider it," she replied and gently closed the door.

Inside she was shaking, a nervous reaction she fought against whenever someone said the name Sebastian Talbot. Sure, she gave her son the same name. Her cousin had called him Harold but she'd called him Sebastian from the first moment she saw him: the boy had his father's face.

She set the little man in his little chair, turned on the TV, and went slowly into the kitchen, set her crutches against the pantry door, and began putting away the groceries.

"I told them it wasn't him," she grumbled, grabbing packs of fruit and vegetables and placing them in the bins inside the refrigerator. "Everybody's got to be an amateur detective! Can't they just leave us alone?"

Finished, she returned to the living room, gathered up her son and together sat on the sofa.

"I keep telling the police he didn't attack me," she said to her son, believing the three-year-old could understand, "but they won't believe me. They think I'm crazy now. They think just because I was in a coma for so long I don't remember anything. But I do. I do remember."

Her son looked up at her, puzzled, then returned his attention to the TV. Her eyes followed his and saw, just above the life lessons of Mister Rogers, the flashing red light on the answering machine. As Mister Rogers and friends headed off to the Land of Make-Believe, Toni Franck pulled herself up and crossed the room.

Ever since she'd left the hospital, people had found her number. They called her a "psycho whore" or "crazy bitch" or "sleeping beasty" or worse. Some suggested she turn herself in for helping the serial killer escape. She hated hearing their angry words but she dared not unplug the machine. She was willing to wait. Someday he would call.

She deleted the first eleven messages with the first hateful word spoken. Tears ran down her cheeks as she stood facing away from her son. The Land of Make-Believe seemed such a happy place, she thought, listening to the characters enjoying their fantasy. Perhaps there was some way to turn back time, to make the past be different. But then, if she did, she would not have this beautiful boy in her life.

Her finger pushed PLAY one more time—three messages still

323

left to play—and a breathy noise rumbled from the small speaker. Her finger twitched, ready to delete it. Then a hesitant voice spoke—"Toni...?"—and she froze.

❋ ❋ ❋

Cassie was on the phone, dialing the number she had dialed so many times before:

"You ain't gonna believe this, but I just saw him. He's at this motel I'm at, same motel—no, I ain't, I'm with Bobby. You know him, from the mailroom. Uh-huh. Yeah, me and him we just got talkin' as we was drinkin' down at th' Tool Shed an' we decided, like, why drive all the way home? so we just pulled in and Got-It-On—yeah, I know! Shit, I guess so. Jeez, I dunno, about five times.... I faked a couple, but—. Yeah, we got protection!— anyway I saw him! You know! *Him!* From work. Yes, goddammit, *him*, that psycho killer guy. No.... Whaddya mean how do I know it's him? It is! It just is! Yeah, I'm freakin' out, too! ...You think I should? What i-if it's like, ya know, a false alarm? They gonna arrest me? And then Bobby's ol' lady'll find out—Okay! I'm gonna leave, like, one of them anonymous tips, see, an' then we're splittin' before any cops can even get over here. Yeah, they gotta catch him! He cain't just get off—yeah, I know! Hey, I gotta call now 'fore he leaves. No—I'm calling anonymous-like. Nobody's gonna know it's me calling in about seeing that killer Sebastian Talbot just walkin' free as a bird at the Greencrest Motel! Really gotta go, gotta speed-dial 9-1-1, and tell'em he's back—bye."

❋ ❋ ❋

Detective Henderson looked up suspiciously from behind the stack of papers that had accumulated on his desk, squinting at the approach of his sidekick, Detective Wilson.

"You're kidding, right?" he asked Wilson.

"I wish I was, but no." Wilson did not know whether to smile at their good fortune or frown at what it would mean to them.

"Seems to be him. Got a good i.d.—one of them IRS girls from way back. She saw him check into a motel out on the east side. Patrol car checked him out, too."

Henderson sat back, taking it all in. For three years they had nothing further to do with the case, thinking that Sebastian Talbot had escape town cleanly. Sure, there had been reported sightings. Half the city knew him, it seemed. He was an Everyman, so he appeared everywhere. So many false leads, he was going crazy.

"If this one's good," Henderson spoke up, "then it's time to get our shit together."

"Amen."

"I mean, I've been trying real hard to put this whole thing out of my mind."

"Me, too," Wilson grumbled, "especially since McElroy went missing."

"Our own man on the list of his victims! How could he ever overpower McElroy? Clever bastard got rid of the body, just like all the others."

"I haven't forgotten."

"And now the bastard's back...."

"They followed him a ways from the motel," said Wilson. "Seems as though he's been living in some abandoned house on the edge of the suburbs. Getting ready to tear it down soon for the mall expansion."

"Then why the sighting at a motel?"

Wilson smiled. "Meeting someone?"

"Maybe. But who?"

"Girlfriend? Co-conspirator?"

"His next victim?"

They looked at each other, then Henderson grabbed his sportcoat and holster.

"To the motel?" asked Wilson.

"Where else?"

✳ ✳ ✳

What he recalled was the two of them sitting on a bench

moments before dawn, there beside the sea, or a lake, a placid surface streaked with brilliant sunrise hues. All that mattered was the endless peace he felt.

"What shall we name this child?" she said, his arm around her shoulders, she snuggling against him.

"Do not name him after me," he said, "at least that."

"You needn't worry," she said.

They kissed and he heard a bird cry out from a nearby tree. The lake seemed to shimmer, widen. It became glassy as the reds and oranges reflected across its surface, and soon the gelatinous ball of sun squeezed above the horizon.

Silence—

He sat the phone down again, afraid to call. After his dream, he'd read the newspaper article again, then began looking through the phone book. His heart beat quickly as he dialed the number, the next number from a list. Another answering machine greeted him. She sounded closer than any of the others so he left his message.

He sat the phone down, hand shaking, breath shallow, eyes closed to the reality he would not accept. Her voice echoed in his head, her words repeating in his ears, wishing a dream to become real.

Curious enough at his message, she had dialed the number to make his dream became real. She was hesitant at first, then cautious.

His hand grasped the phone, raised it to his ear—"Hello?"— and a river of milk and honey ran through the electronic device and entered his heart, calling him back to life.

"I'll definitely meet you, Sebastian," said Toni at the end.

He suggested the Greencrest Motel out on 40 Highway. Ten in the evening.

* * *

"Got it," said Wilson excitedly. He turned to Henderson. "The tap's working. He tried to contact her and she called him back. Now we've got a lock on him."

Henderson sighed, sitting back in his chair. "Bless her heart."

"We've got the sighting at the motel and now we've got them meeting at that same motel."

"Perfect." Then Henderson slapped the desk. "Wait!"

"What? We just go and pick him up."

"No, it's not that simple," said Henderson. "I don't want any shootout at a motel. I don't want Doctor Franck getting hurt."

"I'll send a plainclothes over to stake it out."

"Okay," said Henderson. "I don't want any patrol car within a mile of that place. Let's not spook him."

* ❋ *

Laying back on the bed in the motel room, not wishing to know what this or that stain was, it did not seem as strange as he thought it would be, cold calling a former lover. A lover who had been his psychiatrist. A woman whom he was accused of trying to kill. Some relationship, he thought with a twinge of regret, pondering whether she would welcome his call or not, or whether she would turn him in.

It's the polite thing to do, he decided once evening came.

"Oh, Sebastian," she had said, her words tinged with cinnamon and nutmeg, "I knew you would find me someday. You know, I dreamed of you. I mean, you were in my dreams. I was on an island and we...we were walking hand in hand and...we were *naked*. Yes, really! Just free as birds in the sky, you and me. A wonderful dream!"

"Dreams can be like that," he responded, trying not to be as cynical as he usually was when sentimental talk occurred.

"Now it's real," she laughed, delighted to hear his voice. "I need to see you, Sebastian. I need.... There's something important I need to discuss with you."

"The child?" he asked without emotion.

The line was silent for a while.

"You know, then."

"I read it in the newspaper," he said after a while.

"Oh, Sebastian, everybody still thinks you tried to kill me," she said, weeping, "but I know the truth. It was not you, and I keep telling them, the police and all, it was someone else. They also think I was raped in the attack and that's how I got a child. But I know he was from our last session together. He's a beautiful little boy. And he has your eyes."

"Indeed."

"Is that all you can say? After so long apart?"

"We need to keep this conversation short," he said. "I'm more than curious, but for now, others may be listening."

"What?"

"You never watched a cop show? They always listen to the phone calls of the friends and families of criminals."

"But you're not a criminal! I told them you didn't do it."

"And they, of course, believed you. Especially since you were rather out of your mind, having just awakened from a coma, a coma caused by a blow to the head that should have killed you."

"I remember everything. Really, I do." She paused and he counted the seconds, thinking of the listeners on the line. "Except who hit me. I know it wasn't you because you were not even in my office. I think it was—"

"Chuck McElroy?"

"Who?"

"The cop you were dating."

"Dating? Me date a police officer? That's crazy."

"He let me out of the cell the same night...."

"What?" She exhaled loudly. "Oh, Sebastian...."

"Trying to frame me for it, I suppose. Like I broke out of my cell, hit you on the head, and stole your car—"

"So that's what happened to it. They told me it was wrecked beyond repair, out in the countryside, someone on a joyride."

"It was no joyride. I was escaping." He swallowed hard, then slowly shook his head in disbelief—*What am I doing?*—then launched into his confession: "I was being chased by that cop—McElroy—and I led him to the quarry I told you about, the one with the doorway. I went through it and he followed. We had a fight on the other side and I went my own way and left him to go his way. I suggested he go back the way he came. I don't know what happened to him after that. Obviously, he didn't return to the office or he'd be in the news like you. As for me, I kept going...to a familiar place, eventually recovering from my sojourn on Earth—"

"On Earth? What're you talk—"

"And I continued my life there, on that other world, what I call the Dream Land—what they call Ghoupallesz. You don't have to believe me. I can show you proof when we meet. I could...take you there, if you wish. It's moot now, however, given that I'm stuck here on a little errand. I need to remain a few more days, maybe weeks, to be sure everything works out right. It's a little experiment, you might say, to see if I can change history. Not here. On the other world. I screwed up, and now I've got some people working to fix things—"

"Silly boy!" She laughed. "What kind of game are you playing? Are you trying to cheer me up with your stories again? That's so sweet!"

He held the phone away from his head, wondered how long it had been, thought of the listeners, considered the degree of his paranoia and whether or not it was justified. Who knew he was back on Earth? Only Toni. And she wouldn't tell.

"It's time to go now," he said solemnly. "I'll call you again."

"Wait, Sebastian—"

* ❋ *

Detective Henderson sat on the corner of the captain's desk, pointing to Pink Hill Road on a topographical map.

"We've got a man in the woods," said Henderson, "here...and here. Watching the house."

Detective Wilson stepped back into the office with his coffee and took a side chair.

"And...?" asked Captain Becker, looking at Wilson.

"So far, no sign of activity," said Wilson. "One officer reported a faint light in the house at night but it could be a trick of the moon shining through a gap in the walls."

"Nobody coming or going?" asked Becker.

"Not so far."

The captain exhaled, sat up. "Gentlemen, are we on some goddamn snipe hunt here?"

"No, sir," said Wilson, standing.

"Reports are that he stays in the house," said Henderson. "We don't know how he lives there. We can't get a man close enough to inspect it without raising suspicions."

Wilson grunted, almost chuckled. "He was seen by the pizza delivery boy."

"Pizza boy?" Becker exclaimed.

"Evidently, he ordered pizzas to be delivered to the house," Henderson explained.

"The kid thought it was weird, the house looking abandoned," Wilson added.

"But he said inside, other than Talbot, there were a dozen men, all dressed like video game warriors—"

"Like Klingons!" Wilson interjected. "He described them as 'Klingons'. Or heavy metal groupies."

"I imagined a bunch of bad-ass bikers," said Henderson.

"Klingons, huh?" said Becker. "You mean those *Star Wars* characters?"

"*Star Trek*, sir. They're the bad guys in *Star Trek*, not *Star Wars*."

"Not 'Stargate' or some other shit?" asked the captain, sarcastically.

"No, sir," said Wilson sheepishly, shrugging and glancing at Henderson.

"But the way things are going," said Henderson, "I'll bet somebody's going to be making a movie about some stargate thing soon enough."

"Listen, gentlemen, I don't give a shit what movie they're in," growled Captain Becker, "you're wasting a whole shitload of department resources on this—and, yeah, I'm gonna call it what it is—this goddamn snipe hunt."

"But he's there!" Henderson insisted. "Just a little more time. He'll show."

"We've got a tap on the phone," said Wilson.

"His phone? In that house?" asked Becker.

"No," said Henderson. "He probably calls from the pay phone at the 7-Eleven. It's about a mile up the road."

"I'm talking about his girlfriend, or whoever she is," said Wilson. "The psychiatrist. The one used to be in a coma. The one McElroy was seeing. I think he'll contact her."

"He has nobody else here," said Henderson.

"Nobody here on Earth," Wilson laughed.

The other two stared at him; it was not a funny case they were working on.

"I sure miss that goddamn McElroy," grunted the captain, waving the detectives out.

* * *

The honk of a car horn awoke him and he sat straight up in the sagging bed, sheet tossed to the side. He shook his head, wondering what had been dream and what had been real. With the insistent honking, he climbed out of bed and went to the window.

A bearded hippie wannabe sat behind the steering wheel of a late-model car parked there, cranking the engine over. The noise bore into his brain and he wanted to go out and help the man just to see him drive away and leave him in peace. His hand went to the doorknob as he noticed he was already dressed—or still dressed.

Must've had a late night. He could not recall what he had been doing but it must not have been fun. He grinned sardonically, and opened the door.

"Sorry, man," the driver called to him, "hope I didn't wake you."

The driver got out and opened the hood. The two of them looked at the engine. His friend, Jason Aronstein, had taught him a few things about car engines long ago. So he suggested the driver try it again while he held the fuel injector open on the carburetor. Old cars were easy. The engine finally turned over and roared to life. A stream of black smoke filled the space where he stood and he fell back, covering his face. The driver slammed the hood down.

When the smoke cleared, he saw a woman standing beside the car.

"Hey, thanks, man," the driver called through the open car window.

The woman stopped as the smoke blew away. She seemed awe-struck, like a deer caught in the headlights.

"You!" she exclaimed. "It's you!"

He stepped back, as he always did when someone accused him of something.

"Come on, get in," the driver shouted at her. "Gonna be late for work!"

"You came back!" she shrieked, her face pale, eyes wide.

The driver got out and came around the front of the car to push her into her seat, but her hands grasped the door, refusing to break her gaze.

"You're Sebastian Talbot," she muttered as the guy shoved her into the car.

The guy closed the door and jogged around to the driver's side, jumped in, closed his door, and shifted into reverse, then peeled out of the gravel parking lot, raising a grey cloud of dust that severed Cassie Dorfman's view.

* * *

With his duffle bag slung over his shoulder, he took off jogging across the parking lot, then ran faster down the road, turned onto a side street, and disappeared into a wood between two clusters of newly built subdivision houses.

He came out beside a 7-Eleven, and leaned against the wall, catching his breath. In a flash he knew his cover was broken; police would be descending upon the Greencrest Motel at any moment.

Why did I have to come back to this world?

The mission needed it, he tried to convince himself. His team had to return to Ghoupallesz through the tangents that were on Earth; it was the only way to return in different time zones. And he was the only one who could direct them to the correct tangent for each mission. Yet he had been too cavalier, and now he had compromised his position.

He felt coins in his pocket and pulled out a few.

"Oh, Sebastian, dear, why are you out of breath?" asked Toni when she answered his call on the first ring.

"The motel's not safe," he grunted.

"Where should we meet, then?"

He thought for a few seconds. He hated to suggest it but he told her about the old house down Pink Hill Road, just past the quarry.

"It's back away from the road," he said, "but you can still see the gravel drive in the dark. The house will be dark, but I'll be there."

She was ready to accept anything, any arrangement, and she never suspected any trick. He could have been evil, he realized, planning a ruse to coax her out to some dark house to—

"My landlady will watch him for me," she was saying. "Then I'll be on my way."

"Can't wait to see you," he spoke, much too seriously, calculating how long he had been on the phone, knowing the limits of surveillance technology. "Still ten o'clock."

"See you!"

He stepped back from the phone, his body racing with energy, ready to run more miles to escape the next patrol car he spotted. He knew he'd made a mistake contacting her. They had to be monitoring her phone, waiting for him to contact her. But he could not step away. Now they would be following her out to the countryside, to an old abandoned house set back from the road on the edge of the woods, a dangerous-looking location for the maniac's next murder. Why wouldn't the escaped mental patient want to kill his psychiatrist?

✳ ✳ ✳

"Okay, we got him," said Wilson excitedly, rushing to Henderson's desk, waving a few papers and nearly banging his knee on the desk as he arrived. "Phone tap got him calling Franck. They're gonna meet."

"No kidding," said Henderson, sitting up. "You about had me believing it was all a hoax, or a 'goddamn snipe hunt'—"

"Or mistaken identity. Crazy girl from the Service Center. Always exaggerates."

"She's well-intended."

"But crazy."

"We've got the corroboration of the pizza boy. It's not a false report."

"Look at this," said Wilson.

Wilson showed him the several-page transcript, turned back a page and pointed to the highlighted text.

An officer in blue fatigues, bloused boots, and ball cap, arrived at the open door and, seeing a meeting was on, leaned casually against the door jamb.

"This is Lieutenant Gomez," Henderson introduced the tall, broad-shouldered man with short-cropped hair standing in the doorway, chomping his cinnamon chewing gum. "He'll be leading the assault team."

"Rocky Gomez," said the lieutenant, shaking hands with Wilson, then extending his hand to the new guy: sandy-haired, too-thin Detective Bobby Sawyer. "Happy to be working with y'all."

"I'm sure it'll be fun," said Sawyer.

"See here?" Wilson explained to Lt. Gomez, the SWAT unit commander. "There's an old house outside of town, near that quarry where we tracked him before. Just like the pizza boy said."

"Long time before," commented Sawyer, a replacement for McElroy. He had heard the stories, loved the thrill of the chase, and was eager to participate in the final action to catch Sebastian Talbot.

"Evidently he owns or used to own the property," Wilson told Sawyer.

"Could he really have been hiding out in that house for three years?" asked Sawyer, but they all knew the answer: anything was possible with Talbot, who had outsmarted them on several occasions.

"Look at the transcript. He tells her exactly where to go."

"Then we should go there, too," said Henderson.

"Unless it's a misdirect," said Lt. Gomez.

"I don't think so," said Wilson. "Read the transcript. He sounds sincere, even passionate. He wants to meet her."

"Must've gotten spooked at the motel," said Henderson. "I told them, dammit, nobody was supposed to be there. Do they listen?"

Wilson waved to Sawyer. "Get the map."

"It could be tricky, if Franck shows up," Henderson sighed. "We need to keep her clear of there."

"Let them meet, then get him once she leaves?" suggested Wilson.

"Or keep her from arriving," said Sawyer.

"If she doesn't arrive as planned, he may take off into the woods or something."

"We have to protect her, at all costs," said Henderson.

"Let us handle it," Lt. Gomez spoke up.

Henderson turned to the SWAT unit commander. "How soon can you be ready?"

"Tonight, if need be," replied the lieutenant. "He's just one man."

The two detectives shared a glance.

"Maybe so, but...he's resourceful," said Henderson.

"Don't underestimate him," Wilson added.

"You recall the incident three years ago?" Sawyer spoke, like he'd been there. "He took out a whole team of officers. He had some kind of laser rifle."

"We know the incident." Lt. Gomez grinned confidently, then spit his gum into the wastebasket beside Henderson's desk. "That won't happen again."

Henderson nodded. "I hope it won't."

"Suit up," said Lt. Gomez, cheerfully. "You can join us."

"Cool," said Sawyer.

"I meant these two," Lt. Gomez corrected.

Sawyer blushed. "Sure."

"No thanks, Lieutenant," said Henderson. "I can't be there. You guys do the operation. I got a big family thing going on tomorrow. Father's Day, you know. Some of your men may want off for Father's Day, too, so if we can finish the operation by dawn...well, do what you need to do. Just be sure that woman doesn't get in the middle of a firefight."

"No problem," said Lt. Gomez. "We'll keep her outside the perimeter."

Wilson smiled, entertaining a thought. "Just get a sharpshooter trained on his freakin' head, ya know. Long distance. *Bam!* Then it's Happy Father's Day."

"I like how you think," Lt. Gomez laughed, clapping him on the shoulder, just as McElroy used to do way back when.

❋ ❋ ❋

More than a half-hour late, Cassie Dorfman burst into the section.

"Hey, everybody," she called out. "Guess what I did?"

"What'd you do this time?" her manager, Joyce, asked in a whiny tone.

"I just hit the jackpot, baby!" Cassie sang out in delight. "Fifty thousand dollars! And it's all mine! And what did I do? How'd I get it? You wanna know?"

Others looked up from their work, distracted or amused.

"What?" asked Joyce, on behalf of the section's workers.

"I turned in Sebastian Talbot! Yup, that's right—Sebastian-freakin-Talbot, the IRS serial killer! Remember him? Well, I spotted him out at the...well, out on the east side of town, and I'm the one called police on him. They rushed out to pick him up and right now they're fixing to write out a big-ass check to me. That's cuz I'm the one who gave'em all the 'information leading to the capture' of the fugitive. That's right! Cassie Dorfman is now a crime-fighter!"

Some of them smiled, a few repressed laughs. It was not the first time she had exaggerated the events of her life. A couple of them recalled how Cassie told them about her affair with Michael Fenning—when everybody knew he was seeing Tammy Tucker.

"No, it's true!" Cassie responded to their expressions. "The reward is fifty thousand dollars and it's gonna be mine in a few days. When they finish making out the check, they're gonna be calling me down to headquarters to pick it up."

"Well, good for you, Cassie," said Kate, the comptroller of the section.

"Now can you get to work?" asked Joyce. "You're late already."

"That's what I wanna tell you all." She grinned as brightly as she could. "Y'all ain't gonna believe it, but...I'm quitting! Now, don't try to talk me out of it. I'm gonna be rich so I'm quitting this crappy job. That's why I was late. I was up front getting the papers filled out to quit. So I was still on the clock, Joyce, and ain't nothing you can do about me getting here late cuz I was on time up front."

"Fine, fine," said Joyce, suddenly not enjoying the scene. "If you're still working here, how about starting your work?"

Cassie moved to her desk, sauntered actually, and even Priscilla was impressed.

"You go girl," Priscilla cheered. "I'm gonna be next one outta here."

"I am!" Cassie insisted, with a defiant glance at Joyce. "Soon as I get my check, I'll finish out the pay period and I'm gone!"

"Ya know, girl," said Priscilla, lowering her voice, "fifty thousand really ain't that much. Two, maybe three years is all that'll last."

"Really?" Cassie frowned.

"But, hey, I got my lottery tickets right here," said Priscilla, smiling and patting her purse. "One of them hits, I'm gone, too. With a cool million or more."

Chapter 27

A Round Midnight

It was a dark night in Sorêg, late in the autumn of 1457, close to morning although there was no moon to light the corners of the stable. The *Jêpe* rustled in their stalls, knowing something was about to happen. Two guards got up from their game of cards and went to check the far end of the building, swords in their scabbards, not expecting any trouble—

Two masked men jumped out of the shadows, knives drawn, and easily slashed the throats of the two guards. The bodies were covered with piles of straw. The *Jêpe* calmed after a few *pii*. The two men selected four beasts and led them out of the stalls, tethered them, and the men mounted and rode off.

In the morning, as the gray skies spread sadly over the landscape of Sorêg district, the men arrived at the edge of a wood dividing several fallow fields, greeting two other men who wore the uniforms of the Sekuatean military. The two who had brought the *Jêpe* quickly dismounted and changed into the uniforms the others provided.

Once ready, the quartet waited until another group of mounted soldiers came by and the waiting team ambushed the new soldiers. The attackers assumed the positions of those they had subdued and rode on in the direction the mission required of them. Soon they reached another stand of trees beside a lake and took their posts. The morning drew long and chilly and they began a conversation to pass the time.

"We're not even sure where he's from," said one in gravelly English as they waited beside their mounts, under the shadows of the trees.

"We don't know what accent he speaks," said another.

They debated the identity of their target, deciding that it did not matter so long as they followed their orders.

"We should speak Ghoupallêan since we are here."

"I got so used to this English, I forgot who I am."

"Quiet!" said the third member. "Pay attention. Here they come."

"Remember the plan," the first one cautioned, mounting.

"I will do the talking," said the second one.

The others nodded and the four moved out of the woods and onto the road.

Ahead, paused at the crossroads was their target: a military man of higher rank sitting on a *Jêpe*, seemingly unaware of their approach, perhaps lost in thought, perhaps just lost.

"*Kanê*," the quartet's spokesman addressed the captain. "*Ghou-se y zenmak-fomex d'ubrêsk*"—informing the captain that he was being targeted by rebels.

The captain looked up calmly, squinted at the four soldiers, searching in their faces for some iota of recognition and not finding any.

"*Kanê*," the solder continued, "*Ghou-s'els silden, g'elmas qam læforen.*"

Again the captain stared suspiciously at the soldier.

The captain's face was expressionless, eyes locked on the mounted guard before him.

The guard repeated his concern for the captain's safety. Seeing the captain apparently lacking mental acuity, the guard suggested that the captain might already have been drugged by some rebel, even a member of his own staff. They, on the other hand, the four of them, his personal escort, had not been present at that time and so could not have drugged his food or drink. They could be trusted. In fact, the morning intelligence briefing suggested that a band of rebels were even now waiting for him to enter the woods at the end of the nearby field.

The captain turned to regard the woods mentioned. He

appeared to be recalling a field in the early days of his visit to Sorêg district, when the stalks of *qink* were high and ripe. The guard knew the story, could almost hear the captain's thoughts as he pleasantly recalled walking through them to reach a private place suitable for relieving his bladder. Instead, he had found a young woman writing poetry.

"There," the captain mumbled in some strange language. "There beside the lake." He insisted he had to meet someone there. He raised his hand, pointing to the field, to the dark future beyond the line of trees. "There—over there—"

"*Nê, Kanê,*" the guard interrupted, frustration growing, "you must not go into the woods. It is not safe to go into the woods. You must come with us—"

At that precise instant the guard realized his mistake: English words had jumped from his mouth! Although they had a Ghoupallêan accent, they were English words. The captain's muttering had tricked him. The guard's eyes widened at his error, then focused on the captain's horrified expression.

Suddenly, the captain jerked the reins of his *Jêpe* and bolted wildly past the quartet, galloping down the road as fast as the ungainly beast could be prodded to go.

"After him!" another guard ordered.

They charged down the road, gaining on their target, but rounding a slope covered in trees they lost sight of him. They back-tracked and searched for hoof-prints in the dirt but there were too many to distinguish the right set. They rode along the country roads, first north, then east, then west. They regrouped at the original crossroads, staring south, waiting in silence.

"You idiot," the short one muttered to the spokesman of the group.

"*Sorêjix!*" another guard repeated so their sentiment would be clear.

"You've killed us all!" the third stated succinctly.

And the fourth nodded, then quietly dismounted, knelt in the dirt, and slid a knife deep into his heart.

From her seat beside the low table, the golden-haired woman watched with pained interest her lover discussing the plans with his men in the next room, wondering if it would succeed. No doubt the explosives would detonate. It would be the highlight of 1574. She wondered, however, whether such a dramatic act would have the intended effect. Besides destroying a few buildings and monuments, the blasts were to be timed to coincide with the large gathering of people at the Royal Audience. With luck, the foreigners who ruled over Aivana would be killed.

"You, Jinetta, are like these fake rulers," he had cursed her, though she sided with him.

"But I know what is right," she responded.

"Then you go, ask them to leave," he snarled.

She tried to discuss their options rationally but was met with the snarl at each statement. Lover or not, he was not a polite man. Whenever she suggested a less violent option, he accused her of being a traitor to the Revolutionary Council.

She thought of informing someone of the plot, debating with herself if that were the right course of action. If the foreigners would quietly hand over the keys to the kingdom to some local Aivana couple, then she could see being an informant as a good thing. But that would not likely be the case. Who was she? Just another Voyager, older and wiser. A refugee from an unfinished college program back on Earth, seduced by the chance to play a queen or more. Or less—the lover of a ragged rogue bent on destroying people like herself. In the beginning, it seemed like a good idea, righting wrongs, resetting the world to its proper balance.

Where did he go? She focused her mind on the fading image of her old schoolmate, Sebastian. Ever since she had the dream, ever since the old man made reference to him, she had been thinking of him, trying to remember the early days of adventure they had shared. His face was already dim in her memories. *Is he even on this planet?*

If the situation were reversed, she contemplated, would he come to intervene in this political conundrum?

She got up from her seat and pulled on a shawl to cover her bare shoulders against the cooler night air. The alighting of *i'i* was also a reason to cover her skin when outdoors in the evening. The tiny red flying insects loved to poke their beaks into flesh to suck the blood there. As the air cooled they became especially annoying, moving in small swarms to attack a person. Yet she dared go out, just to clear her mind and weigh her options once more. Perhaps she would not return, she thought as the door caught quietly behind her.

The streets were calm, the daily stirring of people's activities wound down. They were so unprepared for the Royal Audience.

She gazed up at the blue sun slipping behind the coastal mountains, wondering if it was really time for her to go, to move on, to start a new life. This one was done, she decided with a sigh. Two *i'i* landed on her cheek and she brushed them away. *Nothing to miss here by leaving.* Besides, the next place she were to go might be the place where she would once again meet that boy, the one who stood behind her in high school choir, the guy who knew about physics, who suggested they go somewhere else to make-out and instead found the doorway to another world.

"I will let fate decide," she spoke to the sunset.

She returned to the flat, took her daughter by the hand, and left again, vanishing into the desert night.

The cold rain fell steadily through the day and into the evening. The spring of 1533 would become known for its steady, heavy rainfall. In northern climes, especially in Tebbicousimankalê where armies clashed, there would be record snowfalls.

Could they have found a cheaper place to stay? the rain-soaked man thought as he approached the inn.

Few people were staying at the inn that night, so it made a good location, near the great palace of Siti, no longer inhabited by royalty in this nation of Ghoupallæssêa, set centrally within the Ghoupallæssus continent, across the ocean from Tebbicousimankalê. The vast, elegant, royal residence was now an international conference center and one of the most important conferences ever planned was ready to begin.

Customs were somewhat different in the New World, the drenched man now understood as he watched the streets for anyone following him. He was late returning, worried that his comrades would fear the worst. And he did not wish to have any mission failure blamed on him. Not this time, not like the previous mission had ended, with Ikorr-Gulgê committing suicide. Gulgê's team's failure required this new mission. Plan B. This one had to succeed.

The wooden stairs creaked as the man hurried up them, covering his head with a black cape. He went to the door at the end of the balcony and momentarily weighed the key in his hand.

The hotel room door quickly opened and closed, the man stepping inside before any of his comrades could notice.

"All right, I have it," said the intruder, Erutên-Vigasz. "It took longer than I expected to get the information out of our contact. He wanted more money, so I made him a deal: I let him live."

"You're a softy!"

He ignored the insult by his boss, continued: "He will be in the observatory of the west tower a little after midday. That is where he has been taking a nap after lunch. He likes to get the cool mountain breeze—"

"And the woman? What about her?" asked the muscular fellow with a large, curled moustache, Jurrên-Toulorus.

"She's irrelevant now," said Erutên-Vigasz. "She won't be there, anyway. We are to intercept the target only."

"Intercept?" asked Fêg-Louxê.

"Yes."

"Intercept only?"

"Intercept. Hold. Delay. Capture. Kill. Whatever we think necessary."

"The goal remains the same," said another man, blond and lightly bearded, who the others addressed as Number 2. They did not know him by any other name, though he clearly was a trusted confidant of the Captain. Officially, he was the team leader, though he usually allowed Erutên-Vigasz to take charge of their actions. "We must prevent him from meeting with the Zetin ambassador. If he does—"

"The Tebbis will be patsies for the Zetin and—"

"And the war will turn in favor of the Zetin."

"That is unacceptable."

They all agreed—even Fêg-Louxê, the explosives expert, who could be a doubter yet had done good work in previous missions.

Talk turned to the plan itself and someone produced and opened a map of the old palace on the table among them, pushing aside the off-brand bottles of weak *gor* and bowls of old, thickened *tabli*. It was time for work.

The group of seven established the routes they would take to enter the compound, the particular doors they would breach, the corridors they would monitor. Samot-Fênasz marked the small private conference room where their target would be meeting with other leaders to conclude a treaty intended to prevent the Zetin from entering the war on the side of Tebbicousimankalê. Bax-Tovêz and Erzuk-Rêssik briefly debated how that encounter would subvert the meeting between the Tebbi ambassador and the Zetin ambassador a mere two days hence. They marked the room where their target would be resting. Two others reported on the views of that room from other wings of the palace and from the courtyard below. They decided how they would enter that room, with its tall double doors and wide bank of windows opposite the doors. They again went over their escape route.

In less than a day the world would be set right once more.

* ❋ *

The water was cool now and the soap had disintegrated into sludge, so Set-d'Elous decided it was time to end his bath and go to bed for the night.

As he stood, allowing the scented water to run down his body, the maids came to his aid, one bearing a robe, the other a large towel. They dried him and dressed him.

"Thank you, ladies," he said in English, not caring that they would not understand him.

His time in Aivana was coming to an end, thankfully. There had been no Gina, after all, and 1574 would soon come to an end. Since he would be leaving soon, he had no reason to keep forcing himself to speak Rouê. Even reading *The Tales of Anatarka* again was no longer a pleasure, he mused, then bid the maids a good night and stepped across the room to his large bed—

"My large, empty bed," he muttered, sitting on the foot of it. *In America, this would be larger than king size. It would be...an emperor-sized bed!*

He pulled off his robe and threw himself back upon the bed, his body still too warm for him to need any coverings; eventually he slipped into a deep sleep.

In his dream he met Gina, his long-lost love, in a crowded bazaar in Aivana. She recognized him after he innocently backed into her. They hugged excitedly at the unexpected reunion. What're you doing here? Where've you been? What've you been doing? What's up for you next? All the usual questions Voyagers ask each other. They went to a café and talked about their lives together, back on Earth, and the last time at Kipzon on Ghoupallesz. The Revolutionary Council came up, of course, and he asked her why she joined it. Her response seemed reasonable but something she mentioned entirely at random stuck with him.

In the end, they made love—and in the morning he realized it had been one of the palace concubines who had visited him in the night, probably the one named A'o, he determined by the sweet/musky scent remaining with him. It was part of his therapy, Tammy insisted, believing more and more in the teachings of U'Pê, a local Rouê healer. More than once he had ordered that the custom be suspended in his case. Even so, Tammy continued to occasionally surprise him by sending a sleepmate, convinced that he needed one. He wanted to complain again, but lingering thoughts from his dream distracted him.

Pulling himself up for the day, he contemplated it.

In the dream, Gina had mentioned the name of Iadon-Repraxa. He knew the name from his visits to the Selauê Archives. Before 1533, Iadon-Repraxa was the leader of the Aivana ground forces that fought the Sekuatean army, at that time commanded by Latol-Secour. The guerilla warfare waged by Repraxa's men against the Sekuatean Army of the South, as it was known, was effective. He was gaining the support of the people; the royals were happy to be supported by the Sekuatean government, so they had to make a show of resisting the rebels. The scheme was working—including the eventual betrayal of Repraxa by a colleague, leading to his capture. The public execution in the great plaza of Seas was well-known for its brutality.

Now Repraxa was the leader of a rag-tag band of rebels?

That made no sense to him. Unless what he did in Sorêg also affected events in Aivana. He considered that possibility as he dressed for the day. With his act in Sorêg, Iadon-Repraxa, colonel of the 3rd Aivana Volunteers was not captured, did not face execution in Seas, and now was alive and well, available to overthrow the royal family of Aivana—who happened to be his friends from Earth, Tammy and Jason!

And the annual Royal Audience was coming soon! Perfect time for a coup!

Where is she? He thought of Gina as two maids brought his breakfast and arranged it on the low table in the center of the room.

One maid sat beside him and assisted him with the meal, cutting the meat, balling the soft, green *aji*, and dabbing the corners of his mouth and wiping the goblet after each sip. He felt he didn't deserve to be so pampered. He hated being a master— even as he tested them with strange commands, such as ordering one of them to put her thumb into her nose and keep it there while she served him his lunch, or having the other brush her hair so as to cover her face while he changed clothes. He engaged them in conversation, asking them about their plans for the future, or their knowledge of ancient history, or gardening—

Gina must understand the situation if she is to interfere!

The other maid quickly left but was replaced by two buxom musicians, bare-chested and barefoot, filmy green harem-chic pantaloons between. They began a lovely dining serenade for him on a Roûe reed flute and Tigu five-stringed lute.

She must act to stop the plot! Or allow him to do so. Somehow.

The maid assisting him with the meal sensed his tension and, not realizing its true origin, began soothing him by caressing his leg with her hand. Her hand worked down his thigh, then moved to his groin.

"That's not helping," he grunted after a moment. "I need to think now," he said in Roûê, then dismissed the maid.

Perhaps Gina was not even in town, he considered. Perhaps she would not be a part of the terrorist act, after all. Hadn't he changed history? In the greater scheme of things, he had kept her from her intended journey—the diary of her lives was no longer accurate. Perhaps she skipped Iadon-Repraxa. Perhaps she would skip Aivana now. Perhaps, everything was going to be fine.

Except that I'll miss her. Maybe next time. Maybe in her next life.

The door quickly opened and closed, and the men inside looked up, seeing Erutên-Vigasz had returned earlier than expected in rain-soaked Siti.

"The mission has changed," said Erutên, breathless, "only slightly—but significantly."

Chucker got up from cleaning his weapon and pulled Erutên aside.

"Tell me," said the leader.

"Xâta-Mek got the official schedule and it's changed."

"How?"

"The Emperor will not—repeat: will not—be idling in the small audience room on the third floor, west wing at noon, as previously scheduled."

"What?" Chucker exclaimed in a hushed voice, not wanting to alarm his men. They were nervous enough already. "How are we supposed to—?"

"I don't know," said Erutên, shaking his head. "He now *wants* to address the Council of Nations instead of snub them after they invited him to speak."

"Holy crap!" Chucker looked away, thinking of twelve alternative plans.

"In the new schedule he rests in an anteroom near the Grand

Hall prior to his speech."

Chucker's eyes brightened. "Show me."

They went to the map of the Royal Palace and Erutên pointed to the Grand Hall, then to the anteroom down a side corridor.

"It is out of the way, presumably to keep him from being interrupted by those who want a favor or autograph—"

"But it makes him isolated for us, for our purposes!"

Chucker called the group's attention and explained the situation and the need to change the plan. Some grumbled that there had been plenty of changes already. One said he had not signed up for such bullshit. Two others voiced their concern whether or not any of their plans would be effective given the high security of the Royal Palace.

"We need to intercept the target before he enters the Grand Hall," the leader explained. "We do not want a crowd of a hundred national representatives as witnesses. Better he die in his sleep, before anyone suspects what has happened."

They reworked each team member's checkpoints and movements, matching them against the blueprint of the palace. Satisfied, their leader sat back and finally exhaled.

"That'll work."

"What about his mistress?" someone asked.

Sometimes he enjoyed stretching out on the bed, staring at the ceiling, imagining the swirls of plaster were clouds and that between them the sun always shone.

"I can't find him anywhere!" cried Tammy, walking into his chamber before he could get up and dress.

"Chucker's a big boy now," he reminded her. "He can take care of himself. He'll be back in time for the Royal Audience. Probably he needs some boy time—time to be a guy, not a prince."

"You mean he needs playtime?" asked Tammy.

"Exactly." He swung his feet to the side of the great bed, paused to yawn, holding the sheet over his lap. "You didn't see him much as he was growing up. You remember him as a baby, a toddler, a little boy—not as a teenager, not as a youth, not as he is now, a man."

"I know," she said and choked up.

"We live a long time here," he told her, pushing his feet to the tiled floor and rising from the bed, dropping the sheet. He grabbed the burgundy robe on the chair next to the bed and casually wrapped it around himself. "I've got to go to the bathroom, Tammy."

She clapped her hands and the door opened, a maid poking her head in to receive the Queen's instructions. Tammy ordered a lavatory bowl—and in came two maids. One maid gingerly directed the urine flow as the other held the basin. Tammy looked away, continued complaining. When he had finished, the first maid carefully wiped him with a white cloth. The two maids withdrew, presumably disposing of the morning piss.

"I want him to rule with me here," spoke the Queen.

"That's the idea I got from all the lessons you're pushing on him." Dressed in the robe, he sat on the foot of the bed, facing her. "But that's not what he wants. He wants to be a man—a warrior, not a politician. It's not that he doesn't love you. He does."

"Are you sure?" She needed a positive response, he saw.

"Of course, he does. Every boy loves his mother."

He thought about that, wondering. He could no longer conjure a clear image of his own mother. Nor his father. It was almost as though they did not exist, had never existed, and he was born fully grown and already in trouble.

"Maybe after this Royal Audience," he spoke Tammy, "you should cut him some slack. Instead of acting as prince, he could be put in charge of the local brigade of your Aivana Volunteers. That'll teach him some responsibility, military maneuvers and all. Of course, he's been learning a lot from me—and my associates." He stopped, unsure how much he should tell Tammy about her son's role in History, Inc. Chucker had just returned from a crucial mission, after all. "He has a military mind. Give him time," he added.

She gazed up at him, grinning, her mouthful of white teeth shining. "You always know what to say to make me feel good. You always know how to make things right."

"So I'm not a bull in the china shop?"

"Certainly not." She stood and went to him, spread her arms to hug him. "You are so good to me. You always have been. I've never been able to pay you back for everything you've done for me. So I wanna offer you a chance to decide. Tell me. What can I do for you?"

He allowed an innocent shoulder hug, tapping her back a few times as she squeezed him tightly.

"You could let me leave," he whispered into her ear. "Again."

They parted.

Tammy's mouthful of bright white teeth grinned.

"I was thinking something like, maybe, you'd want more ladies, or more beautiful ladies. I could find you a wife, too. You seem so sad sometimes, like you're lonely. You need a good companion. A man has needs. U'Pê says daily sex is important for optimal health. Everyone needs to rid their bodies of toxins and bad spirits. We have some new ladies just completing their training. You could choose—"

"Actually, I don't think I need that," he said, a little embarrassed. He wondered if she meant that she, too, had men to assist her with her optimal health because his friend Jason couldn't keep her satisfied. And what about Jason's appetites? Hmmm. He grinned at her. "No, not any longer. It was just a phase I was going through—I call it Youth. Ah, maybe I'm getting old—older, anyway. Now? I think I have a date with Destiny, or one of her sisters."

"Okay, dear Sebastian, you're free to go. After the Royal Audience." She kissed him. "I'll have a royal ETUR ready to take you to the KOHAX station. We'll say goodbye now."

"Thanks, Tammy." He smiled warmly.

A tiny bell rang and the Queen glanced at the door, opened by a maid.

"Send them away," she spoke in Rouê. "He doesn't want to meet the new girls."

The door closed.

Tammy turned back to her friend. "Where will you go? What will you do?"

He shrugged. "That depends on my dreams."

✳ ✳ ✳

The leader of the A-Team read the report, brought by the archivist, Samot-somebody, who had found it in historical records from the earlier version of history. He had traverse three tangents—Earth to Ghoupallesz in 1581 to get the information, back to Earth to re-enter a new tangent, then back to Ghoupallesz in the altered year of 1533, where they were now—and nervously presented what he felt was so significant.

"*Vâ ben senzenaxii*," the archivist spoke solemnly.

"Speak English," Chucker snapped. "What does that mean?"

Samot the archivist cleared his throat as he mentally threw the switch to change languages. Then: "She is one of the rare people who have a certain mental power," he said, searching for the right words. "*Vai senzenor.* There is no English word for it. She is a *senzenor*. It was not in official records. She can read a person's mind—"

"She's a mind-reader," Chucker growled.

"Not always," the archivist corrected. "The records suggest that when the original incident occurred—"

"When Set-d'Elous first killed her."

"—she may not have been aware of this power. Now, certainly, she is not only aware of it but uses it to great effect."

"How?"

"She seems to be able to control people's thoughts. She makes people do her bidding. At least in a highly suggestible manner. Only those people with whom she can spend some time. Servants perhaps. She needs to get to know a person well enough to bind her thoughts to the person's mind—"

"Could she read our minds as we approach?" asked Chucker.

Samot sighed. "That is my concern."

"You said she needed to spend time with someone to be able to do that."

"With Ghoupalles, yes." He paused and stared at the leader. "With an Earth person, it would be easier for her."

Chucker quickly ascertained the situation: "So you're saying I could jeopardize the mission? She could read my mind and know we were coming for her, so she might escape or call her guards."

"That is my concern."

Chucker rubbed his chin, thinking. Then, realizing his mentor also had the same stupid habit, he stopped and scratched his crotch instead.

"I have to lead the team," he said after another moment to consider the situation. "Is there some way we can block her radar?"

"What I understand of the *senzenor* arts—let us recall Set-d'Elous himself was the consort of such a *senzenor*, with Zaura-Matousz, so we know—"

"I've heard the story," said Chucker impatiently, "but it has no bearing on this mission. He's not even involved."

"Yes, I understand." Samot took a deep breath. "The *senzenor* is not 'on-duty,' we might say, at all times. Use of the power will weaken her. She cannot continue it for a long time. Also, she must concentrate her mental focus whenever she wishes to use the power. When she is asleep, she does not use it."

"So we should act when she's asleep."

"Then she will not detect your approach."

"We will need to alter our plan," said the leader, glancing around the room at the team members.

"We need to arrive earlier," Chucker continued, "catch them both in bed and *bam!* two birds with one humongous stone!" He smiled sympathetically. "We have another change to the plan."

One of the men looked up, reflecting the mood of the others. "We're still going to kill the evil bitch and her idiot consort, aren't we?"

"That part hasn't changed."

"Good! I still want to climb the tower and rappel through the window of their chamber."

"That, unfortunately, will need to be changed."

"How?"

"We will sneak in dressed as one of the delegations."

"That's how women go on a mission—dressing up!"

"The end justifies the means," their leader reminded them.

✳ ❋ ✳

There comes a time, thought Queen Tammy as the platoon of servants washed and bathed her in the quick, delicate motions as custom dictated, when everything will change forever—big changes, grand changes, and nothing is ever bad or disappointing after that. Today would be such a special day. Her son would be officially installed as a prince of Aivana. He would be able to command his own staff. To introduce him to the world, dignitaries from neighboring nations would be attending. A prince of Typeg would present him with a stupendous gift: his daughter as potential bride. It would be a surprise, like Christmas and birthday all wrapped together. He was old enough, she figured; after all, she had Chucker when she was young. He was older than that now, she calculated. But it was all purely for ceremony, a polite political gesture. She was following Roûê customs. Chucker would refuse the bride, naturally, both of them being so unready for marriage. It was the thought that counted in these desert diplomatic diversions. And, as always, her best friend, the man appointed as *Mexas*, Set-d'Elous, would be attending, more to see the boy become a man than to act in any official capacity. There would be some menial business, of course. Her husband, Jason Aronstein, mentioned some silly treaty she needed to stamp with the official seal while the public witnessed it, something about more economic cooperation, her least favorite subject, oh well—

Having no concern about events in other times and other places, forgetting about that former life on distant Earth, the Queen of Aivana glanced about the room, her eyes following the diminutive helpers as they grabbed bits of fiber on the tips of tongs and touched them to her skin, spot by spot, first the moistening, then the drying, then the administering of cologne, piece by piece, from the spaces between her toes, up her body to the hidden places, the covered portions of her body and those visible to the public, to her armpits, neck, ear creases, to the margins of her hair—all in the manner she had heard described by Set-d'Elous.

When he told her how the Lady Jinetta had been prepared to

meet her captor, the evil Zetin warlord Whateverhisnamewas, she thought it must be the most elegant way for a noble lady to be made exquisite, suitable to be worshipped by members of her court. So she adopted the Zetin custom and even had Zetin maidens imported to train her staff. She hired short Aivanans to become her personal staff. They were clumsy at first, hesitant to touch the body of the Queen, reluctant to set eyes upon her royal nakedness, but over time it became routine and only Queen Tammy seemed to regard the hours-long ritual as a divine procedure worthy only of her. To her staff, it was a supreme hassle and they dreaded the days she held audience with her subjects, yet they dared not roll their eyes at her often rude comments or lick their lips when they snuck a gaze at her private parts. Sometimes she noticed. Sometimes she did not seem to mind, even flirted with them just to get them excited only to dismiss them.

In the end, fully bathed through this painstaking poke-a-spot method, she was dressed in her newest outfit: a set of filmy pantaloons in teal, striped in golden *smophê* leaves—'palm fronds' in English, *ha'ep'a* in Rouê—and a matching blouse, puffy and thin, barely extending to the bottom of her ribs, leaving the flat, taut royal belly quite uncovered, all the better to show off the huge, bright blue *tu'pu* gemstone set prominently in her navel, all the better to show off her finely tuned abdomen, sleek and sexy, even for a mother of her age, with so many children—

Ah! This will be a grand audience, she mused, looking herself over.

She adjusted the small pink velvet vest that hung over her shoulders yet remained open enough to display the fullness of the royal breasts, grown round and large in her years of gustatory delights, heavy on the Aivanan dairy products.

I am amazing, she thought.

❋ ❋ ❋

Three men stood around the bed, regarding the figure of the dark-haired woman, crumpled awkwardly there, her bright red blood soaking the white sheets, dripping onto the beige carpet.

"I'm glad I don't have to clean that," said one.

"I thought it would be more difficult," said the leader glumly.

"Was she supposed to fight back?" snapped another man.

"We should have raped her before we killed her," the first man growled.

"She's the devil," the leader rebuked him. "You want to be corrupted like her?"

"I just wanted to dirty her!"

"With your own pollution?" the second man said.

"What's important is she's now dead," said the leader.

They stepped back, fixed their weapons to their belts and scanned the room for any sign of their presence, wanting to leave no mark. Outside, a fourth team member, dressed as a palace guard, stood as lookout.

The room was large and elegantly decorated, the large *qala* set against the wall. In the first instant of entering they were awestruck at its richness. Then they went to work. The woman was asleep when they entered.

Their partner, Xâta-Mek, the only woman on the History, Inc. team, had opened the door for them. She had worked for three years to become accepted and trusted by the Empress, just for this moment. She had brought the Lady's lunch, as scheduled, wearing the maid uniform she had always worn. Xâta, short yet buxom, with long, light-brown hair, stayed as the Lady ate, assisting her with the elegant meal, dabbing a towel at her mouth, participating in polite small talk.

After the meal, at the Lady's insistence, Xâta proceeded to perform a full body massage on her. An affectionate smile crossed her face, playing her role, and began undressing the Lady. She accepted a playful kiss from the Lady once she was nude, but broke away to get the bottle of oil from the dresser. Once on the bed, Xâta followed the Lady's instructions, working her hands up and down the Lady's body from toes to buttocks then on to back and shoulders and neck. She had to admire the fitness and beauty of a woman that age, but she also reminded herself that this woman was the evil Empress.

When the Lady was relaxed on the bed, a nap imminent, Xâta gently climbed off the bed and opened the chamber's door. The team entered quickly and she exited, uniform in hand, without so much as a curious glance back. Her job was done.

They stood at the foot of the bed, their eyes momentarily transfixed on the sleeping woman, admiring her nude body. Then the leader signaled with a nod. The second man pulled out a knife as the third man jumped atop her, grabbing her head and twisting it sideways while clamping his gloved hand over her mouth.

"Where's your lover?" the leader grunted at her in angry Ghoupallêan, her eyes suddenly open, reflecting terror.

They wanted to catch both together in bed. But they had been delayed entering the palace. Obviously, the Emperor had risen already and was proceeding on the day's schedule. Plan C would need to be put into effect. Both Emperor and Empress must be removed, no matter the cost. Tomorrow would be too late.

She mumbled something defiant under the attacker's hand, struggling against the attacker's grip. They could not understand her. She got a few strong kicks in, disabling one of the men. The leader nodded and they finished it: twisting her head until neck bones snapped, thrusting the knife under her ribs, into her heart, then downward across her abdomen. Blood splattered out of her chest and bowels spilled from belly as they climbed off the bed.

"May she turn over and over in the orgies of Ur-tha!"

They watched the blood spread like ripples in a pond through the white bedding, then left.

Chapter 28

Father's Day

Dr. Franck took her son down to Mrs. Gompers earlier and returned to the apartment to prepare for her meeting. For such an important occasion, the reunion with her lover on a balmy summer's evening, she chose a sleek, colorful dress with skinny straps and low-cut V-neck. Not what she would wear in public even in the heat of summer, but she wanted to make an impression on him: gold ear rings that matched the orange and yellow dress and golden sandals. Gazing into the mirror, she carefully put up her dark, curly hair, both to look more elegant and be more comfortable in the muggy evening.

She hurried down to her landlady's apartment—as quickly as she could, using her braces.

"You're going out now?" asked Mrs. Gompers. "It's already so late."

Her son was already tucked in on the sofa, asleep.

"I know it's late but it's very special," Toni explained.

"He's out already," Mrs. Gompers, glancing at the boy.

"We had a good day at the park," said Toni. "I guess he finally wore out."

"What time'll you be back for him?"

"I hope it won't be long. I'm sorry for the inconvenience. The taxi's coming now. Maybe a couple of hours?" She thought a moment, fantasized for a few breaths. "If I'm later, it'll be all right to let him sleep here?"

"I suppose so," said the landlady, "but let's not make a habit of it. I got my own things to tend to."

"I know and I'm sorry." She looked at her watch. "Mon Dieu! It's nearly ten now! Where is that taxi? I need to be there at ten."

After another ten minutes, there was a honk outside. The taxi had arrived. She bid farewell to Mrs. Gompers and gave her sleeping son a kiss, then went out the door.

"Where to, ma'am?" asked the driver.

"I don't know the address," she explained, "but I'll guide you. We need to head out I-70 over to Blue Ridge Boulevard. Then go east on 40 Highway until you get to Lee's Summit Road."

They took off and at that hour found little traffic. Toni instructed him to turn here, turn there, out 39th Street, past the newly built shopping mall, onto some back country road and finally to Pink Hill Road.

"It's a house set off from the road," she told the driver.

They drove ahead slowly.

"What's that?" the driver said.

Toni looked ahead over his shoulder. Two police cars blocked the road, but no lights were flashing on the cruisers as the taxi rolled to a halt.

An officer wearing a vest came up to the taxi with a flashlight, his hand up to halt them. The driver rolled down the window.

"You can't go further on this road. You'll have to turn back."

"Is something wrong?" asked the driver.

"Police business." He shined the light into the back seat. "Ma'am, may I see some I.D., please?"

"Sure, officer." She dug in her purse, retrieved her driver's license. "I know it's expired—that's why I'm using a taxi tonight—but I'll get it renewed soon"—the officer looked it over under the flashlight—"when I can walk without these braces. I can almost walk now but I need a little more time to feel confident—"

"Ma'am, this your real name?" asked the officer.

"Yes, of course." She smiled, trying to be friendly. Ever since she left the hospital she discovered she was famous—infamous, actually. "Yes, I'm that doctor who awoke from the coma, if that's what you're wondering."

"No, ma'am." The officer turned from the taxi and spoke into the radio hanging on his shoulder: "It's her. We got her here, safe and sound."

"Great," came the response, "we can begin."

She looked ahead at the figures moving in the dark beyond the police cars. Only a few yards further would be the field, and at the back of the field would be the old house.

"They know," she muttered to herself.

"What's that?" asked the driver.

"Nothing." She called to the officer: "Should I stay?"

"Yes, ma'am."

"I guess I should stay," she said to the driver and they settled the fare.

Stepping out of the taxi with her braces, she saw two men in suits approach her. They greeted her as the taxi turned around and drove off. They showed her over to a patrol car, gave her a blanket and a cup of coffee from a thermos.

"Doctor Franck," said Detective Wilson, "would you tell us where you are headed this evening?"

"Just out for a drive."

"This late? Wearing a nice dress like that?"

"I was supposed to meet a friend...but I guess I won't be, after all. I think he stood me up. It's happened before."

"Can you tell us about your friend?" asked Detective Sawyer.

Toni let out a long sigh, knowing that things were not going to happen according to plans. She hated that. And these two were obviously onto her, knew more than she knew. But she had to protect him, her lover—whether or not he was actually in that old house.

"He was a good guy, but misunderstood by everyone," she said, staring up at the stars as SWAT members around her were locking and loading.

"What's his name?" asked Wilson.

"His name?" She regarded the detective, could see in his face that he already knew the answer but wanted her to confirm it was Sebastian Talbot. She forced a smile. "He called himself Set."

"Set? What kind of name is that?"

"It's Egyptian, I believe." She wondered. "The name of an ancient Egyptian god, the God of Destruction. That's ironic. I could never be with the God of Destruction, after all. You know? It just wouldn't work out."

"And that's who you were coming to meet out here tonight?" asked Detective Wilson.

"In an ideal world," she sighed, ignoring him, "he and I would be together. Forever."

The Great Royal Hall of Aivana was brightly decorated for the special occasion: colorful ceiling-to-floor streamers and wall-to-wall ribbons, woven baskets of vivid long-stemmed flowers gathered from the far corners of the kingdom, and shield-shaped placards of the royal crest and the triangular banners representing each of the tribes and towns of the kingdom. The marble-like walls and their tall fluted columns were a deep reddish-brown, the placards golden and blue, the banners green, yellow, black, brown, and white, the flowers a myriad of hues. The floor tiles were highly scrubbed and shone crystal blue in the limited light of the room. Guards were stationed at intervals around the hall and at the head of the room.

Set-d'Elous was pleased with what he saw and knew the queen would appreciate his efforts. Everything would go perfectly. Then, finally, he could bow out.

On the dais sat three huge wooden thrones, ornately carved and bedecked with jewels and gold. The center one was for Queen Tammy, who had captured the love of their king and remained to inspire and lead them after his death. The child she and the king had together, a girl named O'Fe'o'pi would stand at her side. On the Queen's right was the smaller throne for her new husband, Jason Aronstein, the now less-obese regent who was building the great arch in memorial to their dead king. Next to him would stand Prince Chucker, who had no royal standing except by the queen's whim. That he was even present on the dais was unsettling to many in the room and a constant source of disgruntlement during the festival preparations. The throne on the left was for the dead king's eldest son, E'Bu'li'rou, whom he had with his first queen, O'Le'e'tu, before he met the pregnant

Tammy on Agani Isle. It was ceremonially proper to provide a throne for the king's eldest son and they honored the custom though he never attended these public events. He avoided the royal court for the life of a playboy in Seas or other cities to the north. Some said he was plotting an overthrow, biding his time, that he had gone to Typeg and collected a group of mercenaries to throw out the foreigners who dared rule in his father's name. It was only a matter of time, Set-d'Elous believed as he stood admiring the elaborate decorations of the room, before they would need to flee in the middle of the night.

To that purpose he had been testing the area around the palace, searching for a tangent he might use to escape. He was often spied late at night moving with great slowness about the courtyards and hanging gardens of the palace—"Doing his midnight Tai Chi," Jason remarked to valets or maids or Tammy, seeing his old friend from a balcony or a doorway. The two of them avoided conversation; it always seemed to lead them into some violent argument. In his movements, Set was nearly nude, arms outstretched, legs and feet touching as many air molecules as possible, waiting to sense the pulse of a tangent. He had come to believe that tangents existed everywhere but that most were hidden by the landscape, the architecture, or restricted to those who knew how to recognize them. He had become an expert.

Meanwhile, in case a suitable tangent could not be found, Plan B was a plain-looking yet sturdy carriage with the quickest *Jêpe* hitched, standing ready to roll—better than the motorized Etur in the narrow streets and certainly better once they went cross-country.

Set-d'Elous breathed in the fragrant air of the Great Hall as the first of the elegantly adorned pre-approved citizens entered through the three-story high doorway, blazing sunlight sliding across the tile floor as the towering doors slowly opened, the squarish block of green light spreading toward his position, then engulfing him and connecting all the tiles to the outdoors. More citizens entered in patient streams, respectful of the Great Hall, solemn and silent. Few guards watched the crowds once they entered, so well-behaved were they. Gradually murmurs arose. He was impressed, having expected a riotous throng.

Standing off to the side, out of the sunlit area of the floor, he regarded his robes, bejeweled belt, short cape and curly-toed boots. What a dandy! How in the world could he and these other ordinary people from a world called Earth make themselves kings and queens here? Luck, of course. The grace of the gods— or their wont to ignore him and his friends. Skullduggery, perhaps. Clever subterfuge, definitely. And endless arrogance. He felt guilty, then didn't.

Eventually the Great Hall was filled wall to wall with the formally dressed citizens of Aivana: those with complaints, favors to ask, or petitions to present; those who had drawn the lottery to be invited, those whose cases were deemed so serious they warranted an audience with the Queen, and those upper-class snobs who attended official functions religiously. Perhaps four thousand people, he estimated, standing shoulder to shoulder. He had become pressed against the back corner of the hall, near the entrance doors—which was fine for him, since he was waiting to leave—but he politely pushed his way out to where guards had split the crowd and made a wide aisle down the center of the hall.

As he reached the edge of the crowd, he gazed across the aisle to his opposite number, a purely random act—merely raising his eyes from the floor where he had been careful not to step on anyone's sandaled toes—and there she was: the golden-haired lady he had so long adored.

Gina? Is that you?

His heart skipped thirteen beats and his head felt light. She was dressed in a glittery golden toga with green leaf-patterned ornaments about her shoulders and around her waist. She was gazing forward to the dais at the far end of the room, like most of the citizenry. He took a moment to study her, to trace the line of her profile, to determine if this woman actually was Gina, his long-lost love. The resemblance was remarkable!

This is the time for her to arrive, he reminded himself. Gina was scheduled to appear in Aivana this year, according to her own diary. And according to a reference in a historical text, written before he had changed history. Yet, considering her rank as the Queen of Fenula—former queen, at least—certainly she should be allowed to attend this privileged occasion. There was no announcement of her arrival, not like the lesser nobility of

Aivana as each entered the hall. There were no guards or escort for her. Just her golden beauty.

Could that be her?

He was about to call across the aisle to her—a rude act in this venue, but he had to know if the woman was Gina—when suddenly a troupe of entertainers entered the Great Hall, acrobats and jugglers performing to the delight of the crowd, blocking his view. He waited patiently but as the entertainers passed, he saw that she had disappeared. He scanned the crowd in each direction from where she had stood, searching for the golden head in the sea of black hair. He stretched up on his toes to look over the heads and saw nothing of her.

Perhaps it was not her. He felt resigned; his eyes were playing tricks on him.

The people around him were whistling, building to a loud volume, and he saw the reason. Out from the red and brown curtains behind the thrones on the dais stepped the young princes and princesses of the dead king: first O'Fe'o'pi, the daughter he had with Queen Tammy, followed by most of the king's previous children by Queen O'Le'e'tu: the five boys— second-eldest son E'Mo'mo, the athletic *Fogo* star E'Li'hou, leg-lamed academy graduate E'Ha'fa (some believed his mother was a palace concubine), the rude and bad-complexioned E'Dou'le (some believed his father was a palace guard), and the irritating jokester E'Ma'lou (half of a set of twins, the other stillborn and preserved in a large vase)—and the three girls: solemn and stately O'Pi'lo, always cute and feminine O'E'di (considered the king's favorite), and the ever-precocious (often slutty, in recent years) O'Ha'fi. The old king's favored eldest son, E'Bu'li'rou, was again absent, as everyone expected.

Out stepped Tammy's pretty blonde daughter, O'Ro'ma'le, conceived one random night with Michael Fenning in the apartment of Set-d'Elous back on Earth, walking hand in hand with her foreign-born son, Prince Chucker (Qi'jou'ka being the Rouê pronunciation). Uncomfortably dressed in flowing purple robe, he grimaced, wanting to be anywhere else but on stage. He wanted to be done with political protocols.

In fact, Chucker had tried to get out of the Royal Audience, insisting he had more important business to do. There had been a big mistake, he told his mother, a serious error that needed his immediate attention. Nonsense, she had replied, waving him to silence. What kind of foolishness could a sweet young man like her son possibly get into? He had tried to continue explaining, even included his step-father, Jason, in the discussion. Nothing could be done at the moment, Jason told him, so might as well do their duty and stand through the Royal Audience. Chucker was steaming, desperate to be understood, but his parents made him wait.

Lastly, out stepped the youngest children, those of Queen Tammy and Jason, her consort: Buffy, Jason Jr., Kip, and Mary-Ann—who each received scant applause, only enough to be polite. They were not in line for the throne, everyone knew, so people were willing to indulge them.

The royal offspring stood stiffly in a line from left to right across the stage as the crowd cheered with customary whistling. The crowd waited, knowing that the royal couple would emerge next. Time passed. The crowd seemed puzzled. Before their beloved Queen Tammy could appear, they must endure waiting for the Queen's husband, Jason, to step out—

"Pardon me, your majesty," a blond-haired woman in golden robe spoke to Jason from an unregally close distance, gently restrained by two guards and their lances. She was comely enough to catch his attention. No one had called him 'your majesty' for a long time, and certainly not in English!

"Excuse me?" said the surprised royal. "Do I know you?"

It was obvious that they had something in common by their mutual use of the foreign tongue, the guards saw and let up their lances.

"I'm a friend of your friend—"

"Then you're not my enemy," laughed Jason.

"—who must urge you to leave the palace with your family as soon as you can."

"Why? Is there going to be an earthquake? An epidemic?"

"No, but...there is a plot to—"

"Oh, I've heard that before," said Jason. "It can't be true, though. The people love us. See that arch out back? That's for them, to honor their king. They love that arch!"

"Actually, they don't. It's kind of the last straw. In fact, I've heard th—"

"What'd you say your name was?"

"I'm Gina."

His face lit up. "I've heard of you."

"Good, then you'll believe me when I say the plot is serious."

"Plot, you say?" He cocked his head comically to the side.

"Yes. Get out now. Don't even finish the audience."

"But we have to!" He glanced at the gap in the curtain, a valet motioning for him to hurry and join the family on stage. "We're committed to this event. Then we'll think of what to do."

"That may be too late."

He nodded, smiled sheepishly.

"Thanks for the, umm, warning, anyway," he said, adding a curt wave.

She tried, at least.

"Good luck."

She turned and brushed past the guards, turning down a side corridor which led out of the Great Hall.

Jason stood behind the curtain, looking across at Tammy on the other side. She had seen him speaking with that blonde woman. He blushed, shrugging, then stepped out onto the dais. The consort stood next to Prince Chucker in the line and the crowd grew less enthusiastic, many hating the vast expense of the memorial arch he had started.

When the audience had become quiet, the Queen of Aivana appeared, as if by magic, in her flowing pale seashell green gown, the golden jewelry shining in the light of the Great Hall. All eyes were on her and whistling erupted again, followed by foot stamping which quickly settled into a unison thumping that shook the hall. She moved before her throne and raised her arms to welcome the crowd. Then she carefully sat upon her throne and motioned for the children to exit stage right. Only Jason, Chucker, and O'Fe'o'pi stayed. Jason sat on his throne and Chucker stood next to him while the girl, O'Fe'o'pi, stood beside her mother's throne. The girl was the link between their king and the present queen, Tammy understood, so the crowd needed to see the girl as part of the royal family.

Queen Tammy spoke from her throne, a welcoming message that led into an impromptu speech about history and commerce in Aivana, ending with some encouraging remarks about the future. That surprised *Mexas* Set-d'Elous, lost in the crowd. He had never heard her speak at length before, certainly not in Rouê. He was pleased, proud. What was more remarkable, was that her speech was in fairly good, almost colloquial Rouê. That alone was worth the price of admission, he snickered.

Next came the long-bearded, long-robed prince from Typeg with a veiled figure in tow. The veil's red cloth was interwoven with gold strands, a shimmering spectacle as they moved up the aisle. Ladies in the audience were delighted, men were aroused.

He was too far away to hear clearly but he understood the ritual. The Typeg prince would throw compliments at the Queen: about her beauty, her good economic sense, her fidelity to her people, and so on, ending in compliments about her son, Chucker, and how he was such a fine young man and now ready to begin a family of his own. The Typeg prince would be ever so grateful were the Queen's son to fancy his best daughter, the young lady under the red veil, and that if such were to be a good match he would provide a fabulous palace for them, into which a beautiful and strong female-child would be created, one who would unite their two lands, and so on. But a male-child would also be welcomed, he added.

Of course, the girl under the red veil would be gorgeous, Set-d'Elous imagined, and Chucker would certainly like the surprise. But it was all statecraft and the Queen would gently refuse the offer, to be reconsidered in three years' time. That would fulfill the obligations both she and the prince from Typeg were required to perform. Still, he could see that Chucker was curious, perhaps also aroused, as he stared at the veiled young woman the whole time she was kneeling before the dais.

Then Queen Tammy deftly included Chucker in suggesting solutions to the problems presented. Listening to the litany of complaints from the people of Aivana, Set gradually slipped out of his attention. As the citizens took turns spilling their guts to the queen, the crowd seemed to wait patiently, apparently also concerned about each of their countrymen's problems. He had heard it all before: personal grudges, unfair labor practices, economic woes, bad deals, unfulfilled marriage contracts, how many *oñacha* for a given price, where to pave a road—and many more. He grew tired.

What could even a king or queen do to alleviate someone's personal problems? And yet, what had he ever done to alleviate anyone's problems? That sobered him. He'd played God, sure, but that had yet to pay off.

Set-d'Elous let out a long sigh. His work was done. That was enough, he thought, ready to leave, ready for the next great adventure. He had returned the boy to his mother, had turned him over to a step-father who made him a man, then mentored the youth in all the knowledge a Voyager needed to know, even trained him to be a fighter and a leader in History, Inc. When this Royal Audience was done, Chucker could return to his team and proceed with the next mission, making the world right again for his and others' families.

He breathed deeply. It was time for him to go, too, he knew, feeling satisfied for the first time in a very long while.

As he cut his way through the crowd toward the open doors, he saw two men trying to enter. Guards were holding them back. That kind of drama was what he expected at this kind of a public gathering. He had no reason to stay so he changed directions, made his way to a side door under the ramparts that held up the staircase leading to the balcony. The guard there recognized him and let him pass, closing the door behind.

There was a commotion at the main doors. Four guards were clasping the arms of two men. One was tall and dark-skinned, dressed in a long beige robe. The other was larger, bare-chested and well-muscled, dressed in leather greaves and a skirt— Roman gladiator style. They were struggling to break free of the guards and other guards were rushing to the entrance.

Suddenly the gladiator person broke free and burst into the Great Hall like a whirlwind, shouting: "Tammy Sue! Tammy Sue!"

"Chuck...?" the Queen uttered.

"Tami'su'o! He'ilo'ye Alebafe!" the gladiator guy cried out in stilted Roûê.

The gladiator fellow ran up the aisle about half-way to the stage before he was stopped by a gang of lance-wielding guards. The man had the crowd's attention. More guards lumbered into the Great Hall, lances poised. The other man, the tall/thin/dark one, shook himself free of the entrance guards and ran up the aisle to his partner. Together they stood amid the crowd of four thousand people.

"Tammy Sue," called the gladiator boldly, "I have returned! I have returned for you! I have braved the harsh life of a slave for you! I have fought my way through Hell for you! I have suffered so much just so I can bring myself to you in purity and love! I can say now, Tammy Sue, I love you!" He fell silent, catching his breath. "Tammy Sue, it's me! Chuck! Your husband!"

The guards surrounding Chuck had their lances pointing at him, unaware that he knew how to handle the lance effectively. His companion, obviously an outlander Rouê, stood outside the circle of spearpoints but had a guard on him as he cowered, a sword pressed against his neck.

The crowd stepped back to give the drama its stage. The view from the dais, so far away, was limited, yet the Queen had stood up and was gazing down the aisle at the intruders.

Then she stepped down from the stage!

The audience gasped.

Down another step, another gasp!

The queen never left the stage during an audience, yet this one had.

And she seemed to want to break yet another tradition!

Queen *Tami'su'o* took the train of her gown in her hands and stepped forward onto the mundane floor of ordinary people, touching her slippers to the polluted surface, the hem of her gown brushing along the dirty tiles as she moved with increasingly quick steps down the aisle to—*gasp!*—where the barbarians were encircled by guards.

Jason Aronstein stood up on the seat of his throne to see Tammy in the crowd, unsure what to do.

"Tammy!" he called after her, remembering the warning he had received. "Wait! Come back!"

Chucker suddenly jumped down from the dais to the common floor, concerned about his mother, and followed her.

Who was this muscular man in loincloth and leather calling out for his mother? Not so polite as a Rouê would be!

Jason waved frantically at the palace guard captain, who waved out a dozen more guards, the team bursting from the curtains behind the dais. They ran down the aisle after her, shoving members of the crowd aside as they surrounded the Queen, like a protective fence, just as she arrived at the feet of Chuck-the-gladiator.

The guards already encircling him pressed their lances closer, forcing him down onto his knees, tightening their circle of spearpoints around his neck and chest.

The Queen breathed deeply, gazing down at the sweaty, half-naked man who did seem a little familiar to her. What had it been, twenty years in Ghoupalle time? He looked just like he did the day she left him—only dressed for some sword-and-sandal movie!

The crowd breathed with her, then erupted in shocked gasps as she spoke the foreign words: "Chuck, you stupid bastard, how'd you find me?"

Murmurs of imitation—*Qiyuk yustupi basu tadoud iyufai dimi*—rippled through the crowd as people tried to interpret what the Queen had said, perplexed by the secret language.

"I have come for you," said Chuck.

"What do you mean, come for me?" she asked.

The audience was shocked that the Queen would engage in a conversation with this half-naked barbarian.

"I followed your friend—that Sebastian Talbot—through an invisible doorway to the desert," Chuck explained. "He said you were here. He said he brought you here. And so I looked for you—everywhere! Tammy, I have suffered through three years of Hell searching for you, always wanting to find you...to bring you back home."

"You mean to Earth?" The Queen laughed.

The crowd was shocked at the sound of frivolity from the royal throat, then joined in her laughter.

"Yeah, Earth! You know where!" Chuck barked. "Where we all came from! None of us belong here! We all need to get home."

"Oh, fat chance, Chuckie!" Tammy sneered, dismissing him with a flick of her hand.

Two guards suddenly stepped into their stance, pressing the lance tips into his chest and throat. Blood ran from the cuts and the crowd gasped.

Queen *Tami'su'o* waved her arms for the guards to stop. They could be so trigger-happy, too easily commanded by the flick of a wrist. She did not mean that they should do anything with the barbarian.

Hah, barbarian! Yeah, he certainly is—but in a nice, ruggedly handsome way.

She fumbled with the Rouê words for 'He's not an enemy' and 'He will not harm me.' But the fifteen guards surrounded Chuck with their lances, bladetips pressed to his skin, encircling his waist, at his throat, and at the base of his skull.

Jason remained on the dais, standing and watching, the guard captain beside him, urging him to remain there to command any emergency action.

Chucker stepped cautiously down the aisle through the excitement, wondering just what the relationship was between the Queen and this ragged man from the desert. Mixed into the gossip he heard from the crowd were questions of their Queen's soft heart for barbarians and how that sort of behavior was not what they wanted from their queen. Their king had never been soft with barbarians. A certain propriety was demanded of the royal family; this foreign queen was breaking all of the rules! She even shared her language with a barbarian! Was she herself a barbarian and not a princess from Agani?

Suddenly there was a commotion in the center of the Great Hall, and three men in brown desert robes had broken rudely through the crowd, bursting into the aisle, each of them lunging at Queen Tammy as they opened their robes to reveal canisters of what Chucker could only imagine was some kind of explosive. They had used similar devices in their History, Inc. missions.

"Mom! Watch out!" Chucker shouted, fighting through the panicked crowd to get to her. "Get down!"

She did not hear him, still looking down at Chuck, her poor misguided husband who was now humbled and apologetic and humiliated and *Oooo* half-naked, and still looking so *gooood* in his shiny, muscled torso, like a Greek hero ready to carry her off the battlefield like some Helen of Aivana and throw her onto a soft feather bed—

Chuck heard the warning and saw the frantic rustle of the crowd escaping from the Great Hall, saw with his police-trained eyes the approaching danger and swept his arms violently upward to fling away the lance tips, ignoring the cuts to his flesh. The guards fell back as their attention went to the three men rushing the Queen.

"Tammy!" shouted Jason, crashing into the crowd and trying to claw his way through but held back by his guards.

Chuck stood and stretched out his arms like a big bear and threw himself forward over the Queen, knocking Her Royal Highness to the dirty floor and covering her sacred body with his profane body—just as the grenades whirred and exploded into a firestorm.

The blast leveled the first rows of people surrounding the Queen, her barbarian lover, and the guards. Torn body parts littered the tiled floor. Those who could, rushed to the doorway or toward the dais, screaming, crashing into each other.

"Mom!" cried Chucker, charging into the mess.

"Tammy! Tammy!" Jason shouted, climbing over bodies to reach her.

Chuck's companion, Godwin, the Good One, who had been first shoved to the floor by two guards, was slapped down hard by the grenade blast. He crawled dizzily across the tiles to where Chuck lay, his body spread over Queen Tammy—and casually placed a fourth canister of explosive into Chuck's open hand, so glad the foreign man had proven to be a good cover for him as his terrorist group prepared for the attack. And everyone had thought they were lovers!

Godwin grinned, near-toothless mouth flinging spittle on the floor, as he crawled backward into the heap of bodies. He paused to wave goodbye to his one-time partner.

In that instant, Chuck wrapped his numbed fingers around the grenade canister, and tried to toss it away as far as he could, but his awkward position on the floor only allowed him to push the grenade a short distance. He had to get it farther away!

Chuck rolled off Tammy, praying she was unharmed but unable in his fury to look back and check on her. The hem of her green dress was caught on his belt stud and the cloth ripped when he lurched for the bomb—just as Chucker, diving to the floor to protect his mother, also grabbed for it. Their hands clenched the grenade canister at the same time and together launched it high into the shadows of the vaulted ceiling.

Chuck glanced at the young man, started to speak—

Once the grenade reached its zenith, it began dropping.

Pulling himself to his knees, Chuck scooped up the youth in his arms and threw him as far as he could across the floor toward the side of the room, not caring that he hit the floor hard and rolled under one of the stone ramparts.

The grenade tumbled downward end over end.

Chuck threw himself back toward Tammy—as the grenade detonated.

Chapter 29

Scene of the Crime

Seeing movement in the darkness outside, Sebastian wished people would just leave him alone. He hadn't hurt anybody, and didn't care enough to bother anyone. But the world kept following him, harassing him, insisting he was evil. In an ideal world everything would be clear; there would be no mistake, no misinterpretation, no misunderstanding.

"But there is no ideal world," he mumbled.

In the distance, out by the road, he saw cars parked. They were trying to hide them under the new moon night but he could spot them. No doubt officers were planted in the field and forest, surrounding the house.

He hated fate, cursed it for a few seconds, then stopped pacing in the middle of the room and listened. He thought of the tangent field, the grid he carefully and patiently constructed, up at the quarry. Plenty of escape routes at the quarry! If he could just get to it. But even a full-blown sprint from the front door of the house would still take him ten minutes to reach the chain blocking the gravel drive, and then another five minutes up the hill to reach the central of the quarry—

Where's the History, Inc. mercenaries when I really need them?

He felt moist irony breaking out under his arms and in his crotch. Not quite two weeks since he had sent them off to their separate missions. He was trying to change history on some other world. What was the point of that? Seemed a good idea at the time. Now he needed to change things on Earth. Back up the clock and not call Toni—

A glance through a broken wall panel let him catch the movement of a battle-dressed SWAT team member, rifle poised, scurrying up to the side of the house.

He knew what the next step would be.

In the basement, there is a feel....

He had always been too busy to explore the possibilities for tangents in the house. Over the years he had grown more sensitive to how a tangent felt and he recalled a similar sensation when he was down in the basement searching for anything useful left there by the previous owner.

Down to the basement he went again, in the dark, feeling not a tangent so much as the cobwebs, the mold and mildew, and the scents of death. Rats, perhaps.

"This is the police!" The rattle of bullhorn cut through the darkness. "Sebastian Talbot. We know you are in the house. We want you to come out through the front door with your hands over your head."

His heart leaped at the sudden retort of the bullhorn but settled into a calmness that surprised him.

"Sebastian Talbot, you have five minutes to come out of the house."

Five minutes? Plenty of time.

He went to the corner of the basement nearest the forest. He reached up to shelves he knew by touch and felt the dusty old Mason jars lined up. Gently pushing his fingers into the spaces between them, he tried to sense resistance. Pickles, peaches, zucchini, hot peppers, apple butter, apricot preserves—he wondered if any it was still edible—then more peaches and pickles.

The sound of a window breaking upstairs startled him. He heard a thud on the floor above his head and guessed it was a canister of gas to smoke him out.

"Time's up, Sebastian Talbot. You need to come out of the house now. Come out through the front door with your hands over your head." There was a pause, then: "We do not want to hurt you, so come out peacefully."

He pushed his fingers between the next pair of jars on the lower shelf, too agitated to sense a tangent now. The fumes were beginning to seep down to him and he held his breath. He looked around the basement, gradually able to see a little in the darkness. Across the room was a door—a coal chute! It faced to the forest behind the house. If he could keep low in the darkness, he might roll across the ground and hide under the propane tank that squatted a dozen feet from the house. Then he could dash into the forest and hide among the boulders there. By dawn he could make his way around the hill and across the road about a mile up, then work his way through the forest to the quarry and escape through one of the tangents.

The front door was kicked in and boots stomped across the floor above him. In a flash, the door to the basement also opened and two sets of boots stepped heavily and cautiously down the steps as he dove for the coal chute doors.

He scrambled up the chute and lay flat on the ground outside, his dark clothing helping him hide. Catching his breath, he inched his body forward, over the grass, moving under the silver torpedo of the propane tank.

"He's not here," came the crackling radio from inside the house.

"What do you mean, he's not there?" came the angry response.

"He seems to have been here recently...but the house is empty now."

"Keep searching!"

From under the propane tank he spied figures moving toward the house from the forest, first two, then another pair, stepping carefully through the field, perhaps expecting booby traps, approaching the side of the house where he waited.

One of the men coming from the woods pointed in his direction and his partner raised a weapon and suddenly there was a flash of light and something hit the ground near his feet.

"What was that?" the radio traffic erupted from the men in the house.

"A shot from the forest."

"This is Gomez. Nobody said to shoot. Everyone halt."

"There!"

"What?"

"They see him—somebody!"

The *thoofmp* of a muffled shot sounded first over the radio, then he felt it hit close to his knee and he could not decide whether to scramble out from under the propane tank and bolt for freedom or to keep still and let them pass. They were shooting at shadows.

"They're checking under the propane tank to make sure nobody's there—"

"Don't shoot at the propane tank!"

"It's got to be empty, after all this time."

He pondered the metal tank above him, fingers gingerly feeling its dirty surface, the paint worn and flaky. How long had it been sitting there? How long since it was last used? How much gas remained in it? How old was the gas? How combustible was—

Another shot dinged the tank, ricocheted off the wall of the house and hit the ground at his shoulder. It nicked him and he flinched. Pain bore into him, his shirt wet with blood.

"I said don't fire at the tank!" shouted Gomez.

He looked toward the road, car lights acting as searchlights. He could never get past them. He squinted toward the line of SWAT members moving toward the house. The one who had fired at him shouldered the rifle, ready to fire again.

Where is a tangent when I really, really, really need one?

"Sebastian Talbot, stand up and place your hands on top of your head. Do not move. We will come to you."

Searchlights from the road crisscrossed the field and the house.

It wasn't so bad being in that mental hospital for the criminally insane, he considered, realizing his options were few and those were quickly running out. He had met Dr. Toni Franck, after all. A pleasant memory of the two of them on her sofa making love swept through his head. Maybe it wouldn't be too bad being sent back there. At least he would get to see her again.

He inched his way out from under the propane tank.

Not a safe place to hide. He decided to aim for a drainage ditch he saw running along side the house, beyond the propane tank. The ditch led to a concrete culvert installed under the road as preparation for the construction of the new housing division.

Then he felt it: resistance, like a bowl of Jell-O, quivering, not yielding at first, then enveloping a spoon, or a finger—or a whole body.

In his excitement, he popped up and quickly reached for the invisible resistance, a spot waist-high, what he hoped was a tangent. His arm disappeared into the air—he thought it did— just as officers spotted him.

"There!" someone shouted and a SWAT member took a shot at him—a shot which, because Sebastian Talbot stretched through the tangent, did not hit him but instead hit the side of the propane tank, piercing its skin and igniting the vapors inside—

His ears went numb. He saw the armed men frozen in their footsteps, yet he could hear nothing but the beating of his heart. His ears burst into pain, his eyes blurred, his head felt heavy and his neck could not hold up his head. He wanted to crawl away, over to the culvert and down the pipe into the new sewer system, but his body was as frozen as those of the SWAT team surrounding the house. He listened for a sound—anything.

The sky and everything around him erupted in a fire storm.

* ✳ *

The explosion shattered the calmness of the night, the house engulfed in flames, the sky lit up.

Toni shrieked, falling out of the patrol car.

Wilson picked her up and they stared at the fire. Toni screamed at first, then sobbed in his arms for a long time after. A fire engine showed up and sprayed water on the house. SWAT team members continued searching the fields around the house and the forest behind, but found nothing of their target.

"Bring it in, men," they heard Lt. Gomez over the radio.

Wilson wrapped his arm around Toni's shoulders.

"I know it's horrible," he spoke to her, "but you have to remember, it's not your fault. He is the bad guy. You got caught up in this, but you don't have to be a part of this any longer. It's over now."

She broke away from him, swayed on her two legs, caught her balance.

"It is not over," she cursed, hands on her hips. "Not for a long time is it over for him, Detective Wilson."

He could have run off with the explosion blocking their view, she imagined. He might have been thrown clear and then gotten up and run into the forest while the police searched the house. She recalled him mentioning a quarry nearby and how that place had a few escape routes. She never believed him, but now she wanted to believe they were real. She wanted to believe he got away, ran from the burning house, across the road, then up through the forest on the opposite hillside, up to that quarry. And even if he were chased he could make it to the quarry and, once there, slip through the doorway he called a tangent. He wouldn't just stand on the edge of the rocks and let himself be captured—or shot. She was willing to believe in the impossible, entertain fantastic possibilities, and open her heart to other options, anything but the obvious one.

By dawn they had put out the fire and searched through the burning timbers and combed the fields around the site. They found footprints, nips of fabric, what looked like a fingernail and possibly a silver filling from a tooth. At the edge of the forest they found a chip of bone and a strip of vinyl from the bottom of a shoe. A squad went to the quarry and searched it. Other than shoe prints, all they found were a few hairs that could be his, some dried phlegm, and a few spots of blood. What could be carried was bagged and sent to the lab for identification.

As the smoke cleared, the SWAT team reassembled on the road for debriefing.

"I guess you were right," said Lt. Gomez.

"How's that?" asked Wilson.

"He is resourceful."

Wilson nodded, then stepped away, returning to the patrol car where Dr. Franck waited.

"We'll take you home now," he said. She remained in a daze. "But we'd like to talk more with you later. Get some rest."

He closed the car door, slapped the roof, and the car drove off.

The radio crackled in a patrol car and Wilson responded.

"You won't believe what just happened," came the voice from headquarters.

"You kidding me? I'm at the site now."

"No, here. At headquarters."

"What? What could possibly happen downtown that's more *exciting* than a house exploding and a man being burned alive? Tell me that!"

"It's McElroy. Detective McElroy is back."

"What do you mean he's back?"

"He fell through the ceiling panels—like, a few minutes ago, right down from the ceiling, like he was stuck up th—"

("I better be getting my check soon," a woman was shouting in the background, "cuz I give you the info on th' fugitive.")

"Ma'am, it takes time to get those processed."

("It's mine, the check! It's for the info. Even if you don't catch him I gave you the info leading to the capture, so I deserve it! And you can't be splittin' it 'tween me and some goddamn pizza boy.")

Wilson took the opportunity for a few deep breaths.

"Sorry about that," said the sergeant.

"Are you sure it's him?" he asked the sergeant. "I mean, how could he fit in that space?"

"We don't know but the weird thing is—two weird things actually—he's half-naked, wearing some leather outfit, ya know, like.... You ever see a gladiator movie? That's how he's dressed, but without any weapons. And he's injured, got burn marks on him, must've been an explosion. And he's got broken arms—"

"And the other weird thing?"

"He keeps crying out for someone named Tammy."

"You sure it's not Toni?"

Wilson turned to regard the smoldering ruins of the house.

"No, it's Tammy. Definitely. Tammy Sue, he says. He's got some green cloth in his hand he says is from her dress, won't let it go. It's got blood on it. He's mumbling about all kinds of shit, a palace, assassins, the desert, some strange words, too, and something about bombs going off, and some guy named Seth Dallas or something. It's crazy. You'd better get back here soon as you can."

"Right," grunted Wilson. "I think I'm done here."

✳ ✴ ✳

"Huh?" mumbled Tammy, raising her head but feeling dizzy.

She found herself in darkness. She felt the surface with her hands: a toilet seat. She stood up and discovered she was in a restroom stall. She burst out of the stall and lights blinked on at the motion. Blinding light filled the room, framing the wide mirror above the basins. She stood stock still before the mirrors, studying herself: the flowing teal pantaloons with the palm leaf pattern across the fabric and the small jacket over the thin teal blouse. At last she understood: she did resemble a harem girl, or at least that Jeannie person from the TV show. The jewels still hung from her neck and sat in her naval. The blue gemstone was safe. Her feet were in ornately embroidered golden sandals, toenails painted turquoise.

Realization grew in her. She went to the door and rushed out, found herself in a large room full of desks, dark except for emergency lights at intervals along the walls. Though she stood in darkness, she knew where she was. The low ceiling held banks of fluorescent lights—which suddenly flicked on.

"Who's there?" a man dressed as a custodian asked. "You awright, Miss?"

"I don't know," she muttered.

Shaking her head, she stepped away from the restroom, not knowing where she was heading—at least going out into the wide corridor that led to other rooms. There had to be an exit somewhere in the IRS Service Center.

She turned a corner and immediately saw three women walking toward her, no doubt heading to the same restroom she had just left. Seeing her, the three halted.

She gazed at the trio and shuddered.

"Tammy?" the big one in the middle spoke.

Their mouths were agape, eyes wide open, faces pale—even Priscilla's brown cheeks seemed white. Kate and Bethany just stared.

"Oh—my—God!" Priscilla exclaimed, then fainted, knocking her coworkers to the floor with her.

✳ ✳ ✳

"Tammy...? Chucker...? Anybody...?" called Jason from the dais in the Great Hall, pulling his robe tightly about himself.

He heard the echo of his voice in the empty hall and stopped to be sure it was real, not merely his imagination. The floor was spotless, the bodies long ago removed, the tiles wiped clean. All that remained was the depression in the floor. He stepped down from the dais and moved slowly, apprehensively, holding the flowing hem of his robe close to his body.

In the center of the hall a wooden fence had been erected to block off the hole from anyone who might get close enough to fall in. The tiles around the hole had been seared by the bomb blast. Everyone believed the Queen had fallen down the hole— much like Alice in her Wonderland adventures, Jason thought. Yet the depth of the hole could not be determined. He had dropped some blocks of wood and balls of metal down the hole, just to test its depth, yet no sound of the objects hitting bottom could be heard. And yet, anyone who ventured to the next floor below the Great Hall would see that no similar hole existed. Gazing up at the ceiling of that level, staring at the underside of the Great Hall, no one could see any mark or sign of the explosion. None at all! There was no hole—not there, and not on any of the other levels. Only in the Great Hall itself did the hole exist!

"Tammy...? Chucker...?" Jason called, stepping up to the fence and staring into the hole. It was exactly the spot where his wife had stood when that big, blonde thug had shown up at court claiming her as his wife! *How preposterous! How—!*

He should have stood up for her, he considered over and over. He could not see clearly what was happening, and didn't want to make a scene. He didn't want to run the risk of being embarrassed or humiliated by the larger man. Then explosions filled the Great Hall with fire and smoke, littering the floor with—*What was the latest count? Two-hundred sixty-three?*—the bodies of the Aivana citizenry torn, decapitated, ripped apart, disgustingly mangled into pulp—

"Anybody...?"

Already the funerals for the common folk were being forgotten, and so were the ones for their Queen *Alebafe*, a.k.a. Tammy Sue Tucker of Raytown, Missouri, and her son, Chucker. Nobody cared what had happened to that barbarian guy.

Jason refused to leave the Great Hall, certain Tammy and Chucker would reappear at any moment. He knew how tangents worked. They weren't dead. They were somewhere else. They'd be back soon—as quickly as a desert whirlwind, they'd just pop back into the vast hall as easily as they left it. He was quite insistent, waiting patiently with little food or drink or sleep, forever calling: "Tammy...? Chucker...?"

Sometimes he would quietly call out the name of that half-forgotten madman: "Set-d'Elous...?"

Chapter 30

Through the Looking Glass [with a touch of] Darkly

The delightful music called silence folded around him like the weighty arms of a nurturing mother. It was not a silence like some insulated compression chamber or the silence of ears that were damaged. He tugged at his ears, nevertheless. Even though the morning he saw outside the windows was brilliantly golden and royal blue, he heard nothing.

Then, gradually, it came: a tingle of light from a distant cloud, mimicking the *ting* of the triangle at the back of an orchestra. He was not sure he heard it so he listened more carefully. Other than the cloud, there was only silence. And into that vacuous hole as deep as a universe came voices: the voice of a child wanting milk, a youth mourning the sports loss, the man complaining about termination from the office, the older man regretting lost youth, the old woman not having a child, the baby resisting separation and shouting to the world, the old man immobile on the kind of bed called death; and the voices of women: a small girl with a scraped knee; a teenager with white-painted face and long black hair standing at the side of the dance hall; the woman all in red walking down the aisle to join a man she did not know, deciding to make a left turn and exit; the woman grunting in childbirth; the woman singing some hymn to a god she made; sisters praying for sons lost to war, mothers crying for brothers lost to war, daughters mourning fathers—

He awoke with a start, straining against the hot, moist sheets, the twisted blanket, and the heavy, embroidered blue quilt with an imperial crest featuring the golden eight-pointed star. Staring at the white vaulted ceiling painted with clouds and birds, he thought the room was chilly.

Soft emerald light streamed in from the four ceiling-high windows that divided the wall to his side of the bed.

He felt a presence beside him. Rather than rush to judgment, he meticulously examined the raised form from the foot of the bed up to the head. A body shorter than his lay beneath the covers, face turned away. He recalled too many times before when he had awakened in a strange bed beside someone he did not expect to be there.

A bare, female shoulder. Strong shoulder blades, a sturdy spinal ridge, taut skin pale and smooth, the skin of a woman. He watched her shoulder rise and fall with her breathing, becoming more audible as she awakened.

Propped on one elbow like a lover at rest for the next round, he gazed at her. Finally, the woman rolled onto her back and regarded him with an affectionate smile. Curly black hair framed her face, tousled from her sleep. The dark eyes, small nose, wide red lips he knew from another life.

What are you doing in my bed, Toni Franck?

She smiled warmly and her arm reached out from under the covers and brushed his cheek. He tried to smile but felt his lips stuck. Suddenly, he could not speak.

She said something in French, cooing and pouting.

He nodded, trying to retrieve some high school French from a locked vault deep in the basement of his mind.

"Tu n'êtes pas l'homme qui m'aime?" she said, giggling.

Again he smiled, hiding his linguistic terror; in his three years of classes his grades were never higher than B.

She stretched up to kiss him and the sheet fell, leaving half of her chest exposed. He recognized the breast. And yet, how could he, or any man, turn away from this stroke of luck? A naked woman in his bed! He laughed and she seemed momentarily offended.

"Pardonnez-moi," he spoke, surprised that the words had come from his mouth. He smiled at the woman, then repeated what she had said, switching the pronoun so it referred to her, not him. He was speaking French. His lover was also speaking French. They must be in some fancy hotel in France, he considered, looking around the elegant room. Probably Paris. He had always wanted to visit. The room had a Louis-some-number appearance to it, stately and ornate, very old-looking yet in perfect condition.

Or it must be a dream.

"J'ai attendu pour tu, mais tu semblez n'apparaissent que dans mes rêves!"

"Huh?" He returned his attention to his mistress.

His throat was dry, eyes tired, as though he had been up all night. Something was not right. Even her *français* was not quite correct. If this woman were really Toni Franck, his doctor, then surely he must be in France rather than on that distant world called Ghoupallesz.

His elbow was stiff, bent against the mattress, so he sat up on the edge of the bed, facing a huge brown armoire with four decoratively carved doors.

The woman rubbed his back. "Vous avez un programme complet pour aujourd'hui."

He supposed that he did have a busy schedule.

Scratching his throat, he felt a substantial beard there, and rubbed his hand over his cheeks to confirm it. As he did, the woman massaged his shoulders. He welcomed her warm touch a moment longer, then stood, letting the edge of the sheet fall to the floor.

Standing nude in the chilly room, he began swinging his arms across his chest, stretching up, then to each side, yawning away the night. He glanced back over his shoulder at her, and noticed a full-length mirror standing nearby. He turned so that his figure filled the mirror and admired his muscular physique.

And there was more! A day of sightseeing was beginning. His mistress had said so.

"Devriez tu préparer pour les grands événements," she said in a rather business-like tone. "Je vais tu rencontrer à dîner."

"Je vais tu voir alors," he spoke absently, somehow knowing what to say—'See you then.'

He went to the armoire and opened one of the middle doors.

Inside were several outfits, most of a militaristic appearance, some suitable for formal dinners. He took one of the uniforms off the hook and lifted it from the armoire. He closed the door and set it on the peg protruding from the door, and examined the khaki jacket and trousers with crimson stripes on the cuffs, powder blue epaulets, bright golden buttons, crimson and gold sash, and brown leather belt. It was not what he would have brought on a trip to France. Perhaps it was left by a previous guest in the hotel. A place this fancy, he thought, must attract a lot of eccentric visitors.

He decided to try it on; it looked his size. He stood in front of the mirror. The man he expected to see was not standing there. Instead, he saw an older man, still fit, the body of a man of action. The man he saw had a full yet neatly trimmed beard and longer, almost shoulder-length dark hair streaked with gray. The man in the mirror looked ten years older than the one he could last recall seeing in a mirror. He pondered once more whether or not he was in a dream.

The woman languished on the bed, pulling the sheet to cover herself, watching him dress and speaking softly to him, words of encouragement, he felt, though he did not want to make the effort to translate them.

Half-way through the dressing, a loud knock landed on the door to their room and before he could say or do anything, the tall, twin wooden doors opened and a uniformed man quickly entered. The man, dressed in the black and gray costume of a staff member, stepped purposefully into the room. The large red ribbon on his lapel, arranged to resemble a flower, marked him as senior staff. The man seemed to know that, looking him over. Perhaps the somber-looking man was the hotel's entertainment director.

With a tablet and stylus in his hands, the man greeted him and his mistress in French, showing great respect yet strictness in his duties. With the rundown of the day's business, the man seemed more like a secretary, though he could not remember ever signing up for any tours or electing to give any speeches. The hotel staff was putting forth all its efforts to make him feel special, so he would grin and play along. He allowed the man to help him complete his dressing so he would appear quite the generalissimo when he went down to the lobby. Perhaps it was a special program he was part of, some kind of role-playing game for hotel guests, a fantasy camp for would-be fascist dictators.

And yet, this secretary fellow did not seem embarrassed being in the same room with the naked woman in the bed. She was not upset either. She rolled with a loud sigh onto her back on the bed, as though she wanted to continue her sleep. Perhaps she was in on the fantasy role playing and was yet another one of the hotel cast members. Or, perhaps the secretary had walked in on so many couples in the course of his duties that he was no longer fazed by the sight.

Satisfied that he was presentable in his uniform, the secretary opened the doors to the corridor and bowed his head as he gestured for him to exit the room and begin the day. It would be something worth telling the folks back home: the day he got to play El Presidente. He wondered where his camera was, had the urge to look for it, but—

She called after him, wishing him a wonderful day.

He playfully blew her a kiss—

"Je t'aime!" she added.

—and only at that instant, between heartbeats, did he realize that the naked woman in his hotel bed was not Dr. Toni Franck, but a different woman: a stranger who had the same curly black hair and dark eyes, a woman he thought had been killed in a nightmare long ago on another planet, a woman named Basura-Kanoun.

"Monsieur," his secretary called, seeing his momentary consternation. Was he fit for duty today?

"Je suis très bien," came his reply, attesting to his fitness.

He recognized that as one of the first phrases he had learned in Madame DuBois' class in high school when the sexy young teacher from Montréal with the low-cut blouses and short skirts went around the room of excitable teenage boys, asking them how they were. She knew how they were—but they were going to learn French anyway! In his mind, the words were already translated into another language that he understood better, an echo of another time and place when he'd had a similar dialog with a blonde cavalry lieutenant.

He listened to the echo, wanted to believe he was home.

Then a valet arrived, at the apparent call of the secretary, to complete his public image by preparing his unruly beard. In the newest fashion, the chin portion was braided in two directions and tipped with crimson dye. The warrior look. The secretary explained that it had been decided he should grow a beard, all the better to present an image of strength and confidence.

A tall, mustached man in burnt-umber uniform with crimson collars, a thick folder of papers in his large hands, arrived immediately. He instinctively reached back to close the doors behind himself, as his mother long ago had taught him. Instead, one of the guards intercepted his hand and grabbed the door handle first, pulling the tall, heavy doors shut. He smiled, only a little embarrassed that he did not know the protocol of the hotel. Obviously, to these people, he was just one of those dumb tourists.

The valet, secretary, personal assistant, whatever he was, spoke to him about the day's activities. He was trying to listen to the detailed timetable. The man addressing him was speaking in French.

Am I in Paris, perhaps? He had no memory of landing at the airport or the limo ride into the city. A glance out the window through the filmy, beige curtains did not show him enough to answer his questions.

As the man with the folder of papers led him, gently yet firmly, down the corridor, a quartet of uniformed guards fell in line behind them and followed.

The secretary continued filling him in on the day's agenda, their pace quickening as they moved down the endless corridor. Following breakfast, there would be a few short briefings covering the customs of the Zetin and the protocols of the Tebbi delegation. Then, because he was considered a hero in this nation, he would take a moment to greet the crowd gathered in the plaza. Later, prior to lunch, he would meet with a delegation from Aivana who had unstated business which they insisted would relate significantly to matters to be addressed in the open session of the conference.

Zetin...? Tebbi...? Aivana...? The words seemed familiar to him. They did not sound French, however.

He tried to follow the words, the ideas, yet, throughout it, all his mind could grasp was that he was not where he was supposed to be, not in the time zone he had aimed for. Why was he here in this uniform, treated as nobility? Why was he ushered to meeting after meeting, greeting admirers, making important decisions? People wanted his counsel, it seemed, and though he was happy to pontificate on matters of little concern to himself personally, he did have some doubts about the consequences of his pronouncements.

*　✻　*

The first order of the day was a formal breakfast with his staff. The people hired to play his staff had prepared a typical Ghoupallean meal of *ruh-flet*, *tabli*, and *drül* (bread wafers to be dipped in a vegetable porridge, and a chilled yogurt drink). He wondered how the kitchen staff would know that. He thought a French breakfast would be different, a croissant and some fruit. Perhaps it was a specialty of the hotel.

As the secretary gestured to his chair at the head of the long table, the others took their places along the sides. At what was presumed to be a signal from him—a random cough—everyone sat. Servers appeared from a side door and brought plates and bowls of food and cups of drink. It seemed a light breakfast to him; French cuisine was usually small on portions and large on plate-size.

The secretary spoke to the staff on his behalf. So it seemed. No one asked him any questions about his wishes for the day. Obviously everything had been planned. He asked the secretary, in surprisingly fluent French, to be sure the woman in his room was also served breakfast. The secretary assured him that it would be done, then noticed him staring at the empty plate before him.

The secretary asked him if something was not to his liking.

He asked for a repeat, listened again, calculated an answer, spoke it in French: "I thought there would be more food." Pleased that he could express himself, he regarded the secretary, continuing in French: "I usually need some meat to start my day. I would've thought you'd know that."

"Oui," said the secretary. He would order a new dish, he announced. He snapped his fingers and a server arrived beside him. They spoke briefly and the server exited.

He asked about the dish that was ordered, confirming he had heard it right.

"Oui," said the secretary.

He nodded, thinking. For a moment the words *issao-rana* stuck in his head. He could not understand the connection, but soon a large plate filled with a lumpy mound of dark orange scrambled egg with a few greenish herbs and a dab of pale-blue cream as decoration was put down in front of him.

How many eggs went into this omelet? he wondered, and smiled, not sure if he wanted to eat it, after all.

The secretary remarked with humor that one egg provided so much food.

He looked up from the plate, grinning. "Only one egg?"

"Certainment," the secretary responded, surprised. An ostrich egg is large enough for an entire meal, he explained.

The staff sitting around the table, having completed their meals, chuckled along with the secretary. He chose not to make a big deal of it, considering that he was a tourist enjoying this Louis XIV fantasy camp. He could let a rude remark go. But why was he served an ostrich egg? Were there no chicken eggs?

After a few bites with a combination spoon-fork utensil, he felt too many eyes on him and he paused. *Perhaps that is enough.* He pushed the plate back and wiped the corners of his mouth before a valet could rush to do it for him. He grinned at the valet's *faux pas*.

Standing, he gazed down the table at each performer in this stage play, smiling and showing appreciation for their efforts to entertain him. It was going to be a fun day!

A guard and two valets led the procession, secretary at his side, explaining the day's schedule once more. Other staff members and guards followed closely.

At the end of the corridor, the space opened into a wide

courtyard set with statues and trees, benches and stone tables, something beautifully unexpected. He paused, staring at the restful scene until the secretary called his attention back to the political matters at hand. He wanted to sit down and enjoy the pleasant morning, so he stepped toward the nearest bench and the secretary once again inquired as to his health, his mood, his will to proceed. To all, he answered that he was robust and ready for anything. He only wished a pause to prepare himself for the next activity.

The secretary, as politely as possible, attempted to persuade him of the urgency of their arrival in an upstairs meeting room.

"Pourquoi sommes-nous parler français?" he asked suddenly, still wondering why they were speaking French. Moreover, he wondered how he could be so fluent.

"C'est à cause de votre commande," the secretary replied quietly. Because he had commanded it: everyone must speak French inside the palace. Did he no longer wish it?

"C'est un palais?" he asked, wondering why it was called a palace.

He laughed, feeling the cameras pointing at him, knowing it was a huge joke someone was playing on him. OK, he would play along. He had thought it was a hotel.

"Non, monsieur, c'est un palais," his side-kick explained. "Le palais royal."

What royal palace?

He considered he was in France and some palaces had been converted into hotels, yet the staff seemed to be appropriate for a real palace, so many doing so many things simultaneously, and constantly.

And who am I?

The uniform bore no rank. He had once been captain of a cavalry regiment in a long-forgotten war that now had never happened, then promoted in the field to *Berron*, the supreme commander of all military forces—

"Je voudrais que vous d'arrêter de parler français maintenant," he said, finally losing the cachet of the language and growing tired of translating everything in his head. Henceforth, he commanded, there would be no more speaking French in the palace!

"Alors, comment devons-nous communiquer?" asked the secretary. Then how would they communicate with each other?

"Que diriez-vous de Ghoupallêan?" he said, suggesting they continue in Ghoupallêan.

The secretary seemed surprised, his face pale.

"We are speaking Ghoupallêan, My Lord," the secretary responded.

"We are?"

The man cleared his throat, then: "*Zil, Kalmonê!*"

Okay, that was Ghoupallêan. Why had it sounded French?

He gave a smirk, embarrassed. There was a moment of pressure on his heart, like a fist squeezing out all of the blood, and just as quickly he was back to normal—or what passed as normal in this elaborate hoax. Fully awake now, he understood what was really happening, but he kept his expression in check so as not to let his personal secretary notice. He finally could see through the filmy beige curtains that had made everything so mysterious. In his gut, he realized the unmistakable truth.

"I'm not in France," slipped from his mouth.

The secretary inquired politely about his remark.

"I must send a message," he announced in Ghoupallêan.

The secretary snapped his fingers and a young scribe appeared, pad of parchment and stylus in hand.

"I want someone in Selauê, one of our ambassadors, not some flunky," he dictated with careful enunciation, "to go to the Martyr's Wall and see what the first name is, the first by date of death. Then fax me the name."

"Sir, what is 'fax'?"

"It's electronic communication. You put a piece of paper in the machine and...."

He watched the expression of the secretary sour. No doubt the man was confirming his insanity. Facsimile technology had not been developed yet on this world.

"Send me the name immediately!"

"Sir, we cannot get a reply until tomorrow," the secretary explained. "Perhaps not until evening. Is it so urgent?"

They probably thought he would explode at that point but they held their ground, aware of their duty to obey and not judge. He considered they were thinking their sovereign must certainly have more knowledge, more awareness than any of the staff. They had to trust he knew what he was doing.

"Avaën Ês-se maxa-d'anno ke?" he grunted, certain that some type of communication device was available in the palace.

"Zil, Kalmonê-se," the secretary responded curtly, clicking his heels.

The secretary turned to the scribe. The scribe confirmed that he had written down the complete message. Another set of instructions and the scribe was off to send the message by the Ghoupallean equivalent of the telegraph, the *maxa-d'anno*. The words would be sent by wire through possibly a dozen exchanges until finally arriving where it could be acted upon. Then the response would be sent back in a similar round-about fashion, possibly to be delivered to him by the next evening. He would have to wait. Only then would he know what to do, how to act, what to say at these official meetings and especially at the Grand Council of Nations.

❋ ❋ ❋

"The first meeting is with the Zetin ambassador," the secretary told him as they moved down the corridor.

"What is this about?"

"My Lord, you requested the meeting."

"I'm checking you," he said with a chuckle. "Tell me what the meeting is about."

"You wish to make an offer of assistance to the Zetin."

"Go on."

"You will offer them assistance in defeating the Tebbis."

"How?"

"You are going to suggest to the Zetin ambassador that when he meets with the Tebbi delegation tomorrow he should require the Tebbis to give a hostage to assure compliance with the treaty they will sign."

"What?" It sounded too familiar, he realized. Had he read it in a history book?

"This is your plan."

"So, we're here in advance of the meeting between the Tebbis and the Zetin to try to disrupt the treaty between them."

"That is your plan, sir. As you previously explained, if the Tebbi and Zetin join forces against the Sekuatean Empire, we will be defeated—"

"Sekuatean Empire?" Did he hear that right? Or were the Ghoupallêan words confusing him?

"*Zil, Kalmonê,*" the secretary replied, "*Sekuatê-drouñ.*"

He stopped there in the corridor, staring down at the ornate design in the carpet running the length of the corridor, admiring the colorful pattern, suggestive of the stories of Anatarka in ancient Danidê. Most of the nations of the Ghoupallæssus, after all, took their culture from Danid and early Ghoupalle history. He recalled Gina, his long-lost love, telling him some of those stories when they happened to meet in their separate travels. *Hah!* He had been waiting to meet her again, he recalled—yes, waiting in Aivana for her to appear, as she had indicated she would in her journal. Now, however, he was about to meet the Zetin ambassador!

"My Lord, did I not say it correctly?" asked the secretary.

He rubbed his chin, feeling the itch of the beard, as he stared at the secretary. He started doing math in his head, even as the secretary urged him to continue to the next meeting. The first name on the Martyr's Wall. Elegant hotel not in Paris but somewhere on Ghoupallesz. The woman in his bed not being Dr. Toni Franck. This secretary guy telling him the day's schedule. The Sekuatean Empire. The Zetin ambassador, the Tebbis, the hostage that would bond them in their common goal of defeating Sekuate. His spiffy uniform, devoid of rank insignia. His quintet of armed guards. His boorish personal secretary. The valets who opened doors for him. His order for the staff to speak French, then stop speaking French—

He gazed at the secretary, then cracked a smile.

"Everything is all right," he said, wanting to shove his hands into his trouser pockets but finding the uniform had no such pockets. He didn't know what to do so he clasped his hands behind his back, maintaining a steady, regal bearing. Evidently he was someone else this morning than he was when he went to sleep the previous night.

Unless he was still asleep....

✳ ✳ ✳

As the Most-Important-Man-In-The-Room, he could recline languorously in the chaise lounge, a valet carefully arranging the tails of his uniform coat so as to affect an authoritarian appearance when their guests arrived. The sitting pillows on the floor were positioned in a diamond pattern, the armed guards set about the eight corners of the room. This small room along a side corridor of the palace served well as a secret meeting place, the secretary told him. All the better to have a private talk with Ut'r-Bkann, the ambassador of the Zetin Union and high priest of the Temple of Something-or-Other—

"So it's going to be like this," the Most-Important-Man-In-The-Room spoke rather brusquely to the ambassador through the half-Zetin young man acting as translator. "The Tebbis are going to ask you to fight alongside them against Sekuate. They will insist that your two nations have a common enemy, and to defeat this enemy you will need to put aside your ancient conflicts and work together. They will offer you some border territory as a reward for your participation. That is what they will say. They hope you will accept that meager token of conciliation."

The chunky, lightly armored Zetin ambassador, kneeling submissively on the burgundy pillow with golden tassels around its edges (a feminine design in the eyes of Zetin), followed the protocol. The ambassador appeared to feel humiliated, which was the intention, and he grumbled in Zetin, more to himself than anyone else in the room. To maintain privacy, the ambassador had been allowed to bring only one other person, a personal bodyguard who also knew the Ghoupallêan language, to assure there was no treachery in the exchange of words.

"What you will do," the Most-Important-Man-In-The-Room said, "is agree to this simple gesture, the offer of land. That is your best move, they will see. But you will demand more. They will want to stamp a treaty. Before you agree to stamp the treaty, you will ask for a hostage. I believe that is your custom, is it not? You will demand that the hostage be not just any person they might offer but a special hostage. You will ask for the Tebbi prime minister's wife as your hostage. Cheer up, she's probably some comely farm wench turned government whore. This point, you will say, is absolutely required for you to stamp the treaty."

The ambassador looked askance at the others in the room. Perhaps he wondered if anyone understood the Zetin customs better than this Sekuatean authority who had him kneeling like a slave girl. Could anyone possibly endure the humiliation of a person of his high rank being told what he would say and do the next afternoon? Who was this pompous bastard to tell him, the high priest of Tjann-Dax, what to do? He represented all of Zetinê! the Zetin Union! the seven nations of the Zetin Empire! and the diaspora in tropical Bæronak and high-plateau Sogoê! and all the remaining oppressed peoples of the western and northern districts of Tebbicousimankalê who had not been able to flee to Zetinê in ancient days! He spoke for all of them!

"The rule you will insist on," the Most-Important-Man-In-The-Room said, after an awkward pause for translation, "is this: the Tebbis must honor the treaty or the hostage will be killed, publicly executed in a most humiliating fashion. This, too, is Zetin custom, is it not?"

The ambassador nodded after hearing the translation.

Custom or not, it may be the best possible retribution for someone so devious as she was, leaving one fine day with their daughter. After he had rescued her from the clutches of this same Zetin ambassador! Who was she to leave him? This time, he decided, he would not be rescuing her—

Where did that come from?

Strange words seemed to echo through his head as though spoken from some ghost. He shook it off, thinking his thoughts of hatred toward his long-lost love were some aberration born of jet lag and bad food. The odd breakfast was disappointing.

"Of course, the Tebbi prime minister will not want to give up his wife as hostage so you must demand that she is the only suitable person. He will not refuse to honor the treaty as long as she is your hostage. Care for her, certainly, or they will have an excuse to break the treaty with you. Understand?"

The ambassador nodded, a fierce scowl spreading across his face. If only he had a sword on his belt he might swoop up from the floor and slice in three parts this pompous bastard from Sekuate! Still, he had his self-defense dagger hidden in the folds of his cape. But what good would that do for the greater future of Zetinê? He had a duty to perform here and, because he represented all of Zetinê, he could not simply act on his individual motives. That much was clear. And yet, how he wished to act!

"All will go well if you follow this plan," said the pompous bastard with a smirk.

"G'D," the ambassador grunted, understanding.

The Most-Important-Man-In-The-Room smiled. "I am the Most Important Man In The Room, in part, because I can see the future. Here is what will happen if you follow this plan: The Sekuatean armies will continue to march toward Siaa and, because of the treaty, Zetin forces will enter Tebbicousimankalê under the pretense of fighting alongside the Tebbis. However, you will only pretend to fight the Sekuateans. You will appear to bog them down in the snowfields. You will seem to hold them and taunt them but you will not actually engage them in any great force. A few minor skirmishes are to be expected. But the major battles are for the Tebbis to engage in at a later time, at the melting of winter. At the start of spring, the Sekuatean forces will enter and conquer Siaa and then—only then—will the people of Zetinê rejoice."

"Why should we rejoice?" asked the distrustful ambassador through his translator. "Why should we wait through the winter and let the world see us as weak? Why should we play this game you have invented?"

The Most-Important-Man-In-The-Room chuckled. He studied his guest. Sensing the weakening of the ambassador's resolve, he pointed a finger at the kneeling man, as if to mark him as an idiot.

"I know you do not trust me," said the Most-Important-Man-In-The-Room. "Yet, you and your people will rejoice when Sekuate occupies Siaa! Because then you will get everything you want. Instead of the scraps of mountainous terrain along your mutual border which the Tebbis offer, I will assure that the Sekuatean forces withdraw from the northern subcontinent. We welcome you and your people to return and occupy it. We will step aside and you may freely annex almost two-thirds of the nation of Tebbicousimankalê—south to the Loulê River. Surely this must please you more than a few hundred *radit* of rock and ice. Remember your history? You will regain deep forests, lush fields, ice-free seaports, many resources of food and fuel, and most importantly, your heritage!"

The ambassador rose spontaneously off the pillow and the guards snapped to intercept him until they were waved off by their leader.

"You offer a fabulous dream," the ambassador laughed. His bodyguard broke into laughter, then translated back to the Most-Important-Man-In-The-Room. "Who should I believe?"

"It is the difference between Tebbi dream and Sekuatean reality."

"Indeed!" the ambassador grunted through his translator. "Yet it is more than a mere man's brain that will call the lot of fate today and tomorrow. There is more to a decision than logical analysis."

"Either way," said the Most-Important-Man-In-The-Room, "I guess you will find the truth in my words."

"I will tell you," the ambassador began, glancing sternly at the Ghoupalle man working as translator for the Most-Important-Man-In-The-Room, "deep in the past night I was called upon a wild *Jêpe* and galloped to the far edge of a world I did not know. There I met a man of another nation. He spoke my language yet with rough accent; I almost could not understand him. He wore a uniform cut from a single cloth and a silver line of jewels ran down his chest to his groin. His clothing was orange, as bright as the winter sunset, and angular symbols were drawn upon his uniform, symbols I cannot remember or decipher. Nevertheless, he spoke to me about the events of today, about this meeting with the Tebbi folk, and the course of my future. He told me he would be watching me."

The man on the chaise lounge found the revelation humorous and burst into an unprofessional fit of laughter.

"It is true!" insisted the ambassador. "This man told me he used to collect taxes. Now he collects moments of history. He told me he would return to collect my moment in history. I think he meant my life. Life is history, is it not? Someday this man would collect my head and heart in a pair of baskets—as effortlessly as he would collect a basket of tax goods. I did not understand that message in the night, yet as I listen to your words today the clouds dissolve and the sun shines clearly on the six winds of Fate—what we call S'TкTкa. Given the importance of dreams, I will take your advice and think on it this night. If I am not visited by the wild *Jêpe* again, there is a chance that tomorrow will be the beginning of a new history for me and my people."

The Most-Important-Man-In-The-Room rose, stepped from the chaise longue. He extended his right hand and the Zetin ambassador, slowly bowing according to protocol, reached out and clasped the hand offered.

"That is what we all want, right?" asked The-Most-Important-Man-In-The-Room. "We all want the world to be in balance."

Ut'r-BkanN gave the hand a firm squeeze, then released.

"Uz'g'zoD!" growled the ambassador in typical Zetin fashion, an utterance full of confidence and agreement.

"Thanks for your time," said the Most-Important-Man-In-The-Room in flawless Zetin.

Chapter 31

Dead Reckoning

"All for the greater good," he sighed with contentment. That was what the voice inside his head told him to say, and it seemed to be the appropriate phrase.

The secretary smiled, seeing his lord once more acting like his true self.

Next he was to visit a balcony overlooking the great plaza where people had assembled to greet him.

"A photo op?" he muttered in English.

"*Ghoumæxii-solamin gal-tilan bram-seren Ghoum-se.*" The secretary's eyebrows happily raised as he told how much the adoring people wanted to see him.

Apparently, he was seen as a unifier, as a rebel willing to take action—what some labeled tyranny—to reunite the people of Zissekap, the old Ghoupalle states, into one giant empire. The people in the plaza were political cousins, descendants of those in Zissekap. They wished to cheer for him, their inspiration. A few minutes waving at the crowd would be good for his public persona. The people here loved him. It was only fair to give them a few moments.

"I can do that," he responded, adjusting his trousers and belt. "It's the least I can do for my fans. Geez, now I know what it feels like to be a rock star!"

The secretary asked what a '*raux-têjir*' was and he explained.

"A famous musician who has the power of a god over an audience," the secretary repeated to confirm it. "And the people will follow his desires, and do what he asks?"

"Yes, that's it."

They had come to the balcony, a wide terrace entered through the parlor. A pair of valets stepped forward and grasped the latches. The double doors opened and beyond he could see the rooftops of the city. The secretary gestured for him to enter and he did so, strutting like a rock star.

"Be aware of your rank, My Lord," the secretary called, acting as his conscience.

"Don't worry," he said with a laugh. "I feel, somehow, like I've done all this before. I feel the routine of it. Strange. Perhaps it was in a dream."

His secretary said something which, at the moment, seemed profound. And yet, as he continued to step forward, up to the railing—the glass panels had been folded back to make the expanse open to the air of the plaza—he felt unusual surges of energy filling his veins. His head felt light, like a balloon, his body floating over the floor. He felt his boots touching the floor but he could not determine his weight. The words the secretary spoke, and the rising roar of the crowd below, numbed his ears.

He knew what to do and lifted his arms in a victorious pose. After all, the whole of Tebbicousimankalê would be theirs by next spring! The forces of the Sekuatean Empire were even now surrounding the city of Siaa, the great industrial center of the northern districts. Nothing could stop them now! Within five years, the whole of the Ghoupallæssus would be bowing before him!

"Ah! So many admirers!" he cried happily.

"Indeed, My Lord!"

He felt another heart beating beside his, another hand holding the railing, another set of eyes seeing much more than his own eyes could see. And the crowds below raised their arms in response, their cheers filling the plaza. He was delighted at their reaction. *I am loved, really loved.* Those representatives he would soon sit down with were so wrong about him. He was not a tyrant! He was not land-hungry, vengeful, or vindictive. He was not an evil person. Nothing could be further from the truth. He had a lovely wife, perhaps some children (he could not recall their names at the moment, nor when he had last seen them), and he had a warm smile which the members of the crowd could clearly see in the noontide sunshine. He was a rock star!

The secretary called to him: his viewing was done. They were limited to seven *pon*. They must move to the next appointment, a short meeting with a delegation from Aivana who wished to address his handling of the Yvo-Dê incident.

"The what incident?" he asked, turning reluctantly away from the railing.

"The army attack on the villagers at the oasis of Yvo-Dê...? More than two hundred women and children were killed...? My Lord must recall the outrage reported. You ordered medical supplies delivered to them."

"Then I am right to be thanked by these people."

He felt a warm sensation grow in his gut, and he called it happiness. Although he had awakened in a very strange place, believing he was in a fancy Parisian hotel with some saucy lass, perhaps a French chambermaid, the day was gradually turning into a rather different adventure. Much better than a fantasy camp, or that Renaissance Fair experience he had back in his college days, dressing up as some knave and playing in a minstrel band.

College? He felt his heart skip a beat. *That sure was a long time ago!*

He felt different—as though he was really, finally waking up for the first time in his life. He could not quite recall the previous day, much less the years before that. They were a blur of impressions, not concrete memories. Perhaps he was growing senile in his late thirties—

Suddenly, he felt all of the haze stop. In a flash he could see clearly the life that he was living—had been living for how many years now? His eyes widened, heartbeat quickening. He stood taller, straighter. He was smart, clever even, and ruggedly handsome, physically fit and sexually attractive; he was a model's model, a political thoroughbred, a social élite, a martial powerhouse! And yet he was still kind to strangers, children, and small animals.

"Let us be on our way, then, to receive our due thanks," he

announced. "Let's kiss some babies! If this were an election year, I'd be a shoo-in!"

The secretary turned pale. Once again, his master's madness was surfacing. A potential disaster was looming.

The secretary reminded him that there were no elections in Sekuate, had never been such public rituals in more than three hundred years.

"And why not? That's the way a democracy is run!"

The secretary grimaced, nodding for their party to exit the balcony for the long corridor.

Out in the corridor, the secretary informed him in a low voice, fearing others might learn of his returning madness, that he was not an elected official, and that once again he was mumbling this strange word, '*dêmax-raxii*'—Was this a foreign term?

"You must be careful what you say in front of the staff," the secretary intoned in a respectful yet fatherly way. "That is the reason for my appointment: to look after you. Too valuable are you to be left alone, or to be forced to make important decisions by yourself. I have been assigned to assist you in these administrative matters."

He seemed to ponder the information, cocking his head to the side as though he were in a cartoon. "Really?"

"Yes, My Lord."

Still wearing a puzzled mask, he asked: "Who assigned you to watch over me? Who appointed you my caretaker?"

The secretary smiled, momentarily afraid to respond. Glancing both directions in the corridor, assured they were safely out of ear-shot, he said, "Your mistress."

"Ah, mistress! Then we are in France. I knew it."

"My Lord, you are in this rather small matter not entirely accurate."

He seemed upset, ready to act, perhaps violently, unprofessionally, like a frustrated tax clerk in the dark recesses of a service center—

"Are you allowed to tell me I'm wrong?"

The secretary cleared his throat, then: "As part of my appointment, I am expected to advise you with regard to the customs and protocols of your office."

"...'My Lord.'" Raising an eyebrow, he gave a smirk. "You're supposed to add 'My Lord,' aren't you?"

"Yes, My Lord!"

"And why do I need a caretaker?" he asked, thinking *as though I need my damn diapers changed and a warm bottle of milk!* "Am I truly going mad?"

The secretary stepped closer, entering a forbidden zone.

"My Lady has suggested that, in your current state of mind, it would be best for me to be ever-present when you are on public display."

The secretary stepped back, exiting the forbidden aura.

"And who is my lady?"

"Pardons, My Lord. This is a convenient example of your troublesome state of mind of late which, unfortunately, is appearing at an inconvenient time. You shared a sleeping chamber the previous evening with your Lady."

"My mistress?"

"Your partner in life."

"My wife?"

The secretary grimaced. "It is a matter of record that no ceremony to join you and her was ever witnessed. Thus, the fact of your alliance as an illegal entity is as yet, according to the judiciary, quite indeterminate. However, the populace believes firmly in your union for both social, political purposes as well as the biological, reproductory functions of such partnerships. Indeed, you and she have thus far produced three children. First, a son named Kag, then a daughter named Mamna and a son named Tomodon—as you know. So, for all intents and purposes, you, My Lord, and your partner, My Lady, continue to very admirably represent yourselves as a formally recognized couple, regardless of the formal laws—which you are most certainly able to bend at your whim. My Lord and Lady act in a legislative capacity, holding executive dominance and sovereignty over the greater geographical region of Sekuate's influence—which in the past several years has grown through military conquest and annexation to become the mighty Sekuatean Empire."

He chuckled, caught his breath, glanced quickly around them for spies, shaking his head in disbelief, then trained his eyes squarely on the secretary's eyes.

"I suppose I don't quite know what you mean," he said slowly, thoughtfully. The secretary shifted his stance, ready to receive the inevitable punishment. "And yet, you might answer me this: What is the name of the one you call my mistress?"

"Her name, My Lord?"

"Humor me."

"I am certainly not allowed to speak the name by which you address her. That is a private word according to our customs—as you know. Ah! I see you are testing me, My Lord."

"Sure, a test." He nodded a few times, pondering the situation. "And what is the title of my job here?"

"You, My Lord?" said the secretary, lowering his voice, "You do not have a job."

"Then what is all of this business?" he asked, gesturing about.

"You do not have a job, My Lord," said the secretary, "because you are the Emperor."

❋ ❋ ❋

He swallowed hard, then coughed to cover his consternation and fell into a coughing fit. The secretary called for the medical attendant on the staff.

"My Lord, are you all right?" asked the secretary, daring to pat the Emperor's shoulder a few times.

"Aargh, all right," the Emperor grunted, coming out of the fit.

He caught his breath and inhaled deeply a few times. He saw that a chair had been brought for him and he sat down there in the corridor, surrounded by his staff. The medical attendant arrived and began checking his vital signs, then looked down his throat. A bottle of a green liquid was produced from the medical attendant's bag of tricks and sprayed into the back of the Emperor's throat. That elicited a few more coughs—

"Ugh, such vile filth!" the Emperor growled.

He started to wipe his mouth with the back of his hand but a valet rushed to him with a white cloth to dab across his mouth. He looked up at the youth holding the phlegm stained towelette. *How they care for me! Am I really so precious to their plots and schemes?* He glanced quickly around the circle of staff members. *What if I were to just get up and leave? Go on vacation? Forget all this administrative bullshit?*

"My Lord," his secretary addressed him, "will you be able to participate in the Council of Nations?"

He gazed at the ceiling as though he had not heard the secretary. The ceiling was decorated with reptilian motifs, the tails of dragon-like beasts curling down the corridors like snakes, the tiny wings sprouting from the shoulders of the creatures, forked tongues flicking from salivating yaws, jagged fangs glistening, talons curled, all of it a bit too Chinese for his comfort.

He had to step out of the present reality and ponder what trick of fate had propelled him into this random variant of history—Ghoupallean history!—and, having thus arrived in this upside-down time zone, how he might correct matters. As he considered the situation, he felt pain growing in his head and just as his attention turned to it, the pain subsided. In fact, whenever he began to have memories of another time and place, whenever he began to think his own thoughts or question his actions, he noticed a pain would grow in his head or sometimes a warm circle would form around his heart and expand to fill his entire body, like a drug being released within him.

His head throbbed again and he jettisoned his own thoughts until the pain stopped.

"There is no reason to change our plan," the Emperor spoke.

The secretary smiled, sighed in relief.

The Emperor attempted to stand and two aides took his arms and helped him to his feet, at which time the Emperor shook off their hands and straightened his uniform. A mirror appeared in the hands of another aide and he gazed at himself, adjusted his collar, ran his fingers through his hair: a touch more gray than he remembered having the night before. The man staring back at him in the mirror he only faintly recognized: a bearded man with only a slight resemblance to someone he had met long ago, perhaps on a deserted road in the northern regions of Zevêna—

Or in an old, abandoned house set off from a back-country road—

Or perhaps in a dream—

The voice had returned, whispering from somewhere behind his ears. A mantra repeating in a vaguely feminine voice, a bit too firm, too parental for his comfort, like the lingering instructions of his mother to be a gentleman—yet decidedly sweeter. He welcomed the soothing tone, relaxed.

The secretary smiled, pleased that his master was ready to proceed.

"Let us go, you and I," said the Emperor in a strangely lilting English voice, "into the sunset, there to die."

He noted how the staff glanced about at each other, eyes rolling in amusement.

"I intended to be amusing," he muttered in English.

The secretary led the group down the corridor, almost strutting with delight that his master was ready to face down the weak and whimpering leaders of small and unimportant nations.

The party arrived at two huge, ornately carved doors and halted.

"Here?" asked the Emperor. "This is the place?"

"My Lord, we are early," the secretary explained. "The Council of Nations will begin soon. We have time for a short audience with a delegation from Aivana."

"Aivana?" He felt his stomach churning. "Since when do we do business with Aivana? That dirty desert kingdom, barbarian queen and bucktoothed barbarians! Most of them are cannibals, I hear. The rest are—"

"They will ask for a special favor," the secretary explained. "They wish to be rewarded for acting for the glory of the Sekuatean Empire by inciting a rebellion in Aivana, which will lead to easy annexation of the kingdom."

"Don't we already control it?"

The secretary grinned, embarrassed. He gestured for the aides to depart. Only the four guards remained with them.

"My Lord, this is a small matter, yet it will pay large dividends to our worldwide reputation."

"How so?"

"If Aivana suffers a rebellion—" The secretary stopped and stared at the guards a moment; they stepped back, then moved down the corridor a short distance. "If there is a rebellion in Aivana, the Sekuatean Empire will need to step in to prevent the usual abuses that occur with such anarchy. We will enforce peace. And the world will hail us as peacemakers. That is much easier than being seen to invade a much smaller nation."

The Emperor nodded, pondering. "I thought of that?"

"Yes, My Lord."

"I'll bet they'll want us to recognize them as the legitimate government once they succeed in overthrowing the current rulers."

"They will be here shortly," said the secretary, "so we have this meeting room set aside for our use. It is private so none will learn of our talk. Everyone will assume you are preparing for your speech at the Council of Nations."

"Sounds like a plan," the Emperor muttered as the secretary motioned for the guards to open the doors so their group could enter the anteroom.

Inside was a circle of large, deeply cushioned chairs, a round table among them, and a bank of windows with beige curtains blocking the view of curious visitors and staff. The wooden floors were polished and a round carpet of khaki and crimson, the colors of the Sekuatean military, spread in the center of the room.

The Emperor stepped into the chamber, a space meant only for freshening up before or during a grand ball or government conference. As an emperor, he had never stood in such a small room. Even the lavatory back in his own palace was larger than the huge bedroom he had been assigned for this visit. He suddenly felt nervous, feeling the walls standing too close. One to his left seemed to move. He looked out the windows through the filmy curtains and saw a garden below, green and brown, tall, leafy growths and colorful sprouting petals. Across the garden was another wing of the palace, with similar rooms, he supposed. He asked an aide to open the curtains so he could see more clearly.

Through a side doorway to a connecting room he spied a huge table set with a map of the world. Curious, he stepped into the adjoining room. On the map were many small tokens and as he squinted at them he recognized them as horses and soldiers and flags. He stepped to the map table. Drawn on the map of Ghoupallesz were military symbols: the target-like circles of enemy forces, the squares of allies' positions, the triangles of

Sekuatean forces, the arrows of campaign movements, and the Xs of battles. Prancing across the land masses were toy *Jêpe*. Marching from nation to nation were legions of toy soldiers. Flags stood in each nation conquered. He stared at Selauê, his adopted hometown, then gazed outward to the edges of the Sogoê plateau in the east, the Alaun plateau in the north, the jungles of Dikondra in the west, and the islands beyond Sanduu in the south. Never had any empire covered so much of the planet!

A sudden flash of fear ran through him like lightning and was gone.

What would they do to him if they discovered he was not their beloved emperor but just some unlucky tax clerk who happened one night to stumble through some invisible doorway to their world and found himself in this body, in this uniform, playing this role they expected of him?

I definitely do not belong here.

He had to be sure to not let his guard down; already he had likely raised their suspicions with his lack of knowledge about the day's schedule, the important events of which he was a part, or the basic customs and protocols of his...*role.*

"My Lord," his personal secretary called gently to him, almost hesitant to interrupt his thoughts, "the delegation is about to arrive. Are you ready to receive them?"

Lost in thought, he had positioned himself before the bank of windows and stared out, but seeing within his mind rather than with his eyes. He contemplated the sum total of his lives, and deciding that no matter which planet he was on, he still could breathe normally. He felt as heavy and as tall as before. He could see everything quite clearly, though everything had a greenish tinge. He held together his many atoms in perfect harmony, and his cells maintained their proper function. That would seem to indicate that he was normal and in a normal place. Anything else must be an illusion. Or a cleverly fabricated hallucination. What had he been given to eat for breakfast?

Issao-rana! The Ghoupalle bird resembling a red ostrich! That was what he had eaten, not an African ostrich egg. He knew he'd recognized the word.

He squinted at the small blue sun shining above the rooftops as the sky turned toward the middle hour and the dominance of the yellow sun. What had he fed himself in the back woods, scraping by in an old abandoned house? Wild quail eggs? Strange leaves? Berries? He felt an uncomfortable sensation growing in his gut. What was on that pizza? After three days sitting in that old house, was it still good? His stomach felt bloated and the wind pressure descended through him and exploded with obstinate fury into his trousers.

The Emperor grinned, knowing his staff would ignore his breach of etiquette.

He stood gazing out the windows at what seemed to be a different plaza than where he had addressed the crowd of admirers. Instead of people pressed from wall to wall in adoration, he saw wooden planks lined up in rank and file, a checkerboard pattern of light and dark wood—

They're boxes, he realized.

He pulled over a chair and climbed onto it, his boots unapologetically marking the embroidered upholstery. From his higher vantage he could better see the plaza below. As large as the one where he had greeted the crowd, this plaza was filled with wooden boxes, all the same size—

Coffins!

He stared hard at the plaza below. A few old men and women moved slowly among the boxes painting crimson stars, the eight-pointed star of Sekuate, on the lids.

Soldiers!

He watched them. As he counted the boxes, he felt the sky expanding—until it burst into a blinding whiteness. A whole universe surrounded him: the potty training gone bad, the boyhood spankings, embarrassment at his lack of athleticism among his neighborhood friends, the beatings by school bullies, the angry teacher with candy and a love of touching, the cheating on standardized tests, sneaking around to spy on girls dressing after dance practice, the forbidden books read under sheets late into the night, the drug *moussalaganê*—

What the...? He had never had that childhood, that youth.

The images continued when he closed his eyes: scenes of military training, riding a horse that became a *Jêpe*, a khaki uniform with crimson detail, the saber practices where he cut arm after arm in a brilliant show of his skill, and the ribboned promotions, crisp salutes, and the long marches into battle, and triumph after triumph, the powder-blue flags waving under the green sky, and the mothers and daughters cheering, the fathers proud of sons, sons proud of fathers, and he riding high in the saddle at the head of the parade, at the head of the legions of horsemen—*Jepêdor!*—and the kaleidoscopic bombs bursting in vibrant colors through the air, the black and gray smoke and brilliant fire, the thunder of siege guns! The walls crumbling, the waves of cavalry slicing through infantry squares, the cannons blasting through staunch lines of enemy forces, bayonets through guts, knives through throats, and the molten pellets burning their way through faces and bellies and backs and groins, and the swords slicing and dropping arms and heads, the fingers clasping the hair of severed enemy heads, and the endless lines of women stripped naked and laid on the ground for the pleasure of soldiers, the ragged children rounded up and put into wagons bound for sale in distant lands—

No! That is not me! I did not do that!

"My Lord, are you all right?" asked the secretary.

He did not answer, could not answer—thinking back, days into weeks into months and years, and nothing stood clear in his mind. No memories existed. Only the most general sensations, like a dark, seeping poison, ran through him: acting without thought, standing and marching and giving speeches and making decisions that had already been made.

A sense of urgency rose in him, a growing belief that—

I am not that person! I am not the sort of person who would condone that behavior. I would not send out my soldiers to make war!

"My Lord, you are the Emperor," spoke the secretary, and he realized his thoughts were mutterings audible to his closest staff member. "We all act upon your commands."

A tear burst into the corner of his eye, another tear in his other eye, and his heartbeat quickened as he gazed down at the rows of coffins.

"I don't belong here," he mumbled.

"Soon this will be finished," the secretary assured him. "They will be very grateful that you attended the Council of Nations. It is a wise choice you have made."

He asked the secretary, posed stiffly somewhere behind him, to confirm the year, and he heard the reply: "One-Five-and-Thirty-Three."

So they were now in 1533, the year of the siege of Siaa in Tebbicousimankalê, the winter before the spring of their retreat—

Impossible! He was supposed to be leading the 102d regiment outside of Siaa, part of the siege—not staring at the stacks of coffins in a plaza of a palace in Siti, far across the ocean. He calculated the difference in years from when he last recalled stepping through the tangent from Earth to Ghoupallesz—as streams of perspiration ran down his face. How could he awaken one fine morning and find himself in such a position, with a history of tyranny trailing him, a history he could not remember?

Am I remembering an altered past or envisioning an impossible future?

And they will demand retribution, he thought. Whatever has been done, they will demand vengeance. After the surrender at Milipour, he recalled from history books yet to be written, the Northern Megan Alliance divided the Sekuatean Empire into quarters, administering it, sucking out its resources and capital until the bill had been paid. He remembered. He hated how it had destroyed his family, so he had decided to do something about it—

Now he was here to speak before the Council of Nations, an angry gathering of representatives from more than forty nations. They would demand that he pull back his forces and make amends. Or, fearing him, they might begin by asking him to explain the need for such military aggression and they might expect him to shrug off their complaints, saying it is the destiny that all Ghoupalle nations be united under the Sekuatean banner.

Then someone would ask: "What about the Danid?" To which he would blithely respond that they will have their own territory: "We will give them a state to rule for themselves; we will give them a homeland." And someone would then insist that the entirety of northern Zissekap was the Danid homeland—

indeed, the prime districts of the Sekuatean Empire. "They are welcome to join us," he would say, "but they will not rule us!" He would strike a defiant pose—which he sensed was in the script, part of the instructions previously impressed upon him and even now draining out of his head. He had been asleep so long! And he would mumble something about how the Sekuatean Empire was not the National Socialist regime and the Danid were not the Jews. And he would believe it. The Council of Nations, however, would be less ready to accept his explanation and reject his strange, fictitious comparison.

He had been called to answer their criticism. He thought it might be amusing. His mistress agreed. So he had come willingly, not to cower under the onslaught of their words but to stand firm against them, to offer a rebuke: they, too, were not invincible against the forces of the Sekuatean Empire's *Gourran Arumê de Remulgar de Sekuate*, once five *coræsz* strong yet now numbering twenty-one *coræsz*. No one was safe, he would tell them, unless they joined him!

"You are weak, all of you!" he heard himself raging, right arm raised stiffly in defiance, as though he had already given his speech and was merely recalling it. "You nations are weak! You cannot defeat us. You should submit to our leadership. Join us! Don't wait for help, for your neighbors have already joined us. There will be none to come to your weak, whimpering, pathetic cries for help! Even so, you, the simpering, pitiful nations of the planet, I will accept you. Yes, I will accept you into my empire—as my boot cleaners!"

And the crowd of representatives will rise as one and shout their indignation—

Still the coffins remained in the plaza below—and a new line of wagons was arriving to unload new coffins. Men were already setting them atop the coffins already marked with crimson eight-pointed stars—

And the flags of Sekuate waved in the back of his eyes, flags of victory hoisted high over government buildings—

Cobwebs! They were melting from his head, opening windows to fresh air, sweeping away the dirt, the shadows, the mysteries. He was awakening at last!

And he saw the coffins below in the plaza open and their

occupants step out, as fresh as the day they marched off to the fronts, and they stood and saluted him *en masse*. He heard them tell of their deaths, the moments in battle when each stood as he was now, seeing the images of his life pass through him. And universal in all their stories was the first sentence, a polemic of the glory bestowed to the honorable acts perpetrated on behalf of the Council, the ruling body of the Empire!

And he, their glorious leader, was saluting them.

The sky was blood red now, filled with dark gray smoke and orange flame, the horizon a line of cleansing fire, the silhouetted buildings a black line of destruction. He shook his head to clear the image but in vain. If he were in a dream, he knew he would soon awaken from it. He knew that no matter what adventures might have been presented in the nocturnal fantasy, no matter the horror or delight, it would always end. It would always come to an end when he opened his eyes.

He took a deep breath, closing and opening his eyes, sensing the movement of the secretary toward the doors, about to let in the delegation from Aivana. What petty request would that silly group have for him? What dull inquiry would prompt them to travel so far to meet with him? He could not work miracles, or grant wishes. He couldn't even be seen in public without his beard properly braided and dipped in red ink. He was a prop, a talking statue. His was a false life, a masque of masks, a joke to be shared at a class reunion, something he could never be certain had ever existed. Except there was some small itch that suggested a bit of truth remained.

Understanding that he was not where he intended to be, where two plus two again equaled four, he called weakly to the secretary: "Have someone check on my...uh, mistress. She might be needing assistance."

"Yes, My Lord," came the reply, and someone opened the doors to the room, to allow the messenger to be dispatched to check on the woman in his private chamber.

When the doors were opened, four figures stood in the corridor.

The secretary lit up: "Ah, welcome Aivanans!"

"*O'loe'me u'ta'io me'Aivana'li ha'eo fo'feo em'de'e ba'Sekuate-drouñ'loe,*" spoke the leader of the brown-robed, hooded

417

quartet. 'The delegation from Aivana has come to speak with the Emperor of Sekuate.'

Instead of a servant slipping out of the room on a simple task and the quartet of robed Aivanans entering solemnly, the room suddenly exploded with chaos as the group sprang into action, ripping off their hoods, drawing weapons from the folds of their robes, knocking down the guards and stomping on their faces with their boots, fatal *puffs* of death from their weapons, voices crying out and immediately silenced—including the anguished cry of his personal secretary—as a spray of blood spotted the windows before him.

The Emperor froze, standing, facing the blood-splattered glass, looking out over the plaza beyond.

He wanted to turn atop the chair, wanted to see what was happening behind him, but a voice inside his head, the same warm womanly voice, told him he did not want to see it, told him to stay as he was. So he remained stock-still on the chair, listening to the horror behind him as he waited for the alarm clock to go off.

"Now you will die!" shouted one of them in Ghoupallêan.

Others cursed him like a crowd of busybodies at the base of a hilltop crucifixion, pointing out his worst faults, his obvious flaws, his long list of ineptitudes, and held up the key to his vault of mistakes, crimes, and mortal sins.

"We will see justice done!" shouted the leader.

"Time for you to die!"

"Just like your wretched whore!"

"She died slowly—and in great pain!"

The news of the woman's murder blasted through his psyche. He raised his arms outward in apparent resignation. Perhaps someone had discovered the body of his mistress and was even now calling for security teams to rush to his aid. He was the Emperor! These things just did not happen to him. Surely there were guards outside the room ready to burst in and save him.

He saw their dull silver weapons reflected in the window panes, glowing orange, their AT guns ignited and ready to fire, their dark brown robes like shadows.

"I'm not the one you want," he spoke firmly, regally. "I didn't do anything. I'm not a bad guy. I'm not even the emperor. Not really."

"Turn around!" growled the leader. "Face your judges!"

"You've been a pox on the world for twenty years!" shouted another assassin.

"No, you're wrong!" He turned his head slightly, trying to see his assassins. "I'm not supposed to be here! I just woke up this morning and found myself here, in this role, but it's—it's not me, not what I'm supposed to be doing—"

"I said turn and face us!" the leader repeated.

"I did nothing wrong!" he shouted at the windows.

"Turn and face us!" the leader commanded.

"It's all a very big mistake!" he exclaimed.

The others shouted: "Death to the Council of Two!"

Chapter 32

The Dream of Future's Past

In the end, the dream is all that remains. It extends
from the past into the future. It is our future's past.

—Set-d'Elous, Emperor of Sekuate, from a speech
(never presented); in Siti, Ghoupallæssa, on
25-Batou: 1533

From the mountaintop he could see the entire world, all its
valleys and rivers, cities and seas, and all of the people that lived
and died, generation after generation, most unaware he was
watching them from on high. Suddenly he was filled with the
urge to invite them all to dinne—

Statesman, diplomat, charismatic speaker of the Grand
Assembly. With his loving, adoring wife. He was in love. He was
happy. Soon he gained the position of ultimate power and the
years that followed grew in intensity. He quickly reorganized
the army in Napoleonic fashion, and embarked on a grandiose
plan to unify all Ghoupalle lands into a single mighty empire. His
beloved wife concurred, applauding his ambition. In 1512 the
future began: waves of annexations, conquests, alliances, battles,
the surrender of crushed nations, treaties and submissions—
until now, in 1533, with the siege of Siaa commencing, when the

meek nations came together to beg him to halt his aggression. He laughed at their weak-willed request. They called for him to explain himself at the Council of Nations. He would humor them, perhaps convince them of his grand vision. No doubt he was hated, as all good leaders are by those who never get to benefit personally. He had many followers; most of the people of the Ghoupallæssus believed in him! And his loving wife believed in him. And their children believ—

Or he was alone in an old house at the edge of the woods, assorted characters coming on stage at will, tricking him, taunting him, playing him for a fool, the audience filled with rabid critics. He knew he would awaken soon—before any harm could befall him.

"I don't belong here!" he insisted.

"It's time for justice!" the leader growled, weapon raised.

The others had their weapons trained on him as well: red-hot, ready to kill.

"I'm not the one—"

He reached forward with one hand, the window pane separated his reality from his dream. He stepped onto the ledge. The coffins were still lined up, stacked up below—

Perhaps he had managed to escape through the culverts the construction crews had installed for the new subdivision. Perhaps he had crawled through the pipes, the rats there becoming his staff and the muskrat his personal secretary. Perhaps he had been able to cross under the road and hide in the forest, away from the police. Perhaps he made his way up to the quarry. Or, perhaps he had been chased and even now stood on the rim of the quarry, looking down at the flat clay basin and the rain pool and the limestone rocks below. So what if they called to him, begging him not to jump? He owed them no reply. So what if they said they wouldn't hurt him? They had fired bullets at him! So what if they considered him dangerous? He was the Emperor of Sekuate! He had a right to go where and when he pleased. One of the many tangents below would surely open and swallo—

"*Mad't!*" he heard the leader shout. 'Wait!'

An intense burning sensation burrowed deep into his body, red-heat spreading up to his shoulders and down to his groin.

He was hit!

"*Sed't!*" shouted the leader, waving for his comrades to lower their weapons. 'Stop!'

"It's Set—"

"—d'Elous!"

"It's me," the leader called to him, "Chucker."

The Emperor nodded absently, and with a raspy groan fell hard against the glass, his elbows shattering the panes, launching his body into the too-thin air. His arms and legs stretched outward, as if spreading on the surface of a lake, a liquid moment hovering in interdimensional time—as his body descended, a lost feather on the breeze...as shards of glass and molten pellets followed him like lonely puppies, striking him like nails, as he dropped, dropped downward, falling so slowly to another place. He waited to hit bottom, waited for the final impact among the stacked coffins in the plaza, for the splattering on the cobblestones, his face mussed against the wet clay of the quarry floor, listening for that damn alarm clock to go o—

And as he fell, drifting like a hang glider riding along the thermals of the Alaun plateau, the winds whistling in his ears, he felt the sensation of soft hands against his cheeks as a woman held his face between her fingers, allowing him to slip into or perhaps out of a drea—

"I must be leaving you," his voice echoed inside his head, hearing the English accent in his Ghoupallêan slipping away. "Forever this time. It has to be. We cannot continue."

The woman squeezed his face tighter. "You cannot leave me, Sir."

"I—We—can't continue—in this manner."

"You will be my lover, my partner...."

She let her delicate weight press against him, directing him deeper into the thick grass at the edge of the lakeshore. Her hips pushed against him, drawing him inside.

"We have united," she said. "Now begins the growing, two halves made whole." She kissed his eyelids. "Together we have created beauty. You and I have met inside the universe, part of each of us has grasped the other. Now we are whole."

"You can't know that," he clamored, understanding her metaphor. "I mean, not yet. It's too soon. It takes about two weeks before you can know. Unless you have one of those devices that show you a blue plus-sign, purchased from any drug store. But they don't make them here."

"It is attaching. Growing, dividing. Growing, dividing—"

"Do you feel it? Or do you *want* to feel it?"

"I have always felt my internal processes."

"How can that be?"

"I am a *senzenor*," she said in a whisper. "I keep it to myself. Some people would hurt me if they knew. They are fearful. Some people think I am a different kind of woman. They might drive me away—or kill me—if they knew."

He froze against her, afraid to think any thoughts lest she sense them. He had known his Ghoupalle wife Zaura was a *senzenor*, and she had worked as a kind of holistic healer but gradually lost her powers with every child she bore. Yet, Zaura could not read his thoughts unless his thoughts were infected with stress or she was in physical union with him.

"How do you know you have this talent?"

"*Senzenaxii* is not a talent, Sir."

"What is it then? The ability to sense another's pain?"

"Yes, and to relieve it." She grinned impishly. "You, Sir, have much pain. I have felt it from the first moment we met. However, soldiers often are filled with pain, so I ignored it. If you wish me to relieve your pain, I will do it."

"I'm not in pain," he responded roughly.

"You are not *in* pain, not like a cut here or a bruise there, yet you *have* much pain that burns along your nerve-strings. You are awake at night often. You feel constant pain...."

As she diagnosed him, he worried she would be able to know everything about him—to know too much. She told him of his meeting with a previous *senzenor*, how she was able to relieve his pain, yet it returned to him again and again. She told him how he travels frequently far distances, and he often tells stories to explain his absences. She told him his life in details that were too close for his comfort.

"Stop!"

Her hands were on his ear lobes, caressing him, drawing out his pain.

"Is it working?"

"No, it's not. I told you, I have no pain."

"You are full of pain. You will die if you do not release it."

He pressed his hand to her mouth, silencing her. Her hands dropped from his ears. Their eyes met.

"I'm sorry for my behavior," he spoke, lifting his hand from her mouth. "Perhaps you are right. I have some pain—guilt, regret, sorrow, anger. Who doesn't these days?"

"Your pain is acute," she whispered. "I feel your strength waning as you allow these pain-things to control you. When we touch, I can know your story, and feel your pain."

"It's getting late. The regiment will be looking for me. How long can a captain go off on his own to play with some young girl in a meadow beside a lake?" He chuckled, but it was insincere and he knew it. "They must be frantic by now."

"There is nothing to worry about, Sir. Our copulation is complete. You may go. Let the seed grow into a child."

"You think it's happened? Just like that? Right now?"

"I feel it inside me, calling me, letting me know he is well."

"He? It's a boy? You know that already?"

"It wants to be a boy—" Her eyes closed, opened. "—yet it is willing to wait to see what will appear between its legs. It will be satisfied either way."

He let out an uneasy laugh.

"That information pleases you?" she asked.

"I think it pleases you to play with my mind."

"It is not a game with your mind. It is your cell and my cell united to create a new cell, which is quickly dividing and growing and gaining consciousness and will be pushed out soon and welcomed into the world and sing praises to the gods and goddesses and live and copulate, eat and drink, make things and breathe deeply, and welcome grandchildren and feel proud of a good life. And people will sing to him when he grows old and brush his hair when life has slipped from him in the darkest hour of the night, when he has just passed the end of his one-hundred-fifty-seventh year. He will be remembered by many people for the goodness he did."

"You feel this now? His whole life?"

"Everything is set, don't you know? Some people can know all, Sir. I can know others' lives but not my own. Do you want to know your life? I can see only flashes, and I cannot see the end."

"I don't want to know."

Her eyes closed and he knew she was sensing him, probing his mind. *That* he could feel.

"You, Sir...are not who you say you are."

He took a deep breath. "What do you mean?"

Her eyes were still closed. Her hands went to his ear lobes, pinched them. Then her fingertip went to the place between his eyebrows for a moment, then moved to the opposite point, there on the back of his head.

"You are not a regimental captain. You...correct numbers, reports...with a pencil, at a desk...among people who have low intelligence...."

"That is a dream I sometimes have—"

"You have a friend who...builds carriages that go very fast, for racing...yet he is a king...and lives in the desert."

"Just another dream. I usually wake up in a cold sweat—"

"You are...not...."

He waited, his heart beating faster.

"I'm not what?"

Her eyes opened and he noticed her face flushed, her skin running with perspiration. It had a greenish tint in the fading sunlight.

"You...are not Ghoupalle!"

"That is a problem I often have," he chuckled, ignoring her horror. "My mind thinks I am two people, so the average *senzenaxii* person is often confused. I am difficult to read. But I do have Ghoupalle blood flowing through me."

"False!"

She struggled to get out from under him, squirming, her face wrinkled in her effort. His hands held her wrists to the ground. Her breathing softened and she relaxed, realizing the need to save her strength. After a while he released one wrist and his fingers brushed her hair as he smiled at her.

"Let me explain...."

She muttered an old saying about the devil always coming with a smile and suddenly shifted into struggle mode, wrestling with him again but soon fell quiet.

"Don't worry," he said, trying to present a confident, sincere voice. "It is a long story but let me tell you the end of it now: I *am* a nice guy."

He shifted his weight to the side.

"I may have been born far away but Sekuate is my home now. I care about this place. I have a family here—*had* a family. They are lost in another time. History does not show an easy life for them. History is not kind to many people. Do you know about history? Can you see what you will be doing in ten years? twenty years? fifty? Can you see what will happen? I have visited the future. I know what will happen. I saw you there. You will wave to the brigades as they march to war! Wars to the south, to the east, to the north, all the way to Bæronak and up to the mountains of Zetinê."

His eyes felt moist. Tears formed and dripped down upon her face, his voice strained.

"I know this because I was there—and I will be there again. I survived the snowfields of Siaa—while my family endured the aerial bombing of Selauê only to suffer death later in the Tebbi invasion! I don't want that to happen again. Yet it will happen if I do nothing. You will send the armies to war. You will order the execution of innocent people. You will bear children who grow up and destroy this land, the entire world you call home. You cannot see it, you said, but I can. Because I am not from here, not from *now*. I have a power, too: I can visit different points in time on your world. And I have returned to this time zone to stop you. I don't want to hurt you; I just want you to go in a different direction, choose a different career path. I have seen the results of your life. You write stupid poetry now, but you will inspire some lunkhead to start a rebellion which brings you and your circle of friends to power. Then you destroy the world! And your actions will destroy my family!"

She was limp in his arms.

He realized then that his tirade had been in English. He started to repeat it in Ghoupallêan but he could not find the right words.

"It doesn't matter," he snorted in Ghoupallêan finally. "You don't need to know what you will do. It is enough that someone stops you."

Tears rolled out of her eyes.

"I don't want to stop it. The embryo must grow. Don't—"

"I'm not talking about that." He shook his head wildly. "How can you think of that? How can you know you're pregnant when we just did it? You're trying to trick me!"

"No, Sir, I am welcoming you."

All of his breath left his mouth and he collapsed, caught himself, and pulled himself up to a sitting position beside her. She hesitated, then also sat up, braced on her arms in the grass.

"You want to welcome me?" he asked.

She seemed to study him, tilting her head from side to side, pondering the future.

"I invite you, Sir, to join me."

He pouted, embarrassed. "Join you?"

A tiny laugh popped out of her mouth. "Do you not recognize the words of joining?"

"No, I'm sorry. I don't."

"Of course, not, Sir. You are not Danid. You are not Ghoupalle. You are not Rouê. Not even Zetin!" and with that she opened her throat and released sweet laughter that filled the meadow and shook the clouds, casting them to the side to let the evening sun shine down upon them. "What are you, then, Sir?"

"I'm like you," he spoke softly, "an outsider, lost in a lost world."

"Then you are perfect for me."

"Perfect? Who, me?"

"At least you are not Zetin!"

"I am definitely not Zetin," he laughed, recalling the time he had dressed up as a Zetin warrior to slip inside the castle KVANN-STA' PO'CIX and rescued Gina, his high school sweetheart. Or was that only a dream?

She leaned toward him. "I ask you to give me your care and kindness, your wisdom and naïveté, your work and play, your support and discrimination, your life and death, all to the adventure that will be a life together. Though you are a foreigner here, we have achieved this union, so it must be the decision of the seven gods and nine goddesses that you and I should join as a family."

"Is that how you see it?"

He noticed her fingers were again pinching his ear lobes. He no longer objected.

"Do you accept?"

"I would rather marry you than kill you," he muttered in English. He recalled suddenly how he had returned to change the war-ravaged history that had destroyed his family, thinking how his trip up to Sorêg might give him the opportunity to do something that would alter the course of that history, and coming to the conclusion that this young woman, a poetess, a student, was the right woman for him to ki—

"You will give me your answer now," she whispered into his ear, gently pinching the lobe.

"Yes!" he cried out as though stung.

She sat up on her knees and reached for him, pushing her mouth against his. They fell back with her atop him, kissing feverishly.

As the evening billowed over them like a snapped bed sheet, they gathered their belongings. The light of the blue sun spread low across the horizon, silhouetting violet trees.

"Where shall we stay tonight?" he asked her, knowing they could not return together to the town.

"Tonight we must be apart, Sir. You will be the captain of a regiment. I will speak to my father about our coupling. He will perform the ritual at the altar in our house. We will meet again here, at this meadow, in three days. Then our future will begin."

"Sounds like a plan," he said with a chuckle.

"I'm glad you like it."

"There's no plan like a sound plan."

"Basura-Kanoun and Set-d'Elous, one family."

She smiled up at him, then took his hand in hers as they walked slowly across the field to where his *Jêpe* grazed.

"Yes," he sighed, "you and me, a Council of Two."

Epilogue

Heaven and/or Hell

To have a beautiful death, he had once read, you must die at an age young enough that the body has not yet begun to decay, while the body is still fit and strong. To have a beautiful death you must be killed in the struggle for justice or in defense of home and family. To have a beautiful death you must bear a smile of satisfaction upon your face when the heart beats its final beat and the mind thinks its final thought. To have a beautiful death, most importantly, you must actually die—

He opened his eyes, saw he was surrounded by splashes of green. With further focus, he realized they were trees and bushes and grass. Sunlight bounced off the leaves, reflected off a small pond. He heard noises: children playing. He felt a breeze. The sky was royal blue, white clouds like soldiers on furlough lined up at the local brothel.

"Hello there."

His eyes shifted to the woman kneeling on the blanket in front of him. A basket sat next to her, and next to the basket was a small boy.

"I thought you would nap longer," she spoke, then turned to the boy: "Ready for a picnic, little man?"

The boy grinned, said something affirmative.

He studied the boy, smiling in his heart, two and two again somehow making four. He stared at the woman, his eyes tracing her figure, returning and lingering on her face, the curly black hair framing her rosy cheeks and the welcoming smile above the beige blouse and olive Bermudas, strappy sandals, curvy legs:

Dr. Toni Franck.

The shaggy-haired boy in *Star Wars* jumper emblazoned with a pair of Jedi knights, light sabers poised, must be, could only be her son—and thus, at least on some legal documents stamped five or six years in the past, also his son. The reality made him feel something like affection for the two people sitting on the khaki-and-crimson blanket spread at the foot of his chair.

She prepared the food, served it on plastic dishes, helped the boy feed himself. Then she filled a bowl and rose to offer it to him. She held the spoon, took some of the food—potato salad— and pushed it against his lips. Her other hand squeezed his mouth open, then the spoon entered and withdrew, depositing the food.

"Is it good? Do you like it?" she asked him. "You needed a day out in the fresh air and sunshine."

He agreed, considered nodding his head.

"A perfect day for our anniversary." She reflected on the passage of time. "How can they still keep you locked up there?" She sighed. "I'm meeting with the lawyers again tomorrow. We're doing everything we can." She spied two men in the bushes. "Look at them watching us. They think they blend into the landscape."

After she finished feeding him and cleaned up her son, she packed away the dishes and sat back on the blanket. They listened to the laughter of children playing. Her son curled up next to her, wanting to nap, and she brushed his hair.

"I like a day that's cool," said Toni, gazing at the sky, "not hot, like it usually is now." She turned to him. "We went shopping before I picked you up. They didn't bother us too much this time. I guess they believe you cannot escape. You won't hurt me, either. You're totally harmless. Finally they feel safe. What a bunch of sissies!"

He watched her lips move.

"Even though they know everything about you now, I think they still fear you." She laughed. "Perhaps you are putting curses on those police men."

She stood, leaned over him. He wanted to scoot away, or get up and run as fast as he could, back to his tangents—but his body would not move. His head tilted lazily to one side, hands in his lap, one foot curled to the right and the other to the left, eyes taking in his condition, mouth dry yet desperate to scream, heart sizzling in terror, stomach a raging inferno, and the sensation of flying, falling, crashing.

He shook his chair, shouting at his legs to move but they refused. Frozen, he shouted again and again—and heard nothing but the breeze rustling leaves, children playing, a dog's barking, birdsong, a squirrel's chattering, the boy's giggling, and this pretty woman's dulcimer words slipping into his good ear.

The woman brushed her lips across his forehead, hovered, then pulled back, avoiding a kiss, teasing him.

"You should never have stepped across my path," she whispered. Her voice was rougher now, dark and throaty, not like Toni's. "Look at yourself! Hah, what an immobile fool! The wars continue, only now they serve me. Let Ghoupalle kill Ghoupalle. And the Danid shall inherit the world—the world *we* made, our planet: *Danid'ta*. No more shall our world be called Ghoupallesz. No more shall the Danid live on Ghoupalle scraps, *Serpan* d'Elous."

He shivered in his seat, seeing the ever-beautiful Basura-Kanoun leaning over him, speaking to him face to face.

She stroked his hair. "*Kai tašiom xes,*" she said in her native language, "*xet gel-ymazk.*" He was not very familiar with Danid, trying to remember what he could from that patrol assignment in Sorêg district that gloomy autumn so long ago, but he guessed her meaning: she was happy with her trick, pleased with her accomplishment.

She kissed his cheek softly, lovingly, and tapped on his cheek a few times, as though he'd been a naughty little boy.

"*Dor-gê vaš-teñ?*" she asked, perhaps testing him. "You understand now?"

She knew he could not respond, that he was locked in his wheelchair, unable to move, unable to speak, yet quite able to feel and think and hear and see the darkness of his future. She paused nevertheless, enjoying the moment.

Then she smiled warmly and said in perfect, beautiful English: "You should never have killed me."

Acknowledgements

Any work of imagination necessarily draws from a variety of sources. For inspiration, insight, and where applicable the gift of insouciance, I am greatly indebted to Roger Zelazny, Michael Moorcock, Robert Silverberg, Gene Roddenberry, and George Lucas—my sci-fi mentors.

Special thanks go to my daughter who not only endured hearing all the tales of the Dream Land but produced the cover art.

About the Author

Stephen Swartz grew up in Kansas City, Missouri where he dreamed of traveling the world. His writing therefore usually includes exotic locations, foreign characters, and splatterings of other languages. Strangers in strange lands is a common theme. After studying music, even composing a symphony, Stephen planned to be a music teacher before turning to teaching English.

The Dream Land trilogy was born from childhood games set up in the playground of a damp basement. Then it was forgotten until the story was reborn in a dream many years later. After many interdimensional voyages, Stephen teaches English at a university in Oklahoma and continues writing fiction at night.

THE DREAM LAND

Book III

Diaspora

THEY'VE CHANGED HISTORY—BUT NOT EVEN AN INTERDIMENSIONAL VOYAGER CAN STOP A COMET!

Set-d'Elous (a.k.a. Sebastian Talbot) finds himself paralyzed and mute, tormented daily by the mocking spirit of the evil Empress— his wife. His only hope is to be rescued, but all his fellow Voyagers have been blown to other places, some back to Earth. They awaken to a world they had left and now cannot comprehend. Tammy's son, Chucker, awakens in the jungle, however, and in his years there realizes what went wrong in his team's assassination attempt on the Emperor of Sekuate: they shot the wrong guy.

Feeling guilty, Chucker tracks Set-d'Elous to Earth, where he is locked up in a prison hospital, let out once a month for a day with Dr. Toni Franck, his former psychiatrist now wife. With the aid of a retired cop, Chucker must rescue Sebastian in order to counter the rise of a violent prophet's cult back on Ghoupallesz. Only a final battle will decide the truth—a truth that permeates the next few centuries....

Legend tells of a comet that will cleanse the world, and governments realize it is near. Fortunately, Jinetta-d'Elous (a.k.a. Gina Parton, Interdimensional Voyager), a struggling mother of two, comes forward to offer assistance. Leading the aerospace commission, she tries to drive forward Ghoupallean technology from airships to interstellar spacecraft in the time remaining.

However, success has its price and as the clock counts down, Gina must rescue her daughter from the evil Overlord and secure seats aboard the last spacecraft departing before the comet strikes.

THE DREAM LAND trilogy concludes in Book III with an epic crash of time lines and an unforgiving planetoid coming to test even the heartiest of Interdimensional Voyagers!

www.ingramcontent.com/pod-product-compliance
Lightning Source LLC
Chambersburg PA
CBHW051511250626
47156CB00001B/55